PRAISE

"James A Moore is the
His work is full of dark ph
desperate warriors and capricious gods. This is fantasy
people who like to wander nighttime forests and scream at the moon. Exhilarating as hell."

– *Christopher Golden, New York times bestselling author of* Snowblind

"Fast-paced fantasy that you simply can't put down. Great action adventure."

– Morpheus Tales

"Gripping, horrific, and unique, James Moore continues to be a winner, whatever genre he's writing in. Well worth your time."

– *Seanan McGuire, New York Times bestselling author of the* InCryptid *and* Toby Daye *series*

"Moore has laid the groundwork for a trilogy that promises to be loaded with terrifically grim fantasy storytelling. I might even call it epic. There is a lot of swift, merciless violence in this book, mingled with an undercurrent of very welcome, if very dark, humor. All of it together takes me back to what made me giddy about epic fantasy way back when. I'd say I'm happy to be back, but I'm not sure that's quite the right word for a book packed with this much violent incident. Let's say instead that I'm bloody satisfied."

– *Rich Rosell for the B&N Sci-Fi & Fantasy Blog*

BY THE SAME AUTHOR

The Tides of War series
The Last Sacrifice • Fallen Gods • Gates of the Dead

The Seven Forges series
Seven Forges • The Blasted Lands
City of Wonders • The Silent Army

The Blood Red series
Blood Red • Blood Harvest • Blood of the Damned

The Chris Corin Chronicles
Possessions • Rabid Growth • Newbies

The Serenity Falls Trilogy
Writ in Blood • The Pack • Dark Carnival

The Griffin & Price series (with Charles R Rutledge)
Blind Shadows • Congregations of the Dead • A Hell Within

Alien: Sea of Sorrows
The Predator: Hunters & Hunted
The Haunted Forest Tour *(with Jeff Strand)*
Bloodstained Oz *(with Christopher Golden)*
Buffy the Vampire Slayer: Chaos Bleeds
Cherry Hill
Deeper
Fireworks
Harvest Moon
Homestead
Under the Overtree
Vampire: House of Secrets *(with Kevin Andrew Murphy)*
Vendetta
Werewolf: Hellstorm
The Wild Hunt
Slices *(stories)*
This is Halloween *(stories)*

James A Moore

THE GODLESS

Seven Forges, Book V

ANGRY ROBOT

ANGRY ROBOT
An imprint of Watkins Media Ltd

Unit 11, Shepperton House
89-93 Shepperton Road
London N1 3DF
UK

angryrobotbooks.com
twitter.com/angryrobotbooks
Everyday a little war

An Angry Robot paperback original, 2021

Cover by Alejandro Colucci
Edited by Paul Simpson and Robin Triggs
Set in Meridien

ISBN 978 0 85766 842 4
Ebook ISBN 978 0 85766 853 0

Printed and bound in the United Kingdom by TJ Books Limited

9 8 7 6 5 4 3 2 1

FSC www.fsc.org MIX Paper from responsible sources FSC® C013056

This one is for Rich Dansky, Jonathan Maberry and Christopher Golden, as well as my wife, Tessa. Thanks for everything, guys.

Special thanks to everyone at Angry Robot who has worked so diligently to make my tales better than they were when they started. I don't say often enough how much I appreciate all that you do.

PROLOGUE

Trigan Garth

Trigan Garth sat at his table in the *Wandering Boar* and ate a meal of meat and cheese with what had to be the driest bread he had ever eaten. There was enough blood and gravy from the meat to make that a forgivable sin. His biggest complaint at that moment was that people kept entering the building, opening the door and letting in the cold.

Most of the people in the place were smart enough to stay away from him. He was Sa'ba Taalor, and that meant he was a warrior first and civil second.

The Sa'ba Taalor were raised as warriors and followed one or more of seven gods. Each of those deities was a god of war. Trigan had three Great Scars upon his face. One split his mouth at a sharp angle. One in his left cheek was high enough to almost touch his eye. The third was on his left side, along the jawline. It was easy to know the warriors. They had gray skin. Sometimes lighter in color and sometimes darker, though no one quite understood the difference. It was very likely a matter of how long they spent in the sun. Trigan Garth had very dark skin. He had traveled through half of Fellein before he reached this place on the southern edge of the continent.

The man who came to see him was unknown to him. He was not small, but he was smaller than Trigan, with tanned flesh and brown hair. His eyes were a pale shade of blue that stood out against the rest of him. He carried a short sword on his hip, a dagger on the other hip and wore a hardened leather breast plate.

He did not ask to sit down, but pulled up a chair and made himself at home.

Only a fool chooses insult where there is none. Trigan was no one's fool and so he ignored the obvious breach of etiquette and took a drink of the bitter ale that came with his meal.

After being ignored for several minutes, long enough for Trigan to finish eating, the man at the table said, "You're Trigan Garth?"

"I am."

"I've been looking for you."

Trigan's silvery eyes looked around the room at all of the Fellein pretending not to listen to the conversation. "I am not hard to find."

The man laughed and slapped the surface of the table with an open palm. "That is true. Are you curious as to why I am looking for you?"

"Did I kill your family in the war? Do you now come to seek vengeance against a kinslayer?" That particular situation had come up several times over the last five years. Trigan was a very good warrior and he had killed many of the Fellein as he rode from the Seven Forges to the throne of the Empire.

"What? Gods no. Your people killed a lot of people, but my family was never reached."

"Do you intend to try killing me?"

"Hadn't been part of my agenda, no." The stranger frowned.

"Then I have no idea why you seek me. Should I be concerned? Or is this a discussion?" His words were in jest. He had no reason to believe he could not kill the stranger.

"Well, I... It's a discussion."

"I am not a man who likes to talk. Say your piece before you bore me." While they had been speaking the people at the tables around them grew less cautious and more actively displayed their willingness to listen in on the conversation. Trigan did not care. They could hear what the fool wanted to say.

"You're godless?"

Those were possibly the worst words the man could have asked. Trigan narrowed his eyes slightly and leaned across the table. "Why would you ask a question like that?"

The stranger kept his eyes on Trigan, as if staring at an angry bear. He was perceptive enough to know he'd made a mistake "I don't mean to offend..."

"Too late. Why would you ask that of a Sa'ba Taalor?"

"I..." The man stared at him but did not back away, did not reach for a weapon, and so was spared a very fast and brutal death. "As I understand it some of your people did not go back to the Forges. They did not speak again to their gods. They have not spoken to their gods in a very long time. I wanted to know if you are one of them."

"I am." Trigan's voice was a low growl.

"Well then," The man smiled as he spoke. "I have an offer for you."

He continued to talk.

Trigan listened.

Lenwig Wickhaven

"We should run!" Jarry made the comment as he bolted past the campsite. A moment before he'd been on his way to find a good place for voiding his bowels. He was young and strong, lean and capable, but he also ate enough for ten men and sooner or later that food wanted to leave his body.

Lenwig looked up from where he was setting up the cooking fire and watched his companion move in long strides that made him look even leaner than usual. Jarry was a playful sort. He did his work, but he never even considered the idea of being serious when he could be cracking a joke, or making a pun, or singing a rude tune as he rode along the way and helped handle the workload. Ten minutes without some sort of off-color remark was a lot if the man was conscious.

Jarry wasn't joking. His voice was very serious. He ran past the encampment and called out his warning several more times to the rest of the gathered riders.

Lenwig stood up, frowning, and looked in the direction Jarry had come from.

There were three men riding toward the campsite. They were of largish build, and wore enough armor and weapons that they very nearly bristled like porcupines.

Two of the men looked normal enough, aside from their weapons. The last one, however, the one who rode between the other two, had gray skin.

The world was a strange place, true enough, but on all of that known world only one race of men had gray skin. The Sa'ba Taalor.

Lenwig had not fought against the Sa'ba Taalor when the war came. He had been wiser than that and had managed to make certain he was not where the people from the Seven Forges could find him. The whole of Fellein was one massive empire and it was a peaceful enough place until the gray skins showed up.

The Sa'ba Taalor were not peaceful and never would be. They had seven gods, and as he understood it, each of those gods was a god of war.

Lenwig looked at the approaching men and shoved his flint and his steel into a small pouch tied to the belt over his ponderous belly. He was not a fighter. He had been when he was a much younger man, but these days he preferred to leave the fighting to those he paid. Like Jarry.

If he lived through the situation, he planned to take his belt to the little bastard for deserting them.

The men came closer still, and he took the short sword he carried, more for appearances than to use, and pulled it from its scabbard. Even as he prepared himself the rest of his group were gathering themselves and forming a half circle around the wagons. Though none of the men looked particularly aggressive, they were paid to defend his property and they were paid well enough to, by the gods, do their work.

Lenwig and his guards were transporting Illian wine to Canhoon. Four wagons of the stuff would make him a handsome profit. There were two boats waiting to do most of the work, but before the boats could take it, he had to get the load to the river. That meant moving through the Wellish Steppes and along the Emperor's Highway. Only a fool would travel the area without protection and Lenwig Wickhaven was no one's fool.

By the time he'd sucked in his belly and done his best to look ready for a fight, the riders were close enough for him to see properly. The men were hard. They were older, and had enough scars to indicate they were survivors. The Sa'ba Taalor was a terror to behold. His skin was dark gray, as if he'd smeared himself in the ashes from a campfire, only the color was smooth and even across his scarred flesh and Lenwig had no doubt it was skin, and not an attempt to appear more like one of the nearly mythical fighters.

The two men looked rather cocky. The Sa'ba Taalor did not. He was casual, yes, but his eyes moved over the entire area even as he spoke softly to Lenwig.

The man spoke with an odd echoing quality to his voice. "There is little to eat out here." That was true enough, they were in the Wellish Steppes and a good day of hunting around the area was likely to yield little more than a half-starved rabbit. Very little lived in the area beyond stubborn scrub brush.

"Not a lot, true, but I have a bit we could share with strangers."

Both of the men snorted. They were the sort that would raid a house and take what they wanted by way of food, property, and flesh without any hesitation. As they were outnumbered that option wasn't overly likely for either of them. The man with them, the Sa'ba Taalor, he was a different story. A man who worships war gods was exactly the sort that might well kill them all just for sport.

The helmet over the man's head was a cap surrounded by scales of metal. It ran down to his shoulders and would likely stop any blade that tried to take his head. The armor he wore was, as seemed to be the case with all of his people, forged specifically for him, and if the stories were true both his weapons and armor would have been forged by his hand.

The eyes of the Sa'ba Taalor should have been hidden away in shadow as a result of that helmet but Lenwig could see them clearly. They stood out, much like the eyes of a cat when the light is just so, and cast an unsettling gray glow.

The man dropped down from his horse with one smooth move and his body weight was enough to make the ground shake under Lenwig's feet. He was a very large man. The leather and metal of his armor was scarred and well worn, but also well-tended. The leather oiled, the metal obviously repaired more than once. This was not a man playing at warrior. This was a warrior who had very likely spent fifteen or more years fighting with regularity.

"We would join you for a meal. I can pay."

Lenwig nodded his head. "It's beef stew. The beef was dried, but the mushrooms and onions are fresh enough."

The Sa'ba Taalor pointed to the sword in his hand. It was held properly. Old, yes, but he'd had his time in the Fellein Army and he'd practiced regularly for years. "Are you planning to kill me?"

Lenwig shook his head. "Just making certain you're not planning to kill me."

The man smiled. His mouth moved the wrong way. Part of it curled up into a proper smile and part of it writhed and split open to reveal uneven teeth and gums that were completely independent of the first mouth. Lenwig had heard of the Great Scars but never seen one. A mouth separate from the main mouth, apparently there solely to let a Sa'ba Taalor's god speak directly to recipients of the scars. There was supposed to be one Great Scar for each god that favored a Sa'ba Taalor. Some of them had two or three. A very few had more. This fellow had at least one. Most of his face was hidden by that helmet and Lenwig could not be certain if he had more than one of the disfigurements. In any event he found the notion terrifying.

"If I intend to kill you, I will let you know first." From all he had heard, the Sa'ba Taalor were strong believers in honor. They didn't lie. Of course he had no proof of that, having dealt with them as little as possible.

Lenwig nodded and put his sword away. He had no certainty that the man was telling the truth, but he decided to listen to him just the same. What choice did he have?

Thirty minutes later the entire group was eating their stew, except for Jarry, who upon his return was sent to clean up after the horses and guard the perimeter.

King Tuskandru

There were some people who still called the area Tyrne, though the once fabled Summer City had been destroyed almost five years earlier, at the beginning of the war. Where that massive city had once stood there was now a mountain of epic scale that dwarfed all of the surrounding landscape. Most of what people saw here was the mountain, and after that the trees, the low hills and, eventually, the sea.

Tuskandru did not care about Tyrne. He had been to the city and he had been the instrument of his God's desires when Durhallem, The Wounder, demanded that the Fellein be taught a lesson.

He was faithful to his god. That was why he was the King in Obsidian, a title of great honor offered only to the person Durhallem chose to be his voice in the world. Currently, he was hunting, along with a dozen of his followers. Stastha was his second and she rode beside him, her spear held in one hand as her mount, Loarhun, grumbled amiably beneath her.

It was a good day for hunting. Brodem moved under him, the mount responding to the smallest touch of Tusk's knees on the beast's sides.

"Where are we going?" Stastha rode up next to him and called out loudly. She knew the answer, but she still loved to hear it from her king.

"We go to hunt and kill the Godless!" He smiled as he spoke and then charged forward, Brodem pouncing, scrabbling and slipping down the mountain's steep angled surface in gigantic strides. Stastha followed, whooping with joy, the curved horns of her helmet hiding the lower half of her face from view. Somewhere behind him Kordha blew the horn he carried to let others know a hunt was on. There was little doubt a few more would join them. Most that did would be doing so symbolically. There weren't enough of the prey for all of them to hunt, but they would have fun just the same.

The bottom of the mountain Durhallem, named for the god that lived in the heart of the volcano, led to the pass, and the pass led to the place called Fellein. A large empire of soft people. If the war were still going on Tusk and his people would have been killing the Fellein without hesitation, but for now Durhallem and the other gods said to wait and so he did. One did not argue with gods, if one had any common sense.

He did not have to ask his gods to tell him where to look. He knew where he would find his targets. They were spread far and wide and thought themselves safe.

They were wrong.

Lenwig Wickhaven

The sun was gone from the sky and darkness had covered the world, save for a faint line of red on the western horizon. They had finished their meal, and the strangers sat around a fire that kept the cold mostly at bay, along with Lenwig and most of his men. The two who traveled with the Sa'ba Taalor still looked at Lenwig and his men with contempt on their weathered faces, but they seemed satisfied with resting their full bellies and that was enough to let Lenwig relax a bit.

"I have heard of the great beasts your people ride. Yet you ride a horse. Why is that, my friend?" Wilom was curious. He always had been. He also had all the manners of a guard dog.

The Sa'ba Taalor looked at him as he finished his third bowl of stew and managed a smile. "The mounts are gifts from the gods. I have not earned such a treasure." Despite his fearsome appearance, the man was pleasant enough.

"So why are you here, and not on one of the Seven Forges with your people?" Wilom asked the question that had been on Lenwig's mind since they'd met the Sa'ba Taalor and his entourage of dubious men. He knew only that the gray man's name was Drusht and that he was traveling the land. That was a nice way of saying he was between jobs as a mercenary.

"The Great Silence."

Lenwig leaned in closer. "The Great Silence?"

Drusht nodded. Currently the man's helmet sat to his left and most of his larger weapons were to the right. There was a spear, a handheld axe, a larger axe and a viciously curved blade that might pass for a sword, or possibly a scythe, depending on whom one asked.

"When your people and mine warred, we listened to our gods. The war ended because the gods stopped talking to us. That is the Great Silence."

Lenwig meant to avoid this conversation, but now that it was started he continued it. "I thought your gods spoke to your people again."

"To some of us. I do not hear the gods and they do not hear me." The tone of voice told Lenwig to leave the matter alone. The two Great Scars on Drusht's face moved on their own, making no noises but shifting and opening seemingly without the man's control.

Wilom, who was not always the most perceptive lad, looked at Drusht and said, "Did you abandon your gods? Or did they abandon you?"

A moment later Drusht had the boy on the ground and was shoving half of Wilom's face into the campfire. Wilom was screaming. Drusht was screaming. Most of the people around the fire were screaming. Thick, powerful fingers held Wilom's face in the blaze and Lenwig watched on, horrified, as the man's face caught fire. His hair was a conflagration. His body bucked, and thrashed, and tried to lift away from the fire, but Drusht held him in place with the whole of his body. Drusht's hand was burning as it held the other man down, but if he felt it, he gave no indication.

Lenwig thought of the sword at his side, the dagger in his boot and then thought better of it.

Without warning Drusht stood, still holding poor Wilom's head in his grip, and dragged the wretch away from the fire. Wilom was either dead or blessedly unconscious, it was hard to say which. Drusht shook the flames away from his hand as he dropped his burden.

The expression on the Sa'ba Taalor's face was enough to stop most people from doing anything at all.

Holder, a longtime friend of Wilom, was not as quick to ignore the situation. He rose from the log he'd been perched on and hurled his dagger at Drusht without hesitation. "Bastard!"

Drusht, who looked large enough to push over trees,

moved his body to the side and managed to avoid the point of the dagger. The blade grazed skin and then the dagger was spinning off into the early evening darkness.

The Sa'ba Taalor bent down, grabbed the shorter of his axes and then buried it in Holder's chest with one fluid motion. Holder's mouth opened and closed soundlessly, and then he fell backward, cracking his head on a rock. His body lay at a position that would never be comfortable for a living being. He was surely dead.

"Does anyone else want to insult me this night?" When he spoke, Drusht's voice was a low rumble, barely above a whisper. The expression in his silvery eyes was enough to make everyone around him calm down in an instant.

The coin he tossed toward Lenwig was pure gold by the feel of it, and worth enough to buy two horses.

Drusht looked at his two companions, who looked exactly and precisely as terrified as Lenwig felt. "Pack your things if you travel with me. I am leaving." Drusht spoke to the closest of his companions who promptly rose and started gathering his possessions.

Jarry, who was tentatively on guard duty, ran past at a very fast pace and yelled, "We should be going. Now! Run now!"

He did not repeat himself, but instead sprinted as hard as he could toward the horses in great strides that tore the distance away.

The shapes Lenwig saw coming were merely shadows in the darkness, save for their eyes. The higher shadows had humanoid forms, though they were large. The figures under them were not human. They were not horses. They were too broad for horses, and too tall, and their movements made Lenwig think of cats stalking prey.

Sa'ba Taalor, and they rode mounts.

The one at the front of the riders moved closer. He was a terror to behold in the light of the campfire. Possibly the largest man that Lenwig had ever seen, he was dressed in leathers and furs, save for his head which sported a helmet shaped like the skull of some great beast and had horns sprouting from the sides of that bestial head.

The creature under the rider was little more than a dark shape, but Lenwig felt a growing cold in his stomach at the sight of it. The eyes of the thing were half hidden in some sort of helmet and yet he could still see those terrifying eyes in the darkness.

Somehow the sword had once again managed to find itself in his hand. Lenwig could see the rider's eyes shift from him, down to the sword, then back up to him again.

"Do you intend to fight me?"

Lenwig heard the words and shook his head. His hand dropped the sword as if it had been sitting in the fire and now seared his palm. "Absolutely not."

The giant nodded his head and the horns of his helmet moved up and down as if to agree. "That is good. I seek only the Godless one. I do not care about the rest of you."

The gray shape of Drusht came close, brushing past two of the men who'd planned to stand with Lenwig.

"You call me Godless? Because I do not hear the voices any longer? Who are you to judge me?"

The horned shadow leaned forward enough to let Lenwig see the broad, scarred chin under that great helmet. "I am called Tuskandru, Chosen of the Forge of Durhallem and Obsidian King. I am here to take you back to your gods, or to kill you for them. Which will it be?"

For a moment that stretched tightly, the only sounds

were the wind shushing across the tents and wagons, and the crackle of the campfire.

Drusht looked around the area and paused, it seemed, to count the number of shapes behind the one called Tuskandru. Finally, he swept up the massive axe he'd settled earlier and roared, "Fuck Durhallem!"

Tuskandru dropped from his ride and stepped toward Drusht, his every move smooth and predatory.

He, too, carried an axe. It was a massive thing, well used and deeply scarred.

When the two smashed into each other the axes met and rang out a scream of metal on metal. Both men grunted and a moment later pushed away from each other.

One of the men with Drusht – Seral, his name was Seral – drew his sword and looked to move in to assist his companion. His body language was clear, and his angry expression said much. The arrow that bloomed from his left eye a moment later was a complete surprise. Seral dropped to the ground without a noise, save the clattering of his sword as it bounced across the stones.

Lenwig turned to face the other Sa'ba Taalor and saw one of them had fired a bow. He could not see the rider clearly, but took the message. He did not move.

Tuskandru and Drusht smashed into each other again. It was not, despite appearances, a bucking contest. Both men held the other at bay with the heavy grip of their axes, the blades locked together. Muscles bulged and they grunted with effort. Drusht was a very large shape, but Tuskandru was even larger. They trembled with exertion and then Tuskandru reared back his head and smashed his helmet into Drusht's bared face. The fangs of the bestial skull peeled meat from bone and drew hot trenches of blood down

Drusht's face. The man blinked furiously as the blood ran into his eyes. He did his best to stay locked in his position against the other fighter.

The second time the helmet smashed into his face one of the long fangs tore open one of Drusht's eyes and part of his nose. Drusht screamed, and flinched, and in the process lost his struggle for survival. King Tuskandru swept the staff of his axe in a hard circle even as he stepped back. Drusht staggered forward and his axe dropped low.

The blunt end of the axe's butt slammed into Drusht's bloodied face and shattered teeth as well as ruining the man's nose. He fell forward and did his best to catch himself on his hands. He managed not to fall on his face, but the act cost him.

Tuskandru stood above him. The king's great axe swept over his head and came down, cleaving through Drusht's shoulder and back, very nearly splitting the poor bastard in two. Tuskandru's boot pressed into Drusht's side and he wrenched the axe free.

Without another word he turned and headed back for his mount. The one with the bow had come closer and Lenwig was surprised to see that the archer was a woman. To the last, the men standing around the campfire and facing the Sa'ba Taalor had dropped their weapons and now held their hands in plain sight, to show they held no means of attack.

Wilom, burned horribly in the fight with Drusht, moaned as Tuskandru stepped over him. The King in Obsidian looked down at the man. "Your friend is badly burned. He is dying."

"We can't save him." Lenwig spoke, barely aware that he was doing so until it was too late to stop.

Tuskandu nodded. "Then show him the mercy of a quick death." The head of his axe had a sharp point above it. He drove that point into Wilom's temple. When he pulled it back out the tip was wet and bloodied. Wilom was dead.

A moment later the gray people mounted their rides and left the area. They did not take their corpses with them.

Lenwig called out to Jarry, who came running, his eyes wide and his hair wilder than usual.

"Jarry?"

The younger man looked at him and nodded.

"Get busy. You're to burn the corpses." There would be no bodies to bring back. Ever since the Sa'ba Taalor had raised the dead, it was generally considered best to burn the corpses and deliver the ashes if one felt like going through the effort.

The war had changed everything, really, and that was a sad thing, indeed.

Not as sad as two dead men who had been friends, but it was sad just the same. Before Jarry could muck up anything else, Lenwig gathered the belongings of the dead men who'd worked for him and put them in separate satchels. He'd return them to the families, along with what pay the men had earned.

Then, if he was lucky, he'd never have to meet another of the gray-skinned monsters in his entire life.

CHAPTER ONE

Darsken Murdro

By day Canhoon thrived. Vendors hawked their wares, and locals and visitors alike bought those goods, often pleasantly surprised at the varieties afforded in the capital of the empire. Veritable fortunes exchanged hands and treasures of every type moved to new locations.

By day the people of Canhoon followed the laws and managed smiles.

By night the wiser people were often off the streets and knew which parts of town should be avoided, although the streets were seldom the issue. The Silent Army moved through Canhoon and more than one ruffian had discovered that the stone soldiers upheld the laws in addition to protecting the city from invaders. They were silent, as their name claimed, and they were merciless. Muggers lost hands, cutthroats lost lives and rapists lost other extremities. Canhoon was very likely the safest place to walk the streets. But the Silent Army did not enter buildings, and seldom walked far from the great walls that were built in three different locations around Canhoon.

There were places that were still unsafe.

Darsken Murdro took care of the places where the Silent Army did not offer protection. Among those places he often frequented was the harbor. For a very long time the City of Wonders had been landlocked. When it lifted itself into the air and moved to its current location in the very center of Lake Gerhaim, that changed. Obviously.

In the years since the war had ended the docks and resulting harbor had come into play quickly, built with careful consideration even as a few tried to make fast work of the growing trade coming in from elsewhere.

The City-Watch was a heavy presence in the area. Too many chances for foul play and theft for that to be avoided.

Darsken looked at the corpse and knew the head of the watch would receive a visit from him in the near future. It was not a visit the man would enjoy in any form.

The two City-Watch standing with him knew it too and were likely grateful not to hold their captain's position in the ranks.

"When did you find him?" He gestured toward the corpse with his walking stick. Said corpse was currently in an unnatural position, legs and arms bent and broken to take shapes they otherwise would never hold on their own. The body was also missing several pieces that had been cut away with great care. Nothing done to the body was random. He knew that much without looking any closer. Skin was peeled away and marked before being placed in new positions, teeth were broken free.

"A fisherman spotted him on the way from the wharves." The man's name was Sarhen. He was efficient and often the one who found trouble in the area. He was currently moving his hands together in an effort to stay warm. Winter was coming all too soon and the air was frigid. His words came out in steaming breaths.

"Where is the fisherman now?"

"He's in front of the *Eel House*. Name's Brenn. He knows not to go anywhere."

Darsken nodded and went back to the corpse. There was half-frozen blood along the cobblestones, but not enough. Likely the murder had happened elsewhere. "The sun is up soon. Please have the body taken to my offices before that happens. Be careful to alter the way the body is presented as little as possible."

Both of the guards looked dubious.

"Do not disappoint me." He made his voice extra stern as he headed toward the pub called the *Eel House*. The structure was less than three years old but already looked like it was rotting and ready to fall over in a strong breeze. As he recalled it had looked that way since the first day it was opened. He came down to the area more than he liked to think about.

There was a stoop-shouldered man squinting from the doorway. He looked decidedly unhappy to be where he was. As the pub was currently closed that was hardly a surprise.

"You're Brenn?"

"Aye." His head bobbed in a nearly violent nod and he squinted harder.

"I am Inquisitor Darsken Murdro. I would ask you some questions." The man swallowed hard and jerked his head in another violent nod.

"H-However I can help." Those eyes regarded him differently after the introduction. Not at all a surprise, really. Most people feared the Inquisitors, not merely because they were the law, but because of the endless rumors about how they could steal secrets from the dead.

The fact that the rumors were mostly true only added to the fear.

Darsken looked at the man and judged him harshly. "Where is your gear?"

"My gear?"

"How do you fish without equipment?"

"I..." The man's eyes flickered unconsciously, very likely looking for an escape route that did not exist.

"The dead man you reported. His clothes were mostly cut away, but someone took the time to empty his pockets. It would be easy for me to ask him who took what was his. Should I ask him?"

Brenn cringed, but stood his ground.

Darsken nodded. Hardly the worst crime, to steal from a dead man, and not one he felt much need to pursue. "You took coin from him. What else?"

"Nothing." The man lowered his head in shame. Sometimes the smallest crimes seemed like sins before the gods. As Darsken was from Louron where no gods were followed, he merely stared hard at the fisherman. Like as not he'd merely stumbled upon the body after half a night of stealing from drunks.

"You reported the body." Darsken stared hard at the man, studying details. Considering the violence done, he doubted Brenn had anything to do with the actual murder. "For that reason, I will overlook your theft, provided you return the coin to me." He waited while the man cringed again and then meticulously counted out four fat coins from a small sack.

Rather than push further, Darsken took the coins and nodded. "Now, did you see anyone near the place where you found the body?"

Brenn shook his head and stared hard at the ground.

"Was he properly dead when you ran across him? Or did he still live?"

"He were dead. How could anyone have lived through

that?" His accent was thick. Not from Canhoon, but far to the east and south. Very likely from Elda.

"Did you touch or take anything else from around the body?"

"No. I swear it."

There were more questions but they got no better answers. When he was satisfied that the man had answered fairly and honestly, he sent him on his way. There were no lessons learned but the money retaken would go to the family if there was one. If not, the inquisition's coffers would fatten by a few coins.

Two hours later Darsken finished his meticulous examination of the body. There was little that the corpse spoke of save degradation and pain. Most of what had been done to the poor bastard had occurred while he was still alive.

When he needed more information, when his eyes and hands had found all the clues they could, he resorted to necromancy.

Darsken made his own marks upon the corpse, using a white paint created from several different plants, the blood of an arrow eel, and grave mold cultivated under careful conditions. In most cases the spirit trapped within the body responded in a matter of minutes, and while he knew the spell cast could cause the dead pain, most were willing to answer the questions to find justice from the other side of death.

In this case nothing happened. Nothing at all. The body did not move, there was no spirit returning from the shores of death. Nothing at all.

Setting aside the paints that should have brought the spirit back, Darsken called on darker, stronger sorceries and tried to force the spirit of his latest examination back into the body, calling out to the powers that could breach the gulf between the living and the dead. The effort was exhausting, as it always was, but the results were unsatisfactory.

When he was finished Darsken left the chamber where the body rested, careful to lock the door. The dead did not always rest easily after being summoned and the room was warded against unpleasant visitations.

Not that he needed to bother. The Second of the Inquisitors walked slowly from his summoning chambers and worried his lower lip as he did so. His dark skin was stippled with perspiration caused by exertion rather than warmth. His thick dreadlocks moved freely over his shoulders and neck, tickling at his flesh, and he pulled them together and tied them into a ponytail without conscious thought. One hand reached into his vest pocket and he pulled free a small piece of dried fruit. He needed sustenance after trying to bring a dead soul back. Magic, even necromancy, always demanded a price. Had the spirit come back the price would have been exacted from the dead, but without a spirit to take the power from it was Darsken himself that paid.

No spirit had come when summoned. That meant only one of two things. Either the summoning had been done improperly, and he considered that possibility and shoved it aside. Had he failed to perform the ritual properly no price would have been exacted and he would not be exhausted. The other possibility was far more disturbing to him.

The spirit had not come back because the spirit had been consumed, completely and utterly. The only thing that could cause that sort of issue was exactly what he had used to try the summoning in the first place: Necromancy.

Not just necromancy but the sort that was expressly forbidden throughout the empire. The sort of dark magic that consumed souls.

Darsken did not speak to anyone as he made his way from the Inquisitor Towers and into the darkness of a cloudy day. The towers loomed above the other nearby structures. The dark stone glistened wetly in the drizzle falling from the storm-drenched skies. He was barely aware of his surroundings as he considered the implications of his failure.

There was someone he needed to speak with. Unfortunately he knew that the First Advisor to the Empire was not in Canhoon at the present time and that he would have to wait.

Nachia Krous

Empress Nachia Krous stared down into what had once been the Blasted Lands and saw the ocean of green foliage that now filled the once desolate valley. Trees as far as the eye could see, all of the growth ancient in appearance. Meandering throughout that lush tapestry was one particular plant that could not be ignored. Once one knew what to look for it was almost impossible not to see the Mother-Vine.

Very nearly a god in its own right, the Mother-Vine was the progenitor of the entire forest that comprised New Trecharch. In the distance, a great ways off, she could see the mountains that had once been home to the Sa'ba Taalor and their seven gods of war. Now those volcanic monoliths lay dormant though she did not truly know if they were merely slumbering or if the Daxar Taalor, the gods of the Seven Forges, had actually abandoned them. How could she hope to know? She could barely keep up with her own gods.

The endless frozen storms were gone, replaced by a vast

jungle. She could not truly say if gods were responsible, only that what she saw now was a miracle.

"I still say this is a horrible mistake, Majesty." Desh Krohan spoke and ruined her moment of silent contemplation.

"Yes, you've made that abundantly clear every hour since we started in this direction."

"And yet here we are, days away from the safety of the palace."

"I'm perfectly safe. I brought my First Advisor with me and he's a fearsome sorcerer. Also I brought the head of my army, and he's a soldier of extreme prowess."

General Merros Dulver, the very head of her army, coughed into his hand to avoid saying anything he'd regret.

Desh was not as generous. "Yes, leaving the City of Wonders half defenseless in these trying times."

"You have your trusted Sisters watching over the city. Merros left other generals to yell at the troops and keep them in line. I have faith in your trusted aides. More than you have, apparently."

Pella, Goriah and Tataya were the three "Sisters" to Desh Krohan, powerful sorcerers in their own right. Any one of them was a considerable threat. All three together were a force of nature in Nachia's eyes. Desh raised his hands in either mock surrender or disgust. His lean face remained neutral, so it was hard to say.

The Temmis Pass lay before them. The easiest and safest route into the New Trecharch valley, it was also the only route where their supplies could come with them. Nachia spurred her horse forward and started moving. The man leading the Imperial Guard got the hint and called for the retinue of ten soldiers before her and ten after to move as well. The small caravan rolled on, and whatever other complaints Desh might have considered were pushed aside for the moment.

He had already argued that as Empress she was too important to risk. She had countered with the simple fact that as Empress she'd listen to her advisors and then make her own decisions. That had been the way of things since she'd taken the throne and she saw no reason for change. She could sit in her palace and wait for information or she could see for herself. It had been five years since the war with the Sa'ba Taalor had come to an end. In that time, she had heard little from New Trecharch and, as she was the ruler of the empire, she meant to rectify that.

Still, her stomach fluttered at a hundred touches of ice as she thought about the people they were about to encounter.

It was possible that of all the countries in Fellein, Trecharch had suffered the greatest losses. The Sa'ba Taalor had burned and cut down everything in their path as they swarmed through the area murdering people, cutting down the Mother-Vine and leaving ruination in the path that was worse than any other part of the empire experienced. The Mother-Vine took care of rebuilding itself. It moved to a new location because the old one was now home to one of the gods of their enemies.

Slightly over five years had passed and the jungle she descended into looked like it had been growing for centuries. Trees towered above them, gigantic and weathered. Deep foliage hid the sun from the ground under a cooling green canopy. Birds of all kinds sang in the deep forest, and creatures moved through the places where eyes could not see, making their own cacophony of noises. Truly Trecharch lived again, despite the impossibility of so much growth.

Merros caught up with her but said nothing. His eyes looked carefully at their surroundings and he was rigid with tension.

"Why are you so worried?"

"There are people watching us, Majesty. Tends to make me nervous when I am severely outnumbered."

Even as he spoke their watchers became more obvious. The people came out of the woods, or rather let themselves be seen. Stepping from behind foliage and barriers hidden by more greenery, until nearly a hundred people stood before the imperial retinue.

She was surprised by the number of weapons aimed in their direction. The war, it seemed, had left the survivors with a strong desire to never lose at combat again. She could understand that notion well enough.

After several moments of staring, one of the watchers stepped forward. He was a tall, lean man with a hard face and salt and pepper hair. His beard was close cropped, and his expression was very carefully neutral. He wore clothes that were designed to blend in with the trees, swirling patterns of brown and gray and green.

"Good day. How may we help you, travelers?"

Nachia was perfectly capable of speaking for herself. That did not stop Desh Krohan from beating her to it. When he spoke his voice rang darkly and, though she did not turn to look, Nachia knew that he had drawn up the mantle of his cloak and his face was buried in shadows. When he wanted to be impressive, the First Advisor could be positively terrifying. Sorcery aided that image and the cloak itself was stronger than the very finest armor ever made.

"The Empress Nachia Krous, the supreme authority of Fellein, calls upon the denizens of New Trecharch to welcome her and show her to the rulers of this land."

The bearded speaker nodded his head and beckoned an androgynous youth to his side. He spoke quietly, and the youth nodded and then jogged deeper into the woods.

"The Empress was not expected. Arrangements are being made, and, of course, rooms will be prepared." The man spoke calmly enough. There were many who were intimidated by her title alone, but he was not one of them. That suited her just fine. She'd long since grown tired of people who were impressed by titles, except when they expedited matters.

The man snapped his fingers and the hundred or so soldiers facing Nachia and her retinue snapped to attention. As a unit they bowed formally and Nachia acknowledged the bow with a nod of her head.

Merros muttered under his breath. "Nice to see a little proper behavior." He said it mostly in jest and she knew it, because the soldiers surrounding them had been obligated to stop aiming in their direction while they bowed. Mostly they held bows, spears and arrows, but whatever the weapons there had been a lot of death aimed their way.

"I'm Marten, the watch commander. Welcome to Trecharch." The spokesman pointed. "If you'll follow me we'll see about a place for you to rest before you meet with the queen." He spoke casually enough, but his eyes stayed locked on Desh Krohan, confirming her suspicions about the great hood covering her First Advisor's head.

It was less than an hour later before Merros, Desh and Nachia were ushered into the chamber where the queen of New Trecharch waited.

In the past, in the original Trecharch, the queen had been in a more traditional palace. The chambers where they met her were palatial, true enough, but appeared to have grown straight up from the ground and the Mother-Vine alike. The walls were alive, as were the floor and ceiling around them.

Everything smelled of fresh, green wood. The furnishings were more traditional, which was probably a necessary evil, really. A chair that was grown from the ground would be hard-pressed to move enough to accommodate a sitting visitor if still attached to a root system.

Queen Tully seemed to have grown into the part she was given despite her own misgivings. At one time she'd carried the spirit of the Mother-Vine inside her body and she'd seemed half-wild. Now she stood erect and carried herself with the proper dignity. Shoulders squared, long, graceful neck straight, and her once short hair now flowed down to her shoulders and beyond.

"Welcome to Trecharch. It's good to see all of you." The young woman smiled and came closer, her expression warm and natural. While half of her advisors and a good number of others in the court would have been horrified by the lack of formalities, Nachia was delighted. She dealt with the bowing and the titles every day and found them tedious. Instead of following traditional protocol or waiting to be called forward with a fanfare of announcements, Tully came straight over to them and offered a friendly embrace. She did not move in to hug anyone, but instead stood with her arms open and a genuine enthusiasm for the people she saw.

Nachia took the plunge and offered a gentle clasp. Merros followed suit and finally Desh lowered his hood and smiled just as brightly as she had ever seen.

There was no royal retinue. The queen entered the chambers by herself and stayed alone.

As if sensing what Nachia was thinking, Tully responded with, "I don't always like ears listening to my words." She leaned in closer. "The Empress comes to see me, I suspect she might like the same courtesy."

Nachia said, "I'm really only here to see how you're settling in. I think it's important to keep contact." Desh snorted, but said nothing. Nachia ignored him.

"I've long since made myself at home. What choice did I have? The Mother-Vine chose me." Which was true. Though no one spoke of it, they all knew that Tully normally spent her time within the massive vine, often times slumbering, as the Mother-Vine planned and changed the area. Being away from the special chamber was an exception and far from normal.

"You've a stronger military than before," Merros Dulver spoke softly. He smiled. "I approve."

Tully's eyes narrowed. "The Sa'ba Taalor still exist. That's all the reason we need."

"That's one of the reasons we have mandatory military service."

Tully nodded. "Three years for the empire. Four years for Trecharch."

"That's long service."

"That's the price of war." Tully shrugged.

"Do you think the Sa'ba Taalor will attack again?"

"I have little doubt." She looked him in the eyes when she spoke, which was different from before she was made queen. The shyness was gone. One could not rule and remain skittish. The two did not sit well together.

Merros nodded and Tully continued, "The Mother-Vine says war is inevitable and so we prepare."

"I agree with the Mother-Vine." Nachia shrugged. They would stay for a while, possibly even the night, but soon they'd be on the way back to Canhoon. What she needed to know she now understood.

"The Sa'ba Taalor are not alone. There is another source

for the coming conflict, one the Mother-Vine does not see clearly."

Nachia reconsidered. Perhaps they would stay an extra day. The Mother-Vine, like all gods, it seemed, was being vague and finding the answer would take time.

Whistler

The day was dying in Goltha, but that hardly mattered at the moment. "Why do they call you the Whistler?" She spoke softly, her face half-buried in a pillow and her large, dark eyes wide in the fading light of the day.

Whistler smiled and leaned in close, nuzzling her ear softly. "Just Whistler. No 'the'. Because it was my job, wasn't it? Back before the war I was lookout for a group of lads that did their own business. I'd special calls for them. One for if the Inquisitors were coming, another if the king's men were nearby. A third for the City-Guard. A fourth to just get them to run from the area."

"What stopped you?"

"The gray skins. Killed most of the boys I was working with." That was the truth of it. The Sa'ba Taalor hadn't been at all picky over who they killed. They'd burned down everyone they couldn't flat out cut apart, and whoever was left when they were done found themselves homeless and called themselves lucky. The war had been as unkind as the City-Guard on a particularly bad day.

"What's your real name, then?"

"Doesn't matter." He kissed a line along her neck and moved his hands over her body. She sighed contentedly and played along. Whistler almost never used his real name. It had no meaning for him. Like everything else from before the gray skins, it was effectively ashes and tasted like the same whenever he heard it.

For a time, she distracted him too much to consider his names, or the ways of the world.

"Well then, what's my name?" She rolled over and looked up at him and issued a silent challenge.

"Auretta."

"You remembered." She laughed and put her arms around his neck, drawing him closer.

"I always remember the important things, my lovely." He chuckled and kissed her mouth and for a time they forgot all about conversation.

Long after they were done, Auretta nuzzled close and drifted in and out of slumber, buoyed on a river of dreams, he supposed.

Whistler listened to the night and the sounds it made. There were other sounds, too – voices, but he knew perfectly well that they were only memories, or dreams trying to capture his attention. At least that was what he tried to tell himself.

He should have been content. He should have been perfectly happy with the beautiful girl in his bed and the money in his purse, and the food on his table, but he wanted more. Needed more. He just wasn't sure where he needed to be looking yet.

"Soon enough," he whispered to himself.

Out in the night, in the darkness, a man with too many blades and a mission to end a life wandered down the street. They would meet when the time was right, and not one minute sooner.

CHAPTER TWO

Trigan Garth

Trigan Garth rode slowly toward the rocky outcropping, not in the least bit hurried to reach his destination. He had listened to the fool's requests and came here now to sate his curiosity.

The fool continued on with him but now rode closer. "This is as far as I go." Koder had traveled half of Fellein with him, leading him to this location, and while he was not particularly fond of the man, he had grown accustomed to his companionship.

"Why?"

"There are others like you that I have to find before the Sa'ba Taalor hunt them down." He turned his horse, ready to go back the other way. "Many of them have gone a great distance. That means I have to travel just as far."

Trigan said nothing more but nodded and drove forward. If this was a trap it was an elaborate one. If not, there was money to be made and glory to be had. The Sa'ba Taalor had little use for money, but he could find ways to spend what he earned.

The stone outcropping he looked at had been recently buried, if he had to guess. Fresh dirt lined all but the crown of the granite, though that area covered several feet the muddied sides rose four feet in the air. What could lift a stone that size he did not know.

There was a single man waiting for him. Not a warrior, by his looks. That was the one his recruiter had called Jeron. He had no doubt. Though his flesh was unblemished by scars, his skin in some places looked fresh, as if recently grown or healed. No hair grew in those places.

'You are Jeron."

"And you are Trigan Garth."

The man was tall and lean with silver-shot hair and a long staff of scarred hardwood. Several shreds of colorful fabric were tied to the staff, though if they served a function it was lost to Trigan.

"You have called for me. Why?"

"I have need of your services. I need fighters, warriors, and fearless men." Jeron smiled softly as he spoke, and walked toward Trigan with eyes that locked onto his own. "There is a war coming. I need soldiers and commanders."

"You are in luck."

"How do you suppose?"

"I am fond of war." He climbed down from his horse. "Where is this army you are building?"

They stood on the Wellish Steppes, an area that was not overly hospitable, which still put it well ahead of most of the Seven Forges. The Daxar Taalor believed that hardship made a person stronger. Trigan agreed. When he saw the small, furry creature come up from between two clusters of thick grass his dagger was out and thrown without conscious thought. The rodent died quickly, and he walked over to claim his prize.

Jeron watched without speaking. After Trigan had his dinner in hand Jeron pointed. "This way. I'll show you where they wait."

The man gestured and the air shimmered for a moment before a trail appeared that simply had not been there a moment before. He followed the trail and saw the shimmer pass behind him as he walked. The only thing that changed was the collection of tents that were suddenly in front of him. A great number of tents.

"I have a tent for you, that is all I can provide. The rest is up to you."

"The tent is enough." It was more than he'd expected. Jeron walked beside him and guided him to his new resting place. The tent was simple and sufficient. He hadn't expected a palace.

Around him men and women alike climbed from their tents to see him. Most were Sa'ba Taalor and that likely meant that they, too, walked without the grace of their old gods. A few faces were familiar, but only a few.

One stood out, Ventdril the Unbroken. He had been punished by the gods, twisted into a Pra-Moresh for disobeying them. Several years later he was given back his true form. Trigan did not expect to see him among the Godless. That he had been given back his true form should have meant he had found his faith again. Perhaps it was easier to lose it the second time.

"What happens next, Jeron?" He gathered his belongings from the horse.

"I ask you to be patient. You will meet with an army soon enough."

Trigan nodded. He was not in a hurry to get anywhere.

When the man moved on Trigan entered his tent and opened his bedroll. He was sore from traveling, and he would rest if he could.

Andover Lashk

Andover Lashk of the Iron Hands did not knock when he entered the building. He merely pushed the door open with a grunt and knocked the fat guard unconscious as the man tried to stop him. He was kind and used his elbow on the man's temple as his fist would have broken bones.

Two Guntha stared at him and considered their options. They were paid to stop people like Andover from causing trouble. Andover was bigger than they were, and he was gray-skinned and scarred like a Sa'ba Taalor. In a very real sense, he *was* Sa'ba Taalor. He had been trained by their gods to become a champion and he had been trained very well, indeed.

If more than a hundred Guntha survived the destruction of their homeland, Andover would be surprised. They were the very first victims of the gray skins and their homeland now rested beneath Wheklam, one of the Seven Forges, the land destroyed and buried by an active volcano. The people who were on that island had either vacated quickly or died a painful death, buried under ashes and fresh, molten stone.

"You can leave if you like." He even held the door.

The two Guntha ran. They were wise.

He closed and locked the door behind them.

Andover Lashk had once been a normal young man. Fate and a fool's actions had changed that. The fool had been a City-Guard who decided he should not look at a young woman named Tega. Purb, the guard, took the hammer Andover used to work metal in a smith's shop and shattered both of Andover's hands.

Tega was apprentice to a sorcerer. The sorcerer met with the gray-skinned Sa'ba Taalor when they first arrived in the capital city, and at her request the sorcerer asked if the Sa'ba Taalor could help mend him.

The gods of the Sa'ba Taalor said yes, in exchange for a favor. For one year he would serve as ambassador between their people. His life changed drastically after that.

He had been an apprentice blacksmith, barely able to afford to eat, and living in a corner of the smith's workshop. No more. The Daxar Taalor worked him like metal. Like the hands he now used, he had been forged by the gods, reshaped and tooled into something so far removed from his past that he was no longer recognizable.

Yes. He was Sa'ba Taalor in all but name, but he lived in the capital, and he dwelled among the Fellein.

Somewhere in this den his Uncle Brann was once again smoking ground Lumba seeds, a cheap method of escaping from his life and finding dreams. Andover did not care, but his mother would have if she'd survived the end of Tyrne. He should not have cared himself as his mother had disowned him long before she died, and yet…

"One last time then. After this, no more." He made the vow again, knowing he would likely not keep it. The man was his uncle, after all.

The woman who ran the place came for him with a dagger in her hand and every intention of cutting his throat. She was easily twenty years older than him and on the heavy side. She also knew how to use her weapon of choice. He was forced to dodge four times before he finally managed to capture her arms and break both wrists. She cursed him in Brellar and he shook his head. He knew the words; he simply did not care.

"Stop selling to my uncle and I will not have to come back here again." Sometimes it worked. There were two houses that currently would not sell to his uncle. There were several more that hadn't met him yet as he went for the cheapest first.

The old woman spit and scowled, then sat down on her rear end, both arms useless. He felt no regret for the pain that lined her face. She had chosen a life that offered risks as often as it offered rewards, and she had chosen to sell to his uncle. Again.

It took five doors to find Brann. Each of the rooms held several people so overwhelmed by Lumba that they could barely move. Some of them were close to death from the stuff, drooling on the floors and sitting in their own waste. He wrinkled his nose in disgust and continued on.

Brann was one of the few good memories from his past. The man had always been kind to Andover, and, when he visited, he inevitably brought his nephew a treat of some kind. Sometimes a toy, or a pastry, or even fresh Pabba fruit on a few occasions.

His Uncle was not sitting in a dreaming stupor. He was dead. Truly dead.

Andover closed his eyes for a moment and thought of the kind man he'd known as a lad and looked at the corpse of that man, shriveled in size from starving himself to afford the Lumba, and made old long before his time.

As he was in the mood to offer favors, he let the people in the rooms know that he was burning down the building before he started taking torches and candles to whatever fabric he could find. He left Brann's body where it lay.

The heavy woman called him several names and he ignored her again. She would find her way out or she would die. He was fine with either result. He felt that way about the entire group of them. They were weak and diseased. If they wanted to live, they would have to be stronger and fight.

There was a chance that the City-Guard would come for him, or the Inquisitors. He would deal with them if that time came. In the meanwhile, the night was open and the air off the lake refreshing after dealing with the Lumba users.

He took his time walking home. If anyone in the seedier part of Canhoon thought of attacking him, they decided against it. That was for the best, really; there was enough blood on his hands for one night.

Pella

Pella smiled despite a quick, jolting trepidation at the sight of Darsken Murdro. He was dressed as always, pants and a shirt and vest, a heavy coat and his walking stick adorned with skulls. His hair was braided into a dozen or more dreadlocks, all of which were pulled back into a thick ponytail of black and gray. His generous mouth smiled from a broad face and his eyes were kind, but the simple fact was that he was an Inquisitor and generated fear simply by existing.

He bowed his head. "May I enter?"

"Of course, Darsken. You are always welcome." He'd have been more welcome if either of her sisters or Desh himself were around, but there it was. Darsken was from Louron and his dark hues were nearly unsettling after the pale skin of so many natives.

She slipped slightly sideways as if afraid his large body would not fit through the doorway. He was a very stocky man – not fat but very wide. Still, she needn't have worried.

"I know that Desh Krohan is not here, but I seek his advice, or possibly yours, Pella." His voice was almost always soft when he spoke, but deep enough to carry just the same.

"Whatever I can help with. We are in your debt." Which

was the other reason for her dread. Darsken was owed a great deal. He had helped them bring back Goriah after she was killed in the war, breaking several important rules in the process. At the very least he was owed a life.

"I find I am dealing with necromancy, true necromancy, and I need to access the right books to find answers. Or, rather, I need them accessed."

Pella gathered her thoughts as she collected tea leaves and took water from the pot over the fire. By the time the tea was brewing properly she had collected herself. "Of course, we can help. Tell me what you need."

"In the last five days I have been tasked with three murders in the old town, Pella. All of them tortured while alive and then tortured again in death. In all three cases there is no spirit left. No soul. The bodies are devoid of any spark of their old lives."

She didn't have to ask how he knew. He was an Inquisitor, one of the few allowed to deal with any aspect of necromancy at all. Even she was forbidden to study that dark art or to practice it. But Desh Krohan, the man who had made certain the practice was outlawed, also held all the books on necromancy. Someone had to be certain to know the signs that the dark art was employed, should any choose to break the laws.

"Desh can certainly look into the matter with more knowledge than me, but if you need the information sooner, I will try to find answers." She had no desire to involve herself, but could not turn away his request after all he had done on their behalf.

His dark eyes studied her for a moment, and the half smile he almost always sported continued on. "There is some urgency, but no great rush. I am merely making certain I understand all that is happening." She offered him a cup of tea and he took it gratefully. It was cold out, and warmth was a wonderful gift to share. Darsken took a large sip of the dark tea and sighed his pleasure.

"Your teas are always a delight, Pella. Thank you."

She smiled in response and settled down across from him. "What do you think you're dealing with, Darsken?"

"I've no doubt it's necromancy. But I am unfamiliar with the sort of spells that can completely pull a spirit from a body." He frowned, sipped his tea and frowned again. "I need to know what is gained from such dark sorcery."

"Power, I suppose." Pella shrugged and took a sip of her own tea. "Magic has a cost, and having someone else pay that cost is always a sought-after reward."

Darsken nodded and frowned more deeply. "That is a very high cost."

"The greater the sorcery, the more power needed."

Darsken frowned and set his emptied teacup down. "What sort of incantation could require three souls?"

"There are any number of summoning spells that could demand three or more souls, Darsken. There are some that require years of a sorcerer's life and rather than risk those years I am certain some would be tempted to make sacrifices instead."

"Are the sacrifices guaranteed to work, I wonder."

"Sorcery is only as good as the summoner." Pella shook her head. "In the hands of an adept the sacrifices would work."

"Are you missing any adepts?" The very question she'd been wondering herself. There were a number of sorcerers in training, but then sorcerers were always in training. One never learned everything.

"Not that I'm aware of, but whoever could perform this sort of ritual would have to be well-trained. You can't simply look at an incantation and work it without years of practice." She sighed as she spoke. It was a simple truth. Whoever was committing the crimes had to come from the only school of magic left. That still left a list of suspects that spanned quite a few names, her own included.

Darsken rose from his seat and nodded. "Please have Desh contact me when he returns. It is of utmost importance that we stop whoever this is."

"Of course, Darsken. I'll get him the information as quickly as I can."

Once again that half smile of his lit the room. He had a wonderful smile. "You are very kind."

"No, just kind enough, I think." She smiled back and watched as the Inquisitor left. Her stomach wanted to knot itself. This was a dangerous time. Desh Krohan would be furious. The very notion of anyone using necromancy to aid their cause was reason for dread, but three bodies? Blatantly put on display so that everyone saw them and knew what was happening? It was more than an insult, it was a challenge to the council of wizards, such as it was. The school would very likely come under suspicion, as it should.

They lived in Canhoon, the only city where a sorcerer could commit an act of necromancy and possibly get away with it, simply because there were too many with similar talents. The Inquisition was looking at the sorcerers with a wary eye.

That did not bode well for anyone.

Desh Krohan

Three storm crows came down from the sky at the same time. Not unheard of but also not likely. The birds almost never gathered together when flying. Desh knew that as he'd studied the birds extensively.

He held up one arm and the closest of the great gray birds landed on his wrist. Pella looked at him from within the bird. Not ten feet away Merros Dulver cursed softly under his breath. He was a man who hated sorcery and always would. It took only seconds for Pella to share her conversation with Darsken Murdro. The news was hardly relaxing. Desh felt his shoulders tense and the start of a headache reached for him, clinging to his temples.

They had climbed back up the Temmis Pass and passed the small town of Hallis. They were well along the Jeurgis River now, headed for home. The soldiers with them did their jobs well, but that was hardly relaxing when one considered the news that the Sa'ba Taalor were hunting in the area. Officially there was no war going on, but that didn't mean anyone relaxed when the gray skins were on the move. Twenty soldiers, even the best trained, were more of a warm-up for the Sa'ba Taalor than an actual threat. Soldiers were trained. The gray skins were literally bred for combat. Unfair of him to think that way? Yes, but still it happened. There was nothing he could do about it, either, and he knew he wasn't alone in his thoughts.

The Imperial Guard were better than average soldiers. They were trained by Andover Iron Hands, who had managed, with the help of the gods of the Sa'ba Taalor, to learn the ways of the gray skins. He had, in fact, bested Desh himself in a fight. It was a memory he tried not to dwell on.

Pella stared at him with one dark eye, and then flapped her wings and was airborne a moment later. One of the other great birds dropped and landed on his wrist a moment later. Goriah. She stared in his eye and conveyed her message: something was wrong in the Wellish Steppes. The great stone that had rested there for as long as anyone could remember had changed and was pushing itself from the ground.

Desh frowned at that news. There had been a time when the stone was above the soil. Ages of wind and erosion had pushed that stone down into the ground until little remained but a small hump of rock above the surface.

The stone was marked a thousand times over, had been marked by Desh himself when he first placed it over the resting place of the Overlords. He preferred it stay where it was and not rise from the ground. Whatever was under there needed to remain lost to the ages.

Goriah rose from her position on his wrist and soared into the wind, rising easily. Tataya did not land, but instead circled with her sisters and rose higher into the air. In moments the three Sisters dressed as storm crows were on their way, headed back to Canhoon.

Whatever secrets she had acquired would wait. For now he had enough to consider.

Nachia rode next to him, and looked his way with a silent demand for knowledge. She was the Empress. He would tell her when he was ready. First, he had to figure out *what* to tell her.

She looked at him expectantly. "Well?"

"Well what?"

Nachia shook her head and, given the chance, she might well have snorted angrily, but there were too many witnesses for her comfort. "I know full well that those birds were talking with you. What did they say?"

"You heard them yourself." He allowed himself a small smile.

"Don't test me, Desh."

"One of them might have cawed."

Her color reddened a great deal and he sighed. "Let me compose my thoughts, Majesty. It's a lot to take in."

She said nothing more, but made it a point to keep pace with him when he tried to ride past her.

He waited until they'd set up camp and were gathered in the largest tent to eat before he finally clarified what he'd heard.

Desh's knife deftly cut a Pabba fruit into sections that he set out on a platter on a small table between himself, Merros and Nachia. Merros took an offered slice and chewed eagerly at the succulent treat. Nachia took a piece and nibbled daintily.

"So, first it seems that someone is performing necromantic rites in Canhoon." Desh spoke with slow deliberation. "We don't know who as yet, but it is being investigated."

"What does that mean, Desh?" Merros eyed him as he continued chewing.

"It means that a sorcerer has stolen at least three souls from the bodies of recently tortured people." Just that fast the general's appetite faded.

"How could that be allowed to happen?"

"No one allowed anything, no more than we allow assassination. Some things simply happen and are dealt with. The Inquisitors are investigating the sorcerer's guild as there is no one else with the sort of knowledge needed and even among sorcerers the use of necromancy is forbidden."

He made sure to stay calm as he spoke, but it was a challenge.

When he continued, he added, "The bodies were publicly displayed. It's not going to get easier to handle."

His knife cut a smaller wedge from a slice of the fruit and he ate it before continuing.

"More significantly there has been a change in the resting place of the Overlords."

Merros frowned. "The who?"

"The Wellish Overlords. They were a threat a very long time ago."

Nachia shook her head. "I would swear you once told me they were only a story to scare children." Her voice carried an accusatory edge.

"That's all they've been for as long as anyone can remember, including me. I know that at one time they were a threat, but it has been centuries, Nachia. Probably a thousand years."

Merros shook his head. "So, what has happened to their resting place?"

"They were buried a long time ago. I… We thought they were dead, but the very worst of them would not stay buried and their corpses would not burn. No matter how hard we tried, we could not give their flesh to the fire."

Desh Krohan stared out into the distance beyond the wall of the tent, troubled by the words he spoke. "I've said it before. I am ancient, far older than you understand. I don't remember everything from my past. I know that the Overlords are real. I know I dealt with them and that they fought against Fellein. But I know that in the same way that a man remembers his childhood. I have scattered memories and little else to go on. I don't clearly remember the Overlords, not any more than I remember the first anniversary of my birth. I can't recall if I ever saw them while they were alive."

The sad part was he was telling the truth. When he tried

to think of the Overlords, he got a nervous flutter in his stomach and little else.

"The thing to know, to understand, is that the Overlords were real and very dangerous. I mean they came close to taking all of Fellein. I remember that well enough." Desh stared at Nachia for a moment and then looked past her, trying to remember more of the Overlords through the haze of centuries.

"So what do you remember about them, Desh?" Nachia stared hard into his eyes, did her best to freeze him with her glare.

He stared back. "I remember that they were not like us. They are at least as smart as we are, but they aren't human." He had a vision of long, nearly wiry limbs that bent in too many places. "They're like nothing I'd ever seen before."

His first look at the things was a distant memory, but he could still remember the chill that had coursed through his body when he saw them revealed. The way the flesh of his scalp crept tighter at the sight of them.

Maybe it wasn't just age and the centuries. Maybe he simply didn't want to remember the Overlords that clearly. That thought filled him with dread.

"They don't think like us. They are not like us in many ways, really. What they want, what they seek from us, it's not just about taking over the land." His brow knotted as he tried to think. "I'm not sure what it was that made them different. I have to research the Overlords when I get back to my library," he muttered to himself, but loudly enough for the others to hear.

"So, not much then?" Merros smiled as he spoke.

Desh blinked and shook off the fog of distant memories. "Say again?"

"What do we need to know about the Overlords the most?"

"They're dangerous. They are everything we should fear." Desh Krohan looked away from the general and stared at the sky. "I'd rather face the Sa'ba Taalor again."

The humor drained from Merros's face. That was a threat he could easily understand. In that context he suddenly knew how bad the situation was.

Jeron

The stone parted before him and Jeron walked into the mound where the Overlords still slept.

There had been a time, long ago, when he regarded them as enemies. That had been a mistake and he understood that now.

Behind him Tymin hesitated. Tymin was a good man, but not the bravest he had ever met.

"Come along, Tymin." His tone allowed for no argument, and the nervous man nodded his shaggy head and followed. They had met only a few months earlier and in exchange for a few meals a day Tymin had proven a loyal aide. Not overly bright, certainly not a shrewd conversationalist, but loyal.

"Do you suppose they're awake yet?" the man's voice shook. He had glimpsed more than a mere shadow of the Overlords and they worried him a great deal. He was right to be worried. They were not kind.

"We would know, Tymin."

"We would?"

"Oh, yes. We would know if they were awake. You would be able to feel it in your bones." He wasn't completely sure that was true, but he suspected it. Jeron had faced the Overlords back in the past, when he was a much younger being and capable of foolishness without provocation. He had stood side by side with Desh Krohan and the rest and cast his sorceries, for all the good they did.

Wisdom comes with age. This time around he would work with the very things that nearly conquered Fellein in the past. The curving wall of the tunnel offered support, and Jeron touched the surface, grateful to have something to lean on as he felt the questing gaze of the Overlords move through the very earth in search of him. He wanted to stop but didn't allow himself that luxury. He wanted to run but forbade himself. The fear he felt was potent, and he let it wash over him.

Tymin moaned and tried to back away. Jeron reached for the right sorcery and took control of the man's legs. "No. Come with me. You have to be stronger than this, Tymin."

"Please, Jeron, no." The man's voice shook with fear.

"They will not hurt you, Tymin. I won't allow it." He forced his companion to walk forward, a puppeteer with a marionette. Tymin moaned, and began to pray under his breath.

"No!" Jeron spun fast on the man and thrust a finger that struck Tymin hard in the chest. His voice echoed and bounced along the winding passage. "Whatever gods you pray to, stop yourself before you offend them. The Overlords will not have gods in their way again."

Tymin licked thin, nervous lips and nodded his head, eyes closed tightly. His breaths came in rushed gasps. They descended for several minutes in silence save for Tymin's continued whimpers.

Tymin had never been into the chamber, but for Jeron the area had grown familiar in recent days. The walls around them were lit by a dozen small torches. The sconces holding those torches shook, and their flames flickered and danced as Jeron stepped lower on his way into the vast chamber where the Overlords still rested.

A thousand years of decay crept across the walls and dripped to the floor of the chamber. It fairly grew like mold as it slid in frozen rivers down to the heavy ground. On the floor of the cavern the dark decay wavered in the breezeless confines as if seeking something new to corrupt. Jeron stayed well away from the dark patches. There was a stench to the area that Jeron knew would linger long after he had retreated back to the surface.

Tymin looked around and let out a long, low moan of fright.

Jeron ignored his companion and stared at the huddled shadows where the Overlords rested. They were buried in a deep caul of wet-looking darkness. Whatever it was that actually covered them refused to drink in the light from the torches, but instead stretched blackly from the center of the chamber toward the western wall.

How many of the Overlords still lived he could not have guessed. The shapes beneath the blackness seemed nearly fused together, crushed into one another and frozen with outreaching hands and stranger, unknown limbs. Each looked to be suffering, though he felt no pain from them, only hunger and rage. They had moved since last he had been down. Even their slumber was restless now. They grew impatient.

Tymin saw them and fell to his knees, his head turned so that he looked away from the seething darkness where the Overlords rested. Jeron understood the desire but could not offer himself that luxury. His new companions did not respect fear.

Without hesitation he forced Tymin to stand. The

marionette danced to his tune, regardless of what it wanted.

"No! Please, Jeron, do not do this!"

Jeron sighed. He hated to do what must be done but the Overlords made demands.

Tymin let out a wail of pure fear as his legs moved him forward. He pissed himself as his treacherous feet walked closer to the dark shape that seemed already to be reaching for him. He was screaming in terror by the time his forehead pressed against the outstretched hand in front of him.

The darkness that covered the Overlords flowed faster as it touched living flesh. Like the corruption that slowly dripped down the walls of the cavern, that black caul spread from the groping fingers of the Overlord and slapped over Tymin's face, moved down his neck and over his skull, drawing him into the black without warning. He fought back, tried desperately to escape, but the darkness held him and pulled him slowly into its depths.

Jeron watched it all silently, not speaking, not daring so much as a gasp lest he catch the attention of the Overlords in the wrong way. He served them, yes, but he also knew they were not human and doubted they thought of humans as equals. He also knew that for all his powers, they had greater strengths than he could dream of.

So far, he had fed the Overlords a dozen living souls and twice that number of dead souls. It was a challenge, pulling the lives from the people he killed, but he knew the right rituals, understood the power of necromancy that Desh Krohan sought to deny. He also knew the power of fear, which was why he'd started leaving some of the bodies in different places around Canhoon. It was easy enough to move them when he was done. Hardly a challenge at all, but he knew the dead were frightening sights by the time he'd finished with them, and that fear could be a powerful motivator.

Jeron. The voice felt like a distant whisper in his skull, but he knew the source was much closer. One of the Overlords spoke to him.

He lowered his head for a moment and answered, "I serve, my Lord."

We are pleased with your offerings. We awaken soon. Before that happens, we shall reward your patience. Come forward.

Jeron hesitated only for a moment. They would reward him or kill him, but either way he had little choice save to approach and receive whatever blessing or curse the Overlords offered. He had served faithfully. It would have to be enough.

The black shape of a hand moved toward him as it had toward Tymin, and Jeron stood his ground. That vile blackness touched him and he fought against recoiling. There was nothing natural to it, nothing that promised anything but pain. He had seen a dozen men taken by the very same hand, pulled into the darkness and swallowed as easily as a frog takes a fly.

Had anything ever felt so cold? Surely not. Jeron stopped himself from screaming as the fear frosted his guts. Pain tore at him, but still the sorcerer refused to scream. It was never wise to show weakness to predators.

Darkness crawled through his mind, his body, every last fiber of his being.

The darkness changed things. Changed him. Changed the way he saw the world. Jeron drank in that darkness with every breath he took and embraced the transformation.

Why had he ever hesitated? Why had he ever doubted the Overlords?

The darkness burned away his doubts and changed his very body.

Truly he was blessed by the Overlords.

Jeron screamed as the blessings began to warp his body and his mind alike.

Whistler

The voices were louder.

They had been lodged in his head for as long as he could remember, possibly as long as he'd been alive. They were in his head as the sun was in the daytime sky. Whether he paid them any heed, they were still present and inevitable. Sometimes they were the faintest whisper, and others were a conversation he had to strain to hear beyond, but now? They were impossible to ignore.

"What do you want?"

He didn't expect an answer, but he got one. "Come to us. We have need of you."

Whistler sat up on his narrow bed and opened his eyes. The room was familiar. The same walls, the same floor, the same collection of threadbare clothes. Some things simply did not change.

But the voices did. For the first time ever, the words were clear enough for him to hear without straining. He thought about the last of his skin of wine and decided against it. He did not seek to escape the voices, merely to understand what had changed.

"You need me, but I have no need of you. Go away."

He closed his eyes, half expecting pain for his insolence. When he had worked as a whistler he had always expected pain if he disobeyed. He had the scars along his back from when he had been whipped for his insolence. He had dared sleep on his watch once, and Doven had taken a belt to his back until it was raw and bloody.

There was no pain, but the voices grew louder, more insistent.

They only dimmed to a tolerable level when he considered the notion of leaving his home.

"Not yet. I have things I must do first."

He closed his eyes and sighed. There was a feeling in his guts, a nervous twist that told him he should be afraid of speaking against the voices, but Whistler did not react to fear the way he was supposed to. He never truly had. He was far likelier to attack what scared him than he was to run from it.

Sometimes he wondered why he was still alive. He knew his reaction was wrong but could not change what he was.

"Soon." The voices very nearly roared the word but Whistler knew they were only in his head.

They had always been there, for him and for him alone.

They were his blessing, perhaps, or just as likely his curse.

Outside of his small apartment, his neighbor Lowel was arguing with someone. Lowel had all the manners of a swine. He would roar out in his loudest voice whenever it suited him, and never consider the consequences. That was because Lowel was a large man, and believed that everyone was afraid of him.

He also smelled like he had last bathed before the war. Maybe it was the voices that made the man's existence so annoying, but Whistler found himself dressing quickly, pulling on his boots and picking up one of his knives.

Lowel was arguing with a man who trembled, but stood

up to the larger, doubtless smellier, neighbor. "I do not care if you feel you've paid your debt to me. I say you still owe seven Denouli."

"I have paid you." The man was sweating, his eyes wide, his body very nearly rattling in the cold morning air. He was dressed in a heavy coat that looked two sizes too large and was probably older than Whistler. If he had seven Denouli to his name, he'd need it just to repair his wretched clothing.

Lowel stepped closer and grabbed the man by his lapels, shaking him and wrenching him from his feet. "You will pay me, or I will break you."

"I cannot pay what I do not have. Please!"

"Then I break you." Lowel snarled the words, but he grinned as he did it. That was the thing with Lowel. He liked to hurt people. He liked to scare them.

The man flinched, but could go nowhere.

Whistler cleared his throat, and both men looked his way. "I don't want to hear your screams, Lowel. It is too early in the day."

"I don't care what you want, boy. Go away." Lowel glowered, offended by Whistler's presence. He was almost always offended by Whistler. Offended was simply the way the man lived his life.

Whistler stepped forward and drove his blade into Lowel's forearm, skewering the flesh, driving between the bones.

Lowel dropped the man and screamed in shock or pain or both, his eye wide and his jowly face shaking.

The blood flowed from his arm as the dagger's tip burst though the other side of his limb. The man he was holding dropped, completely forgotten.

Whistler yanked his dagger from Lowel's forearm and stepped in close. The blade punched nine holes in his neighbor's stomach in short order. Each elicited a gasp and little more, as the point was aimed upward and drove deep into the man's lungs.

Whistler looked at the thin stranger. "Run away."

Wisely, the stranger ran. He did not look back.

Whistler watched while Lowel collapsed slowly to the ground between their apartments. There was little he needed, but he'd not be coming back here. Returning meant dealing with the City-Guard, and that was not in his plans.

He pulled the body into his neighbor's small collection of rooms and wiped most of the blood away. Then he collected what he needed from his own rooms and moved on. It was not the first time he'd left a place he'd called home. He doubted it would be the last.

CHAPTER THREE

Darsken Murdro

Five bodies scattered through Canhoon and only two of them had been found by citizens instead of City-Guards. That was a blessing of sorts, but a small one. Two bodies meant a lot of talk, but not complete panic. The City-Guards had been put on alert. They were to look, to find, before anyone else managed to do the same.

In the meantime, Darsken Murdro had his work ahead of him as well as to his back. He had studied all five bodies, and though the markings were different on each of them, they were all victims of necromancy. He had no doubt it was the work of one person. The challenge was finding that person and stopping the continued crimes.

He walked across the grounds of the Imperial gardens, careful to stay on the path between the different rare plants and flowering bushes. The ground was level and it was easy to see anyone approaching. He was there to think, to reflect on what was happening, not to deal with possible trouble. For that reason, he tapped his walking stick to the ground with every step his left foot took. It was a warning that he was nearby. It was also a warning to the wise to leave him be.

Most took one look at his shape and decided against any possible attack. He was a large and imposing figure. Not a giant of a man, to be sure, but stocky.

The wind from the lake was cold and damp, a reminder of the season changing, and he was glad he'd bundled himself in several layers of clothing. Louron was to the south and so much warmer than Canhoon or the surrounding areas. How anyone walked the colder nights in only a shirt he would never understand, though he saw people doing it every day.

The sun had set, and the sky was lit only by stars. Several lanterns burned along the paths of the gardens, offering illumination if not warmth. Though it could not be seen past the massive inner wall that separated Old Canhoon from the newer parts, Darsken knew the lake was close; even now an evening fog was creeping into the city, hiding sins and sinners alike. Somewhere, near or far, there was a murderer who was taking lives and souls. That thought haunted him. He needed to resolve this madness before the murderer could strike again.

"This place invites madness." He spoke only to himself, but someone listened and responded.

"The gardens? Or do you mean the city itself?" Darsken recognized the voice. It was Desh Krohan who spoke.

"I was beginning to wonder if you would ever return to Canhoon." He smiled softly as he spoke, grateful to hear the man's voice.

The First Advisor to the Empress stepped before him, dressed in his robes of office, which is to say dressed to intimidate. Darsken did not understand the sorceries involved, but when wearing his robes the wizard was not only nearly indestructible, he also generated fear in a way that was far from natural. Even knowing that sorcery was involved did not help. The man seemed taller, more menacing, and capable of almost anything at all when his robes were on and the hood was drawn up.

Darsken managed not to shiver, but it wasn't easy.

"Pella and Tataya both told me you wanted to see me." Desh's face was lost in a darkness that was more than mere shadow. The robes shifted in the breeze but seemed to writhe with menace.

Darsken looked around for any possible witnesses. He could see none. "There is necromancy involved, Desh. I need your help to identify the source."

"Necromancy is forbidden. You know that." He could not tell if the man was jesting or sincere in his words. He decided to assume it was a sincere statement.

"There are always those who would break the rules for their own benefit." He sighed. "If not, I would not be an Inquisitor, but a fisherman instead."

"Tataya took me to see the bodies." Desh stepped closer, his voice not quite a whisper but close enough to stop anyone from eavesdropping. "It's definitely necromancy, but I can't find a clue as to who is responsible. I've already been by the Hall of Wizards seeking evidence."

Darsken pressed his lips together and said nothing. Speaking out against Desh Krohan's abilities would hardly be his wisest move.

The sorcerer put a familiar hand on his shoulder. "I haven't stopped looking, Darsken. I simply haven't had success yet. There are only so many questions I can ask at a time and I can only ask the people I see. Since the military started using sorcerers for communications, I've had to spread my people out across the whole of Fellein, and that makes conversation a bit more challenging than it used to be."

"Are there any sorcerers who are not a part of your academy?" It was an odd thing that, as an Inquisitor, Darsken could use necromancy, but knew almost nothing of the sorceries that were permitted in Fellein. The wizards were not fond of sharing information about themselves. Desh Krohan was an exception to that rule, but sometimes he wondered if the man helped because of his position or because he wanted to.

"It's always possible, but not likely. Wizardry is a challenging thing at the best of times, and learning anything more complex than a glamour isn't likely without a teacher." Desh leaned in closer and Darsken managed not to flinch. "Frankly, I've made it very difficult for most to learn without a teacher by keeping tight control over the books needed to learn."

That made a certain amount of sense. Even the simplest necromancy required a great deal of study with an instructor who was adept. There were no books, not for the Inquisitors. Written instructions on necromancy were forbidden to all but the most powerful sorcerers.

Someone moved up ahead and both of the men stopped speaking and listened. A moment later a young woman and her paramour moved from the bushes and onto the pathway. Seeing Desh Krohan and Darsken Murdro on the path, they chose to walk in the opposite direction.

Desh continued, "You know how hard it is to learn necromancy, but there are still a dozen or so wizards who were trained in the art before it was outlawed. I can control who learns from books, but if someone truly wanted to study, there are other ways. I have extensive knowledge of my own and I have access to the books. By all rights I am a suspect."

"You would be, but you were out of town and had witnesses for several of the murders."

"Have you identified the victims?"

"Three of them. All were merchants. One of them was also in charge of the merchant guild for Canhoon."

"Welan Parse?"

Darsken nodded. "None other. His death has already had ripples."

Desh sighed and shook his head under the cowl. "No doubt. What a pity, he was actually good at his job."

"I am doing what I can to investigate, but a list of those capable of performing the rituals would be most beneficial." Darsken made his point as clearly as he could.

Desh Krohan nodded somewhere inside of his robe and his hood moved. Even that simple gesture was menacing. "I'll have a full list for you soon. I have to contemplate who would and would not have that sort of knowledge."

Darsken tried to formulate a question that was delicate. It seemed the First Advisor was hesitating.

Before he could ask, Desh Krohan answered. "It's always best to be certain before accusing a sorcerer of anything untoward. Some of them have tempers. Any who could work this sort of necromancy wield a great deal of power."

"Understood."

"We will speak again soon, Darsken." Without another word the man vanished. He did not move away into shadows. He simply disappeared.

Darsken suppressed another shudder. The darkness had settled in properly, reinforced by a heavy shroud of fog. The Inquisitor tapped his way through the night and toward his home. He took comfort from the thought of his fireplace and the blaze he would soon set in it. The night seemed as cold as the dead, and if anyone would know, it was him.

King Swech

Winter was coming. The fire in the great hearth was warm and Swech reveled in it. She stretched her legs and her arms and moved her body in ways designed to relax tense muscles. It did not pay to ignore the aches in her body. Being prepared for fighting was essential, of course. She was a king these days and it would never pay to think that meant less work or preparation.

Jo'Hedee mirrored her moves, as did Valam. Her friend and her son. Without warning, Swech shifted her stance and delivered a kick to Jo'Hedee's side. The woman moved to block the blow and was partially successful. Without another word spoken, the other woman charged, feinting with her left hand and then delivering a savage strike with her right elbow. Swech blocked both of them, grunting at the impact from the elbow.

Her return volley involved two strikes with her right hand and a knee that sent her friend staggering backward. Swech pushed her advantage and struck the younger woman again before she could roll away and recover.

Valam watched, not speaking, but instead drinking in each strike. He was too young to fight with either of them, but he was never too young to learn.

Jo'Hedee fell to the ground and used her new position to sweep Swech's legs. Swech dropped obligingly before delivering a brutal axe kick into the other woman's stomach.

Jo'Hedee rolled to her knees and waved a surrender as she gagged and tried not to vomit. Swech climbed back to her feet and waited patiently for the other to recover enough for another round of combat. She also kept her attention on her surroundings as Jo'Hedee was not above inviting others to attack the King in Mercury. It came with the territory.

She saw the movement from the corner of her eye and dropped down to the ground, rolling out of the way as three darts cut through the air where she had been standing. Swech continued her forward momentum and struck with her left heel, delivering a blow into the groin of the would-be attacker. Hotches dropped to the ground and groaned, absolutely unprepared for the attack.

He should have been. Swech knew he was better than that.

Her knee delivered another strike, this time on his temple, and Hotches dropped, unconscious.

Jo'Hedee came in from the left and landed a hard blow to Swech's ribs. Swech moved with the strike, lessening the force that connected, and slapped a hand across Jo'Hedee's eyes blinding the girl for a moment. That was long enough. While Jo'Hedee flinched and tried to see, Swech drove a knee into her stomach and dropped her again. By the time Jo'Hedee was recovering, Swech was sitting on her throne and staring into the molten heart of Paedle, looking down into the chamber of molten stone that should have incinerated them all by right. Paedle kept them safe and let them see the glory hidden from most. Valam tried to climb into her lap and she let him. The fighting was done for now.

Jo'Hedee nodded and settled herself in another chair.

Swech was silent for a moment as Paedle spoke to her. The god spoke to all of his people, but more to his chosen king.

Swech listened carefully, and obeyed. "Gather nine others, Jo'Hedee. Make sure they are prepared for a long journey. We leave with the dawn."

The woman nodded and rose from her chair. "Followers of Paedle?"

"To the last."

Paedle was the God of Silent Combat and God in Mercury. Silence and poison were his greatest gifts and what he expected from his followers. Swech was his King and would do as he ordered without question. Currently that meant heading for Canhoon. She did not question the gods; she simply obeyed them.

"Jo'Hedee?"

"Yes?" She looked back at Swech, her head slightly tilted as she listened.

"Make them followers of Wrommish as well."

"A god with whom I must once again study," Jo'Hedee said, as she ran a hand over her bruised ribs.

"Wrommish is as close to Paedle as I am." Swech nodded. The God of Unarmed Combat was indeed a sibling to Paedle. It was wise to study under both gods, even if their kingdoms were no longer as close as they once had been.

That was the wisdom of the Daxar Taalor: the kingdoms were farther apart than they had been in the past. Traveling between them was a challenge. There were ways around the issue, but they were fraught with dangers of their own. No task laid out for the Sa'ba Taalor was meant to be easy. The gods sought to make their chosen people stronger through challenges. A life of ease was what had made Fellein so very weak.

Swech moved her hand through her son's fine blond hair and wondered whether she would see his father, Merros Dulver, again. Years and years and still she could not keep him from her thoughts. Foolishness, of course. The man was not Sa'ba Taalor. He did not follow any gods and he was the general in charge of the Fellein armies. By rights she should never think of him, should never have been with him, but there was something about him that captured her attention and worried at her mind.

Not that her thoughts would stop her from following Paedle's wishes. Unlike Merros, she was faithful to the gods of her people. They had never failed her, and she did her best to return that favor.

Canhoon would soon be back in her world. Merros lived in Canhoon.

Anything was possible, if the gods allowed it, and they had always been so very kind to Swech.

Merros Dulver

There weren't a lot of warriors in Canhoon that scared Merros Dulver. He had never run from a fight in his life and he knew that he could match if not exceed most fighters he met, simply by virtue of how long he'd been an active soldier and mercenary. He was alive, which said a great deal about his skills after the number of conflicts he'd been in.

Andover Lashk of the Iron Hands? He scared Merros more than he wanted to think about. Andover had literally been trained by gods of war to be the most brutal fighter possible. He had fought countless enemies until he was honed like a fine blade. With or without weapons he was a terror on the battlefield, which was one of the reasons Merros had hired him to train the elite warriors of Fellein. He had learned a great deal under the younger man's tutelage.

Currently Andover was waiting patiently for Merros to tell him off. They both knew what the man had done and why it was wrong.

"Were you expecting me to deny it? They killed my uncle with their poisons." Andover's voice was perfectly reasonable through the odd sibilance that accompanied all of the Sa'ba Taalor when they spoke. That was the Great Scars, the mouths that grew out of their faces when they were accepted by one of the gods. In Andover's case he had seven Great Scars that ran along his actual lips in neat succession. Apparently, something that only happened when they'd been accepted by all seven of the gods of the forges.

"You can't just go around burning down houses, Andover."

Andover shrugged his broad shoulders, sending ripples through the preposterous levels of muscle on his body. "It needed burning." While he spoke, Andover sharpened the edge of a massive battle axe. It had a single blade and a curve to the handle. Merros guessed it would cleave a horse in half with remarkably little effort. Currently the man's longish hair was tied back with a leather cord.

Merros had resisted the urge to bring a dozen soldiers with him. He doubted Andover would be impressed, and he didn't need to give the man an excuse to use that axe.

"Andover..."

Those silvery eyes looked on his and stared hard. "I only had the one uncle and he's dead. I see no reason to burn down any other houses. That is the best you will get from me. I refuse any claims of guilt. They killed first."

Merros considered the words carefully. No one had died save, apparently, the one uncle, despite the fire being deliberately set. The only structure ruined belonged to the filth selling poison to foolish people.

Finally he shook his head and sighed. "I suppose that will have to do."

Andover continued sharpening his blade, but it was just possible that he'd relaxed a little. "Then I am pleased that we had this conversation."

Merros put his hands together and clenched them. "Andover. Please, the next time you have a complaint, bring it to me first."

"You are the leader of the Imperial armies. You have more pressing matters."

"First and foremost, I do what I can to keep the peace. I need you. I do not need you locked away for murdering people."

There had been several pressing cases where that was exactly what happened. In each situation the deaths were, if not necessary, at least justifiable in the eyes of the law. Despite his sheer size being a deterrent to the wiser people who approached Andover, there had been a few fools who were either drunk enough or stupid enough to see him and decide to take out their anger against the Sa'ba Taalor on him.

Andover was not Sa'ba Taalor. He was from Fellein. He looked like one of the people of the forges, however, and that was enough for a few fools. He had also, as has been stated, been trained by the Daxar Taalor, the very gods of the Sa'ba Taalor, to be a very effective warrior. In most cases he'd killed his attackers and then gone home to wait for the City-Guard to come for him. He had not resisted arrest even once, for which Merros was extremely grateful.

"If people do not try to kill me or mine, I will refrain from returning the favor."

"I expect that's the best I'm going to get from you."

"You are right." Andover looked him in the eyes, that odd glow coming from beneath his heavy brow.

Andover put down his whetstone and rose to his full height, holding out his newest weapon and shifting his grip until he could hold the weapon in his open iron hand, perfectly balanced. The blade was large and shone dully in the afternoon light. So did his fingertips.

"You should try making your own weapons, Merros. There is something very fulfilling in it."

Merros grinned and shook his head again. "We've had this discussion. I'm not a blacksmith."

"I could teach you."

"I believe the Empress might have an objection to me taking the time from running her armies."

"She can make more generals."

"That's a horrible idea. Then I'd be in daily arguments about how I'm doing everything the wrong way."

Andover chuckled and set his axe down. "You like being in charge too much, I think."

"It has advantages." Merros smiled and put a hand on the larger man's shoulder. Then he put on his stern face and matching voice. "I mean it. No more taking matters on yourself, Andover. You have another problem, you come to me. Or I forget about our mutually beneficial arrangements and look at having you locked in a cell for a few years."

Despite his size and his astonishing combat abilities, the fact was that Andover Lashk was still a young man. He nodded and said, "Yes sir," automatically.

"I'm sorry about your uncle."

Andover's gaze slid across the area slowly. "He was the last of my blood. I'm alone now."

Merros gave the boy's shoulder a squeeze. "I have been without family for some time. I understand all too well." He knew there were differences. He did not have the physical markings of a Sa'ba Taalor to separate him from everyone around him. There were many soldiers who knew and respected Andover, but none likely to spend time with him. He was simply too different.

Still, he had no answers for Andover, and so he went on his way.

Andover would go on as he had for the last few years, undeterred by his differences. At least Merros hoped he would. The notion of losing the man as an ally was daunting.

He walked the short distance from Andover's rooms at the palace – better to keep the man close by was the philosophy Merros shared with Nachia and Desh – and back to his own offices. He spent all of ten minutes looking over his notes before he was summoned to the Empress's court.

He arrived in the latest barrage of argument between Empress and First Advisor. Desh Krohan wore his robes, but the hood was cast back, leaving him less intimidating than the mage would have liked by a stretch. When his mantle was up the man inspired terror. When it was down, he had an average face with salt and pepper hair and his voice was merely a human one. Sorcery was only as effective as the limitations placed on it. Merros tried to tell himself that every time he encountered magic. He hated the stuff. Happily, the man who embodied the most powerful uses for magic was actually a decent human being.

Nachia Krause, the Empress of Fellein, was a gorgeous woman with auburn hair and blue eyes. He'd studied her beauty more than once and remained convinced that she and her family were bred as much for looks as they were for wealth. Her brother, Brolley, was a handsome enough lad and had the courtesan followers to prove it.

This was a closed court affair, meaning that Empress and First Advisor alike were not on their best behavior.

Desh shook his head, his lips pressed into a thin line. "You can argue the point with me as long as you'd like, Nachia, but the facts remain the same. Either you find a husband, or at least a mate, or your family will choose your successor when you die."

"My cousin chose me." She sighed and stared hard to make her point.

The sorcerer stepped back and gave her a hard glare. "Yes, he did. And several of your other cousins and relatives fought me very hard regarding your ascension to the throne."

If the Empress was at all threatened by his expression she hid it behind a mask of calm that was impenetrable. "Well, you'll simply have to fight again if the time comes before I have an heir."

Desh sighed and seemed to wither within his robes. "As I was reminded only a few years ago, Majesty, there's always the chance that I won't always be here. Death comes to all of us eventually, and I am very far removed from being a young man."

She tsked her response.

Desh shook his head. "Nachia, this sounds like a jest to you, but I'm extremely serious."

"I have no intention of marrying just to have a baby." She shook her head and her lips pressed into a thin line. "I'm the Empress. I get to put in my personal opinion for time to time."

Desh crossed his arms. "Not as often as you'd like."

"More often than you seem prepared to understand, Desh."

Merros cleared his throat, hoping desperately that the conversation could be sent in another direction. He had no say in whether or not the Empress found a mate and he was perfectly fine with that.

"By the gods, Merros, talk some sense into her," Desh spoke, and Nachia fired a preemptive glare in the general's direction.

Merros quickly made a gesture of surrender. "There are some wars that I am not in control of. This is decidedly one of them."

Desh Krohan humphed in response. Apparently, they'd both reached the point where guttural sound effects were all that was required to make their positions known.

"I was summoned, Majesty?" It was all he had as an argument.

Nachia looked momentarily puzzled, which was really far better than irritated, in his eyes. Then, "Yes. Desh wanted to know how you feel about using more sorcerers with the army."

"Much the same as I did before." He looked to the First Advisor. "Nothing personal. I don't like sorcery."

"I'm not overly fond of axes after taking one to the chest, but I still see their benefit."

"An axe kills exactly one soldier at a time." He crossed his arms. "An axe cannot accidentally hit an army."

"I've never once missed when aiming at an army. Believe it."

"It's not your aim I worry about." Even if he did, he'd never admit it. He had seen the sorcerer burn a two-mile swath of forest and people with a volley of lighting that left him half blinded. The people he burned had already been dead and brought back to false life by the gods of the Sa'ba Taalor. He had been spared the horrors of trying to kill something that could not easily die by the First Advisor. He could not hope to guess how many soldiers had also been spared by that gesture. Still, in the hands of a less sorcerer, the same sort of power was frightening. One sorcerer had frozen the whole of Lake Gerhaim during the war. Only one though, and under duress. It was an argument he'd used before.

"Merros, we've had movement at all of the Seven Forges." Nachia spoke softly, and her eyes took on the distant look they always got when she was considering how best to argue her point. The simple fact of the matter was that the Empress often left him in complete control of the armies. That was the task she'd appointed him to, and it was the task she expected him to handle. But the look and the tone of her voice said she was ready to debate the situation, and strongly.

If she did, he would lose the argument. It was her empire. He was just in charge of part of it and he could be replaced.

"Majesty, it's not Desh Krohan I doubt. It's not his abilities I question. You know this. He knows this. I have made myself very clear, or at least I've tried to. The sheer power that sorcerers employ is simply too great."

The First Advisor shook his head and crossed his arms. "One man holds a sword, two hundred carry sticks. The man with the sword has a power that is too great."

"More like one man has a catapult with burning oil. Everyone else is a child with a toy." Merros sighed and moved across to the table in front of the Empress. The table was laden with fruit and breads and cheese. As Nachia had, on several occasions, made clear that the food was for everyone, he plucked a small cluster of grapes from a platter and started eating them one at a time. "Again, my problem isn't with you, Desh. I worry about the others, who may not have been taught as well as you."

"I'm in charge of the academy of magical arts, Merros. You presume I don't take my teaching seriously."

There was simply no way to win the argument. Not unless he wanted to have a bloody duel with the man, and there was no chance of that happening.

Nachia spoke. "Ten more sorcerers to start, placed with

the battalions that Merros chooses and Desh approves. Each of these sorcerers to answer directly to the commander of Merros's choosing." She waved one hand in the air. "Make it so by my command."

That was the end of the debate. Except, "I want regular training sessions for all of them. I also want to meet them all before I approve their placement."

Desh nodded "Done."

Merros nodded too, though he was hardly happy with the situation. The Empress had spoken. That was all there was to say about the matter.

"They're subject to the same rules as any member of my army. They disobey and they are punished."

Desh opened his mouth to speak and Merros pointed a finger. "That means I expect you or one of the Sisters to be ready to administer punishment when necessary. Do you agree?"

"Well, I suppose I must."

"Then ten sorcerers added to the armies is acceptable for me."

Nachia reached for a hard cheese and smiled. "I'm glad we're all in agreement." She nibbled an edge of the cheese. "What other business do we have?"

"There's the matter of your courtship, Majesty."

"Not today, Desh. I'm in too good a mood."

"Sooner or later, Majesty, you will have to make a choice."

"Sooner or later I might actually find someone who strikes my fancy. Until then, you should prepare my brother for possible ascension to the throne."

"Brolley?" Merros and Desh spoke at the same time.

"Yes, Brolley." Nachia looked from one to the other several times in quick succession, gauging who she should direct her ire toward first.

Desh stepped forward to take the full brunt of her anger. “Nachia, Brolley may not have the same sense of diplomacy as you do.”

“Brolley is much better than he used to be.”

“And that’s true, but I am not certain he’ll ever be as wise a leader as his sister.”

That stopped her anger. It was hard to argue with a sincere compliment.

She waved her hand again as if chasing away a persistent fly. “That’s why you should begin training him now.”

“Since I am here, and before you two begin this argument again in earnest,” Merros spoke quickly before they could lose themselves in Desh’s latest obsession, “I think we should consider the matter of the temples.”

Desh rolled his eyes, already frustrated. Nachia’s jaw clamped down.

“So, we’re all in agreement that things are going poorly?” Merros reached for a piece of cheese that looked particularly savory and bit into the small wedge, the sudden rich flavor working well to complement the grapes still in his mouth.

“Only if the various temples joining forces to push for more political power is your idea of a poorly handled situation.” Nachia leaned back on her seat and then scowled. She sighed and stood up, restless, apparently.

“I remind you, Majesty, that the laws allow for religious gatherings of any size.” Desh spoke with a certain wariness.

The Empress of Fellein made an obscene hand gesture and said nothing. Merros managed not to laugh. He had already annoyed the most powerful sorcerer in the empire enough for one day.

“So back to the Sa’ba Taalor then. What sort of movement has been spotted?”

"Armies are gathering, according to our observers."

"By which you mean the sorcerers who are keeping watch?" They had learned the hard way that observers spotted near the various mountains of the Seven Forges tended not to report home. In fact, they were never seen again. The Sa'ba Taalor were not a forgiving people and they liked their privacy.

"For all we know they plan on fighting each other."

"True enough." Nachia took another tiny bite of cheese and then continued. "For all we know they plan on starting another war with Fellein."

He wanted to argue, but truthfully, she was right.

King Tuskandru

Brodem let out a companionly rumble and Tusk rubbed his mount behind the right ear, a gesture nearly guaranteed to put the beast in a good mood. Brodem's head pushed against his fingers and palm, urging him to continue, and Tusk did so even as he looked around the area.

Durhallem, the mountain, was also rumbling, but there was little that could be called companionly about it. Though everyone was safe enough where the tribe was settled, great gouts of steam bellowed from the top of the mountain and pushed toward the north and east, compelled by the ocean breeze.

Far below, a dozen figures approached, riding on horses. That told Tusk all he needed to know about who was coming into his territory. He looked over Brodem and saw that his weapons were still where they belonged. It was time to descend and see what the humans wanted. He expected he already knew.

Most of the humans who came to Durhallem hoped that, somehow, they could reach the ruins of Tyrne. They came with plans to dig and find treasures left behind when Durhallem chose that city as the place to move his mountain. Sometimes they asked permission and other times they simply began digging.

The answer was always no. Those who did not ask first were punished for their insolence.

Stastha rode past him on Loarhun, who let out a friendly growl in Brodem's direction.

"We have visitors, Tuskandru."

"Yes. I know. I am headed there now."

"You are slow," she called out mockingly.

"I wasn't aware we were racing." He smiled and climbed on Brodem's back. His hand had barely captured the front of his saddle before the mount was moving, taking the distance in leaps, the better to catch up with Loarhun and his rider. He sensed his mount's amusement at his annoyance. A moment later he was smiling. The thrill of the race, the prospect of combat, those were the things that he lived for.

Stastha saw him and let out a raw laugh as her mount started racing. She was a good second. She challenged him constantly, but was also wise enough not to anger him with those challenges, or to contradict any order he gave.

Tuskandru was the Chosen of Durhallem, the Obsidian King. His place was his until his god decided otherwise or he was killed in combat, whichever came first. It would be foolish to question his ways. He was the voice of Durhallem and the champion of his god. Durhallem was the Wounder. He believed in punishing the foolish. Tusk agreed with his god's philosophies.

They raced down the mountain toward the gathered

Fellein, both riders and mounts putting their all into the race. Brodem let out a low rumble as Loarhun beat him. "He had too large a lead." Tusk patted his mount's neck and then reached for his axe.

Stastha managed to put on her horned helmet before she dropped from Loarhun's back and pulled her own axe free.

Twelve men on horseback looked at the two riders and mounts, and then fought to keep their horses from panic. The mounts were large and very predatory. The horses were wise to be nervous.

Tusk got directly to his reason for descending the mountain. "Why are you here?" His axe rested across his broad shoulder as he spoke. His free hand held the massive skull-shaped helmet he usually sported and he placed it carefully, half expecting Stastha to make a comment that was not forthcoming. She might mention it later, but for the moment her king was speaking to trespassers. It was not the time for playful jests.

"We've come to speak to King Tuskandru." The man who spoke was older, with gray hair and a thick white beard. He had enough scars on his body to show that he was a warrior. Though his horse was nervous, the man himself was not. His left eye was covered with a patch, and his face around that patch was heavy with scar tissue.

"I am King Tuskandru. Why are you here?"

"We wish to barter with you."

Now Stastha spoke, though she did so in the language of the Seven Forges, not in the common tongue of the Fellein. "Perhaps they will share whatever wealth they can dig up from under the mountain."

Tusk smiled and gave no other indication that he had heard her words.

"What do you wish to barter for?"

"Safe passage through your kingdom, along the old Emperor's Highway." The man pointed to the south where, though it was currently unused, a paved road ran for miles to the north and south. "Tyrne is gone, but Larnsport is not far from here and mostly cut off from the empire. There is also the land where Roathes stands, where we have been rebuilding for over two years."

"Interesting." It wasn't what he'd expected to hear. He'd had no doubt that the men wanted to dig beneath Durhallem and seek treasures long since destroyed.

"What do you seek to barter with?" Stastha asked the very question that he would have asked himself. At the moment he was considering the possible difficulties that might arise, and he was also waiting to hear what Durhallem might decree. The god did not always involve himself in the mundane but there was always that possibility.

"We can offer whatever you'd like."

Tusk paced slowly in a small circle, considering the possibilities. The easiest response was to kill them, of course, but Durhallem did not demand that and, for now at least, there was no war.

War made decisions much easier, really.

"We have no need of these fools, Tuskandru." Stastha got directly to the point, as she often did.

Tusk nodded absently and continued his pacing. Durhallem was silent, but it was a baited silence. Tusk knew his god was listening in and waiting for his response. He could kill the interlopers, or he could draw a bargain of some kind.

"You wish passage past Durhallem." Tusk looked at the scarred man. "I want four hundred horses and two of yours to teach my people to ride them."

"Four hundred?" Though the man kept a calm expression his voice wavered a bit.

"You come on behalf of your empire to see if I will let your people pass by my lands without attack," Tusk stopped pacing and stared hard at the man. "The answer is yes. But the cost is four hundred horses and trainers." Tusk smiled under his helmet and continued staring. "That is my offer. Go discuss it with those you answer to, if you must."

It was one of the men behind him that answered. "You're a fool. Four hundred horses? Fifty, perhaps."

Tusk smiled. "And now you insult me? Five hundred horses. No less."

The older man spoke. "My son is unwise. Forgive him."

"I follow the god Durhallem. He is called 'The Wounder' because he is unforgiving. I cannot forgive an insult. Adding more to the cost allows me to spare your son his life for insulting me." Tusk moved his hand in a gesture that looked like he was imitating waves. It was the equivalent of a shrug for the Sa'ba Taalor. "Four hundred and I fight your son. Five hundred and he is free to go."

The old man looked back at his son. "Erig carries no weapons."

Tusk looked at the younger man and made his hand gesture again. "We can fight without weapons, or five hundred horses. It is all the same to me."

Stastha spoke in the language of the Sa'ba Taalor. "Why do you want horses, Tusk?" She sounded both amused and exasperated. She was used to her king's ways.

He responded in the same language. "We have mounts. I do not know that there will ever be more. Time will see the answer. There have been no new mounts for a few years, yes? For now, horses to add to our traveling abilities." He thought about it. "That, or food for the mounts."

The scarred man answered at the same time. "I must consult with a few others, who would have to help me procure your price."

Tusk nodded, but he looked at Erig, the younger man, as he did so and smiled. His expression was enough to offend the boy, which was exactly what he expected.

"Father. I will fight him." Erig's voice was a low rumble past bared teeth. He was offended enough by Tusk that he sought combat. Tusk always sought combat.

"No. You will not." The older man spoke without bothering to look to his son. While he spoke, the younger man climbed down from his horse.

"Stastha. Teach him." He stayed where he was, while his second set down her axe and stepped forward. Then to the boy he said, "Stastha will fight you on my behalf."

"A woman?" Erig sneered.

"No. My second." Tusk smiled. Any fool who thought a woman less capable deserved to learn what a woman could do. Stastha was a capable teacher.

Erig walked closer, ignoring his father when the man called for him.

Stastha stood her ground and took a deep breath, relaxing her body. Her hands slid up into defensive positions.

Erig came in swinging, expecting, to judge by the expression on his face, to end the fight quickly. His right fist came around in a savage arc. Stastha brought her left arm around and blocked his swing, her arm catching the full impact of his attack and stopping it cold. Even from a distance Tusk could see the hard bands of muscle at play under her skin. She was his second for a reason. She had earned that position. Her left hand moved and caught her enemy's arm at the wrist. She moved as she had been taught by the followers of Wrommish, and her fingers slid over Erig's wrist until they locked down and twisted.

The man let out a yelp of pain, and Stastha stepped back, releasing him.

"Bitch!" He tried to strike her with his elbow and she slipped out of the way, dropping down and using her left knee to connect with his stomach. The man bent over, doubled by the unexpected blow, and then grunted as she brought her own elbow down on the side of his head. Erig, fully a head taller than Stastha, dropped to his knee and hands in front of her, shaking his head to clear the dust away. He let out a groan and followed it with a low growl of anger, more insulted than hurt, apparently.

His hands reached out to capture her ankles, but Stastha danced back from the attempt and waited for him to get to his feet. Tusk shook his head. She was toying with the man. It wasn't a wise thing to do, even with a Fellein.

As soon as the man was standing, she stepped in again, striking him hard in the throat with the ridge of her hand. He fell back gagging, both hands moving to his throat. Stastha hit him again, driving her elbow into his chest and sending him staggering.

Had she been serious, she would have ruptured his throat. Tusk felt himself tensing, growing angry as she played with the Fellein. He could understand her reasoning, she was trying to prolong her fun. Still, now was not the time.

"Finish the fight, Stastha!"

She did not question her king, but instead responded. Erig charged forward, arms spread wide as if he were attempting to hug her. Powerful arms grabbed her and pulled her into an embrace that was anything but kind. Erig let out a grunt and did his best to crush Stastha.

Her hand delivered a brutal blow to Erig's face and changed the shape of his nose. Blood fairly exploded from his face, and he dropped her, too stunned to keep his grip. Stastha landed easily on her feet and then one hand caught the back of his head as if she were going to kiss him. She struck his face with her elbow once, twice, a third time. Each blow was hard enough to rock his head back. The final strike saw Erig fall to the ground, broken, his face ruined. He did not get up, but he still breathed.

Tusk nodded. "Four hundred horses. In good health. No old ones or lame ones."

The eleven men still on their horses were all staring at Stastha as if they had never seen her like. Tusk chuckled and said, "The women of the Sa'ba Taalor, they are like the men. They are trained for life in war and all things related to war. Do not make his mistake."

The man with the eye patch snapped his fingers and pointed over his shoulder. Two men climbed from their horses and gathered their bloodied, unconscious associate. As they carried him over to his horse to drape him over the saddle, the one-eyed man said, "I'll discuss this with my employers. I expect they'll agree. Horses need saddles and blankets. I'll make sure they include them in the price."

"When will I hear from you?"

"If my son lives, you'll hear from me when I return to the camp and make the request. If he dies, considerably sooner."

King Tuskandru laughed out loud. "I like you! You are very funny."

"Not joking. But we shall see." He whistled and turned his horse. The others followed suit and a moment later they were headed back the way they had come.

Stastha took off her helmet and brushed her fingers through her thick black hair. "He is angry."

"He's a fool. His son is a fool."

"Just the same, we should post watchers for a few days."

"We already have guards."

"Yes. But they should be told to actually guard the mountain."

Tusk nodded and watched the riders as they disappeared. "If we see them again, I want to know. Then I'll decide if they have to die." Stastha nodded and headed for her mount. Tusk watched her for a moment and then followed.

Morten Dunraven

Morten Dunraven rode the highway and refused himself the opportunity to look at Erig. When they stopped would be soon enough. They were almost at the campsite.

The boy could be so damned foolish! Why would he challenge a king? Why would he think there could be a good ending to that sort of challenge? If he had done that to any of the monarchs in Fellein he'd have been whipped to death, if he were lucky, or even burned at the stake.

Still, the boy was his oldest and he loved him.

Fourteen different merchants from Canhoon and Goltha were paying him handsomely to negotiate on their behalf. Trade routes needed to be opened. Roathes wanted to be a country again, a kingdom that could trade as they had in the past. For now it was a gathering of merchants and misplaced

Roathians that held the future of the Emperor's Highway as a possibility. If all went well Queen Lanaie would involve herself and there could even be a title in it for his efforts.

"Four hundred horses." He nearly spat the words. Was it possible? Of course. Was it likely to happen with ease? No. But they wanted to know Tuskandru's price and he found it. The rest was up to them.

There likely weren't four hundred horses to be found between Roathes and Canhoon, but they could be brought in and perhaps, if the gods were generous, the damned highway could be opened again. Using boats and ships wasn't as convenient as the occasional caravan. The problem currently was that any attempts to ride past the great, black mountain Durhallem was met by Sa'ba Taalor. The gray skins were not known for anything but bloodshed. The bastards hardly ever seemed to sleep. Didn't matter if the caravans crept past long after the sun had set, the Sa'ba Taalor found them.

The camp eventually showed itself and Morten scowled as he climbed off his mare. She took his shifting weight calmly and he in turn pulled an apple from his bag to thank her.

Erig was conscious by the time he reached the boy, but he was still addled from the fight. He resisted the urge to yell, preferring to save his anger for when it would do him good. Also, he was too relieved to see his son conscious after the beating he'd taken. The first man who mocked Erig for losing to a woman would get the lash. He promised himself that pleasure.

Delar and Jalle helped Erig to his tent. Morten thanked them both and made note of their actions. They did the deed without being asked, and several others simply went about their own affairs. A kindness was a kindness and his father had always said that kindnesses should be remembered and repaid.

Delar came to his tent less than ten minutes later. He waited until he was called in before speaking. "He'll be fine, Erig will. Took a beating but he's a strong lad."

"He's a fool. Lucky he didn't get his head cut off."

Delar nodded and offered a weathered smile. "Aye. True enough. Still, he made his point before..."

"Before he was beaten for a fool."

Delar scratched at his bald head and then nodded. "Aye."

The lads started making their noises twenty minutes later and Morten expected to meet a sorcerer, so he climbed back out of his tent. There were three men waiting, two of whom looked unfamiliar. The third was a welcome one. Lenwig's round face broke into a smile when he saw Morten and he grasped the man's arm warmly.

"You're alive. I suppose that means negotiations went well."

"They went. Not perfectly, but they went."

"This is Corin, he's going to help us with the meeting." He pointed to a thin man of average height. There was nothing average about him in any other account. Dark, curly hair and beard and mustache, ceremonial robes the likes of which so many of the sorcerers wore. He carried a sword on one hip and walked with a short spear as a walking stick. He had no particularly scary feature, but he was unsettling just the same.

Morten offered another arm grasp as greeting and the man accepted. "The last of our number is Darsken Murdro of the Inquisition." The dark man smiled warmly and Morten did his best to offer an arm he feared might be taken from him.

The Inquisitors had a reputation for finding every hidden sin, and while Morten tried his best, he had a few secrets he didn't want discovered.

The man grasped his arm with a firm hand and accepted the greeting. He smiled throughout the process and Morten grimaced in return. What if he could read minds? Nonsense. If they could see into a man's thoughts no one would allow them to live.

The man's smile seemed to grow even wider as he let go of Morten's arm. "I'm traveling through and have to be on my way soon."

"Where are you headed?" The question was habit. It was always polite to ask and to offer warning if you knew of dangers.

"Down to Louron."

"The roads are treacherous, my friend. The Sa'ba Taalor have a tight grasp on them."

Murdro nodded and his dark eyes drifted lazily over the area. "They do. But I have my own ways past them."

"Might be a time soon when you don't have to worry, but for now have a care."

The Inquisitor took his arm again and then did the same with his traveling companions before heading down the road toward Durhallem. Though he traveled on foot, he covered the distance at a remarkable speed.

"Lenwig, I didn't expect you here."

"It seemed easier to show Corin the way than to describe it, and my caravan is only a few hours distant and getting closer."

"Will you be joining us?"

"If you'll allow it."

"I'd be glad of the company." He spoke the truth.

"Where will you have your meeting, Morten?" Corin spoke softly, but no one had a problem hearing him.

He gestured to his tent, and the wizard nodded before heading in that direction. "It is time, good sirs."

When they entered the tent Corin had already begun his preparations. Within minutes the meeting had begun.

CHAPTER FOUR

Whistler

He walked along the streets of Goltha, his boot heels clacking softly on the cobblestones, and whistled softly to himself. All around him the streets were busy, and the people moved with purpose. Although there weren't as many people chattering away as usual. Too many deaths, he expected. Bodies found flayed open and marked with dark sorceries. "Sure to make people less talkative, I suppose." He spoke only to himself, and as no one was close enough to hear him, no one responded.

Whistler was not overly tall, but he was thin enough to make him appear that way, especially as he wore no cloak or coat, despite the chill, and the lack of those layers made his physique more noticeable. He eyed the people around him, and in his hand the hilt of his dagger nestled comfortably.

In the marketplace he stopped at Hashan's stand and bought two sticks of roast. The meat was well seasoned and the cuts were generous enough. The vendor offered bread with the roast and he took it. Some he used to fill the empty places the roast did not cover. Some he saved in a pocket, for later. Not to eat himself, but for the birds near the water.

He liked feeding them and liked their antics when they flew in close to snatch the prizes he offered away.

Illia was at her father's stand again. "Where is your father today, Illia?"

She looked up with a half scowl on her face, but recognizing him, that expression became a smile. Long, nimble fingers ran through her brown hair and she took a step in his direction. "He's not feeling well. The cold catches him more every season." She shook her head as he plucked an apple from one of the baskets, and then another.

The fruit she offered was fresh, and he added a Pabba. Illia's smile was as bright as the sun above them.

Goltha was his home and he knew it well, but Whistler expected that to change in the near future.

He knew that he would be leaving soon. The voices in his head told him so. There were many, many voices; so many that he could not count them all. They talked, they sang, they laughed, they cried. They were a constant cacophony, and he reveled in them the same way he reveled in the first blooms growing in the spring, and the way the cooling rains felt against his skin on a hot summer day.

Still, the endless noises could be distracting, and he knew that if he didn't leave Goltha soon they would overwhelm him again, as they had last night when he considered staying in the town he loved.

His blade deftly cut through the hard rind of the Pabba fruit, and he offered a thick slice to Illia. She took it and bit a wedge from it without hesitation. That was one of the things he liked best about the merchants in the area. They had no time for pretense or protocols. They were busy selling their wares, and eating was something they did when they could.

Not twenty feet away from where he stood, a man was glaring at the stands around him as if they had caused personal offense. He was large, well muscled and scarred by the life he'd lived. His face was broad and the start of thick jowls marred an otherwise strong jaw. That was the same with his body, really; the flab was sneaking in to hide the muscles.

Whistler disliked him immediately.

"I'm looking for Nedoun, the smith." The man looked at Illia as if she must surely know the answers to any question he might have.

Illia shook her head and frowned. "Can't say as I know the name. He's not around here."

"He told me he's in the western market."

"This is the western market but there's no one around here by that name."

The man let out a deep sigh and stared harder, as if he could use the force of his will to change her mind, "Nedoun. Nedoun the smith."

"Aye, I heard you. He's not here." She offered a very quick, apologetic smile. "I've worked here over three years. No one by that name works at any shop around this area."

The man's face grew stormy, and he leaned in closer to her. "He's got to be here. He has money of mine, and I'm expecting him to finish what I paid him for." The man looked around as if afraid someone would hear him and glean from his words what he had hired the smith to make for him.

Illia opened her mouth and then closed it, obviously uncertain as to what she could say to the stranger.

Whistler smiled. "Nedoun is not here. He never has been."

"And how would you know that? Are you a merchant?"

The man's dark eyes locked on him. If he'd been aiming a crossbow, Whistler would have been worried about walking away from the conflict intact. Instead, he merely smiled as he considered the jowl-faced stranger. "Do you know Nedoun?"

"I know a smith of that name. He's in the southern market. He's been there as long as I can remember."

"He told me the western market."

"Then he lied to you." Whistler's smile grew wider, and his teeth gritted together. "Lied, lied, lied." His voice bordered between a sing-song and a taunt.

"Why would he lie to me?" He couldn't have been more offended if Whistler accused him of being a gray skin.

"Because Nedoun is a poor smith at best, and known to lie when he wants to make money with no effort. He thinks you're likely to let him walk away with your money."

"What? Why would I do that?"

"I didn't say you would. I said he thinks you will. I don't know you. I can hardly say why he feels that way."

The stranger's face was red, his eyes fairly bulging from his skull, and his hands clenched into fists and relaxed again and again. "I don't like thieves."

"None of us do." Illia tried to catch his attention, but Whistler kept staring at the larger man, fully aware there was a chance the man was looking to punish him for offering bad news.

"So what am I supposed to do, then?" The man's posture was like a tightened fist. He wanted to lash out, and Whistler knew it. Better, however, to have the man angry with him than with Illia.

"Go to the southern market and find him. If you must, call the City-Guard to help you."

"You think I need the guard to handle my disputes?" He reared back as if slapped.

"I don't know or care what you need." Whistler's smile grew wider, and he stared hard at the man, locking eyes in challenge "No one here cares what you need."

All of the anger faded back in the man's expression as he considered the very obvious response to his posturing. What he'd expected was not what he got, and that made him hesitant to continue. Pity, really, Whistler was looking forward to the idea of spilling the man's innards.

Without another word the man nodded and backed down. In moments he'd faded into the crowd. Illia said, "I was taking care of it."

"I know. I just didn't like him very much."

"The problem with you, Whistler, is that you don't like a lot of people. And the ones you dislike tend to get bloodied."

He considered the blade he'd slipped into his hand when the man was getting confrontational, and slowly nodded. His smile did not go away. "I know. I know, Illia."

"One of these days the City-Guard are going to be in the wrong place, and what happens then?"

He winked at her. "Well, then I guess they'll have to do their own work for a change. Wouldn't that be nice?"

Without another word he counted out the coin he owed for the fruit and placed it carefully in her palm. Whistler took a moment to look at Illia's face one last time. He did not think he'd see her again, as Goltha was no longer to be his home. That decision was made in the moment, and though there were things and people he would miss, Whistler started on his course, heading away from the market and the faces he knew and even loved.

He did not know where he was going, exactly, only that

he had to head across the lake, in the direction of the setting sun.

The voices were speaking, and when they spoke together, it was time to move on.

Lenwig Wickhaven

Three faces were missing from the meeting. It was an odd affair to be sure, as the merchants and mercenaries all met in a single room that none of them actually occupied.

"We are absent Welan Parse, Eidar Hopsig and Tomlin Strom." It was Brolley Krous who spoke, not as the brother of the Empress, but as one of the heads of his house, which for better or worse was tied in with the merchants of Canhoon.

The one-eyed mercenary they'd hired to negotiate with Tuskandru growled in his throat and shook his head. "Why are three such… prestigious members of our gathering missing?"

Brolley spoke calmly. "They have been murdered."

Every voice started up at once and the Empress's brother crossed his arms and waited for the outcry to calm down. When it finally did, he answered, "The Inquisition is seeking answers even as we speak. They were murdered. That is all we know for now."

"Yes, but–"

"That is all we know. Asking again does not change that fact." He looked around the room calmly and focused on Morten. "How did your meeting with Tuskandru fare?"

"He wants four hundred horses, saddles, blankets and trainers."

The murders hadn't created that much outrage. Every voice cried out at once, save Brolley, who stood in the same spot and nodded slowly. He once again waited quietly while the voices around him did their best to drown each other out. Finally, he spoke. "What choice do we have? Would you rather try sneaking past the mountain? Would you prefer risking your goods on the river?"

"Four hundred horses!" It was Darris Longsmile who spoke. As the man likely to replace Welan Parse on the Merchant's Guild his voice carried a decent weight to it. "Where will we come up with four hundred horses?"

"A small portion from each family will cover the cost. No one family is responsible for the whole sum." Brolley spoke as calmly as any man ever did, but a few of the men present still didn't want to listen.

"Let the Empress pay the fees!" Longsmile scowled as he spoke.

Brolley never raised his voice. He didn't need to. "Then she'll have every reason to bring a harder burden of taxes upon the merchants."

All around the gathered merchants complained and shook heads and waved halfhearted fists in the air, but the end result was never in doubt as far as Lenwig was concerned. They'd pay the tithings and get their road back. It was the easiest way.

"And who will deliver these horses? And when?" Longsmile was starting to sound like an ass. Really, that was hardly unique in Lenwig's experience.

"I will. It's what you're paying me for." Morten Dunraven was an old soldier and carried himself like one. That is to say he was battered and scarred and most of the men in the meeting would back down from anything he had to say. Because he was alive after the punishment his body had taken and he was still spry for a man of his years. "I'll return to speak to King Tuskandru tomorrow and make arrangements. I'd recommend each of you gather your horses and equipment and have it brought here."

"Why bring it here?" The speaker was one of the men unknown to Ledwig. He was also an idiot.

"Because I am not in the business of driving livestock. I'm in the business of negotiation. I'm risking my head talking to a madman on your behalf. You'll have to deliver your own horses to me, or you can take them right up the side of the mountain, whichever is easier for you." Morten's one eye glared at the man who talked. The man had the good sense to shrink back from the old soldier.

For the next hour they worked out the details of doing business in an area that was now under the watchful eye of the Sa'ba Taalor. Business costs money and a dozen horses was a price he was willing to pay, especially after seeing Tuskandru when he was in the mood to kill.

CHAPTER FIVE

Jeron

The night settled over the Wellish Steppes quickly. One moment the sun was visible and the next it sank too low to do anyone the least good. Twilight was a short span of time and quickly overtaken by true darkness.

Jeron rose with the night, came from his hiding place in the tunnels and moved at a steady pace over to the grounds where his mercenaries waited with mixed patience. They had food and shelter. They were promised wealth. It was enough for now, but he knew some of them were growing restless.

He blamed the Overlords. Even while they rested, their presence was unsettling for most.

He had adapted of course. Had been made to adapt. He looked at his hands and marveled at how much stronger they appeared. How much younger. He was ancient. He had walked the land for over a thousand years, had traveled to other lands, studied sorceries barely even remembered by his peers, and been privy to secrets few could comprehend. He should have been dead, by now, or at least borne the scars to show his long history. Instead the Overlords had changed him again, given him a new appearance, a fresh vitality.

He was blessed by his new masters.

And they were his masters. He could not deny that. They had but to beckon him and he would come running, grateful for the opportunity.

Something shifted under his flesh, a small lump that slid and moved itself from his wrist to his elbow before vanishing. That was a common thing now. He should have been worried. Things were happening under his skin that he had no control over, but there was no doubt, no concern. Whatever might occur, it was likely a blessing of the Overlords and he accepted the unusual changes as part of what he was becoming in service of his new masters.

Jeron stepped into the main area of his hidden domain and looked at the mercenaries gathered there. The numbers continued to increase. Several of the mercenaries looked his way and one of them stepped closer. None of the Godless seemed the least bit concerned, but the humans grew restless.

"How long do we stay here?" It was Darus Kestle who spoke up. Darus was a violent man who wanted to draw blood. He didn't want to wait around, he wanted to cause harm.

He was also the sort of dog who needed to have his leash tightened.

Jeron looked at him and felt his left eyelid twitch. Everything about the man's demeanor was offensive to him. The patience that he should have been experiencing was gone, peeled away when the Overlords remade him.

"Do you wish to discuss battle strategies with the Overlords, Darus?"

Darus was no larger than Jeron, but he was hard from years of combat and living in the sorts of places wise people avoided. He'd been a mercenary, a soldier and more often than not a raider, the sort who preyed on anyone foolish enough to look weak. The Overlords weren't even a consideration for him. He was here for money and easy prey.

"Who?"

"The Overlords. The Wellish Overlords. They're here to take Fellein and remake it. They're the ones paying you."

"I haven't been paid, Jeron. I've been waiting here a fortnight for anything to happen, but I have not been paid."

"Look around you." Jeron swept his arm in an arc. "There are almost four hundred men here and more coming every day. All of you are waiting, but you wait in comfort. You have food and supplies. You sleep under the calm stars. Be grateful."

"Aye. I've food and shelter. But I was promised more than that."

"You want to draw blood? Would you try yourself against the Godless?" Jeron smiled at the thought and before the man could respond he called out to Trigan Garth. "Trigan!"

The brute rose from where he was examining the blade of his sword, and nodded.

"Trigan, we have restless warriors here."

The Sa'ba Taalor walked closer, his steps calm and confident. "What would you have done about it?"

"I would have you and yours train them. Make them better warriors."

Without any more direction Trigan strode toward Darus, who retreated. "Now wait a moment," Darus said.

Trigan did not wait. He pushed into the mercenary and shoved him backward. "Fight me!"

Darus tried to draw the sword at his hip and Trigan

knocked him sprawling. All around them mercenaries took note and rose from where they had been. Several called out, wanting to see what would happen next.

Trigan called out to the Godless in his own native tongue and they responded, drawing weapons. Seventeen Sa'ba Taalor gathered themselves in rough formation behind Trigan Garth, drawing weapons that ranged from swords to items unknown to the Fellein.

Jeron spoke up, his voice carrying over the muttered calls of the mercenaries. "It is time to prepare yourselves. We are soon going to war. Trigan Garth and his fellows will be training you to prepare for the coming battles."

A few people started to speak up and Jeron silenced them with a hard gesture. "Don't complain to me. Fight! Prepare for what comes next!"

Trigan spoke. "Stand in formation. Line up!"

The mercenaries muttered amongst themselves and several obeyed while others looked skeptically at the gray-skinned Sa'ba Taalor. When Trigan spoke again it was in his native tongue and the other Sa'ba Taalor broke ranks and moved among the mercenaries, grabbing and pushing the Fellein into rough ranks. A few protested and were immediately struck down for their comments, not killed but knocked to the ground and offered a chance to defend themselves in proper combat. The fights were short-lived and the Sa'ba Taalor were victorious in each case.

The rest decided they wanted to keep their teeth and quickly obeyed. They were mercenaries, not fools. Those that had not fought the Sa'ba Taalor before had certainly heard of them and virtually all of the people there had seen at least a half dozen fights between the gray skins. They fought constantly and they fought hard. Man or woman, young or old, the Godless fought and trained.

The mercenaries fought, too. Most listened to their new instructors. Those who did not were struck down.

Jeron watched on, a smile on his face. If nothing else came from this, at least the mercenaries were reminded how to stand in formation.

Kallir Lundt

Where once a vast forest rested there was now a black mountain. Truska-Pren loomed over the farthest northern region of Fellein, an active volcano that rose as far as the eye could see, the top wreathed in clouds. Below the clouds, where the air was thin and clear, lay Prydiria, the Iron Fortress, the seat of power for the Iron Kingdom. It was from there that the King in Iron, Tarag Paedori, looked down upon Fellein.

Kallir Lundt stood by his side and studied the world below, the world that he had once belonged to before Tarag Paedori and the god Truska-Pren had healed his face from the damage done to it and saved his life. All they asked in return was his fealty, and he'd offered it eagerly for the chance to live again. To have a life beyond a ruined face and shattered jaw.

They had a friendship of sorts. It was not always easy to be a friend to the King in Iron. The man was burdened with being the sword of his god. His was the voice that commanded all of the armies of the Sa'ba Taalor. There were seven kings, but in times of war all answered to Tarag Paedori. The king was a brute. As was often the case with the Sa'ba Taalor, he was larger than most of the Fellein, both in height and in build. Kallir himself was a fairly slender man, and stood a full head shorter than the man he spent most of his free time with. There was little doubt in his mind that if Paedori wanted him dead he would die quickly.

Happily, the man didn't seem to follow that desire. Instead they talked of Fellein and the beliefs of the people there. They spoke strategy and contemplated the next possible war and the best ways to end any conflicts.

In other words, Kallir was an advisor to the king. He was satisfied with his lot in life. He could never return to Fellein and be accepted, but here, in Prydiria, he was respected and appreciated.

It was the iron face that made the difference. Before he ever met the Sa'ba Taalor his face was taken by a savage beast, one of the Pra-Moresh, a nightmarish creature that fought and killed and then ate whatever it managed to destroy. He had thought the animals frightening before encountering them, and then come to realize they were so very much worse than he believed. Sometimes, late at night when sleep eluded him, he still felt the claws of the beast ripping his face from his skull.

The Daxar Taalor, the gods of the Seven Forges, had their own ways. When Tarag Paedori asked the gods to mend Kallir they did so. Truska-Pren rewarded him with a new face. This one, however, was made of iron. The metal moved like flesh. He could see through the iron eyes. Eat and speak and taste with a mouth made of iron, but though the Sa'ba Taalor accepted him, Kallir knew his own people would never be able to look past the metallic face he now bore.

He had seen their reactions the one time he ventured back to Fellein. The children had stared, the adults had stared. To them he was the stuff of nightmares. To the Sa'ba Taalor his iron mask was a sign that the gods had favored him with a blessing. They had cured his ills. To the Fellein that made him a monster.

So be it. He would be a monster. He could accept that. Here he had home and friends. He even had a lover, Desta, one of the Sa'ba Taalor who spent time with him most days and trained him in the ways of her people.

Above them the mountain grumbled. Not just above, but everywhere. Nothing fell and no one really reacted. Truska-Pren was alive, but that did not mean the sounds were a threat. The mountain, the god, was merely stretching. That was the best way to consider the situation.

Kallir reached out with his mind and felt the god's presence. As with the Sa'ba Taalor, he found that presence comforting. Being able to speak with a god was reassuring.

Tarag rose from his seat on the iron throne and strode over to the window closest to him, looking down and out toward the distant Wellish Steppes. His long black hair was shot with silver and gray, leading him to look even more as if he were made of iron himself. At present he wore dark pants and a red tunic. His silvery eyes glowed faintly in the shadows that kept the sun from his face.

He pointed one thick finger into the distance. "There, Kallir Lundt. There is the threat we face."

Kallir moved closer and followed the line from finger to distant ground. He could see the swelling earth. It was not much to see, really, but like Tarag he was familiar with what should be seen and what was newly changed.

"What is it, my king?"

Tarag shook his head. "I do not know. I only know it should not be there. Truska-Pren wants answers."

Kallir nodded. "Shall I go there my king?"

"Perhaps." He turned his head slightly and looked at Kallir. His gaze softened briefly. "Yes, I think. But do not go alone. Take Desta with you."

Kallir smiled. He felt his lips shift, knew that his teeth were made visible. Iron on iron. Metal moved and reshaped itself to mimic the face he'd been born with and had been taken from him. "I shall leave right away."

Tarag nodded. "Take enough water. The Steppes are surprisingly dry."

"I have traveled the Steppes many times." There was truth in that. Before Truska-Pren grew from the ruins this had been Trecharch, the land where Kallir was born and raised.

Kallir moved from the throne room and to his quarters, sorting out what he would need to take with him. The list was short, and within half an hour he was seeking Desta. She was not hard to find. Desta was in the courtyard, as she was most days, training.

She was short and lean, with hard muscles and scars running over her body to show every battle she'd walked away from over her twenty-four years. He knew most of those scars, had traced them with his eyes and his hands alike. Her hair was kept fairly short, and was tied back with a length of cloth. She had four Great Scars upon her face, and a portion of her left ear was missing from the war with Fellein. The man who had taken her earlobe had paid with his life.

The staff in her hands moved in thrust and parry and jab as she fought against one sword and two smaller staffs. The two fighting her were as deadly serious as she was, and one of the small staffs slipped past her defenses and slammed into her shoulder with bruising force.

Desta grunted and then pushed her entire body forward, the staff in her hands bending forward and then moving to strike at the stomach of her opponent, who scrambled back and defended against the attempt.

The sword lashed out, and sliced into Desta's staff, became stuck in the hardwood. Desta threw herself to the left and pulled the sword and its bearer toward her. The man holding the sword – his name was Atranno – released the blade and retreated before she could strike him. She managed to maintain her balance and Kallir kept his silence as he watched. The Sa'ba Taalor allowed him to train with them, but if he were being truthful, he knew that they fought differently with him as they coached him to their levels. He was a skilled fighter, but most of the adults among his new people easily overshadowed his talents.

Feeling the fresh scars along his knuckles he knew they did not treat him as a child, merely that if they exerted the full force of their blows he would likely have been maimed for life.

Desta moved toward Atranno and then reversed the trajectory of her staff. The undamaged end fired at the last player in their dance and struck him directly in the forehead. He fell back hard and crashed to the ground, unconscious.

While she was busy with her armed opponent, Atranno slid forward and grabbed the end of her staff that was still holding his sword. He did not try to wrest his weapon back, but instead pushed the staff lower. While she tried to compensate, the man stepped closer and struck a savage blow across her face. Staff and sword fell from her grip and Atranno caught her in a hold that locked both of her arms into a painful position, effectively crippling her attack.

A moment later she signaled her surrender and the three

combatants were all discussing their fight in technical terms. If any of them harbored ill will toward any of the others, they hid it remarkably well.

Desta smiled in his direction, her great scars showing bared teeth and gums. "Kallir, I was not expecting you."

"The king has asked me to examine something happening in the Wellish Steppes. He asked that I take you with me."

Desta nodded and stepped closer to him, ignoring the damaged weapon she'd had knocked from her hands. "When do we leave?"

"As soon as you are prepared. We have only a few miles to travel."

"Then I am ready now."

As she spoke she looked around and found a heavy club that bore one rounded side and an interior sharpened into a serrated blade. Curved hooks were on both sides, half-hidden and nearly decorative, but deceptively barbed. Near as Kallir could tell, the entire thing was made of bone, very likely from a Pra-Moresh. A jaw, perhaps, or a hip that had been filed down. In either case, it was a formidable weapon. There was a long leather loop at the handle end of the club. She slid her wrist into the strap and then started walking toward the Steppes. Kallir caught up with her quickly.

Heading down the side of the mountain was easy enough as long as one used caution. Kallir had learned the hard way that the paths were deceptive. He took his time and Desta moved with him in companionable silence.

The paths through the ruins of what had been a vast forest were clear. One merely had to walk those paths to avoid the mountain of burned wood and ash. Trecharch was dead. Trecharch lived again elsewhere but had left behind a corpse when the Sa'ba Taalor burned down the vast forest.

What remained was ruination shoved aside by Truska-Pren's eruption from the flaming ground. The mountain pushed everything into new positions when it rose from the soil. The Sa'ba Taalor had no need of what remained and cared little to remove the debris. Instead they made use of the deadfalls and found new places to watch for strangers among the shattered trees and numerous stumps.

Not that they need worry about the situation. Only a true fool would trespass in the Kingdom of Iron. Kallir had dwelled in the new area for five years and only at the very beginning did he see anyone come to examine the new mountain. They did not leave. Their remains still rested within the ruined forest, a warning to others.

The Seven Forges had been a distant mountain range the first time he'd heard of them, and now he resided in a kingdom on one of those very volcanic mountains, said mountain having moved to a different location as the gods deemed necessary.

Desta's voice brought him away from his musings. "What are you doing?"

"Hmm?" He cast his eyes toward Desta.

"I speak of training and you stare off into your dreams." She was not offended, merely amused.

"I'm considering how much the world has changed in only a few years."

She nodded. "The gods demand change."

"Why now, I wonder?"

"I do not question the Daxar Taalor. I merely obey."

Kallir nodded absently. He understood. Where his own people had trouble remembering the names of gods, the Sa'ba Taalor quite literally spoke to their gods and had conversations. In his time Kallir had thought himself devout, had worshipped the Mother-Vine and considered the possibilities that gods existed and decided that surely they must, even if they offered no proof beyond old stories. Then he had seen the relationship between the People of the Forges and their gods. He had, in fact, been healed by one of the very same gods. That left no room for doubt in his mind. Faith came as easily as that. He had but to touch the iron of his face to know that gods existed, that he had been blessed by them. He had but to listen, and Truska-Pren's voice was there, a soothing tide of faith.

"I do not question. I merely observe."

Desta scanned the horizon. There was little to see once they passed the old ruins of Trecharch. The land was low and mostly level. Fifty miles to the south there were variations on the Steppes, but this far north there was little except scrub grass and an occasional plant.

There were no horses in the area. If they showed themselves they'd likely be carrying riders or they'd end up as fresh meat for the Sa'ba Taalor. Kallir had a mount but had not yet decided if Frakka would come along this time. In the name of expediency he made his choice and called to his traveling companion.

"We take your mount?"

"I think it wisest. We do not know what we face, and we might need to get back here quickly."

Desta looked at him and smiled. She had not yet had the chance to earn one of the beasts. He had been offered the opportunity as a way of proving himself to Tarag Paedori. Despite his fears he'd managed to best Frakka in singular combat. Really it had been a matter of endurance more than skill, and he was stubborn to a fault, as Frakka often reminded him.

As was usually the case, Frakka wandered where he wanted. He was not a beast of burden to be locked away, but a friend, an equal, who did as he pleased when not asked to serve. He was obligated to obey, but only a fool would make the great beast a captive. Frakka moved closer at his summons. Kallir smiled at that thought and at the beast he called a friend as it came closer. Frakka was not wearing a saddle or armor, but that was just as well. They didn't need the extra noise that would come with the burden.

"Can you carry two of us, Frakka?"

In response the mount looked at Desta and then butted her gently with his face, like an oversized cat displaying affection. Desta managed to keep her balance with an effort and a laugh. When he'd first seen the great mounts, he thought they were like horses, intelligent enough, but dumb animals. It was only later he discovered that they were as intelligent as humans. He would no more assume Frakka was in the mood to carry two burdens than he would assume his mother wanted company for dinner when he was younger. It was simply best to ask.

He climbed on first and Desta slipped into place behind him. With no reins he grabbed a thick hank of Frakka's mane and felt Desta's hands grip at his waist. A few moments later they were on the move, balancing themselves on the mount's back and relaxing into the rhythm of Frakka's stride.

Desta leaned in closer and spoke, "What are we searching for, Kallir?"

"Something is happening in the Steppes, Desta. There are changes taking place and both Tarag Paedori and Truska-Pren would know more of these changes."

"Then we seek answers to worthy questions."

"I would think any request by a king or god worthy."

Desta made no response, but her arms pulled her body closer to his and she leaned forward until her chin rested on his shoulder. He let himself get distracted by the feel of her warm body pressing to his, but not to the point where he lost himself in the sensations. Frakka made no sound, but showed his approval through their connection.

The ground rose slowly, which in itself was a change from what Kallir had seen in the past. He had stood more than once on his balcony and watched the rains wash ashes and debris from Trecharch's ruins down the slopes into the Steppes and, eventually, the Freeholdt River. There should have been a gradual dip into a proper valley but instead the land lifted in a gentle slope that he could see up ahead became steeper. By the time the ground began to rise he could see their goal, a large outcropping of stone rising from the ground like a broken bone through flesh. It was fresh and raw, the layer of soil pressed toward the sky by the open wound.

Kallir called for a halt to their progress and he and Desta dismounted. Frakka settled himself in the dried scrub brush and panted softly, taking the opportunity to relax.

Desta and Kallir moved slowly, observing everything around them, both old and newly revealed. There was nothing to see but dried grasses and the occasional plant. There wasn't a threat here that he could see. Norhun was two days ride south, at the very least, and Stonehaven five days.

This was new. The wound in the ground could almost have been an accident, but Kallir could see the shimmering distortion where the ground was most exposed to the air. There was an entrance of sorts; a cave, perhaps.

He had no doubt that sorcery was involved. What was hiding behind that sorcery was the challenge, and one he was not sure they were ready to examine. Truska-Pren asked a service of him and he was glad to accommodate, but the simple fact was that he was a soldier first, and not accustomed to magic. He had seen sorcery in action and had a healthy respect for the power.

Desta tilted her head and examined the same shimmering area that had caught his attention. Her left hand tapped the war club lightly against her thigh and hip, and she moved forward without another word. He already knew what she was thinking: the gods would protect them, or they would not, there was nothing else to consider.

He could find no flaw in her thinking, and so he moved as well.

The entrance was obvious as they got closer. The ground here was broken, but where the earth was at the highest height there was a tunnel entrance. The hole dropped down into darkness in seconds, leaving the world of light behind. The fresh soil was dark, and the corpses of a hundred or so bugs lay in the light, drying and decomposing slowly.

The opening was large enough to accommodate the both of them and so they walked together into the darkness.

Andover Lashk

Dala Hemistry smiled as he looked toward Andover.

"It has been some time since I saw you, Iron Hands."

Andover smiled and felt all of his Great Scars respond by splitting themselves open. "I did not expect you, Dala."

The bald man moved closer and offered his hand. Andover

took it and gripped the forearm carefully. Iron hands meant always being careful. He had come to accept that quite some time back.

Dala blew out a breath that plumed in the cold of the day. The wind stole the breath away as quickly as it could. "I'm here to receive new orders."

"Indeed." Andover nodded and searched for the memory of where the other man was assigned. "You no longer need to watch the northern trails?"

"I go where I'm told, Andover. The life of a soldier is following orders."

"More than just that." Andover eyed his student carefully. "There is also the fight."

Dala nodded. His stance changed and Andover smiled again. The way he stood now was in readiness. Had Andover attacked – and he'd been considering just that – the man would have been ready to defend himself.

Dala had lost weight, but in the best possible way. When they'd met, he'd had a layer of fat around his guts, and that was gone now, replaced with lean muscle. He had followed Andover's advice, perhaps, or simply been where supplies of food were limited. Andover didn't care which; he was simply glad to see a student of his doing well. Most he simply did not see again, or not often.

"The fight happens less often right now, but we both know that can change." Dala walked over to a low wall and settled himself against it, leaning on the stones and trusting them to hold his weight. The wall did not betray that trust.

Andover looked around and sighed. "I expect changes to happen soon. The seven kingdoms make motions. The gods speak of change."

"You hear their gods?" Dala frowned in his direction.

Andover nodded. "The Daxar Taalor are with me, as always. If I listen closely, I can hear their words. If I do not listen, it is like the the ocean's waves, there but only as a sound that never leaves." He shrugged. "The gods speak, but they seldom speak to me. They have many others to talk to, I suppose."

Dala crossed his arms and sighed deep in his chest. "It is good to see you, Andover."

"I did not expect a visitor today, Dala," Andover repeated. "I am pleased by your visit, but what brings you here?"

Dala smiled. "I remember your lessons, Andover. You taught me different ways to look at fighting, and I am grateful for the changes."

Andover felt his face flush with blood. He was not used to being embarrassed but he was pleased by the sensation. "You are one of Merros Dulver's chosen warriors. If not, I would not have trained you."

"But you *did* train me Andover." The man stepped in closer, his eyes locked on Andover's. "I am better prepared because of you, and I think I'm going to need that. I am hearing rumors of a new army forming. If it's true I will go to fight them. If I do, and we are victorious, you are one of the reasons for success."

"I have not heard of a new army." Andover brushed aside the thanks. They made him uncomfortable.

"To the west. Mercenaries, and I am hearing the Godless are involved."

Andover scowled. "Beware the Godless. They may be without gods but they are not without abilities."

"You are Godless, and I would not fight you." Dala laughed as he spoke, and his callused hand gripped Andover's shoulder.

"I will speak with Merros about these Godless, I think." He looked toward the great stone wall of the castle proper. "They are more dangerous than anyone suspects."

"Why is that?"

"They are trained as warriors, but they have no masters. They are like war dogs without a leash, I expect."

"The general would be wise to hear you, Andover." Dala brushed the words aside and Andover silently acknowledged that the man did not understand he was close enough to the general to speak with him freely. Dala was a warrior, yes, but he fought in distant areas. He did not know Merros Dulver well enough to speak with him as he pleased.

Just as he considered explaining to Dala, a messenger called to the man. Dala smiled an apology and then they shook hands again. "Be well, Andover!"

"Be well, Dala, until we meet again."

Dala walked over to the messenger who eyed Andover as if he just might be poisonous, and then whispered his message to Dala. Andover took no offense.

A moment later the two men were gone, and Andover looked over the courtyard and sighed. The world was growing smaller on him. For five years the courtyard had been enough, but now it seemed to close in from all sides and he wanted to fight back against it. He did not want to be crushed by the familiar. He wanted – needed – to have more.

Without another word he turned toward the castle and started across the area he had virtually taken as his own. He would meet with Merros and learn what he could about the Godless and the mercenaries. If there was a war coming he would know of it.

Whistler

Canhoon was not as impressive as he'd expected. Oh, it was ripe with massive towers and statues, and the Silent Army was fascinating to watch, of course, but somehow Whistler had expected a place with more grandeur and less pickpockets.

Case in point was the little shit that had just stolen his bag of coins. Or rather thought she had. Mostly what she got for her troubles was a few pebbles and two old arrowheads that rattled around the right way.

What Whistler got was amused. Instead of being angry, he decided it would be more fun to follow the thief. He was very good at sneaking when he wanted to be. Had to be good at that if you wanted to survive the parts of Goltha where he grew up.

Best not to dwell on that. Sometimes, when he least expected it, the recollections of his earlier days brought about the sort of anger that was hard to quell. He liked that well enough in the right circumstances, but not now. He needed his calm for the moment, his quiet. Trailing a thief was hard work, especially if one didn't want to get noticed.

The girl he was following was very good at what she did. She made it look easy, but he knew she was looking around and surveying where she moved. She'd also signaled at least two other cutpurses as she moved along. He wasn't quite sure what her signal meant – they seldom meant the same things even in different parts of towns, to say nothing of different cities – but they'd communicated without a single word being spoken. All he knew for certain was that she wasn't aware of him.

Not yet, at least. If she were she'd have long since been gone. One didn't live long if one was followed by the very people one had robbed. She would have vanished, and fast, if she knew he was there. It was a matter of survival. She couldn't know he wasn't ready to cut her throat for taking from him.

The alleyways were narrow and getting more so as they moved from the edge of the docks and deeper into Old Canhoon. Whistler was aware of that, and of the lad who slipped into the alley behind him. Could be he was wrong and she knew he was there. Could be she'd sent for a friend to put a blade through a sweet spot on his body.

It would hardly be a first. Best to assume he'd made a mistake and keep himself properly aware of those around him. He had no desire to lose the girl in the crowds, but he also planned to keep himself intact.

The boy followed him, doing his best to be discreet. He walked with the same subtlety as a draft horse, which is to say none at all. Whistler pretended not to notice him and went about his hunt. The girl was either not aware of him or very good at pretending. He couldn't quite decide which.

The boy behind him came closer and Whistler let him. Just a little closer and he'd strike. The girl he followed was mostly hidden behind a hooded cloak. He'd spotted brown hair and a rounded chin, and if he had to guess she was at the cusp of being an adult. Likely if she were caught she'd be punished by the City-Guard. Not swatted on her bum and sent to her parents, but truly punished. He knew a few thieves who'd been fortunate enough to run across a Guard who was gentle, but they were the exception. There were plenty of cases where a Guard gave a beating or worse when they caught a thief.

The boy made his move. He was fast, give him that. The knife practically grew out of his wrist. Whistler slipped sideways and felt the boy's blade cut into the thin coat he was wearing. A look of triumph had started on the urchin's face but it was replaced by surprise when all he caught was the coat.

"Not smart."

The boy dropped the blade even as Whistler caught his thin wrist in a hard grip. Before the would-be assassin could pull free, Whistler applied pressure from one thumb to the back of his hand and twisted the hand sideways. It was a simple wristlock, but very effective.

"If you move, boy, I'll wreck your arm." A little pressure made his point. The boy stayed quiet, but winced in pain.

The alley was narrow enough, and the shadows of the day were half concealing the both of them. Whistler caught the boy by the neck and pulled him deeper into the shade. "Why are you trying to cut me?" The urchin's mouth opened and he sucked in a deep breath. "Scream and I ruin your arm."

That ended the attempt at a scream.

"Answer my question." Whistler looked hard into the boy's eyes. The face that looked back was too thin, and the brown eyes that should have been afraid were instead filled with anger. "Be honest, or I'll whittle away your face." The hand that had been holding the boy's neck moved and to show the boy he was serious Whistler put a thin blade along the boy's nose. "Why were you trying to cut me?"

The boy's foot stabbed forward in an effort to cut into Whistler's shin. The blade on the shoe was long enough to cause serious harm.

Whistler slipped to the side and cursed under his breath

as his anger flared. One thing to try for a quick mark. Another thing to try to maim him. There was no logic to his way of thinking, but it was his and he never questioned the sudden rage. His hands did exactly what he'd warned the boy against. Sudden hard pressure on the captured arm shattered bones and the squirming would-be assassin let out a loud yelp before he sagged toward the ground. Either he had fainted dead away from the pain, or he was faking. In either situation the result was the same, he was maimed and would need the best physicians in Canhoon if he ever wanted to use his arm again.

Whistler let the boy fall where he was and moved on. The girl was long gone, which was unfortunate. Still, he was in Canhoon and the voices seemed satisfied with that notion.

"So be it." Whistler smiled to himself and looked around the gathering of alleyways and winding, narrow roads. "We are here and here we shall stay, for now."

He walked on, fully aware that he was being followed by at least two more shapes. Time would tell what their plans were. For now he only knew that they moved with him, extra shadows in the sun-deprived alleys where he walked.

Darsken Murdro

Darsken Murdro walked the late night streets of Goltha and scowled to himself. While he had been busy looking over the bodies in Canhoon he had never considered that the same might be happening on the other side of the lake in the largest city in Fellein.

The layers of Goltha rose above him like waves of stone. Each rise of the hills around him had more of the city.

Currently he walked near the docks, where, so far, no bodies had been left. Small buildings, towers, great edifices, the castle of the king, all loomed higher in the murky evening, lit by hearths and torches, candles and braziers; a thousand stars close enough to touch.

Rain fell from the skies, light and misty, adding to the chill in the air. Four bodies had been left in the city on nights exactly like this one, when rain kept most people from wandering far from home, and few people would be around to witness atrocities. The bodies were all violated, cut and marked, twisted and scarred with a hundred marks that tore spirits from flesh.

Etredu Moiren walked with him and said little. Another Inquisitor, this one in charge of the city they occupied, he had called to Darsken when he heard about the corpses in Canhoon. Etredu was lean and tall and very good at his job, but as with so many of the Inquisitors, he was quiet and carried many secrets most people would never understand.

"Why do you expect a body here, Etredu?" he spoke softly and in the language of their people. Few outside of Louron spoke the tongue.

"The cutthroat has placed one body in each district. This is the next place one should appear, if the pattern holds." Etredu's voice was soft and melodic, his face was as stone, and bore scars from when he had fought against the Sa'ba Taalor and the Shimmer did not accommodate his pleas for aid. The Shimmer was a gift. With little more than a thought the Louron could move between worlds, or ride the Shimmer to move faster than should be possible. It was a week's ride on a good horse to reach their homeland, but walking the Shimmer a person could reach Louron in a single day without being exhausted. The ability to use the Shimmer was unique to the Louron, and it was rare, indeed, that the ability failed one of their people.

Etredu was burned when the Sa'ba Taalor razed a large portion of the city. He either offended the Shimmer or did not call on it in time. In any event, he bore the scars without protest.

Etredu's hair was gathered in braids and flowed loosely around his head. He was younger than Darsken, or at least had less gray in his hair. The walking stick he carried was adorned with a half dozen serpents that writhed around each other, each scale carefully carved on some and missing on others. Years had been spent already on the details and many more years were likely to pass before he was finished. A lifetime of contemplation had gone into the making. Even as he looked, Etredu held the stout shaft of wood in his hands and his lips moved, speaking silently into the staff, mumbling words not meant to be heard by a human being.

Darsken let the silence wash over him, then heard the sound of the waves rushing toward the shore, the call of the wind, the scrape of feet on cobblestones and along the piers and dock, the creak of ships moving on the water. Here and there a conversation took place.

He let his senses expand as best he could. He was not a sorcerer. He could not call on the Sooth to help him. He could, however, ask the spirits of the dead to aid him, and he did. He begged them to watch over the living and let him know if any were in danger of having their lives taken, and, more importantly, their spirits stolen away.

The spirits can be fickle, but that night they offered help. He heard their whispers at the same time that his ears picked up the sound of a struggle.

Someone said, "What's that then?" A woman, by the

sound, and then there was a scream, or rather the start of one. The voice rose in pitch and volume and then vanished as easily as a thief in heavy fog.

Without a word to his partner, Darsken cut to the left and ran up the low hill separating the streets. Etredu's heavy stride echoed off the buildings and found Darsken's ears. The man was following. That was good.

His stomach clenched at the thought of what he might encounter, and Darsken lowered his head and ran faster. Better to face whatever fears he had than to surrender to them. He was an Inquisitor and that meant he dealt with things others would find too frightening for words. He was not going to let himself become the sort of man who fled from the darkness, not when he was supposed to find his way to whatever that darkness hid.

The cobblestones were wet, and his feet slipped in that dampness. He caught himself and continued on, but it was not easy, and he heard Etredu fall behind him before he could offer a warning. The sound of his body hitting the ground was accented by his gasp of pain.

Up ahead a cloaked figure crouched, revealing little but shadows in the darkness. The shape must have heard Etredu's grunt of pain because it reared up and turned toward them at the same moment.

There was little to see but the hood and cloak. A heavy blade was held in one hand and it was dark with use.

The tip, the edge, were bathed in crimson gore. The hand holding it was withered, wrinkled, but not with age. The flesh was mottled as if diseased.

Whatever the case, the form beneath that cloak hardly seemed at a disadvantage. Without any warning the shape crouched low and then jumped a solid twenty feet into the air, vaulting over the low wall of the closest building and onto the roof in a leap that was physically impossible.

"Stop where you are!" Darsken knew the words were wasted but he tried just the same.

He considered trying to follow, but it was already too late. The shape jumped again, soaring over the rooftop and onto the next adjoining building. A third leap as he followed with his eyes and the shape was gone, leaving behind only the grisly work that had already been done to its victim.

The woman was dead, her throat cut and her body already cooling in a pool of blood that trickled down to the cobblestones and painted them. A quick glance at his foot showed red marks on the sole of his boot.

Darsken felt his lips press together as he moved closer to the corpse and examined the wounds. A blade to the throat ended her life. The same blade left several markings on her pale skin.

There was no doubt in his mind that he had just seen the necromancer. He cursed softly as he looked around. Whatever he could say about the murderer, he could not deny the physical prowess.

His hand reached for the pouch inside his jacket, tucked away on the left-hand side of his body. His fingers opened the pouch easily enough and a pinch of the fine black powder inside spilled into his palm.

Etredu came toward him, already trying to apologize, but Darsken held his free hand up to silence the man. He'd been caught unawares more than once in his life and could hardly blame the other for the same error. "Should I ever be free of mistakes, I will chastise you, Etredu. For now, I want answers more than anything else."

Etredu nodded and then crouched down, his right hand

on his walking stick, which was directly in front of him.

Darsken tossed the fine dust across the face and head of the corpse and muttered his words softly, lest anyone be close enough to hear. The powder changed her. For the moment, dead, slack skin tightened on her face, and a semblance of life moved across her features. It was a mockery, a lie, but a necessary one.

The dead woman's mouth opened, and she inhaled a deep gasp of breath. Dead eyes flew open wide and looked at nothing. What the corpse saw was not certain to Darsken.

All that mattered was what she had seen, not what she now observed. "Ask your questions." Her voice was a cold whisper.

"Who killed you?"

"I did not know him." An edge of anger at that thought of her life taken by a stranger.

"What did he look like?"

"His face was covered. His hands were marked, the skin peeling away." Those dead eyes grew wider and rolled wildly in their sockets. "He had such darkness to show me."

"What did he say to you?"

"He spoke no language I know. He chanted and sang dark songs." Her voice grew softer and Darsken knew his time with her was limited.

"Do you know why he chose you?"

"I walked alone," she cried the words softly. "Alone and so cold." The corpse's head shifted until she stared directly up at Darsken's face and a long, shuddering breath escaped her mouth. A second later he felt the spirit leave her. He could call her back if he had to, but there would be a cost.

"Call your City-Guard, Etredu. Have them take her away."

Etredu nodded and rose from his crouch without a word.

A moment later the man was gone, sliding quietly into the growing fog coming off of the lake. Darsken waited by the dead woman as his associate went to find the City-Guard. She had been alone long enough and, if the necromancer was waiting, he might want her back. She was dead and he could not change that, but he could keep her spirit safe from the sorcerer.

Darsken had hoped there was a reason for why each body was chosen, but according to the dead woman it was merely that she was available. The dead could not lie to him. She said what she believed.

He reached over to the corpse and closed the eyes, the mouth. He read the runes carved into her flesh. They were the start of a curse, a trap laid to capture her soul and steal it away. He was glad that the bastard had failed.

His skin chilled into gooseflesh as he thought about the necromancer and wondered where the man was now.

As much as he wanted to know the answer, part of him was fine with not finding out too soon.

The corpse and the night were both silent as he waited for Etredu and the City-Guard.

Andover Lashk

Andover stared at the map of Fellein and considered the Seven Forges in their new places on that map. Traveling to the volcanic mountains would be a challenge for anyone leaving Canhoon. The closest of the volcanoes was days away and those would be days of hard rides and little rest.

Still, he expected he'd be riding soon, moving from one mountain to the next across the land. He could feel it. The gods themselves wanted him to leave Canhoon and travel to the wonders that each mountain held.

He had been to all of the mountains before. During his time away from Fellein he had seen each mountain, spoken to each god, been given gifts by the Daxar Taalor. That made him unique among his people.

The map he stared at was a tapestry that adorned the vast hall where formal functions took place in the palace. Currently there were no functions planned. He merely came to the area to see the map and contemplate his place in Canhoon and Fellein as a whole.

He was paid well to train the troops chosen by Merros Dulver. He was paid well enough as a blacksmith on those occasions when he chose to hire himself out and make weapons. His swords and other tools were sought by many and only a few ever got to hold those blades. Most of the time he preferred to make weapons for his personal use.

Andover would even say he was content with his lot in life, if not exactly happy. Happiness had always been about finding the right person to share his world with, and there was no one in Canhoon that suited. Had he made mention of that fact, there was little doubt that Merros Dulver and Desh Krohan would seek to find the right person to fill that void. If they kept him happy he would not leave and if he did not leave he would be their personal triumph, a teacher for their pets, and occasionally a man who could answer their questions about the Sa'ba Taalor and the gods the gray skins answered to.

He sighed and crossed his arms as he considered that thought. It was hardly fair. They did what they could to make him feel at home but he was not like the people of Canhoon, even if he'd been born among them. He was changed. He was at least as much Sa'ba Taalor as he was Fellein. He certainly looked the part.

In the back of his head the gods continued their conversations and he listened to the constant song of the Daxar Taalor. Their words soothed him, even when he couldn't understand exactly what they were saying. The gods spoke constantly, and the sounds were an endless whisper. If he focused, he could hear exactly what they said, though the fact was the words were not for him. On those occasions when the gods wanted to speak to Andover the words were louder and clear as could be. He could not mistake words obviously meant for him and no one else.

"I didn't expect to see you here, Andover."

The words rang out loudly in the vast hall, and he turned to look at the Empress as she walked toward him.

She had once again found her way to where he was without seeming to enter the area by any of the doors. He had heard that several hidden passages existed through the castle, and he had little doubt that it was true. The Empress managed to surprise him more often than not, and that was not an easy task.

"Majesty." He bowed low and held his arms far away from his body. The move was traditional among the Sa'ba Taalor, a sign that no weapons were drawn or ready to be used. It was as close to a formal greeting as the gray skins usually managed. "I was merely looking at the map."

"I could have a map drawn up for you, if you'd like." Nachia Krous moved closer and Andover stiffened. She was the Empress. She controlled all that surrounded them. With a word, his world could be shattered or made better. He was very aware of that fact.

"Thank you for the offer, but really I just like to look. I

like to see the world outside of Canhoon and to consider it."

"Have you considered going back to the Seven Forges? Or seeing the rest of Fellein?"

He stared into her eyes for a moment and then looked away. "I have often thought of both."

"There's nothing to stop you, Andover. You could travel where you like, and you would always be welcome here."

"I fought your champion. I fought for the Sa'ba Taalor. Why would you welcome me back?"

"You fought because I chose a battle between champions over a prolonged war." She smiled briefly. It was a pleasant expression, but not one meant to convey anything. He wasn't quite sure how she managed that. "I can no more hold that against you than I can hold it against Desh Krohan."

It had been that very wizard who fought Andover. There was some debate about who actually won the fight. All Andover could say for certain was that the sorcerer burned his body severely before the fighting was done. Most of the battle was a jumble of half-remembered movements.

"Desh Krohan did not betray his homeland on behalf of the Daxar Taalor."

Her laughter was genuine, and she put a hand on his arm. "You just said it yourself, Andover Lashk. *Gods* asked that you fight for them. What could you say but yes?"

"You are a kind woman and a kinder Empress, Majesty."

"I try to be fair. Had gods made a demand of me, I'd be listening very carefully."

Andover nodded as they fell into a comfortable silence. She hesitated a long moment before drawing her hand away from his arm.

"Do the gods still speak to you, Andover?"

"Aye. Though not as often as you might think. They speak

to all of their followers, and I am fortunate enough to hear them. Their speech reminds me that there are gods in this world."

"What do they say to you?"

"Right now, they tell me that I will be moving on soon."

"Where will you go?"

"First I shall travel to the Iron Fortress, Prydiria, high on the slopes of Truska-Pren. I must thank the god for my hands again, and ask what he seeks of me."

"And if he seeks war with Fellein?"

"Then I will know why, and you will be told why."

Nachia Krous lowered her head and then nodded. "That is all I could ever ask, Andover."

"I will not attack anyone without reason, Majesty." He paused, trying to find the right words. "I have paid my debts to the Daxar Taalor. I would need a very good reason to attack."

"If you go to the Forges, I would like you to ask the Daxar Taalor and their kings if peace is possible between our people. I have no desire for another war."

Andover already knew the answer. The Daxar Taalor were gods of war. Still, he said, "I will ask, Majesty."

He watched the lady move away from him. "Thank you, Andover."

"I am pleased that I can aid you, Majesty." In truth he was puzzled. Five minutes earlier he hadn't been completely certain about his plans, and now it seemed he would be visiting the seven kings. He heard the approval of the Daxar Taalor move through the endless whispers of the gods.

CHAPTER SIX

Jeron

Jeron crouched in the darkness of an alleyway and shook his head. Failure was not permitted. He had plans for the night and those included another sacrifice to the Overlords. Was it necessary? Yes. They were growing more demanding as they came closer to awakening. Their sleep was a powerful thing, but hunger was replacing the torpor they'd endured for centuries.

He looked down at his hands, at the flesh that was even now peeling slowly away, revealing the metamorphosis taking place within him. Clusters of muscles deep inside his legs and arms ached as they changed, but it was a pain he accepted willingly.

"Where are you, Roledru?" He called out for his assistant even as he reveled in the transformation taking place under his peeling flesh.

He was reborn, made again in the shape the Overlords felt was more efficient and why not? He was stronger than he had ever been. He was faster than he'd ever been, and the changes were still occurring. He saw so much more than he'd ever thought possible.

The winds off the lake pushed fog across the ground and

buried the world around him in shades of gray. When he spoke again his voice was exactly as strong as before, but carried with it the sorcerous ability to only be heard by one man. "Roledru, come to me."

Roledru was a competent enough follower. He obeyed and seldom made errors grievous enough to generate ire. It was only a matter of minutes before he showed himself through the thickening fog.

He did not show alone but rather with a bound form slung across his shoulder. He strained with the effort but made no complaint. Without a word he set the breathing form down on the ground in front of Jeron and backed away.

A man, badly beaten but alive, which was all that truly mattered. Jeron moved forward and examined the unconscious form. A simple spell was all it took to silence the man's ability to scream or speak. A moment later he began cutting, and the wretch woke up, eyes flashing, mouth drawn open in a wide scream of pain that made no noise.

The first mark was easy and unexpected. The second brought about the struggles Jeron had prepared himself for, and which tested his newfound strength as he used both hands and legs to pin the poor fool in place. "Help me hold him down," he called to Roledru, who immediately obeyed, thus freeing Jeron's arms. A moment later he began cutting more marks into unwilling flesh. He spoke the words softly, felt the power in them wash over him and flow from his body into the man struggling for survival.

Three sentences spilled past his flaking lips and the victim of his ministrations stopped moving; his muscles strained and fought to no avail. Roledru's dark eyes trailed over the man's form and then looked to Jeron for a moment before he started examining the entrance of the alleyway. Jeron understood. Best to make certain they were not disturbed. Roledru's hand went to the long dagger at his waist and he turned completely away from Jeron and his latest sacrifice. It was nothing he hadn't seen before.

Jeron worked in quick, deft strokes, marking flesh, cutting into muscle and watching as blood pooled on the ground beneath his latest victim. He felt the life drain from the body, felt the life force rise, captured that essence in his grasp and pulled it away from the cooling corpse.

His prize had to be kept and so Jeron pushed the stolen soul into the amulet around his neck. A simple stone, polished and rounded, was sufficient for the task.

As much as he enjoyed playing with his kills, there was no time. Inquisitors were looking into his murders. The Overlords were demanding, but Jeron understood their needs. They were building an army, after all.

A small portion of the stolen life was all that he required to open a portal back to the Wellish Steppes. Jeron and Roledru walked through the rift in space together, and moments later stood before the opening in the ground where Overlords and mercenaries alike waited for them.

The air was much drier and the fog that followed in their wake quickly dissipated. Roledru shook his head and stretched his arms. The knife at his side stayed sheathed and he walked toward the entrance of the underground hideaway Jeron had created.

The entrance was obvious from a short distance, but was nowhere near any of the main roads through the steppes. That was just as well.

"You should hide that better." Roledru waved his hand at the entrance point as he moved toward it.

"No. It would be easy to be too careful."

The man stopped moving and looked back at him. "How?"

"The mercenaries. Some of them are smart enough, but others may have taken a few too many blows to their heads. They would walk right past and keep going."

Roledru smiled but shook his head. "You are too judgmental."

"I've spent lifetimes observing people. They are often foolish."

Roledru pulled his hair back and grimaced. Jeron knew the problem. The man's hair was growing out and was the exact length where he could not yet tie it back.

"Jeron, you are a good man." He paused. "Mostly. Mostly you are a good man, but you must remember that you are older, from a different time. Most soldiers these days have actually fought in a war now. They're not as foolish as you think."

Jeron was considering a scathing response when the first of the Godless showed up. He had seen the man before but did not know his name. No. Wait. Trigan Garth.

The Sa'ba Taalor was one of the largest men he'd ever seen, which seemed too often to be the case with the gray skins. Generations of endless fighting had forged the survivors into beasts instead of men. They were taller, stronger and faster than most of the men from Fellein.

"I would speak with you." Trigan didn't block his path but stood next to it. Several more of the Godless waited nearby, apparently having chosen Trigan as their speaker.

Jeron eyed the man and nodded. "Then speak."

"We are here because we were promised war."

"And you'll have war. But you must wait a bit longer. The forces you will join with are not yet here, but they are coming."

"What forces?" Thick fingers brushed dark red hair back from a heavy brow and silvery eyes regarded Jeron without trepidation. It was an unsettling experience, because he'd had centuries of deference.

"The Overlords are rising from a sleep unlike any you or I could ever hope to know. They have been buried in the ground for centuries. They wake soon, and when they do they will lead us into glorious battle. They will crush their enemies and we are the heel they will use to grind meat and bone."

The man's eyes narrowed. "Your words are pretty, but they mean nothing."

"They mean *everything,* Trigan Garth. You have forsaken your gods." He held out his hands to show he meant no offense. "Or they have forsaken you. In either situation the Overlords will help you. They will guide you into glorious wars. They will destroy everything that stands, they will burn Fellein and break the Seven Forges."

The brute leaned forward until their faces were inches apart. "When? How much longer must we wait?"

And there was the biggest problem. He had no honest answer. "Soon. They stir now. They are waking and they are rising from the earth. Until then, there are ways you and yours can stay busy."

"How?"

"The mercenaries from Fellein have fought your kind before, yes?"

"Some have. Some have not."

"Keep preparing them for war. Teach them your ways and how they can be better ready for the coming conflicts." He paused only a moment and then added, "Find the weak among them and point them out to me. The Overlords would mend them."

Trigan Garth rose back to his full height and looked over his shoulder as if he could see all of the mercenaries where they waited. His scarred face pulled into a mask of thought that practically looked painful to the sorcerer.

Finally, he spoke. "Some of your mercenaries would not survive if we trained them. Several have already died."

Jeron smiled and nodded, "Then they do not deserve to fight with you. Teach them, Trigan Garth. Make them better fighters. Separate the weakest from the pack."

The man nodded. "So long as you are aware."

"I expect stronger soldiers. The weak die if they must."

Trigan said nothing more but turned on his heel and walked back the way he had come. Jeron paused as something painful slipped along his lower back and moved in his left hip. The changes were growing more apparent. He wondered if he would be crippled soon.

Not likely. The metamorphosis was happening for a reason, and he had to accept that the Overlords knew what they were doing. There was simply no choice in the matter. His senses were different. Not better, exactly, but changed. Oh, he could still see, but colors seemed distorted. His ability to smell was sharper. He could easily tell people apart by their scent.

Shooting pain wove into his head, and Jeron closed his eyes and did his best to ignore the sudden agony moving through his skull.

He failed. A wave of nausea pushed through him and he very nearly collapsed before Roledru was there with a strong arm to hold him steady. The man spoke softly, "No sign of weakness, Jeron. You are watched."

Jeron sighed and stood taller, lowering his head as if to avoid any possible light. The Overlords may well have plans, but they did not stop the pain from trying to crush him. He heeded Roledru's words and started walking, making certain that his limbs did not shake, that his eyes did not tear up at the nearly blinding pain.

There was only one place where the pain could not crush him and that was in the arms of his new masters. Jeron walked slowly into the charnel darkness of the pit leading to the Overlords, where they slowly clawed their way back toward consciousness. He could feel their hunger long before he reached them, and wrapped one hand around the stone where he carried one precious life.

He would offer it up soon enough. First, he would secure himself in his place of rest, the only place where peace even seemed possible these days.

The dark shapes of the Overlords remained hidden behind a caul, a deep black that pulled the light from even the few torches he'd left burning. Jeron, who could kill with little more than a thought, who could steal the very souls from people, crawled into a place at the feet of the Overlords and closed his eyes, taking solace from the presence of the undying creatures he had foolishly feared for centuries.

Kallir Lundt

Kallir and Desta moved carefully, sliding from one shadow to the next. They had spent two days in the camp of the Godless and the mercenaries, listening and moving in the shadows. Desta excelled at being silent; Kallir… managed not to alert anyone to their presence.

They had learned a good amount. The gathered forces were called together to help people called Overlords. The name seemed almost familiar to Kallir, but he could not find anything in his memories. The one called Jeron was in charge. The Godless moved among the people with impunity. For two days they had crept among the growing numbers, and now it was time to leave. Tarag Paedori would want his answers. The King in Iron had been patient long enough and Kallir wanted to return to his home.

Desta eyed their surroundings and nodded her approval. He had suggested leaving and she wanted to study the area carefully before they did so.

The sun had set, and they moved into darkness. Frakka waited nearby. It was enough. Soon they would be on their way home.

One of the mercenaries stumbled across them and started to speak. Desta's club silenced him very well. She settled the fool in shadows, and they moved on, quickly leaving the encampment. They were outside of the shimmering portal before everything went wrong.

His footing failed him when the ground beneath his feet surged and jumped. Kallir shifted his body in an effort to keep his balance and failed. The ground bucked and both he and Desta fell. His palms throbbed with the impact of striking hard rocks as he tried to regain his feet.

The ground continued to protest and shift under them, and Desta wisely moved downhill, even as the earth slid under them. Kallir was not as quick to regain his balance and so was caught when the rocks pushed upward.

The ground broke beneath him as stones shoved up toward the stars. His stomach clenched and he caught the closest rocks with his hands, desperate to find a steady grip.

The crust of dirt around the chosen stones broke away and Kallir held on tightly, his feet scrabbling for better purchase as the stones shifted and rose, thrusting into the air.

He heard Desta calling for him and feared he might well have made a horrible mistake.

His hands held tightly but the ground continued changing under him. Rocks shifted, dirt fell away as the vibrations increased. Somehow the world jumped away while he was focused on his hands and his feet lost their points of purchase. He was hanging over a sheer cliff before he fully understood what was happening, and Kallir swung his legs in an effort to find better support.

If the rocks had changed and grown at the same speed, he might have been safe, but they did not. His left hand kept its grip on the stone and his right hand fell slowly lower, until he had no choice but to let go his grip and try to fit both hands on the blade of stone holding his weight. Kallir knew he was screaming but could not hear himself over the rumbling noise of the ground breaking beneath him.

Dirt cascaded down from above him, followed by a stream of pebbles and small stones that banged off his metallic face and skittered away. Anyone else would surely have been knocked senseless by the avalanche and Kallir was thankful that the back of his head, the part that was still flesh and bone, was protected by the same outcropping that supported his hands. He considered dropping from the growing madness around him and realized he was high enough that he could well kill himself if he bounced against the growing stones.

Oh, yes, he screamed. One thing to fight an enemy and die in combat, but it was entirely different to have the earth beneath him growing taller as he held on for all he was worth.

A great shadow came for him from above and Kallir closed his eyes, fully prepared to die if whatever was falling his way hit him. There was simply nowhere to go.

Frakka's teeth caught his tunic and pulled him away from the growing mountainside.

Kallir yelped and moved his arms until they locked around his mount's neck.

Frakka made not a sound as he pounced and jumped, bouncing from one location to the next until they were down the growing slope of rock. A moment later Kallir was lying on his back and Frakka was crouched next to him. They watched together as the rocks kept pushing up from the ground, cutting free of the soil.

Then they moved back as the shaking got worse and the earth around them cracked and broke. Kallir climbed onto Frakka's back and looked for Desta. He spotted her where she moved several hundred feet away from them, doing her best to keep her balance as she ran.

They moved and the ground continued to shake, to rumble, as fissures split the skin of the land. Frakka lowered his head and charged across the shaking soil, passing Desta to their far left before he slowed down and finally stopped.

Kallir looked back, past his friend, as the ground continued its shaking. Easily seventy feet of stone had pushed its way from the earth, a hill coming from beneath them and moving upward, a mountain growing from the ground.

The rumbling stopped. The rocks ceased their upward growth.

Desta continued running until she reached them, panting hard from the exertion. Kallir had never truly seen her winded before.

"I think we can call that a sign to report back to Tarag," said Desta.

"If a sign were needed, I would agree. Let's get back as quickly as we can. The king will want answers."

"We don't have answers. Just more situations."

"We have some answers. We know this is the work of a sorcerer."

"This Jeron is a wizard?"

Kallir nodded. "I heard his name many times when I was growing up. He is a powerful sorcerer, from all the stories. Almost as great as Desh Krohan himself." What could sorcerers do? There were endless tales, but the truth of their abilities wasn't known to Kallir. He was a soldier. He heard only rumors. He had never seen a wizard in person before he saw Desh Krohan, and that had been only in passing.

Desta climbed on Frakka's broad back and once again held on to Kallir as the beast started running. It was not long before they were back at the palace and heading for the hall where Tarag Paedori saw most of his people. Long before they reached that spot, they saw the increased activity. Obviously the shaking earth had been felt here as well, though likely not as violently.

Several of the Sa'ba Taalor were gathered in the courtyard and speaking as more of the people gathered. "Where is Tarag?" Kallir asked one of the men he knew, and the man confirmed that the king was waiting for him. He was expected back.

He and Desta moved directly to the hall, and there they found Tarag Paedori speaking with a gathering of his people, some of the top warriors in the kingdom. They listened as their king spoke, and Kallir and Desta waited patiently until the discussions were finished. The gathering broke up, the warriors heading in different directions and Tarag standing still, watching as they left his side.

"You have returned." Tarag gestured them closer. "Tell me what you learned."

"There is a sorcerer named Jeron. I have never met him, but he was one of Desh Krohan's closest."

"I know a Jeron. I thought I'd killed him."

"I don't think it's an unusual name, but this one hides in shadows. I never saw him clearly."

Desta nodded her agreement and spoke softly. "He is diseased. His skin peels like the hide of a rotten fruit."

"A mountain is growing from the ground." Kallir shook his head. "It grew beneath us."

The king spoke absently, his brow heavily knitted and his eyes distant. "Yes, I am aware. We felt the ground shake even here. I am glad you were unharmed."

Tarag Paedori strode across his throne room, as he often did when he was thinking. His eyes shifted through the windows, looked toward the freshly hewn stone as if he could see clearly into it from their distance. It was little more than a bulge from here, only a slight difference showing where the rocks had risen from the earth. Still the King in Iron stared.

Without preamble the king removed his vest and headed toward the heart of Truska-Pren. The chamber he entered glowed a deep, bloody red. The heat from the entrance into the area was a blast from an opened oven. He stopped long enough to remove the rest of his clothing and then moved deeper into the fiery chamber.

Though he had watched a hundred times before, Kallir looked on as the King in Iron walked into a field of molten stone, his body slowly sinking into the lava as he communed with his god. His flesh did not blister. His hair did not burn. The King in Iron slowly disappeared into a heat that should have broiled him alive.

He would return when he was finished speaking with his god. Kallir knew that king and god could speak without the close proximity, just as he could speak with the god himself, but there was something more to what passed between Tarag Paedori and Truska-Pren. The King in Iron would return invigorated. The silver and gray in his hair would be less. He would return more energetic, less worn down by the crown he wore. He was literally in the presence of a god. How could he not be changed by that?

Kallir looked into the blazing heat and slowly nodded. He would wait where he was. At least for now – it might be days before Tarag showed himself again. There was no way to know for certain, and he did not second guess gods or kings, but for a while he would wait.

Desta stood beside him and did not move.

He was pleased to have someone to wait with him.

Swech

Swech moved carefully through the rain and fog. Canhoon slept under heavy storms. There was no lightning, no thunder, only wind and cold rain.

She had not been to the palace of the Empress of Fellein in some time, but she was here now, and she would do as she was commanded by her gods.

She was to meet with one man and hear his plea.

The opening into the castle was obscured in shadow. For a moment she wondered if the hidden entrance was still there, or if it had been found and sealed. She needn't have worried. The stone slid smoothly to the side and Swech slipped into the darkness with ease. She did not have to use her eyes to remember the passages. She had spent weeks moving through the castle again and again without being seen, and her memories were clear.

Still it was the voice of her god that whispered to her, told her where she had to go and made certain she did not take the wrong passages through the vast network of concealed tunnels within the complex. Paedle spoke and she listened.

The object of her attention was sleeping when she entered his chambers. She had no intention of startling him. Her plan was to see him without being seen by others, but she was not foolish enough to want to catch him unawares.

"Andover." She spoke softly.

His eyes opened in the darkness.

Andover Iron Hands rose from his sleep and moved into a crouch as he looked over the room. Swech stood perfectly still and let him adjust to her presence. Had she meant him harm he would already be dead, and both of them knew it.

"My king," Andover bowed and left his arms wide apart, his hands held toward the ceiling.

Swech waved aside his bow and settled herself against the wall closest to his window.

"Paedle says you are planning to see all the kings of the Seven Forges."

"The gods have made it clear that I should."

Swech nodded. "I am here. You are the only person in Canhoon who knows this. I would keep it that way."

Andover nodded.

"You will seek the kings for your own reasons? Or will you seek the kings for the Fellein?"

"I plan only to seek each of you and pay my respects. If the Fellein would ask for more, then I will abide by their wishes. Already the Empress of Fellein has asked me to bring a message to each of the kings. She would ask if there is a chance of peace between the Sa'ba Taalor and the Fellein."

Swech looked at the man for several seconds. He was not the same boy she had met in the past. She'd known that before she saw him, but the reality was still unexpected. "If the gods demand war, we war."

"I would expect no less, but I ask as the Empress has requested."

"I am here. I follow Paedle's wishes and do not know how long I will be here." Swech moved closer to Andover and stared into his eyes. "You have been here for five years and the gods still speak to you and of you. You have earned their trust, Andover. You have earned my trust. You are always welcome in Paedle's domain unless that trust is broken."

"I will seek your audience again, Swech. I know this. I know they will ask more of me as the armies of the Sa'ba Taalor move."

"We do not move yet."

"The sorcerers say you will." He shrugged. "And you are here."

Swech said nothing, but she nodded.

"It is good to see you, Swech."

"Why do you stay here? Is this your home now?"

Andover sighed and did not answer.

"So. Visit the other kingdoms first and then come to see me."

She stepped back to the hidden door in his chamber and opened it. A moment later she was once again in the darkness.

Andover weighed on her mind as she left the palace. He was neither Sa'ba Taalor nor Fellein. He was favored by the gods. They watched over him. He trained the Fellein in the tactics of the Sa'ba Taalor, and took neither side of the conflict.

Swech could not decide what to think of him. Ultimately she decided as she almost always did: that the gods offered the best example. If Paedle said he was a good man, then he was a good man.

Desh Krohan

They gathered in the central courtyard; first only a few, but soon the people were overrunning the pathways laid out by the gardeners and were congregating in the well-manicured lawns and between the bushes as the priests spoke of gods and the best way to appease them.

Estre spoke first, calling for blessings from Plith and thanks for the bountiful harvest. The city had food in abundance and the cost of fresh fruit was reasonable even in Canhoon, and so many offered their thanks to the god of the harvest.

Theor offered a prayer to Etrilla, the god of cities and towns, and everyone present grew silent and still in contemplation of the god's power. Was Canhoon not proof of all that was well and loved?

Ornel spoke blessings from Tyrea, the god of the wild, and many took the sweet berries offered with the blessings, a sign of the god's favor.

Fantohl moved among the gathered and marked any outstretched hand with ash and sand, a sign that Lalos the Wanderer listened to all prayers. Canhoon was a city of commerce, and many of those who frequented the markets traveled great distances to bring treasures from far off places. Blessings from Lalos were always considered fortunate, indeed.

Lariso offered thanks to Kanheer, the god of war, for his continued slumbers. All who served or had served in the Imperial Army were gifted special blessings. There was a moment of prayer for those who'd served and fallen in battle in previous wars. There was a time when no one would have considered that prayer a necessity, but the ghosts of the fallen still haunted the living in Fellein.

Ovish the beggar made prayers to Luhnsh, the Beggar King, asking protection for the weakest, and many offered coin as their way of thanking the god for their good fortune.

Finally, beautiful Ahdra offered prayers to Vendahl, the god of wealth and good fortune, and many voices joined in, for most in Canhoon considered themselves among the fortunate, even those who were not wealthy.

Throughout the ceremonies, twelve of the Silent Army stood and watched over the procession, expressionless and stoic. Each of the stone soldiers faced the priest or priestess who made blessings, but otherwise remained still.

Three times as many members of the City-Guard watched the proceedings, moving among the many celebrants and keeping alert to possible dangers. The Empress had demanded their presence, and they obeyed.

Desh Krohan made his way through the crowd, his hood down and his presence barely noticed. It was rare for anyone to recognize him, and there were no exceptions here.

When the gathering started there were perhaps fifty people. By the time the prayers were finished they numbered closer to six hundred. Ahdra promised another meeting the next night at the same time, as the sun fell toward the lake and the day came to an end. The merchants in the area had already closed their stands and put away their wares. The locals took advantage of the distraction offered, and heard from the priests.

In the history of Canhoon, Desh had never seen the priests of the different gods unified as a force before, save when the Pilgrim raised the faithful together to call forth the Silent Army. If he had needed proof of miracles, that day was all he ever had to remember.

He had helped create the Silent Army when he was a young man. He and the other sorcerers who created them had never planned for a day when the gods would call them back to action. These days the Silent Army did as they had in the past and served as a force to preserve and protect the people of Canhoon.

They just did so of their own volition. If anyone could be said to command them, it was the Empress. Otherwise it was the gods.

The representatives of those gods were unified now, a fact that bothered Desh a great deal more than the Silent Army. People were far less likely to defend the city, and far more likely to cause troubles, in his experience.

The crowd began to disperse, and from the middle of that crowd he saw Merros Dulver looking in his direction. The general's expression mirrored his own thoughts, that the meeting was not as harmless as it likely seemed to most people.

The general was dressed in civilian garb, with dark pants and a heavy sweater under his thick cloak. Like many in the military, his hair was kept short and his face was clean of moustache or beard. He nodded toward Desh and walked in his direction.

Despite his attempt to look casual, the people around him parted to let Merros through. His stance, his bearing, made clear that he was not to be trifled with.

"You're well, Desh?"

The wizard looked toward the general and sighed. "I am alive. That's enough for the moment I expect."

"And what did you think of our gathered priests?"

Desh made certain no one was paying them particular attention and then walked further before he answered. "I can see why you've been worried. They have collected more people than I expected."

"Twice the crowd I saw before, at least."

Desh nodded and looked around. More people were leaving the area, heading for their homes or other places. The air was cold and that was enough to drive several of the smaller groups away. The weather was promising more rain as well.

"They're better organized than anticipated."

"I'm telling you, Desh; this is a problem, or it will be."

"Yes, but what to do about it?"

"Limit them to their proper churches instead of the imperial gardens."

"There are any number of places where people can gather, Merros. Certainly nothing to stop them from gathering in the marketplaces."

"I'd say the vendors might have an objection."

"Oh, they might, but we spend money when we gather." The voice came from his left and Desh looked over to see Ahdra and Ovish both looking his way. Ahdra was dressed in finery and Ovish was dressed in rags. Ahdra was lovely. Ovish had dirt ingrained in the wrinkles on his face. Ahdra represented the wealthy. Ovish celebrated the Beggar King.

It was Ovish who spoke. "Gather together and offer nothing to vendors and they will certainly be upset, but if two hundred gather and only one hundred spend something, that is one hundred more sales than would happen otherwise." He polished an apple on his dirty shirt, and then took a bite of it, chewing noisily.

For her part, Ahdra nodded and smiled her agreement.

Merros looked at each of them, his brow slightly stormy, but his expression otherwise calm. Anyone who didn't know him wouldn't think he was reacting at all.

Desh nodded.

Ahdra spoke up. "We are gathering for the glory of the gods, who helped us in our time of need. How is that a bad thing?"

"It isn't," Merros answered. "But when large groups gather in new places, I worry that the City-Guard might need to watch carefully."

"Does the City-Guard gather when there is a concert?" Ahdra smiled.

"Yes, actually, they do." Merros smiled back. "It's what they are paid for. Surely it's best if we're prepared for pickpockets and cutpurses."

"Of course, but that is one of the reasons we have these meetings in different places, to avoid just that sort of problem." Ovish this time. He continued, "And many who would steal from a concert might think twice before stealing from the gods."

Desh responded, "I was unaware that the gods have purses."

Ovish's dark eyes were surrounded by wrinkles as he smiled back. "'Those who serve the gods are blessed with good fortune.' At least according to Luhnsh. Who am I to argue with a god?"

"Well, simply tell me when and where the next meeting takes place and I'll make certain that the City-Guard is on hand to keep everyone safe." Merros spoke softly and kept a calm demeanor.

Ahdra kept her calm demeanor as well. "We don't want to become a burden, General Dulver."

"I can't imagine anyone seeing you as a burden."

"Me alone? Not likely, but six hundred or so devotees can make anyone feel as if they've been tasked."

Ovish chuckled to himself and a moment later both of the religious leaders were on their way, leaving Merros and Desh on their own in the growing darkness.

Merros sighed. "You see? A problem."

Desh nodded but said nothing else. There was simply nothing to add at the moment. He was far too busy considering the best possible ways to put an end to what was, so far, a simple social gathering.

After a few minutes he said, "She's not going to be happy about this."

"Nor should she be. This will not go well for the empire."

"Why do you say that?"

"It's seldom a good thing when someone else comes along and tells the locals how to think. If that someone is a god or two, I can't see how the Empress can easily out-argue the situation." Merros sighed. "I've had enough trouble with a few soldiers who wanted to argue what I said with what a god supposedly claimed."

"And what did you do about those soldiers?"

Merros patted the bullwhip he kept on his hip. "I find five or so lashes tends to end most insubordination. The mere threat does wonders. But that's with a man in a uniform, not with the average citizen on the street."

"And what would you do with the average citizen?"

"Leave them to the City-Guard, of course." Merros shrugged. "Might work in these circumstances, but I'd hate to be the one to argue with a mob that numbers in the hundreds."

"The Sa'ba Taalor always follow their gods. That's what I've heard."

"True, but their gods speak to them directly."

"Let's hope that never happens here." Desh sighed. "It'll be very difficult to get anyone to listen to the Empress, or the City-Guard."

Merros Dulver looked away from him and stared at the thick stone inner wall that separated the imperial grounds from the rest of the city. Just to the left of where they stood was one of the heavy gates that were always left open in times of peace. Merros said nothing about wondering if they should be closed again, but Desh sighed just the same. Merros always seemed interested in easy solutions that solved problems before they became more difficult. Nachia would not approve.

That was the problem with having an optimist sitting on the throne. Her cousin had been the same way, and in the end that optimism had killed Pathra Krous. He just needed to make certain the same didn't happen to Nachia.

CHAPTER SEVEN

Jeron

"Move them down the hillside. Have them bring their tents with them." Jeron's long fingers rubbed at his temples as he spoke to Roledru. As was most often the case, his assistant did not acknowledge his order, but Jeron knew the man was listening and would obey.

"The hill, will it continue to grow?"

"Almost certainly. Whatever the Overlords are doing I expect they are nowhere close to finished with the changes they plan to make."

Roledru tilted his head to the side and looked away, a sure sign that he had something to say that he did not relish.

"What bothers you?"

The man's dark eyes regarded at him for a moment. Sometimes his assistant forgot who he dealt with. In his long life Jeron had forgotten more of body language than most would ever know. Each person spoke it, but none in the same way. It was a language with countless dialects.

"The mercenaries want to get paid."

"Of course, they do."

"I can handle the matter, but I'll need the funds to pay them."

"Ah. Send Trigan Garth to me, please. And two more of his Godless."

Roledru left without question, and soon enough the hulking warrior stood in front of him. The others were only a few steps behind.

"Trigan, the mercenaries wish to be paid."

Trigan made a wave motion from his fingers to his wrist several times. "I would think they'd need to fight first."

"I'd feel the same way, but coin is the only loyalty most of them know." He smiled. "I would ask that you and these two with you stand by Roledru while he doles out payment, lest anyone decide to get greedy."

"I will kill any who try to take too much."

"Thank you."

The Sa'ba Taalor all stood at ease better than any military man he'd ever seen, and yet they also fought better alone and in groups. The relaxed muscles of the gray skins seemed to move faster than the tensed muscles of the Fellein. He wondered if there was a correlation. In time he might try a few experiments to find out. "How many soldiers come?" Trigan asked. "How many of these mercenaries?"

"Within the next two days there will be several hundred more arriving by boat. Our camp is about to become much larger."

"Do they bring their own supplies?"

"They bring horses and weapons. I have called for a company of cooks and supplies. They should be here tomorrow."

"Good. Most of these mercenaries could not hunt a rock."

Jeron offered a genuine laugh. "You are a fine man, Trigan."

The man nodded at the compliment and left to handle

business. From outside the tent he heard the deep voice calling for Roledru. As far as Jeron was concerned he had found a worthy leader for the forces.

He rose from his seat and tested out the new limbs where his legs had once been, pondering what the Godless and the mercenaries would think if they knew how much he had changed. His robes hid most of the obvious transformations, and the few no longer concealed were subtler than most. Mostly his fingers appeared substantially longer.

Of course, the changes were still happening. He did not know how far this would go. He did not care. In a matter of minutes Roledru would be guaranteeing the loyalty of the troops already present.

The rest would fall in line quickly enough when the select few chosen for rebirth emerged from their cocoons of darkness. He could feel them down below, buried deep with the Overlords. He could sense the changes in their very minds.

The longer he served the Overlords, the more impressed he was with them and their strategies alike. What had he ever feared?

All he'd had to give up was his humanity, and he'd been working on that for as long as he could remember. After all, humans were mortal, and he was already becoming so much more.

Darsken Murdro

It was rare to see more than two members of the Inquisition at the same time. There were exceptions, but Darsken could not recall a time when he had ever seen twenty in one chamber.

The Grand Inquisitor, Alacrid, had summoned them, and no one hesitated to show their loyalty to the woman who led them. Alacrid was a heavyset woman with white hair and an amiable smile. She was their leader because she had earned her place. Her determination in pursuing investigations was legendary, as was her willingness to hunt down the guilty parties.

"We have troubled times before us," she said, once they were all gathered in the tower chamber. "There are murders unsolved, and someone is using the Dark Art against the very people they are killing." The room was silent, but the shocked expressions on the faces of the Inquisitors spoke volumes. The use of necromancy was a bad sign. It meant that even the most highly regarded members of the Inquisition had to be considered as suspects.

Alacrid nodded slowly as the Inquisitors considered the situation. "Because of this, all Inquisitors must now work with a partner. We cannot afford to take chances. None will work alone, not even me."

Though a few were surprised by the decree, none could debate the logic. That was reason enough for Darsken to know the measure was unnecessary.

He said nothing, of course, but knew that the people in the room continued as they had before, uncorrupted by the temptations that necromancy sometimes offered.

It was power. It was a form of sorcery that promoted abuse. Most magic required a sacrifice of energy. Necromancy allowed a sorcerer to pull that energy from the dead. Even the Inquisitors used the life force taken from the dead to fuel their talents, though the amount taken was minimal. The spells cast by Inquisitors were less involved, less intrusive than some. Speaking with the dead was easy in comparison to stealing from them or bending them to a necromancer's will. Still, power was sought, and often necromancy made that power easier to capture.

"Who leads the investigation?" Samsal asked the question. The man was brusque by nature.

"Darsken Murdro has been investigating. He has made good strides, but the Necromancer eludes him so far. Etredu Moiren also investigates. There have been deaths here and in Goltha. The two Inquisitors have worked together to try solving this investigation." Alacrid's faith in him felt unwarranted after so many setbacks, but Darsken knew the words were her truth. She did not make false claims to ease his mind. It was not how she thought.

Samsal looked his way and nodded, satisfied with the answer, apparently. The Inquisitor was a wanderer. He did not have a city he looked over, but rather a territory. Like most wanderers, he preferred it that way. Cities were too restrictive. It took a particular mindset to prefer living in a city to exploring. The Louron were wanderers by nature, though, inevitably, all returned to their native land whenever time permitted. Samsal looked for Etredu and frowned when he saw the man was not present. Darsken frowned as well. He'd been looking forward to seeing Goltha's lead Inquisitor.

Alacrid continued, "This necromancer must be found. He has already killed here, in Canhoon, and in Goltha. Souls have been stolen away. This cannot be allowed to continue." She paused and looked round the chamber. "Darsken, did Etredu not say he would be present?"

"He did, but I have not seen him." His frown deepened as he answered. Etredu was not the sort to miss a meeting where he was summoned. Still, there was nothing to be done at the moment. Etredu would hardly be the only Inquisitor who missed a meeting while on the hunt for answers. He would seek the man out when the meeting was finished, if only for his own peace of mind.

"Have any of you found bodies marked with runes in your areas? Bodies where necromancy is the obvious culprit?" Alacrid asked the question but likely already knew the answer. There were few among the Inquisitors arrogant enough to consider approaching the situation without reporting a similar crime. Darsken was second only to the Grand Inquisitor, but he reported the situation to her immediately when he discovered the loss of souls, just as he'd alerted Desh Krohan as quickly as he could.

The sorcerers had to know, had to be prepared if it was one of theirs who committed these heinous offenses.

"Etredu is dead." The words were spoken softly. Daivem Murdro spoke them. Daivem, his sister, who was another wanderer. She had literally just walked into the room.

"Why do you say that, Daivem? What have you seen?"

"I have seen his body, Darsken. I have seen the markings carved into his flesh." Daivem was younger, but she looked older by a decade at that moment. "They killed him slowly, I think. I feel they made him suffer a great deal."

Darsken was not easily angered, but he ground his teeth and felt his hands clench into fists. "This cannot be allowed."

Alacrid spoke softly. "I agree. We go now to see the body of our brother. We will find his killer. This has gone on for too long, and cannot be forgiven."

No one disagreed. Daivem led the way to where Etredu's body lay buried in shadows. No one spoke. They were too busy examining the corpse of their fallen and looking for clues that might be hidden away.

There were secrets lost in that darkness.

The Inquisition was driven to find answers as they had seldom been before. The clues made themselves known, though it took most of the night and the next day.

Trigan Garth

The expected cooks and supplies did not arrive. Instead there were hacked and bloodied bodies floating on the waters of the Freeholdt River. The weather had grown bitterly cold and snow flurried its way to the ground.

Trigan studied the corpses as he and his gathered Godless pulled them from the waters. Someone had taken from them and that would not do.

"Godless! We ride!" It hadn't been long since he'd nearly killed a man for calling him Godless, but now, oddly, he was beginning to think differently. When he first heard the term it wounded him. The Daxar Taalor had abandoned him, to his way of thinking. These days, however, he understood that he was the one who had abandoned them. They had lied. The gods of his people had sworn to always be there, to always answer questions and offer guidance. They had failed in that vow; through their own fault or someone else's was irrelevant. According to some of the others, all he had to do was present himself to the lying bastard gods and he would be accepted.

No. They should present themselves to him and beg him to return. He had never offered the gods silence before they offered it to him.

Trigan mounted the horse he was offered by Jeron and turned to follow the river upstream. They would find the thieves. They would kill the thieves. Not that he was angry about what had happened, but because they needed to suffer for what they had done. He no longer followed the gods of war, but he still agreed with their philosophies of life. Let no one go unpunished who richly deserved punishment.

The gathering moved quickly, and Harlo, a lean, vicious fighter, rode ahead, looking for any signs of their enemy. He had worked with the man before and let Harlo scout ahead in complete comfort with the man's abilities. He was a follower – no, had been a follower – of Paedle. He was well trained in scouting.

He was also deadly.

After nearly an hour of hard riding, Harlo brought his horse to a halt and then dropped from the saddle. He gestured, and the rest of the riders followed suit. Trigan observed, and followed Harlo's directions. There was no question about who was in charge at that moment. Harlo understood what was needed better than Trigan did, and so he led the party. He had seen the Fellein in action, and that was something their culture could not understand. That, he suspected, would be the downfall of their empire if the Sa'ba Taalor ever warred with them again.

Harlo pointed to a cluster of shrubs near the top of a gentle slope to the north. He showed the tracks of their targets, left clearly visible for all to see. They were killers and thieves but made no effort to hide themselves. That spoke of arrogance. The tracks themselves spoke of numbers.

No weapons were drawn as they moved up the slope toward the tracks left behind. They would use their hands if they needed to fight. Unarmed combat was quieter. It would be foolish to assume there were no guards watching. For that reason they moved as quietly as they could.

Harlo moved over the top of the hill first, and after almost three minutes he waved the rest of them forward. There had indeed been a man on watch. That man was now dead.

The remaining thieves were looking over their bounty, the vast supplies meant for the mercenaries working for Jeron. There were live animals aplenty, and crates of supplies. The thieves had not really hidden themselves, because they felt safe. They felt they had the numbers on their side. There were thirty of them, a much more significant gathering than Trigan would have initially expected.

He scowled as he considered the gathered men. They were hardened and hungry. The majority of the group was currently eating freshly cooked meat and focused on little besides their meal. One man cooked, throwing slabs of meat onto an iron pan over a fire. Everything looked as if it had been rushed, from the location of the stolen goods to the fire they used to cook. More of the group was waiting to eat, and none of them looked patient about waiting for the fire to finish the process of cooking.

There were five of the thieves for every Godless. Trigan felt his body preparing itself for war. His heart beat loud and strong, his blood sang, and he waited for the signal from Harlo.

He did not wait long. Harlo used gestures, not words, but the command was clear enough. It was time to attack.

Trigan let out a loud battle cry and came toward the encampment from the left. The men they faced turned in his direction, some staring gape-mouthed with surprise and others quicker to respond, rising from their positions and drawing weapons.

Trigan and two others moved into them, roaring and making as much noise as they could. The response was everything he wanted. The first of the Fellein rose up and grabbed his spear, alert and ready for bloodshed. Trigan moved in without hesitation, grabbing the spear before its wielder could bring it around to cause him harm. The man was unprepared for his quick action, and grunted as he tried to pull the spear away. Trigan kept his grip on the shaft of the spear and threw his weight into twisting it away from its owner. The man let go of his prize and Trigan brought a knee up and drove it into the fool's ribcage.

Panicked eyes looked into his face. Trigan spun to the right and swept the spear with him, smashing the previous owner in the skull with the butt of the haft. Long before the man crashed to the ground, he was driving the point of the weapon into another man's throat.

The element of surprise was gone. It had served him well enough. He blocked an attempt to strike him in the side and pushed back against the attacker. The man was using an axe, but he did it poorly, sweeping the weapon a wide arc as if he were chopping down a tree. There was no consideration of failure in the gesture, and it left the axe-man off balance.

Trigan backed away as a second warrior attacked, and parried the blow sent his way. His face pulled into a grin as he fought. This was truly when he felt most alive. The tip of the spear drove forward and into his enemy's shoulder. He twisted the blade and ripped, tearing away meat and gristle. His enemy screamed and pulled back from the sudden pain. Trigan pushed forward and stabbed the point into the man's chest. Bone caught the end of the spear. He let the weapon go.

The next attacker was the cook, who wielded a large knife already bloodied on the animal the Fellein were eating. Blocking a blade was easier with a weapon, and Trigan pulled the war club from his side and dodged back as the man lunged at him. The club came down on the man's arm and broke his wrist. The knife fell to the ground and Trigan grabbed the broken wrist with his free hand and twisted bone and meat to the side.

Something hot burned across his shoulder. Trigan grunted and pulled the screaming cook toward him. The man stumbled in closer and Trigan pushed him toward the source of his pain. The man who'd successfully stabbed him with a dagger fell back as the cook crashed into him, and Trigan brought the club around again, this time pulping the head of the dagger-wielder.

He was aware of the fight around him in a peripheral way. The Godless were all engaged in combat now. The two who came with him were in hard combat, driving into the Fellein with what looked like reckless abandon. They had drawn the attention of the Fellein for a reason. They were loud fighters. The quiet ones came in from the other side and took advantage of the distractions they provided.

Hrothrun, a Godless he had known most of his life, and a woman to be feared in combat, brought her blade around and cut a man's head off. She let out a scream that was nearly deafening as she did it, and most of the people around them blanched as the blood from her enemy coated her in crimson gore. She took advantage of their hesitation and brought her blade back around, carving through the cheek of her next opponent. The man fell back screaming.

At the same time, one of the Fellein stepped forward and buried the blade of his sword in the stomach of Deillor, who had come from the other side with Harlo. It was a good cut and Deillor fell back, bleeding freely from the wound that opened his guts to the world. Deillor stumbled and landed hard, both hands engaged in trying to keep his innards where they belonged. The swordsman looked at the fallen enemy and at his sword, as if having trouble believing that he had just killed one of the Godless. While he was busy working out the details, Trigan beat in the back of his skull.

And just that quickly the fighting was done.

Deillor looked up at Trigan and shook his head feebly before he vomited blood. Trigan stared and knew that the man was dead. Most of his bowels had spilled into the dirt. He would not survive.

Hrothrun ended Deillor's suffering with a sword stroke across the throat.

They didn't take care of the wounded Fellein the same way. Let the bastards suffer. Instead they gathered their one dead companion and left the dead and dying enemies alone. They had come to take back their supplies and that was all that mattered.

"What happens to him now?" Hrothrun spoke softly.

"To Deillor? We burn his body." Trigan spoke just as softly. He didn't like to think about what dying meant. He never had.

Hrothrun shook her head. "I'll take him to Truska-Pren."

"I think he was closer to Wheklam."

She looked to the south, as if she could possibly see Wheklam's burning mountain from where they stood. "Then I will take him to Wheklam."

"You will not be welcomed."

She sighed and cast her eyes toward him. "I grow tired of not hearing the gods. I would have them with me again."

Trigan nodded. The silence from the gods still weighed on him. He understood.

Harlo scowled. It was possible he might have argued with her about her choice, but Trigan discouraged him with a look.

Trigan helped strap the body of his dead companion to the horse he'd ridden. Within five minutes Hrothrun and Deillor were on their way.

Harlo said, "Jeron will not like this."

"Jeron is not Sa'ba Taalor. He does not matter."

"He pays us."

Trigan shook his head. "Gold and silver do not come before the gods."

"We're Godless."

Trigan looked at the other man. "For as long as we choose to be, or as long as the gods choose it. If Paedle speaks to you right now, what will you do?"

"I'll answer."

"And if Paedle tells you to come home?"

"I will go home."

Trigan nodded. "We are Godless only because the Daxar Taalor allow it."

Harlo looked at a loss as to what he should say, and so he stayed silent.

"I am angry with the Daxar Taalor. I am also wise enough to know that the gods can punish us at any time for any reason."

"What if they can't? What if they can no longer see us?"

"They are gods, Harlo. They can move mountains. They can heal wounds. Best to believe they can find us if they so desire."

Harlo nodded in silence, and then they moved to gather the possessions stolen by river thieves who would never steal again.

Jeron and his Overlords might have great powers, but there was no doubt in Trigan's mind that the gods had greater abilities.

Time would test that belief.

Nachia Krous

"You're joking, of course." Nachia stared hard at the sorcerer. He was wise enough to have his robes in position, but she was not intimidated. Well, not much. She'd grown used to his ways.

With a wave of her hand she sent her retinue scattering like leaves in a howling wind. They left quickly and quietly. Even Gissamoen, who was as close as anyone came to a confidant these days, outside of Desh himself and Merros.

"Of course not. The first dozen suitors are merely waiting to be seen."

She refused to look at Merros Dulver, especially because the man was trying his very best not to make a single sound as he laughed silently.

"I could just have you imprisoned, Desh. Or killed. It would be easier."

"Neither would go very well, Majesty."

"I have far more pressing matters to deal with, old man."

"You take this too lightly, Majesty. We need to prepare an heir to the throne."

"I do not have the patience for your games, Desh Krohan."

"It's not my intention to make you laugh, nor do I jest."

"I've named my heir."

"Brolley does not have your wisdom."

"He grows wiser by the day."

"There is a difference between running the family business and running an empire, Nachia."

"We have troubles that are far more pressing, I assure you. We have a murdered Inquisitor. We have citizens whose souls have been ripped from their bodies by necromancy. We have troubles brewing in the Wellish Steppes. Sa'ba Taalor have been seen there, and there's a mountain growing from the ground. For all we know the gray skins have decided to start another war."

"The Sooth say no."

"The Sooth have been known to lie."

"Well, yes, but not often."

"Often enough."

"Majesty. I don't think I can stress how important it is that you choose a proper heir, or birth one."

"No one said I had to get married to have an heir, Desh."

She shook her head as the man moaned. "Not this again."

"I have no intention of being courted by an army of buffoons to satisfy your desire to see me with child."

"I assure you, Nachia, some of the men I've brought to court you are quite competent."

"And I assure you, Desh, that I'll gleefully execute any of them that aren't."

"You know it isn't always easy to know when you're making a jest."

"Best to imagine I am not then, don't you think?"

Desh glared.

Merros Dulver coughed into his hand and looked away from both of them. The poor bastard had to find them deeply absurd.

"If I may, perhaps you should focus on the immediate

threats for a moment. I feel it necessary to investigate the Wellish Steppes and the new hill growing there."

"Hill, Merros?" Nachia stared at him.

"It's hardly a mountain, Majesty."

"Nor is it a bump. I hear the mound is over seventy feet taller than the land around it."

"That is true, Majesty, but it is far smaller than any of the Seven Forges."

"So are the majority of the mountains around us."

Merros nodded, "Mountain it is, then."

"Relax, Merros. I'm joking."

"If the Empress wants to make a mountain from a hill, then I will follow her orders. I'm fairly certain it's the law."

"It certainly should be."

Desh shook his head. "Yes, by all means. Let's make it a decree. Now, about your suitors."

"Send them away."

"I don't think you're giving the situation the gravity it deserves."

"When I decide to have a child, I'll let you know."

"Majesty..."

"Enough! I'm growing tired of this conversation, Desh."

Much as she loved him, the First Advisor tended toward trying too hard in many cases. She would not be forced into decisions she did not agree with.

Merros cleared his throat and said, "Mountains. I believe we were discussing mountains and investigating their appearance. I'm thinking of going out to the Wellish Steppes myself."

"You're the general in charge of all my armies, Merros. I can hardly have you wandering off into the wilderness."

"Said the woman who decided to go exploring instead of

being an Empress." He winced as he said it. Desh laughed out loud, and Nachia sent him an ugly scowl in response. "My apologies, Majesty. I have overstepped my position."

Nachia rolled her eyes. "Really, Merros, I don't know when you became worried about offending me. Please. If I decide to take offense, I'll let you know."

"I just. I don't want anyone thinking they should look to me as an example of how to speak to the Empress, Nachia. I don't want anyone deciding they can take liberties."

"Merros, if I ever have a problem with how people speak to me, I'll take up your example and have their hides for their efforts." She mimicked hitting someone with a bullwhip. "Seems to work for you when it comes to discipline."

"Well, yes, but it's expected of me."

"I'm perfectly willing to be as harsh as I need to be, Merros. Don't stop being you around me, please. You and Desh are very nearly the only people I trust enough to relax around, and Desh is growing tiresome."

Desh waved a dismissive hand.

"Who can we send to the steppes instead of you, Merros?"

"I fear I'm in the same position as you, Nachia. There really aren't that many people I trust to make a proper report."

"For the love of all the gods," Desh shook his head and glared. "Either find better people to work with, or lower your standards. I can send any of the Sisters and have answers for you within the day."

"We don't all have your luck with assistants. I, for example, only have a withered, old, First Advisor. He's dubious at the best of times."

"Truly your wit will save us all from the dire times ahead."

"If neither of you find a better solution, I'll still head

off into the steppes." Merros shook his head but he was smiling again, relaxing, which was what she wanted. She had enough people around her who would do as she said without consideration. She wanted people she could trust to be honest with her. It was a rarity at the best of times. The majority of the friends she'd had before her ascension to the throne were no longer trustworthy in her eyes. Far too many of them either wanted special favor as a result of knowing her for years, or seemed resentful of her status. More importantly, she wanted to have people who simply treated her as if she weren't made of spider webs that would blow away in a strong wind.

Gissamoen was the one exception she allowed herself and, while her secretary was very competent and capable, she had all the personality of a glass bauble.

"Let me send Pella. She needs a good reason to leave the city for a while."

"By all means, send her. I can find many ways to occupy myself." Merros shook his head.

"There. That very expression, Merros. That is why I chose to ride to New Trecharch. I refuse to be locked away in this castle for the rest of my existence."

"Oh, come now, Nachia." Desh started speaking and she shook her head.

"No, Desh. Pathra said more than once that not seeing the empire he ruled was one of his greatest regrets. I will not follow in his shadow."

That was the end of the argument for the moment. She knew there would be more debates to come.

Once the men left her chambers Gissamoen returned, like a shadow when the clouds move away from the sun.

Gissamoen was an annoyingly ethereal woman. She was

graceful and lovely and dressed in the very finest fashions, all while having to deal with Nachia and her endless moods. She didn't know what she'd do without the woman.

"Should I arrange quarters for any visiting suitors, Majesty?"

"I suppose yes, but don't be in too big a hurry. Desh will have his way, but I won't make it easy for him."

Gissamoen smiled and nodded but said nothing else for the moment. She liked to jest, but always waited until she was certain Desh was nowhere around. The man scared her half to madness. That was justifiable. Even after all the time she'd been working for Nachia, she did not know the First Advisor very well. It was a sign of exactly how powerful his reputation was. The fact that rumors continued to state he could turn his enemies into toads, or worse, merely added to the desire to stay on his good side – and, frankly, Nachia didn't doubt the man's ability to destroy lives with little more than a gesture, though she was suspicious about the whole "human into amphibian" phenomenon.

Merros Dulver

There were forces gathering along the Freeholdt River in the Wellish Steppes. They had to be investigated and dealt with. The news was what he expected, but he did not like to hear it.

Pella was an excellent source of information. While she could not see everything going on, she could point out what he likely would have missed himself, mainly that there was a gathering army hidden away. Not a force he would be worried about attacking Canhoon, to be sure, but a force just the same. One that could easily destroy any number of small towns. One that was growing and hiding in an area that was not known for seeing travelers. A careful group could grow an army if one were to remain unwary.

"How many did you say, Pella?"

"Well, I had to use discretion, I'm afraid, but I would say there could easily be a thousand warm bodies in the steppes that were not there a season ago. More importantly, they are hiding where the Wellish Overlords once rested. I do not think that's a coincidence, Merros."

"Yes, but the Overlords? How much of a threat can they be?"

"I'm in the same position as you, Merros. I was not alive when they were considered a risk. All I know is what is written in old books. They were very dangerous in their time, a serious challenge to the much younger empire."

He nodded absently, considering the possibilities. No one had thought the Sa'ba Taalor were a viable danger at first. There were certainly less of them than there were Fellein, but they had spread across the map leaving death and devastation wherever they moved. The Overlords might well be just as dangerous, and he had to consider that seriously.

"Pella, could you possibly find some of these books for me to study? I want to know more about the Overlords. I want to know if they're a hazard."

The Sister frowned and looked toward him. "I'll find what I can."

"Thank you, truly. I don't imagine there are many sources more reliable than the libraries you have access to."

"The books are mostly a collection of first-hand reports from a very long time ago. They can be helpful, but they are only as reliable as the ones who wrote the information down."

"Do you think that's a problem? I thought the sorcerers were adept at recording information."

When she spoke, Pella's voice could not hide a scolding edge. "There is a difference between recording experiments and finding new sources of spellcraft and the reports of events that have recently taken place, Merros. I would trust you to tell the truth in a written account of a military encounter, but some of your predecessors were notorious for coloring the details of conflicts."

"What do you mean?"

"General Houda was in charge of the Imperial armies only three decades ago. According to his reports there was a war between Goltha and Danaher that, frankly, never happened."

"I'd have certainly heard of a war…"

Pella shook her head and grinned. "His gift for exaggeration was only rivaled by his desire to get Goriah to bear his children." She pointed toward him. "And if you were to repeat what I just said around anyone at all, I might well be forced to remove your tongue and teeth."

Threats? He chose to ignore them. Some of the sorcerers had unusual ideas of what was amusing.

"I'd rather you not."

"I think I can find a few reliable accounts for you. It's a pity Desh doesn't recall those times as well as he used to. He has likely forgotten more than we will ever know."

"I still don't understand that, you know. Has he grown more absent-minded?"

"No." Pella rose from the seat where she'd been sitting and walked over to the fireplace where she was once again brewing one of her teas. Very nearly always when he saw the woman she offered him another tea and he always accepted, because it was polite, and because she had such a staggering variety of flavors.

She did not ask, but instead simply poured a cup for each of them. He accepted gratefully.

"Desh believes, and I am tempted to agree, that there is only so much space for memories in our minds. Like there is only so much room for tea in your cup. More than what fits is wasted, or spills away to be lost forever. He has lived for longer than there has been an Empire of Fellein. His mind has been filled to overflowing. The older the memories, the less he clearly remembers."

Merros nodded and tested his tea. "What a horrible notion."

"Not really," Pella looked into her tea cup. "So much of what we can remember are details of a slow and often boring life. How much of your life is filled with marching, and tents, and digging pits for latrines?"

"Well, when you put it that way."

"Precisely. Desh remembers those things he finds important. For the rest he has the Sisters to aid his recollection."

"How do you help him?"

"In the very same way I will be helping you. Desh already has me researching the Overlords to aid him and to help both you and the Empress with understanding how serious the threat they represent might be."

"And what do you believe about them right now?"

Her eyes seemed very nearly to draw him in, and Merros found himself staring at Pella, surprised to realize she was unsettlingly lovely. He tended not to think of the Sisters as he did other women. They were not human, not in the way he often thought, at least. They could wield power far greater than he liked to think about, and like Desh Krohan, he often considered them as too dangerous to be merely mortal.

Pella offered him a brief smile and spoke. "I believe that whatever they were, the Overlords were dangerous. I'm not sure what is left of them, only that they do not die. I've visited the place on several occasions where they were buried and nothing about them ever changed during that time. Now, however, they have stirred. I don't know how they've transformed themselves. I can't quite see them when I am in the area, but I can sense them. They are awakening. I think they're very, very dangerous."

"Why weren't they destroyed before? When the war ended so long ago?"

"Because no one could find a way to destroy them. They are not like us. They do not die, or if they do, they don't die easily."

"I don't understand."

"They were defeated, Merros. They were imprisoned. There were plans to kill them, but whatever efforts were made, they failed." Pella shrugged and looked away. "They did not burn. They did not suffocate. Swords and spears would not kill them, and so instead they were buried deep in the ground, and they were left to waste away."

"And that is why I don't trust sorcery." Merros shook his head and scowled. "Dead things shouldn't come back, and buried things should stay buried."

"You oversimplify things, General. Sorcery is a means to an end." Pella looked out the window of the chamber where she and Desh and the Sisters most often met with people, and her eyes drifted out across the palace grounds. Snow fell from the sky and danced past the view. Merros kept his silence. It wasn't that very long ago Pella had been thought dead and brought back by sorcery. His words probably offended her, but he could hardly take them back.

"The Overlords are dangerous, if they are truly coming back. That's all I can tell you with any certainty. Something is happening in the Wellish Steppes, and there are forces gathering there. It might be that they are mercenaries. It could just as easily be a force of Sa'ba Taalor. Whatever the case, they are hidden from me. Powerful magic is being used to keep me from seeing beyond that rising earth."

"Thank you for your assistance, Pella."

"We are here for the same reason, Merros. We serve the empire."

A moment later he was on his way from the chambers and to his offices. The Empress did not want him visiting the Wellish Steppes. Very well then, he would have to find someone to go in his stead. There were plenty of capable officers who could lead a force, it was simply a matter of choosing the right one.

He found he had no desire to think about his options. He simply wanted to handle the matter himself. Perhaps he was simply tired of the business of running an army. It was exhausting in many ways.

"You know, there's nothing to stop me from going. I can bring one of those damned sorcerers with me for communication."

He spoke to himself.

He was not the only one who listened.

Andover Lashk

Andover looked at the side of Durhallem and started to climb. He'd ridden Gorwich as quickly as he could at a hard pace and they were both tired. Gorwich could now rest. He could not.

The ground was rich black soil, with a scattering of fine onyx mixed in. Andover walked when he could, and climbed when necessary. His hands made short work of the business of digging. Metallic fingers sank deep into the earth and found purchase with ease. Still the mountain was very large, and the path he chose was deliberately challenging. He didn't want Tusk or any of his people to see a simple method of climbing. They preferred challenges that were worthwhile, and he was visiting their home.

A third of the way up the eastern slope of Durhallem he found Tusk waiting for him. The man sat on a large outcropping and chewed on a sizable piece of roasted meat. He stared down at Andover with a smile on his broad face.

Tuskandru was a walking map of scars. The story of his life was laid bare in the old wounds that accentuated his form. He was a large man, and very possibly had the broadest shoulders that Andover had ever seen. His arms were thick, and it was harder to find a place on them that had not been injured in the past than it was to find still more scar tissue.

"We have trails, you know. And the gateway." Tusk spoke and then tore a bite of meat from his meal.

"Sometimes a man has to challenge himself." Andover dusted himself off and moved closer to the spot where Tusk sat. "It has been a long time, King Tuskandru."

"The last time I saw you, you were a boy." Tusk's eyes looked him over appraisingly. "You are now a warrior." From Tusk, that was high praise.

"The gods blessed me with many lessons."

"I remember." Tusk offered his food to Andover and he took it gratefully. Several hours had passed since he'd eaten anything. He took a chunk of the meat and offered the rest back, but Tusk waved it aside. While Andover ate, Tusk brought out a skin of wine from a small sack at his waist. When the wine was offered, he accepted that as well.

The two men sat in silence for several minutes while finishing their repast. When they were done Tusk asked, "Why do you come to Durhallem?"

"I have been gone from the Seven Forges for a long time. I wanted to speak with the gods."

Tusk nodded. "You would ask favors of Durhallem?"

"I would ask if Durhallem sees any way to peace with Fellein."

"Fellein can surrender to my will for Durhallem. Otherwise, no."

Andover nodded. "I expected that answer."

"Durhallem has no desire for forgiveness. He does not offer it. He does not ask it. We have warred with Fellein. What else is there?"

"I only ask on behalf of Fellein's Empress."

Tusk looked hard at him. "You are a messenger now?"

"No. But I was asked to convey that message and get answers."

"So you are a messenger."

"I am not a king."

"You are the chosen champion of the Daxar Taalor." Tusk stood up and scanned the area. It wasn't in his nature to relax for long. None of the Sa'ba Taalor believed in relaxing. Not in the same way as Fellein did. "You were trained to serve as a champion."

"If the gods should call on me, I will serve them again. They have not called."

"You are here. Are you so certain they did not call?"

Andover considered the words but did not answer.

"The gods don't expect you to do anything, Andover. You served when you had to."

"I served because they asked me to, Tusk. I would do so again."

"You come here to see if the gods have any need of you." It wasn't a question. Tusk was the voice of Durhallem. He spoke the words of the god in a way that was unique. Durhallem spoke to all of his followers, yes, but the decisions he wished to make clear were often voiced by his chosen king. "They did not choose you so that they could set you aside. That decision is yours. You are their chosen voice for the Fellein."

"I know this."

"You do not!" Tusk turned on him as fast as a snake ready to strike. "For five years you have walked with the Fellein and trained them in our ways. The Daxar Taalor would have you be their tongue, do you understand? You have lived in the palace of the Empress, when you should have been speaking to her." Tusk's face grew dark with anger. "You are the champion! You defeated their greatest warrior. Why have you taken a place as a servant when you should be their ruler?"

"I am not a king!"

Tuskandru smiled and swatted Andover's shoulder. "I know this. But I ask to see if you know this."

Andover shook his head and Tusk laughed out loud. "You are a funny man, Andover Iron Hands." Tusk kept walking, moving in a small circle restlessly. "We are not at war with Fellein. That might change. Until it does, the Empress has nothing to fear from Durhallem and his followers. If we should go to war, the Empress will know it."

Andover watched the man for a moment, never quite certain what to think of him. Tusk had his own ways, and they were often mercurial.

"I was not a servant, Tusk. I was a teacher."

"I know this. And I am glad of it. The Fellein are too… structured. They cannot adjust to the unexpected quickly enough. It is a weakness that I gladly exploited more than once, but it makes them less of a threat. I prefer an opponent that can adapt."

"You just called me a servant."

"And you let me. What does that say?"

"That I won't attack a king over an insult."

"So does that mean you are weak? Or that you know your place?"

"I don't know what it means, but you offend me."

"And how does Durhallem say you should deal with offense?"

"Durhallem is the Wounder. He would say I should decide if the offense is worth taking your life." His hands balled into fists.

Tusk was facing away from him and turned his body until he could see Andover over his shoulder. "Is it, Andover? Have I offended you enough to demand blood?"

"No."

"Then why are we talking of the matter?"

"I want to know your reasons. Do you want me to attack?"

"If I wanted you to attack, I would have already hit you." He spoke calmly. There was no edge to his voice, there was no indication that Tusk was angry.

"You confuse me."

"Durhallem says you are welcome here, Andover. But that you have other kingdoms to see. Other kings and other gods."

Andover did his best to balance the words against what Tusk had already said to him. "I have six more kings."

Tusk grunted an acknowledgement. "If you should see the Godless, Durhallem asks that you confront them. They must either return to the gods or they must die."

"Die?"

"They do not show the same respect that you do, Iron Hands. You would come before the gods and ask to speak with them, even though you can talk to the gods." Tusk shook his head and frowned heavily. "The gods have given them life and yet they cannot pay this simple courtesy. Durhallem is unforgiving."

Andover nodded. It was what the gods asked, and he would do it.

"It feels wrong now."

"What feels wrong?" Tusk walked closer to him.

"The way to the gods. There is a distance to travel, but no Blasted Lands."

"You miss the great storms?" Tusk eyed him skeptically. "You miss the endless cold and wind?"

"I…" He thought about it and nodded. "Yes. Where is the challenge of finding the gods if anyone can reach them?"

"Not anyone. If I did not want you here, do you truly think you would be speaking with me? Many have tried to reach me before and failed. Many have tried to speak with Durhallem and found me waiting. You are here because you are welcome here."

Andover considered the words. "Still, I miss the winds."

"You traveled the Blasted Lands once and you miss them. That is a strange way to be."

"I am neither Sa'ba Taalor nor Fellein. I am a strange person."

Tusk laughed. "You are Sa'ba Taalor in all the ways that matter, Andover Iron Hands. If you were not, you would not be welcomed by the gods or their kings."

He found himself warmed by the words. "Thank you, Tusk."

"The Blasted Lands are not gone, Andover. They are sleeping."

"Sleeping?" It was Andover's turn to cast a skeptical glance.

"The gods have many plans. The Blasted Lands are a whetstone. They existed to sharpen the edge of the Sa'ba Taalor. Do you think we have enough challenges to keep us ready for war?"

"We can never be too ready for war."

Tusk's smile grew broader. "So. The Blasted Lands come back soon. You will see. The time is coming when all that the Daxar Taalor do to prepare us will be revealed." He tilted his head, and for a moment he looked away. When Tusk found Andover's gaze again, his smile grew sharper. "No. Durhallem says that you have asked and now is as good a time as any to reveal. You wanted the Blasted Lands and the gods provide."

Tuskandru gestured to the foot of the mountain and, as he motioned, the wind screamed.

The dust came from nowhere, and rose into the skies at the very base of the mountain. The winds he heard could be seen as they caught that dust and hurled it toward the skies. The temperature changed around Durhallem, and despite his shock, Andover felt himself grinning.

As far as he could see around the mountain a storm grew and raged. The howl of the wind was a familiar sound, and one Andover remembered with unsettling fondness.

"The gods prepare, Andover. The world wants to change, and the gods make their own adjustments. The Blasted Lands are here. They will not go away again."

Tusk laughed, and his heavy hand slapped Andover's shoulder.

Andover found he was smiling, though he could hardly have said exactly why.

Perhaps it was simply that he could understand Tusk. Or, just as likely, that being around the man made him feel like he had come home after too long away.

Whistler

Hard to say exactly when things went wrong, but they were definitely going in the worst possible direction. He ran hard as the voices of his pursuers echoed off the walls.

They were in the new part of Canhoon, where most of the darkest crimes took place. Seemed a lot easier for the deadliest elements to be where the Silent Army was not.

Whistler was doing fine in town, learning the new area and the rules, as it were, right up until someone accused him of crippling a boy named Makley. The fact that he had actually done the crime hardly mattered. He'd been defending himself from the little bastard's attempts to kill or cripple him. He had all the defense he needed, as far as he was concerned.

The people in the town did not agree, and so he was on the run.

Angry as his pursuers were, you'd have thought he'd killed the Empress.

A rock skimmed the side of his head, leaving a hot rail of pain just over his left ear. Had it hit him properly he'd have likely been knocked unconscious. Instead, he was warned that someone had a decent aim.

He ducked into the leftward bend of a side alley and glanced around for any possible escape route. His best chance, and it wasn't much of one, looked to be climbing.

There was a gathering of crates wrapped in canvas and ropes against one wall that lead halfway to the roof. He didn't bother to check it for anchors. Instead he ran for it and started scaling. Nimble hands made short work of the obstacles, and his feet in their soft leather boots managed to find purchases as he went, praying that the shifting pile under him would hold his weight. At least one of the gods must have been smiling because he didn't fall back to the ground amid a pile of uneven crates.

In very little time he was at the top of the collection and reaching for the edge of the roof. He had to jump, and in the act of jumping he knocked the center from his piled footing. The collected boxes and bundles of scrap fell down in a rain of heavy destruction, bouncing across the narrow alleyway and falling to the wet passage between two buildings.

He wished he knew the town better, wished he knew where he was standing, as he looked around at Canhoon. No. Nothing around him seemed at all familiar. That was a definite disadvantage. In Goltha there wasn't a solitary alleyway that wasn't as close to him as a childhood friend.

Here? Nothing was familiar. Nothing at all.

That was a bad thing, to be sure, but not the worst situation he'd ever come across. Down in the alleyway, several people were now looking around and one of them was looking up in an effort to find him.

Time to leave then. The alley was narrow on this side and narrower still on the far side of the building. He chose to head in that direction as a voice cried out, "He's made it to the roof!"

He didn't have time to spare a dagger for the eye of the one who spotted him, so he ran. There were patches of ice that made his work harder, especially since the sun was slipping lower by the second and most of what he could see was reflected light catching those patches just so. By another miracle he managed to make the far side of the roof without landing on his backside, and he took a leap toward the next building, landing on both feet and not slipping his way to his death.

Luckier than he had a right to be, that was for certain.

The next building over was only one story tall, and he managed to jump down the difference without breaking a leg or twisting an ankle. After that he was running again. He climbed one wall, scaled down another and then dropped into an alley so thin he had to twist his body sideways to slip out of it.

By the time he managed to get free of the tangle, he was alone.

Alone except for the voices, of course. They seldom left him in peace for long.

He thought about his situation and decided it was time to find a new place. Canhoon was not likely to work out in his favor.

Surprisingly, the voices agreed and told him to head west again. He was gone from Canhoon long before the sun rose.

Swech

The men walked along the lakeside, talking of business, of

women and of how they planned to spend their winnings. In truth it was Millan Larne who'd made the big win at the dice pit, but he was feeling generous and so he offered to share a little of his bounty with Harum. Seemed only fair, as Harum had done the same for him on a few occasions.

Besides which, Harum was willing to work with him on moving a great deal of merchandise to Roathes, now that the passage through to the kingdom was open again.

The chain let out a soft whistling noise as it cut through the air, and then rattled faintly as it caught the edge of Harum's neck and wrapped around him close as a lover. The man had enough time to know there was a problem before Swech reeled him in closer.

The tug of the chain was enough to get him moving. Harum staggered back, coughing silently. He'd likely have made a great deal of noise if he could have, but the chain was choking him too well.

Harum was not her target, but he was close enough to see what happened and so he had to be silenced. Swech dropped down from the low rooftop and landed on Harum's back. He fell forward, red faced, and the chain pulled tight. It wasn't a very thick series of links, but it was thick enough to serve her purpose. Harum's neck broke as she pushed off him and hauled the chain with her.

The other end of the chain had a weighted hook on it. The hook snapped through the air and sank into Millan Larne's shoulder. He let out a proper scream as she hauled him back from the edge of the water and sent him staggering. The uneven ground did the rest of the job for her, and the man fell with all the grace that a drunken Fellein could manage.

There might well have been someone around to see what

was happening aside from the unfortunate Harum, but she had not seen anyone.

Swech pulled the chain taught as she stepped closer to her target. "You will stop screaming, or I'll kill you. Understand?"

Millan Larne looked at her with eyes as round as a fish's and nodded his head. He did not scream, but he whimpered a bit.

"You are Millan Larne of Larnsport."

He nodded again. "I'm not rich. No one will pay a ransom for me."

"You lie badly." Swech crouched closer to him and shook her head in the way of the Fellein. "You own many things and a ransom would be easy. But I do not care about your money."

"Then, what do you want?"

"Your promise."

He frowned. "What am I promising?"

"I will tell you when the time is right. For now you only need to know that when I come to you again, I will have instructions for you. Do you understand?" To make her point she gently tugged on the hook in his shoulder, causing him to wince in pain.

He nodded his head vigorously. "Speak to no one about this, and you will live comfortably. Speak of this affair and I will cut you into many small pieces, understood?"

"Yes. Yes, I understand," he whispered his response.

With one deft move she pulled the hook from his shoulder, he opened his mouth to scream and then thought better of it.

"You learn quickly. Do not scream. Tell no one that we have met." She wore a veil over the lower part of her face, and all he could see in the night was that she had dark skin. Doubtful he could even be certain she was Sa'ba Taalor by her appearance, though her accent would give her away if he had ever dealt with her kind previously.

He nodded his head and when she came closer, he flinched and closed his eyes.

By the time he opened his eyes again, she was out of his sight and hidden away.

After he was absolutely certain that she was gone, Millan Larne rose to his feet, swayed a bit as he examined the wound in his shoulder, and then half-ran and half-staggered toward the next main road away from the docks.

Where he went, Swech followed. The gods had deemed it necessary and she never questioned the gods. She had prepared Welan Parse in similar fashion several years earlier, but someone had killed the man and torn the soul from his body. The gods wanted their servants ready to serve, and that included those among the Fellein that they chose.

CHAPTER EIGHT

Kallir Lundt

The gods had their own ways of doing things. That was always the way with gods, he supposed. Kallir looked down at the clouds below and shook his head. They had not been there before and when they suddenly rose from the ground like a wall built of sand and dust, he was surprised.

The view from the throne room had been enough to let him see the growing mountain previously, but that was done with. Now there was grit and ice and more dust, and little else beyond the foothills of Truska-Pren.

The Blasted Lands had returned, it seemed. He had no idea how or why, and apparently all that most needed to know was that the gods had deemed it necessary to restore them in their new fashion.

Tarag Paedori looked upon the raging storm at the lower end of his mountain kingdom and acted as if nothing unusual had happened. Then again, for him it really wasn't anything out of the ordinary. He was used to gods and miracles and, while Kallir had grown more accustomed to both over the last few years, they were still unusual enough in his mind to give him pause.

Tarag stepped closer to him. "You still wonder about the storms?"

"Five years they've been gone." Kallir looked to his king. "It seems odd to restore them. That is all."

"Truska-Pren wanted them back. He wants another defense before we meet the ones raising another mountain."

"Does he know what abides there?"

"The Overlords. We have met them before, long ago." Tarag crossed his arms and looked at Kallir. "This is one of those moments we've discussed before, Kallir. This is a time to have faith in the Daxar Taalor."

"I do, my king, But I am of a curious mind. I want to know more. I always want to know more. If I see a hill, I want to know what is on the other side and if I should see a hill become a mountain, I want to understand how it happens."

"A curious mind is a good thing, my friend, but do not let curiosity become something different. Do not doubt that Truska-Pren and the other gods have plans and know what they are doing."

"No, my king. I merely find I am puzzled by the timing of all that happens."

"The gods do not know everything. There are surprises for them as there are surprises for us. But they know more than we do, and even the unexplained holds little mystery for them. Do you understand?"

Kallir nodded. A child might know many things, but most of the time they knew less than adults. A grown man might understand many things, but a grandmother would understand the world that much better. How much more then, would a god know in comparison to even the wisest and most venerable wizard?

"How will we find food and forage through the storms, Tarag?"

"The way we have for as long as the Sa'ba Taalor have been here, Kallir. We move through the Blasted Lands and we hunt."

"Hunt what? Dust?"

Tarag Paedori laughed softly and struck him a playful blow on the shoulder. "Did you think the gods would forget to supply us with good hunting prey?" He leaned in closer. "Have you not heard them in the storms at night?"

"Heard who?"

"Who else? The Pra-Moresh?"

He had not. He hadn't paid the least bit of attention.

Pra-Moresh, savage creatures at the best of times. It was one of their kind that had torn his face away with a single swipe of a massive claw. Five years later he could remember the pain clearly. His nightmares were filled with the recollection.

"When do we go hunting, my king?" There was little he would like more than to hunt down and kill each and every one of the beasts.

Tarag Paedori smiled with all of his mouths. "That is what I like to hear, my friend." The King in Iron looked toward the windows and stared out at the raging storms that would forever darken the landscape. "Gather your hunting tools, Kallir. We'll go hunting right now."

There had been a time when the notion of the Pra-Moresh had filled him with fear. That time was long gone. He no longer thought of the animals with dread – except in his dreams – but rather with anticipation. They would be a welcome addition to any meal he ever ate. Not that the meat was particularly flavorful, merely that he liked the idea of killing and eating his enemies.

The people of Fellein didn't understand that notion. The Sa'ba Taalor did. Another of the many reasons he remained in the Seven Kingdoms. He owed so much to the Sa'ba Taalor and the Daxar Taalor.

Perhaps fifteen minutes passed before he was ready for the hunt. Frakka stood waiting, saddle in place and several spears in their quiver strapped to his right side. There were other tools, of course, but Kallir had an affinity for spears and they were his preferred method of hunting.

The king smiled when he saw him and threw a heavy cloth veil his way. Kallir, moderately ashamed of himself for not considering the need, nodded his thanks and quickly tied the veil around his neck, keeping it lowered for the moment.

"The dust is thick out there, Kallir. If you don't want muddied teeth, that veil is for the best." Tarag's amusement was obvious.

"I had forgotten that part, my king."

"I know you spent a great deal of time in the Blasted Lands, but it is easy enough to forget the essentials." Tarag finished strapping his weapons into their locations on Prawlah's side. The mount looked toward Kallir as the king did his work, its eyes glowing silvery in the daylight.

"How long will we be gone, my king?"

"For as long as it takes." Tarag looked his way. Prawlah yawned, baring teeth as large as daggers.

There were four others with them, each dressed for the storms they were about to enter, with heavy cloaks and thick clothing.

Kallir resisted the urge to run back to his chamber and hide. This was a hunt, and he intended to do his part, no matter how the memories of losing his face bothered him.

The thick scar tissue around his face itched horribly, but he knew the pain was in his mind and not a reality. That was the cost he paid for being saved. It was a very small price.

Tarag fairly leaped onto Prawlah's back. The beast didn't even seem to notice despite the king's size and weight. Kallir took his time and climbed the stirrup onto Frakka's saddle.

Within moments the six of them rode into the storm and were swallowed effortlessly.

The difference was immediately noticeable. On the mountain the clouds were held at bay by the gods alone knew what. The winds were dulled and the sounds muffled before they rode across the border of whatever it was that kept the raging storms quelled.

Once they moved through, however, the effects were immediate. The second lids that the gods gave the Sa'ba Taalor closed over their eyes, and Kallir felt the difference. All of his face was made of iron. By rights he did not need a secondary eyelid to add protection, but through the power of the gods his eyes were also as sensitive as a normal human's, and the dust and grit would have caused him great discomfort and that pain very likely would have blinded him as the tears fell to wash away the irritation. He remembered well the trouble he'd had when he first entered the Blasted Lands so long ago. It had taken over a week for his eyes to adjust to the constant irritation, and even after that week he had constant bouts of tears and temporary blindness until he learned to squint just so.

Now? The inner eyelids slid into place and the dust and wind faded from his thoughts.

They were replaced by a deep and abiding sense of wonder. The storm was not merely a storm, there was so very much more going on. For one thing, he had but to look around himself to see all seven of the volcanic forges. Some closer, some further away, but all of them within his visual range for the first time in half a decade.

Impossible, yes, but there they were. He had no doubt in his mind that if he rode toward the great mountains he would reach them in a matter of hours at most. Tarag Paedori looked around and laughed deep in his chest, a sound of pure joy and wonder that matched what Kallir himself felt.

Truly, the gods were great and powerful.

Andover Lashk

Andover's boot heel caught the first of the poachers in his knee. The joint bent the wrong way with a loud crack, and the man fell down screaming, his left leg rendered useless by the blow.

The second of the men who'd followed him let out a loud battle cry and charged him, swinging his sword with all the finesse of a toddler. Andover knew better than to think a child with a blade was harmless. He stepped back, twisted to avoid being struck and then drove three of his iron fingers into the man's throat, crushing the tender flesh there into a new shape that did not accommodate breathing. The man fell down, face reddening, and dropped his sword, reaching for his own neck in an effort to fix what Andover had done to him.

The rest of the men slowed down and considered him very carefully as they circled slowly. Two of the men rode horses. The rest were on foot. One of the horseback riders swept a long chain through the air over his head, looking for the right moment to strike. He was calm and he was dangerous, and Andover did his best to keep him in sight while watching the rest of the sorry lot.

The riders were in better shape. They were larger men, well fed and likely very adept at fighting. The men on foot were scavengers. If he had to guess, it was the riders who decided that hunting down Gorwich was a wise thing to do.

Gorwich, his mount, was wounded, and currently stood shakily, watching all that transpired. Three thick arrow shafts were in his flank and if Andover had to guess, they were tipped with a poison of some kind. The mount did not fight, did nothing but shake his head and try to keep his balance. The wounds were not bad enough to cause him that much distress without help.

A third came for him. This one was a brute of a man, solidly built and seemingly capable of actually wielding the spear he was carrying. It was a short spear but large enough to cause a killing blow.

The man's wide face was smooth enough, but his arms both bore heavy scars, and his left hand was missing two fingers. All that remained where the last two digits should have been was a mass of scar tissue. He still seemed capable enough with his weapon.

Eight Fingers came forward, eyes locked on Andover, and thrust hard with the spear. Andover dodged the weapon and then slapped it aside with one palm. The man responded by stepping in closer and trying to use the dull end of the spear as a bludgeon across Andover's face.

He dodged again and then backpedaled as the man quickly reversed the spear and very nearly impaled him. Rather than stopping with his single thrust the man bellowed and charged forward, stabbing again and again, keeping Andover very busy indeed.

Almost too busy to see the chain-welding rider come in closer for a strike. He blocked the chain, or tried to, and cursed himself a fool as the chain wrapped around his forearm and tangled with his iron hand. The chain caught his fingers properly and the rider backed up, dragging Andover forward. Blood flowed down his forearm as the chain bit flesh.

The spearman was prepared and jabbed the sharp blade of the spear at his thigh. Andover winced as the very tip slid through flesh, and then he attacked. One step forward and the spearman was now the one suddenly on defense. He grunted his surprise as Andover caught the spear with his free hand and crushed the head of it between his fingers and palm. Andover continued pushing forward and ran his broad shoulder into the spearman's chest, sending him staggering.

His chain-wrapped hand clenched into a fist, and he stepped forward, kicking his foot against the spearman's hip. The first result was that the man lost his balance and fell on his back against the hard ground. The second was that Andover was sent in the direction of the rider. The chain grew slack and Andover hauled it closer to him, pulling the rider off balance.

The horseman cursed and tried to maintain his balance. Andover pulled again and threw his weight into the maneuver. The rider came free from his perch on the saddle and Andover pulled harder still, dragging the rider through the air.

All around him the remaining poachers watched and edged forward, eager to do their part in killing him. Two of them broke away and headed for Gorwich. Andover called to his mount through their mental connection and the great beast turned quickly and swept one massive paw at the first of the men. Injured or not, he was a killer. The closest target never even had a chance to scream before five thick claws carved through his face and throat, then down to his navel.

Andover pulled the dehorsed rider in closer and stomped down on the man's head with all of his strength. Bones broke and softer tissues were pulped under the force of his action.

And it felt good, so very good to be fighting again after trying to remain calm for so long. Andover grinned with his seven mouths, but said nothing.

Several of the fighters let out cries of surprise and horror, and while they did, Andover pulled the chain from his dead enemy's hands and then whipped the end at the closest of the men.

Gorwich reared back, managing to keep his balance despite the arrows, and ripped at the next of his targets. The man screamed as Gorwich pinned him to the ground and then bit down in his enemy's stomach.

The chain caught in the thin man's hair and cut across his face. Andover pulled and the man screamed like his fellow as chain links cut his flesh. Andover stepped forward, struck with one elbow and broke the man's collarbone.

He used the chain again, this time unseating the other rider. The man was pulled down to the ground and died as his horse rode over him in an effort to get away.

Blind luck saved Andover from the archer. He was in motion and the arrow fired at his chest whizzed past him and bounced off the ground a dozen yards distant. By rights he should have been impaled, but now and then the gods smile down. His chain slapped across the man's bow and knocked it aside. He charged and drove his hand into the man's sternum, breaking bone and cartilage.

By the time he looked up from his latest attack, most of

the men still standing were doing their best to be elsewhere. Two of them ran hard toward the wall of dust in the distance. They either did not understand the Blasted Lands or feared him more than they did the territory beyond the barrier that kept them safe from the endless storms.

He let them run. Gorwich was more important.

"You are hurt, my friend. How badly?"

The mount looked at him and huffed out a long breath. *I am injured, but not dying.* The words settled comfortably in his brain, and Andover nodded.

"I thought the arrows poisoned."

I think they are, but I think it is a sleeping poison, not a deadly one.

"I should hunt them down and kill them."

Kill them another time. Gorwich grumbled amiably and then let out a low growl as Andover's metal fingers caught one of the arrows and carefully pulled it free from the wound. *Gently. That's tender.*

"Oh, quit your crying. I'll have them out in a moment." Andover smiled as he said it and pulled the second arrow free. "One more and then we can clean this out."

With what?

"I have water. It will suffice."

Let it wait, Andover. Let's move into the Blasted Lands proper and I will worry about the rest after we reach our destination.

"What if the poison is worse than you think? We need to cleanse the wounds."

Gorwich stood and shook his entire body like a dog climbing from a river. *I trust in the gods, Andover. They will keep me if I am to live or take me if I am to die.*

Andover sighed. He could hardly argue the point. "As you say."

He did not attempt to climb onto his mount. Gorwich might feel he was strong enough, but Andover was capable of walking beside his friend. His legs worked perfectly well.

It's as well you feel that way. You've grown fat and lazy.

"I should leave you behind."

Gorwich swayed hard to his left and very nearly knocked Andover off his feet with his gesture of affection.

A moment later they walked into the great storm. As they approached, the winds picked up and the grit started pelting lightly at their skin. Their inner eyelids dropped and protected them from the worst of the winds and dust.

Andover looked into the skies just after they entered the storm. From where he stood, seven mountains could easily be seen, each distinct in shape and color. "We move for Wheklam." He spoke with his mouth but didn't raise his voice. To anyone else the sounds would have been lost, but he spoke to Gorwich, who shared a unique connection with his rider.

Instead of answering, Gorwich merely turned his body and started in the direction of the great, gray mountain. Wheklam was a long way off. In the regular world, beyond the newly risen Blasted Lands, the mountain was several days' ride away, and, even after getting close, there was a need to catch a boat or ship to reach the island where the mountain rested.

This was not the world of Fellein. This was the world of the Daxar Taalor. The rules were not the same here. Somewhere ahead of them, or nearby at the very least, three men had run from Andover into the storm. Where they were now was something he didn't care to guess. They were lost from sight, likely blown off course by the wind, or taken by whatever might rest within the endless storms.

Andover and Gorwich did not suffer the same fate. They moved on through harsh winds and sand and ice. They saw Wheklam, the mountain, and moved forward, undeterred.

A day passed and a night. The winds raged and the storm continued on, growing stronger as time passed. Still, by the morning of the next day, Andover Lashk and Gorwich walked out of the raging tempest and found themselves at the foothills of the great mountain, the sun beating down upon them and the gentle sea breeze blowing the worst of the grit from their bodies, if not their hair.

There was little to do but consider their situation. After several moments of staring at the towering slope closest to them, man and mount began their arduous climb, fully aware that they were observed.

CHAPTER NINE

Jeron

He was not the same as he had been. There was simply no denying the changes taking place in his body and in his mind. Jeron had spent hundreds of years studying sorcery and at least as long making certain that his body changed in the ways that he wanted. Now, after only a few months with the Overlords, he felt as if those centuries had been wasted.

His body was newly shaped, twisted to suit the needs of his new masters.

Jeron looked down upon all that he was creating and smiled.

Below him fifteen armorers were busily working to craft enough supplies for a rapidly growing army. Their hammers slammed into metal, formed weapons, shields and occasionally actual armor. Most of them were Fellein but four of them were Sa'ba Taalor, and they worked tirelessly to hand out weapons to the newcomers who were not prepared.

It was easier than expected. Most of the mercenaries came with their own equipment, but they were all tested by the gray skins. If the weapons were in poor condition they were replaced. If the soldiers were in poor condition, they, too, were replaced.

Roledru smiled and nodded as he looked down at the men working. "Gurnae blades."

"What's that?" Jeron had no idea what the man was prattling on about.

"They're making Gurnae blades. Roathian swords. They're excellent tools for cutting and excellent weapons for slicing. Just about the best swords for an army, if you ask me."

He hadn't asked, but he trusted the man to know what he was talking about. "What makes them so special?"

"It's all in the weight. A swordsman spends decades learning to be the best with a fine weapon. But for the purpose of hacking open an enemy, Gurnae blades are weighted the right way. They can slice through most armor and they'll do the job even in the hands of an oaf."

"Good to know." Jeron stretched his neck and turned his head. The new vertebrae along his spine creaked, popped and aligned themselves properly. "Do we have many oafs?"

"No. Most of the men here have been tested in battle and they'll do the hard work. The Sa'ba Taalor are making sure of that."

"I don't like depending on any one people too much, Roledru. I find that sort of dependency can lead to troubles."

"Agreed, but if you must lean on soldiers you could do much worse. The Godless thrive on war. They want to win and they want bloodshed. They'll follow whatever orders you give 'em, and the ones they won't follow are probably not the wisest choices."

Roledru looked around, his eyes scanning the cave that shouldn't have existed, that wouldn"t have existed if Jeron hadn't forced it into existence. The amount of energy he used was staggering, but all of it was also stolen, ripped from the souls of fresh victims. He'd be leaving soon to acquire more.

The power, he had to admit – if only to himself – was addictive. Small wonder necromancy was outlawed in Fellein. Sorcery required sacrifice under most circumstances and that meant self-sacrifice, not the sort where stealing from another was allowed and encouraged. Creating the hidden lair that he now stood in would have been months of power, if not years of his life, before the necromancy. Now? He had killed in the name of his masters, and used the power he stole from the dead to bend reality to his will, on their behalf. And he'd done it in days. Days!

The smile in his mind came back and twisted his new visage into a grin.

"I'm still not used to the changes in you, Jeron." Roledru looked at him and shook his head. "You're becoming something entirely new in my world."

"I'm becoming what they want me to become. I've grown so very much." He looked at Roledru and truly studied the man. He was a good second, a wise and careful advisor and servant. He did not make casual mistakes and he served with the knowledge that his was not the final say, but merely an extension of what best pleased Jeron and the Overlords.

"Does it… Does it hurt?"

"No." He considered his answer carefully. "No. I find it enlightening."

Within his robe his body continued to change and adjust in small, subtle ways. His second set of arms moved, and he felt the ways in which they moved and reveled in the sensations.

Below him the sounds of small hammers pounding metal continued, and Jeron looked down to consider the sword blades his second said were the best for their needs. He knew nothing at all of swords beyond what he had learned as a child. He had different weapons at his disposal, far more powerful weapons now that he was willing to simply break the rules he'd allowed to keep him hostage for so long.

"I have to leave again, Roledru. I'll need you to come with me."

"Yes, of course."

"We'll be gone for several days, I think. You should put Trigon in charge. Make certain he understands that for now secrecy is important." Roledru walked away to handle the matter and left Jeron alone with his thoughts. He was comfortable in solitude; he always had been.

Roledru returned after only a few minutes, and as he approached, he asked, "Where do we go this time?"

"As amused as I am by driving the City-Guard in Canhoon into a lather. I think it's time for a new city. Danaher, I think. I've not been there in a very long while."

"Never been there. I have no idea what we'll face."

"Nothing we cannot deal with, I expect." Jeron waved an idle hand at the notion and prepared his enchantments. Covering the distance quickly was a must. He could have shaped them into Storm Crows, or used another form of transportation, but instead he bent reality to his whim. With seven steps they covered the great distance between the Wellish Steppes and Danaher, a city that was across the continent from where they started.

The same collection of spells allowed them to move quietly, unseen and unheard, even as they moved into a crowded, narrow street. People shifted around them, parted like water around stones in a riverbed. But never touched them, did not see them. That was the way of sorcery. He was there, but even those who sensed him did not observe him.

The sun was in a different position above them. It was as unsettling as anything Roledru had ever seen, apparently, because he looked at the sun and then looked away, his eyes wide and frightened.

Jeron did not explain that the world moved in its own ways. Instead he let the man contemplate the nature of the world and the universe. If he was curious enough, he would ask and Jeron would explain.

Danaher was not the same as Canhoon or Goltha. Despite its age, the city was smaller. The streets were narrower and most of the buildings were no more than a story tall. Orchards existed in the town that had been there for as long as man remembered, and there were cemeteries, far more cemeteries than anyone would have expected. These days, with the new laws enforced, they were very nearly abandoned, memorials to the past and not places where the newly dead would be interred.

Generations of families lived in the same places, often building onto existing structures or replacing older buildings. In any event, the result was a chaotic mixture of old and new. Smaller towns had merged together into one larger city spread out across land that had been used in the past for little more than farming.

Danaher was alive in a very different way. It was not the sort of place where hiding between two towering buildings was easily accomplished. Oh, to be sure there was a castle, but even that was very different from what the two men were used to.

"I can't see much I recognize." Jeron shook his head.

"When were you last here?"

"It's been a few hundred years."

"Beg pardon?"

"I'm older than I look, Roledru."

"Obviously." Roledru shook his head and fussed with putting his hair into a proper ponytail, the better to restrain it. The people around them barely took notice of Jeron or Roledru, lost as they were in their own business. The night was coming quickly, and the clear skies were darkening.

"Do you have a preference, Jeron?"

"No. Alive is all that matters."

Roledru nodded and his lips pressed together as he started truly observing the people around them. Jeron relaxed against the pitted stone wall of the alleyway where they'd stepped into the city. He would be patient. There was no need to hurry. When Roledru was done with his hunting he would bring back the latest victim and Jeron could take the sacrificial energies into himself, both for his own needs and those of the Overlords.

He closed his eyes for a moment and felt the city around him, in the same way that some might feel the wind, or hear the sounds of waves crashing near the sea. People walked nearby, many of them scurrying to get to their homes, as if the darkness might hold a greater threat than they had anticipated. The darkness held no special threats for Jeron. The night might try to hide a blade or cutthroat, but Jeron was no longer fearful of either. Why fear a knife when the wielder of the weapon was easily killed?

All around him the people moved on, unaware of his attention. They walked, they chatted with each other, they moved along their paths heading for homes in some cases and pubs in others. It was the time of day when people wanted to unwind. The work was done, it was time now to relax.

One person stared back at Jeron, which took him by surprise. She stood in a different part of the city and she *saw* him as no one else around him did.

Jeron stopped where he was and tried to focus on her, to find out where she was exactly, and how it was she could see him. It should not have been possible. He'd worked all of the right wards to make certain he was unseen by the people around him and yet she watched him as casually as he watched the people walking near him.

"Who are you?" The question intruded on his mind, forced itself into his attention. He pushed back against it, unsettled, resisting the query that was as loud as any thought he'd ever had, as intrusive as a sword into an exposed belly. He could not resist the question, could not ignore it.

But he did not have to answer.

Jeron pushed back again, forced the attention away from his mind, annoyed that anyone could catch him unawares. He was one of the most talented, powerful wizards in the known world. He should not have been noticed when he did not want to be seen. He should not have heard the question that forced its way into his mind.

"WHO ARE YOU?" The question was louder now, like thunder detonating in his brain. Jeron pushed back again, forced the words from his mind and reinforced the defenses he had built over time. The words that had seemed so loud faded to the merest whisper.

He sought the source of the query, reached through the connection and tried to find the woman who dared ask him questions, but he had no luck, no success.

Whoever it was that sought him out was elusive, quick to

hide away and powerful enough to make certain he could not find her.

This would not do!

"Where are you, woman? Who are you to ask questions of me?" He forced that thought out from his mind and into the subtle magics that played against him. Somewhere out in the night was a person with enough power to unsettle his control of the world around him. Someone strong enough to gain his attention and careful enough to hide exactly where she was.

He didn't much like being played with.

He'd settle this soon enough.

Roledru set the bound man on the ground at Jeron's feet. He grunted with the effort of carrying his latest victim, a man at least as large as he was, and in excellent physical shape.

Jeron did not see him for a moment, he was too lost in his pursuit of the woman who dared question him.

Darsken Murdro

"There are no new bodies." Darsken stared into the shadows of his office and sighed. "I do not trust that news."

He shook his head and stood up, moving away from the desk and chair where he did so much of his work. It was better, he thought, to be out in the world right now and not to stare into the shadows. Sometimes the shadows held answers. Other times it was the world outside of those very shadows that had the solutions to any mysteries.

The bodies were adding up. The rituals used to kill the victims, to steal their souls, were old and forbidden. That meant nothing. Whoever the killer was, the rules did not matter to them and the age of an incantation meant precisely as much as the laws around them. Nothing. A book with the right words would tell a person with the right knowledge how to perform a ritual.

Despite his belief that he did not need to know everything about the ritual, Desh Krohan had shown him the books that held the necromantic sorceries. In a matter of a few hours Darsken had learned the necessary spells. He could have performed them himself if he were so inclined. That thought disturbed him more than he wanted to admit.

The night in Çanhoon was darker than usual, which suited his mood very well.

The winds whipped off the lake and pushed leaves from trees, drew clouds to cover the stars above and shrouded the city in a deepening gloom. There would be more rain soon.

Darsken moved into that night without hesitation, comfortable in the darkness as he was in the light of day. His cloak and hat kept him warm enough despite the bitter cold of the evening, and he walked along the cobblestone pathways with the rhythmic tap of his walking stick to keep him company.

The dead were there too, of course, moving through the streets and watching him with silent judgement.

They were not real. They were not ghosts, but they haunted him just the same. They were the failures, those poor wretches he had not yet given peace. They were not avenged.

He meant to change that.

As he walked along the streets he was aware of the people around him. Most did not matter. Not really. They were alive, yes, and they were likely just as aware of him, but he was not there to consider them, unless he found that they had blood on their hands, and the ones that saw him were quick to look elsewhere. There might be places where an Inquisitor was not recognized, but Canhoon was not among them.

"Darsken." A single word and he stopped. It was the voice, of course. He recognized the head of the Imperial armies by his voice alone. Merros Dulver was a powerful man.

Darsken put on a smile and turned to face the man. "General Dulver. How may I help you?"

Dulver stepped closer, a striking figure, though he was dressed in casual clothes and not in his uniform. The man moved with the grace of a cat, emerging from the shadows into the light of the closest streetlamp. His hair was dark and shot with gray, his face was all angles and shadows in the night.

"I'm sorry. I didn't expect to see you. I'm afraid you caught me off guard."

"I did not mean to." Darsken smiled.

"No, of course not. It's just that I was thinking about," Dulver's voice softened, "about the murders and wondering if there was anything the City-Guard could do to help you."

"They are already helpful. They've found most of the bodies and moved them before more people could see the worst thing done to them."

"That much is going right at least." He paused a moment and then said, "Did you hear? The great storms are back. The Blasted Lands have returned, only this time they surround each of the Seven Forges, like a damned barrier to stop people from getting too close."

"I was told of this." Darsken shook his head. "I do not understand the reasoning. Why would their gods bother?

We are hardly in a hurry to visit any of the mountains ruled by the Sa'ba Taalor. Well, I am certainly not in a hurry at the very least."

Merros Dulver smiled. "I have yet to meet anyone who actively sought an audience with any of their kings." Darsken was enough of an Inquisitor to know when he was being lied to, and that last had been a lie. He was also one of the few who understood the complex and unkind history shared between the general and one of the Sa'ba Taalor, though he could not remember the woman's name.

Rather than dwell on the situation, he said, "I had heard you were leaving the city, off to investigate possible troubles to the west." Which was true enough. He'd heard two riders discussing the possibility near the stables.

Dulver nodded again. "I am. That is, I will be. I leave in the morning, but for now I find I'm restless. It's been too long without answers about so many of the rumors I'm hearing." Dulver stepped closer. He was a tall man, and in excellent shape, but not as large as Darsken always expected. The man was smaller than the reputation he carried with him.

"What rumors are haunting you the most?"

"The murders." The General looked into his eyes for a moment and then looked away. "The spirits of the victims are gone, torn away." He shook his head and his lips pressed into a thin line. "I would think that's the worst possible fate."

Darsken nodded. "That is why I want the killer found."

"I want to make an example of those responsible." The general's hand moved to the heavy bullwhip at his side.

"If I can find him, you will have your chance, General."

The man smiled and took the hand from the whip. "How goes your investigation?"

"We are being toyed with, I think. The murders have stopped in Canhoon and there are no new ones in Goltha, so far. The most recent deaths are a week old, and that means the killer should be at his dark work again soon, if not already."

"Let me know if any help can be given, Darsken. We're counting on you."

"I will, General. For now, however, I think you'd be wise to get some rest before you travel."

Dulver nodded absently. He would likely rest when he was finished with his latest quest, and no sooner. It was the mark of many of the people Darsken met. Normally the ones who were most successful in their fields.

"You are a wise man, Darsken Murdro. When I return, we should meet again and discuss strategies."

"I would very much like that, General, if it is not an inconvenience."

The man flashed a grin. "Not at all. It would be of benefit to me. I want to understand better what it is you do."

"You are only going to investigate rumors, yes?"

"Yes."

"Then if you'd like I can come with you: we can investigate those rumors together. Perhaps we can learn from each other."

"I didn't want to stop your investigations."

"I think, General, that we can help each other. No more deaths have come to my attention and I have ways of learning if they do."

Merros Dulver looked at him with hard eyes. His face was calm, but the mind inside his skull was likely working to understand all the possibilities.

"Meet me in the morning, at the royal stables, as the sun rises."

"I'll be there, General."

"Please, by the gods, call me Merros."

"Merros. Call me Darsken."

"I'll see you at sunrise, Darsken."

The man turned and walked away.

Darsken watched him as he moved into the night and wondered if he was making a mistake. He had heard many stories about General Dulver. Most of them were favorable. He was a man who held the ear of the Empress and the First Advisor. He was very powerful though seemingly without full measure of just how much political clout he held. Either he was naive to a fault, or simply did not care what others thought of him. In any event, Darsken liked him. Perhaps he even liked him enough to learn from him. Time would tell.

Swech

Rooftop to rooftop Swech followed her prey. He remained oblivious to her, which was as she planned it.

The gods watched over her. At one point, as she dropped down fifteen feet to a lower roof, her foot slipped to the side and she came close to falling from her perch and landing much further below. She managed to maintain her balance, and fully blamed the gods for their kindness.

She worked twice as hard to prove herself worthy of their blessings. When her target reached the intersection of Market Way and the Imperial Gardens, her fingers captured the wet tile at the corner of the building where she stood and she descended nimbly into the alleyway.

There was no light here. There were torches nearby but

nothing at the spot where she moved. That was just as well. She preferred not being seen.

The man she followed was young and cocky. He moved with the sort of easy grace that belonged to youth, though she had seen plenty who carry themselves with the same abandon. It was almost a trait among her people, but here? Among the Fellein? The strut was less a common thing.

He bristled with weapons. The man carried no less than a dozen daggers and moved from spot to spot with the confidence of a master warrior.

She stood perfectly still as her target passed by, and then moved to follow him, to shadow his movements.

He remained oblivious to her.

Another fifteen paces down the street and he turned to the left, exactly as she had expected. She'd followed him for several days now and he rarely broke from his routine. He caught her from the corner of his eye and turned sharply to look at her.

"Who are you?" The words were out of his mouth in a soft purr, and his eyes narrowed.

The blade in her hand cut his throat before he could ask anything else.

Dark eyes grew wide, and his mouth gaped as he tried to draw in a breath past the bleeding, hissing wound under his jaw. His need to strut bled across the ground.

Swech stepped back into the darkness and watched as her target died slowly. No one came to his aid. No one entered the area, though there were people only a dozen paces away.

When he was dead, and she knew he would not struggle, Swech caught the dead man's wrists and pulled him deeper into the alley. A single gesture from her and Hotches slid out of the shadows with Laowan. The two men worked quickly to secure the corpse and move it away from the area. Swech nodded to them and moved on. Her part in the task was finished.

Jo'Hedee would mark the body.

The gods sought confusion. Someone in the city of Canhoon was killing people and disfiguring them. The gods wished that trend to continue, and so Swech did as the gods asked.

The dead seemed to have no complaints about the situation. Even if they did, they were not her concern.

Merros…

She needed only concern herself with the gods and their wishes.

Three more of her people moved nearby. Most of them were subtle and quiet. One of them wore the flesh of a Fellein and had for several years. It was that one who slipped into the alleyway and rested near where Swech stood.

"My king."

"It has been too long." She smiled and spoke softly to her friend.

"As the gods would will it." Swech nodded. "Still, I have missed you, Swech."

"And I have missed you. We are together for the moment."

"The gods have not spoken to me in some time, not directly."

Swech nodded and moved closer. Her hand moved up and touched the smooth face, felt the flesh that was as unfamiliar now as the last time they'd seen each other, before the war ended.

The god wanted the contact and the end result was a soft, wondrous smile on the other. "Oh. Oh, at last."

Swech had suffered the Great Silence along with all of

the other Sa'ba Taalor. She had felt the vast emptiness that swallowed her serenity. She had felt that same joy when the voices of the Daxar Taalor came back to her, but unlike her companion she had not waited years for the silence to be stripped away.

"Your faith is rewarded. The gods have not abandoned you."

Desperate fingers clenched at her wrist and held her hand close to a face that would never truly belong to her companion. Swech had worn another's body at one time, had lived for months in another life, as if wearing a suit that did not quite fit properly.

"What must I do next?" The eyes that looked her way were dark and lovely, but as false as the face that held them.

"You must listen to the gods, as always. You must lead, as you have done for the last few years."

The face that looked at her nodded softly and the lips that kissed her fingertips smiled warmly.

"Yes. Oh, I hear them, Swech. I hear the gods again after so very long."

Swech smiled back.

The gods were kind. They always had been.

Hrothrun

Trigan Garth would have been disappointed, perhaps. Or merely amused. He had warned her, after all. Taking Deillor back to the gods was a fool's quest in his eyes. She did not feel the same. The gods were gods and the dead belonged to the Daxar Taalor and always had. She understood that even if he did not want to. He was better than some, Trigan, but he was also not as wise as he felt he was.

Four days of riding passed before Hrothrun decided to risk the storms. She rode along the odd contours of the Blasted Lands and considered them for a long while before making her decision. It was not fear, exactly. As with most of the Sa'ba Taalor, fear was very close to an unknown concept. The gods spoke to them, schooled them in what was right and what was wrong, and taught that fear was a wasted emotion. It was wise to be cautious, but foolish to be afraid.

So why then, had she waited so long before coming back to the gods? If it wasn't fear, what was it that kept her away? The gods had not betrayed her; they had merely grown silent. As she understood it, those who returned to the Seven Forges were embraced by the gods anew, returned to their good graces as if nothing had ever happened.

Ah, but something had happened, hadn't it? The Great Silence. The loss of the certainty brought by having the gods with you at all times was removed, and much as she wanted to dispute the notion, there was an odd comfort in that silence, at least during the times when being alone didn't bring with it a freezing, crippling doubt.

The silence had been horrifying when it wasn't liberating. There was peace to be found in that quiet.

There was guilt in having the gods listening in to every thought, wasn't there? What if they heard something in her mind that they did not like? Would there be punishment?

There never had been, not in her entire life, but what if that changed? What if they knew that she'd felt fear during several of the battles with the Fellein? Would that merit being outcast, or worse? Better, perhaps not to risk it.

Still, Deillor would want to be seen and claimed by his gods.

And so, with Deillor in her thoughts, Hrothrun returned

to her people, walking into the Blasted Lands without any further hesitation.

It was an odd sensation. From outside, the storms raged and there was little to no breeze, merely a thickening in the air, a deep and abiding sense of pressure. When she walked forward, however, the pressure eased almost immediately and was replaced by howling winds and a bitter cold that she could not escape. Her entire life, since she was deemed old enough to defend herself, Hrothrun, like all of her people, had moved into the Blasted Lands to hunt. The cold was familiar, the winds were familiar. The sounds and scents of the endless storm were ingrained within her. Moving back into that storm brought with it a deep sense of familiarity that was comfortable, even if it was not necessarily welcome.

The storm roared around her and she bowed into it, fighting to keep her footing even as the horse that carried Deillor fought for a moment, wanting little more than to flee the area.

Within twenty minutes she surrendered to the inevitable and released the horses. She could fight them, kill them or let them go, and in the end it was easier to carry the corpse of her friend than it was to fight two animals that wanted to flee.

Wheklam called for her. She saw the great mountain, the plumes of black, volcanic smoke spitting from its crown, and heard the roaring winds howling around the sides of the god's heart. Deillor's dead weight pressed at her shoulders and neck, tried to bend her and force her to her knees, but she'd have none of it. The only weight that mattered was the crushing guilt that nearly consumed her as she looked at the god she had walked away from.

Tears burned at her eyes, slid past the inner eyelid that shielded her from the sand, ash and ice.

"I come for you, Wheklam. I bow to you. I beg you, take me back." The words were lost to the wind but she did not care. They did not need to be heard by ears for the god to know of them. At least she hoped that was still the case. The storms continued to rage and she walked, ignoring all but the shadow of Wheklam.

Wheklam waited and likely grew impatient, and so she moved faster.

Breaking free of the raging storms was easy. She merely walked through them until the gods freed her from their grasp. The winds faded to a whisper, and the wall of sands that had assaulted her vanished with it.

She set down the dead man she had been carrying and sighed her relief.

Wheklam was above her. She could see up to the crown of the great mountain, could make out the form of another pilgrim scaling the rugged heights, doubtless seeking the war god's attention.

She rolled her shoulders and took a deep breath before reaching for Deillor's weight. If he was to be offered to Wheklam, he must first be carried to the very pinnacle of the mountain.

Her hands had only briefly touched the dead flesh before the pain came upon her and brought a scream of surprise to her lips.

Deillor's body shifted, pulled and warped before her eyes, even as her fingers and toes began to twist and change. The pain moved quickly from there, reached her wrists, her knees, her spine. Bones grew and shifted and Hrothrun let out a sound that was both a cry of pain and a warped giggle.

She had been seen, by Wheklam, it seemed, and likely by the other gods as well. She had been judged and found wanting, but that judgement was not truly unexpected. She had known even when she started her quest that there was a price for defying the gods.

Still, the pain was so much larger than she had expected. It hit her like a hundred hammer blows, concentrated first in her bones and joints and then across muscles and nerve endings.

The sounds coming from her mouth continued and her mind grew foggy, even as she wept-cackled and fell to her hands and feet. Clothing split and fell away, and weapons she'd carried for years were discarded, even as her nails thickened into heavy claws and her teeth grew longer and wickedly sharp.

The pain faded away, replaced by a deep, gnawing hunger. Beside her the dead man shook his head and stood, towering over the height he had known in his previous life.

The Sa'ba Taalor were the chosen of the gods. Those who failed in their life were punished, and the punishment was considered fitting by gods and gray skins alike.

For five years the Blasted Lands had ceased to exist but they had returned. How then could the Pra-Moresh, the scavengers and hunters of the Blasted Lands, not return with them?

Her name no longer mattered. She remembered it, but it was a faint whisper in comparison to the raging hunger that tore at her guts and fueled a nearly blinding anger.

Beside her, the male of her kind moved and giggled, sliding back into the endless tempest as the scent of live prey caught his attention. Had she kept words, she'd have remembered the word *horse,* but like all sentient thought, that was a thing of the past.

For now all that mattered was that the male was correct,

there was meat to be found in the distance and she intended to find it.

Had Swech seen what had occurred, she would have nodded her satisfaction.

The gods were just, after all, and merciful in their own ways.

CHAPTER TEN

Desh Krohan

"You're a fickle woman, Majesty." He spoke without worry. The Empress was not the vindictive sort, despite the numerous promises she had made to see him suffer.

"I'm not fickle. I'm tired. As you wish, Desh. You may send in your suitors. I make no promises to care but I will at least entertain the notion."

Her agreeing made the entire affair less pleasant, of course. Nachia Krous was not the sort who gave up fights easily, but she might lie about her decision to stop a proper debate. "Listen, it's not that I don't want you to find a spouse and have a baby, but you're actually making me nervous now."

"Of course I am." Nachia smiled.

"I really hate it when you grow agreeable."

"You can't have it both ways, Desh. Either I agree to your foolish conditions, or I don't. If I change my mind it merely means that you've worn me down."

"Mountains wear down after ages, Majesty, but I've yet to see proof of the same happening to you." He moved closer to the large table in front of her, where she had a very detailed map of Fellein and the surrounding Seven Forges laid out. There was a figure on horseback that rested approximately where Merros Dulver and his entourage of soldiers rode from the city.

"Are you worried about him?"

"Of course I am. I didn't want him going in the first place."

"I expect he felt the same way about your last excursion from the city."

"I know he did. That's why I let him win this argument." She sighed and shifted on her throne. "You know, Desh, I know what you did to this damnable chair, I'm going to have it burned."

"The enchantments placed on the throne are there to keep you safe."

"And humbled."

"Humble goes along with safe." He waved her arguments aside. Long ago he'd enchanted two thrones, one in the Summer City and one in the palace. They were identical enchantments designed to protect the reigning Emperor or Empress, and also to cause them discomfort. Nothing too severe of course, but enough to make sitting on the throne an uncomfortable experience. It was best to make certain that no one grew complacent.

The only problem with that was simply that Nachia knew about it. He'd told her long ago, before there was much chance of her ever becoming the Empress.

"Just the same, I should have the damned thing destroyed."

"Or you could try a new cushion."

She sighed and rose from her seat.

"What is happening out there, Desh? Why are there storms surrounding the Seven Forges?"

"Because their gods wanted them, apparently."

"Can't you stop them?"

"No, Majesty. I am no match for a god, and certainly not for seven of them."

"We have people out there whose main agenda is to open negotiations with the seven kingdoms. How are they supposed to get past this new obstacle?"

"Well, technically it's not new. It's just showing up again. We've had people traverse the Blasted Lands before, and while I'm not certain, it seems there are fewer of them to deal with this time."

"What do you mean?"

"I mean there's a narrow strip of storm surrounding each of the forges. How bad could it be?"

"Desh, every report coming in so far says that if you look around in the storm you can see all seven of the forges, no matter which of the areas is entered."

"Well then, that could be an obstacle to consider."

"Yes, exactly the problem. Now, what are you going to do about it?"

"Not a solitary thing. As I've already said, I'm no match for seven gods putting up obstacles."

"But–"

"Honestly, Nachia, sometimes I don't think you hear a single word I say. I'm barely allowed to use the sorcery I have. There are laws put in place to prevent me from using most of my more powerful spells, and even without those laws, I can't do much of anything without being drained by the end of even the simplest incantations. I've told you a thousand times, magic has a price." He sounded testy, and he didn't want to sound that way, but after having the same conversation a dozen or more times, he had grown very tired of the situation.

"Well then, work some sort of magic with your Sisters

and a few more wizards. Work together to make things go the way you'd like them to, but fix this."

"It's not a bird I can pull from the sleeve of my robes. I can't use a deck of cards to create an illusion here, Majesty. This is a power the likes of which I can never outdo. This is the work of gods, Nachia. Gods!" He leaned in closer to her, stared hard at her eyes, and despite himself felt his temper flaring.

Sadly, her temper was at least as volatile as his, and she did not have centuries of buffering her ire to help her appear calm. "Make it work, damn you! These damned gray skins have cut off any possible trade routes to themselves and barricaded substantial passages that have existed for as long as there's been an empire."

"I am an advisor, Majesty, not the solution to every problem you have."

"You are the First Advisor to the Empire, Desh. I expect you to advise me and to have actual answers, real solutions, not suggestions that I get myself with child as quickly as possible."

"That's called advice, Nachia, and it's very good advice. You need to secure your claim to the throne and prevent any of the other members of your family from working hard to end your time as Empress."

"My claim is secured. I'm sitting on the damned throne." She was pacing, but he decided not to point that out.

"Without an heir, there's a much stronger chance that a member of the Krous bloodline could decide you need to be removed from the throne by any means necessary. It wouldn't be the first time in history, nor, sadly, would it likely be the last. The Krous family, your family, is notorious for removing obstacles by means of assassination. I'm trying to protect you."

"What do you know that I don't, old man?"

"I have spies everywhere, Nachia. I have spies and I have the Sooth, and both tell me you're in danger."

"I'm always in danger, Desh. It's the one thing that remains a constant in my world. I knew that the day I accepted the throne." She sat back down on her throne and winced as she did so, but she stayed there to make her point.

"Find a proper suitor. Then, perhaps, I'll consider using my sorcery to try finding a way around the Blasted Lands."

"I'm not known for making compromises, Desh."

"All the more reason to be worried for your life, Majesty."

Without another word he left the throne room, annoyed that there had been yet another debate, but delighted to have finally gotten the last word in one of the many arguments he had with the Empress.

Morten Dunraven

It wasn't going as well as could be expected, but Morten had prepared for as many contingencies as he could. That was part of being a businessman and a negotiator.

The winds were everything he'd been told to expect, and he had been told to expect a punishment fit for those who offended gods. Ice was crusted into his hair and beard, and as often as he thought to break the damned stuff away it came back until he finally just gave up.

The lanterns were of little help, but he kept them lit just the same, and made certain that the shields were up to stop the raging storm from simply snuffing them out. If nothing else, they helped when the time came to make a fire and try cooking.

And then, as easily as it had started, he found himself on the other side of the endless storms. The air was still cold, but not freezing, and the winds died down to a whisper as he looked up to see Durhallem before him, and a gathering of the gray skins, including the massive brute they called a king.

Morten walked forward and led the horses with him. The men who'd been brave enough to join him kept moving forward with more horses. They'd all be getting something extra for their efforts as this had been a much worse trek than expected.

The Sa'ba Taalor waited patiently for the most part, though more than a few of them looked like they preferred the idea of beating the men heading toward them to death. They were, to the last, some of the scariest bastards he had ever seen, and he wanted little to do with them. That included their women.

Tuskandru, their king, stepped closer. Morten looked the man over from head to toe and wondered what had ever led him to threaten a return if his son died. Good thing he hadn't. Morten didn't think he'd have lived past the first few seconds of any fight.

"You have brought the horses." The man's mouth worked into a smile, and the scars along his face opened and closed of their own will, making small noises even as he spoke. He would never get used to that. All of them were that way, too, with smaller mouths that just did as they pleased.

He made himself look away from the scars and speak. "Would have been here sooner, but there's the storms to deal with."

Tuskandru raised one arm until it was leveled before him, and then moved his hand in a motion that mimicked waves on the sea. "The gods want storms, and so we have storms again."

"Well, who can argue with gods? Not me, that's for certain. I barely argue with my wife."

Tuskandru nodded amiably. "Four hundred horses, and what of the trainers?"

"Oh, aye. They'll be along. Put them at the end of the train, so they could make sure to capture any stragglers. Horses don't much like the storms, it seems."

"Your safety is guaranteed by me. Passage to the Empress's Highway." Tuskandru smiled again and gestured in the direction of the mountain.

The woman who had beaten his fool son half to his funeral pyre stood nearby and came closer as the king pointed. She looked from Morten to where Erig was dismounting. Erig looked back and nodded humbly. At least the boy could learn a lesson now and then.

The woman spoke, not to Erig, but to Morten. "The king would like you to lead your horses up the mountain. We have a place for them."

"Aye. Lead on, then. We'll follow."

She nodded and walked away, heading up the side of the mountain. It wasn't steep, not really, and Morten followed, feeling as if he was walking into an oven. Not that it was hot, not in the least, but he had no doubt that wherever they were going, it would be the sort of place where a wrong move would get someone injured or worse.

Best not to make any wrong moves, then, wasn't it?

The gray skins did nothing. None of them moved out of the way, or interfered. They simply watched as he walked past. Though a few of them spoke to each other, they spoke in their own tongue and he didn't know so much as a single word of whatever that language was.

Their king watched but said nothing at all as he led the first of the horses up the mountainside. There was nothing to be done but to finish what he'd started; still, Morten wanted nothing so much as he wanted to run from the area. They were a frightening people, and he could think of little else besides that notion.

Behind him more of his people came from the unnatural storm, covered in frost and ash. Ahead of him the mountain beckoned.

And around him the people he was here to impress looked absolutely unimpressed by his actions.

It was going to be a long day, if he had to guess.

CHAPTER ELEVEN

Andover Lashk

Wheklam was a long climb and Andover was exhausted by the time he reached the pinnacle. So was Gorwich, though it looked like his wounds were scabbing over nicely. Whatever the poisons the poachers had on the arrows, it was not a deadly mix. Though it had taken time, Gorwich was doing better, was more alert and seemed stronger than he had since being injured.

From the top of the volcano, along the edge and away from the smoke, they could look down on Wheklam properly and see the vast cities that had been built near the water's edge.

They would go to the city soon enough, but first and foremost Andover was here to pay his respects to a god. It was to that end that he'd climbed to the very top in the first place. Wheklam did not need him to make the climb but doing so was a sign of respect.

The winds were strong at the top of the mountain, but Andover was not afraid of them. He was here to visit a god. He was protected. That was the way of it. If Wheklam wanted him dead, he would die. If the god wanted him alive, he would be unharmed. The smoke did not obscure his vision or force him to cough. The heat rising from the heart of the volcano did not cook the flesh from his bones.

Andover stared down into the vast bowl of the volcano and then crouched on the very edge and spread his arms in supplication. "I am here, Wheklam. I offer myself to you."

The god said nothing, but he felt the welcoming embrace just the same, a powerful sense of peace. For twenty minutes he stayed in the same spot, testing the strength of his legs as he crouched over the yawning well of molten stone below him. The winds caught his hair and lifted it in a constantly stirring breeze.

At the end of that time, having heard no words from the god, Andover rose and started back down the long slope leading to the crescent-shaped city near the edge of the ocean far below. His body moved, but the sense of peace stayed with him.

In the last few days he had traveled long distances, fought against a dozen men, been injured and now embraced by one of the gods he willingly followed.

He felt truly alive, and it was a wonderful sensation.

Are you sorry for your time in Canhoon?

Andover shook his head. "No, Gorwich. I am glad of it. I had to know where I belonged, and I had to offer time to the people of my past life."

Is that all they are, Andover? Your past?

"I don't know. I only know that I don't want to be in Canhoon any longer, at least not as I have been. I've waited five years. I've trained a great number of the soldiers there, hopefully well enough to make themselves capable fighters."

They weren't capable without you? He felt the amusement in his companion's words.

"No. You know better. But most of them are so... rigid

in their ways of thinking. It's such a different way from the Sa'ba Taalor."

They walked for most of the day and night before finally reaching the city near the water's edge.

Parhallo. The throne for Wheklam is here.

"I have been here before, you know."

Have you? It was before we met, I think. Once again Gorwich spoke with an edge of humor to his words. *Did you exist before we met? How can I be certain?*

"It was. Just the same, I've been here and to all of the capital cities." Andover grinned as he spoke. That was a rarity too, and he rather liked it. Smiling should be a common thing, not an exception. He'd known that once, long ago, before Perb ruined his hands and he started on the journey that led to being who he was.

He shook his head. Sometimes Gorwich's philosophies polluted his head with existential thoughts. He had to remind himself not to take the mount's philosophies to heart. Certainly, Gorwich never did. They were merely a way of keeping himself amused.

The city was spread across a great area. Along the water's edge there were docks holding the massive black ships of the Sa'ba Taalor fleet. He had no idea how many ships there were in all, but he knew that for every one of the twenty or so vessels he could see there were likely twice as many out at sea.

Along the docks, and spreading into the low buildings in the area, he could see hundreds of Sa'ba Taalor wandering about and most of them looked to be working. There were few people in the area who looked like they were relaxing. That was the way with the followers of Wheklam as far as he could figure. On land they were constantly in motion and looked like they sought a way to be comfortable. At sea they seemed less active, but more at home.

The king met him as he entered Parhallo. Donaie Swarl stood as tall as Andover himself, and her skin was a study in healed wounds, adorned with scars on nearly every inch of visible flesh. Her face bore five Great Scars and she wore leather breeches, a vest and a bright blue sash, along with a heavy sword, a long dagger and a knife that looked well used.

She did not smile when she saw Andover. Then again, he couldn't think of a single time he'd ever seen the woman smile. She was usually too busy.

He held his arms away from his body his palms facing the sky and bowed formally. "My king, I am here to pay my respects."

She looked at him carefully, and then nodded. "I have a ship heading out today for Wrommish. You can come with us if you like."

"In all my life I have never been on the ocean."

"Then your training will never be complete. How can you fight on the waves if you have never been on a stormy sea?"

He bowed his head a second time. "I will accept your offer with thanks."

"Come. I'll find a place for you and your mount."

Together they walked toward the docks and the vast black ships that waited there.

Darsken Murdro

Darsken sat on the saddle as carefully as he could, and looked at the ground. It seemed a great ways off. He was used to walking wherever he went, but General Dulver had offered him a horse, and not accepting might be deemed rude.

The horse was a gentle animal and seemed unbothered by his weight. He could feel the play of muscles on the creature as his swayed gently side to side, moved by the animal's motion.

There were a great number of cavalry riding with them as they headed to the west. He didn't bother to count, but it was well over a hundred soldiers.

The latest information said that there were more murders. Darsken had spent half the night examining the body of a well-known cutthroat in Canhoon. Like the other bodies, he had been cut repeatedly, marked by blades while he was alive and while he was dead. He had been moved, placed in the marketplace closest to the docks, his body displayed for all to see. Happily, he had only been seen by the City-Guard, who wisely took the body off display and sent a runner to come get him.

The difference was simply that this body, while marked appropriately, had not had the soul stolen from it. Andle Harper was a well-known brawler and thief, and he was suspected in half a dozen murders over the years. He had almost always evaded getting himself caught by the City-Guard and had escaped the one time he was captured.

And now he was dead. On the better side of the coin, he confessed to several murders while Darsken questioned his corpse. On the darker side, someone was actively imitating the murders that were already plaguing the city and the surrounding areas.

"Do you think we'll find any more of your murders out this way?" Merros Dulver rode next to him.

"It is possible," Darsken nodded. "There are enough small

towns between here and the steppes." Which was true enough. Goltha was the name of the city on the far side of the lake, but it encompassed not only the city but the many small towns around the shorelines and along the four rivers that surrounded Lake Gerhaim. As was often the case, where there was water, there were people. The four rivers running into the massive lake were no exception. The towns often had their own government, but all of them were seen as facets of the whole.

Since the war's end, and the shift of Canhoon's position, a great number of people had also moved along the river's edge, from areas farther way from the capital all the way to Inborough. There was little between where Canhoon had rested at the mouth of the Jeurgis River to where Canhoon had settled in Lake Gerhaim, that wasn't now occupied by settlements and farms. The Emperor's Highway had been built before the change, of course, and it was still there, as far as Darsken knew.

"I'd never have imagined so many towns appearing after the war." Dulver shook his head.

"It makes sense." Darsken pointed along the highway ahead of them. "All of this land was simply too far away for convenience in most cases and now the largest city in the empire and the capitol city are both in the same area. Why wouldn't people move closer to feel safe?"

"I expect the City-Guard could point to a few reasons on any given night." Dulver chuckled and then shook his head. "I jest, of course."

"There have been more marauders of late." Darsken shook his head as well. "I hear the reports and we do what we can. But they do not stay long in any one area. They move around, the better to find fresh victims."

Dulver nodded and swept a hand across the area. "There are stragglers everywhere, of course."

"Stragglers?"

"I don't know what else to call them. People moving from one area to the next or working their way along the roads at different farms, in different towns. It's been suggested that I send recruitment teams through here and gather them up to get new soldiers for the ranks."

"Do you have a need for new soldiers?"

"No. Nothing has changed. Three years of service is mandatory. Of course, there are plenty who say they've served their time and never do."

"Is there a punishment for that?"

Dulver chuckled. "Of course. Three years' service or three years' incarceration."

"I imagine most prefer to serve."

"The catch is, we have to catch them in the lie."

"How hard are they to catch?"

"Honestly, it's easy in most places." Dulver looked around the area and pointed to a group of people walking the highway up ahead. As the horses drew closer the people moved to the side to let them pass. Easier for them to move aside than for battalions of cavalry to do the same. "But the stragglers, the ones on the move, make it more challenging. The local towns have lists of people who have served and are getting to the right age to serve. If they move, it's harder to know one way or the other."

"No one to keep proper records?"

"Exactly so." He gestured to the crowd they were passing. "Look at this group as an example. There are four lads there who are of that age. They've served. Or they're close to the age where they should. If those lads are coming from Canhoon, moving on, there's little I can do to make certain."

"There are some peoples who mark their service, yes?"

"With tattoos?" Dulver frowned, "I know some of the soldiers do, but not all of them."

"You could make it mandatory."

"I never thought of that."

"If you make them bear the mark of their regiment then you know they've served. Problem eliminated."

"All my time, Darsken, and I never once thought of that."

"I'm an Inquisitor. It's my job to look for the marks left behind, the trails that can tell a story. If I were looking for your soldiers, those that have served, first I would look for tattoos and then I would look for scars." There were other ways to tell, of course, but they were good indicators.

"I might well implement that as a way to handle the matter." He pointed to two of the young men in the crowd. "Do you think either of them have served?"

The first one was lean and hard and carried a sword that looked like it was general issue. If he had to guess, the lad had served. He walked like a soldier. The second was shorter, but moved with wiry grace. He had a smile on his face and his eyes were in constant motion. Might be he had served, might be he was simply from one of the darker areas in Goltha. He had that look about him. He did not carry a sword, but Darsken expected that if they were to stop him and check, they'd find no less than three blades hidden on his body somewhere.

"The blond lad. Yes. The darker one, back a few paces? Possibly. But I'd think not."

"And yet he's the right age. By all rights I should be stopping him and checking, but I simply do not have the resources."

"You have a hundred men with you, General. What are they if not resources for checking?"

"They are soldiers on the way to a possible battle post. We don't know what's ahead of us. If that lad hasn't been in service and is avoiding that service, I don't have enough soldiers with me to send him away with a couple of my men to escort him to where he needs to be."

Darsken nodded and moved over to where the gathered people on foot were walking. He pointed to the dark-haired young man and gestured for him to come closer.

The young man looked at him for a moment, one eyebrow raised in question and then stepped forward.

"What have I done?"

"Nothing that I know of. Have you served your time in the Imperial Army?"

"I have not." The young man looked back at him and grinned.

"Why not?"

"Figure I did enough during the war."

"You could not have served during the war. You're too young."

"Already said I haven't served. I did my work during the war."

Merros Dulver moved closer and listened but did not speak.

"How did you serve?"

"I was a whistler." The grin on that face grew even brighter.

Darsken was familiar with the term, of course. Whistlers were a part of the informal watch in Goltha. They often watched over neighborhoods, but just as often served as early warnings when the City-Guard came into an area, hired by whatever street gangs roamed a territory to alert against the authorities.

Darsken let out a short bark of laughter. "That is hardly serving."

"Depends on who you ask. The lads who paid me to whistle also paid me to tell 'em when the gray skins got too close."

Darsken chuckled and so did Dulver. The young man looked at the two of them and his eyes gave away absolutely nothing. Darsken had no doubt that the whistler had already sussed out any possible methods of escaping if they tried to capture him.

"You see, General? He has already served, in his own way."

Merros Dulver stroked his fingers across the edges of his newly growing moustache and smiled. "I suppose he has." He looked at the young man and his eyes scrutinized carefully.

The young man nodded and slowed his walking pace down. In a matter of only a few seconds he was already fading into the crowd.

Darsken looked back at the general. "Your men could take him."

"No. He'd be gone before they dismounted. I know the type."

"Yes he would. But they could find him. There is only so far he could run in this area."

"True, but who knows how long it would take?"

"If you truly wanted to check, you could always bring a few extra men along on these journeys, who could take him back with them to Canhoon and have him properly inducted."

"I could, but it's not worth it to me. I have plenty of soldiers and the ones who truly do not wish to serve are the ones I least want to have in my army." He thought about it for a moment and added, "There are areas where I might try that, however."

"You are wise, I think."

"Seldom accused of that crime, Inquisitor."

"What are you looking for, where we are going?"

"Signs of a military buildup. There are rumors of a lot of mercenaries heading in this direction. Specifically heading for the steppes and not for any of the towns out this way."

"Why would they choose the steppes?"

"Can you think of a better place to hide? No one comes out to the Wellish Steppes without a good reason." In fact, the last time Darsken had been to the steppes it had been to make certain the Overlords did not awaken. From what he had heard, there was a very real chance that the offering he'd made was not enough to satisfy the creatures that had once threatened the entire empire.

"There is a long-standing tradition, General, to offer a sacrifice of sorts to the Overlords in order to keep them resting in their tomb." Dulver stared at him, not saying a word. Darsken sighed and continued. "Handling that matter has been my task for the last eight years. I have never failed. By all rights they should be asleep."

"Why do you tell me this now, Darsken?"

"Because if something has gone wrong, if the Overlords are stirring, I might yet be able to settle them. The cost would be heavy but I could possibly manage it."

"Do you think they're waking?"

"I think it's a possibility." He frowned and gestured to the west. "There is little that would cause problems in the

Wellish Steppes. They are insignificant except for the fact that the Overlords are buried there. The closest thing to a threat in the entire area is the Sa'ba Taalor to the north."

"It's not them. We'd know. They have their ways and they've recently decided to protect their kingdoms by summoning a storm around each of the mountains." He shook his head, and the expression on his face said he was having trouble with the notion that storms could be called upon as if they were well-trained hounds. "But they've made no gestures of war that I know of, and I'd hear about them if they did." He pointed to where one of the sorcerers rode along in silence. "I'm not allowed to travel without an adept along to keep me informed of what happens in the empire."

"It is possible that the Overlords have awakened." Darsken shook his head and felt his frown grow heavier. "I know so little about them. Only that keeping them from waking has been the task of the Inquisitors for as long as any Inquisitor can recall. If I have failed, then the empire is in danger."

"We'll find out soon enough, Darsken."

"I have heard it said that necromancy was first learned by the Overlords and shared with select humans."

General Dulver looked at the adept for a moment and said nothing, then turned back to Darsken and spoke softly. "I have it on solid authority that only a few people outside of the Inquisitors have access to that sort of power."

"No one is supposed to know outside of the Inquisitors. That does not mean anything, I fear. The books that teach it are not solely in the control of the Inquisition. The sorcerers have their own books, their own ways of learning that have little or nothing to do with how we are taught."

"How many ways are there to learn?"

"How many ways can a man learn to fight with a sword?"

"Well, yes, but there are so many types of swords out there."

"And there are so many schools of sorcery." He shrugged. "It wasn't that long ago that the Inquisitors were required to collect any book believed to hold spells."

"Did you collect a lot of books?"

"Thousands. Most only held references to other books of spells, but Emperor Pathra was very strict about who could learn magic and how they could learn it."

"Thousands?" The general shook his head. "I hate sorcery."

"As with all things, it is only as dangerous as the hand that wields it. I know enough of necromancy to kill a man with a few words and a gesture. Since this unfortunate investigation began, I have learned even more of it."

"You've learned more?"

"The markings, the rituals, I have learned enough that I could imitate them easily."

Dulver stared at him in quiet horror.

"I would not use what I have learned."

"Why not?"

"I can think of nothing more horrible than torturing the dead, General. They have suffered enough."

"How so?"

"They've lived, haven't they? And their lives are stolen away from them. Whatever is supposed to happen to the dead after they have left the world, for these victims it never happens. Not ever. They are consumed, not just in body, but in spirit."

"Do you know what happens after death?"

"I have suspicions. I do not know for certain. I only know

that those taken by necromancy will never reach whatever waits beyond death."

"I'd have thought that if anyone would know…"

"Like I said, suspicions. I have no desire to know. I will learn when the time is right, and no sooner."

"You mean when you die?"

"Just so, General."

"Please call me Merros."

"I will do my best to remember that."

They rode in silence for a time, and Darsken contemplated the actions of the necromancer while he rode. It took his mind off how uncomfortable the saddle was on his backside.

Whistler

Whistler relaxed as the soldiers slipped past, riding their horses and looking down on everyone else. Them and the Inquisitor.

He'd spoken only the truth to the dark-skinned man. It was best never to lie to Inquisitors, who supposedly could steal a man's soul if an untruth were told. While he wasn't much of a follower of gods, and he'd never heard exactly what a soul was for, he felt it best to keep his for the present time.

They were heading in the same direction as he was, and after the men on horses came the wagons of supplies, followed by more soldiers on horseback. Wouldn't do to leave their food unprotected, would it?

They were headed west. They went the same direction as the voices told him to go, and they would be getting there sooner than he would, that was a sure thing. Walking was his only option, as he had no horse and had never learned to ride one of the great beasts, besides. Like as not he'd fall on his ass the first time he tried, or break his skull on the rocks if the thing decided it didn't like his weight.

He kept pace with the wagons. Wasn't hard to do.

Down the road a distance he could see what he needed by way of distractions, and he smiled. There were four wagons set up with trinkets, cloth, fruit and other notions. There was even a man up there working hard to make two puppets dance. He had half a dozen more in a small cart, and though not everyone was stopping, a proper crowd had gathered to pay attention to his dancing couple as they bobbed and moved to his whims.

It was enough. Whistler kept walking and admired the man's skills with his marionettes. One was a man with an evil grin and a large nose and pointed chin. He sported a wizard's robes and a wand in his hand. The other looked a great deal like royalty, a woman with hair the same style and color as the Empress. He knew, because he'd seen the woman only a few days earlier, during his very brief stay in Old Canhoon.

Seemed like everyone was distracted by the dancing puppets, and that was good enough for Whistler. He moved between two of the wagons and then climbed onto the back of one. He was lucky. No one was inside it. Just supplies aplenty.

There was blessed silence and no one else around, which meant that he could hear the voices again, and could try to decipher what it was they were saying. Mostly it was gibberish, an endless stream of words and sounds, none of which seemed intelligible until he had time to actually listen, truly focus. Then, with luck, the streams of noise merged and became a coherent river. Without that concentration it was just noise, and frustrating noise at that. Incessant noises that made his skull ache and his mind seek an escape.

That was the case now. Whistler closed his eyes and lay back and listened, and slowly the words became words and the noises made sense.

The message was the same as before. He had to go west, and he had to get there soon. Whatever was supposed to happen, it would happen within the next four days, and he would have to move quickly if he was going to get there.

Four days. That was hardly any time at all, really.

Time to find a faster method of travel, he supposed, even if that meant doing something deeply foolish, like stealing a horse from the soldiers.

He considered the possibilities as he continued riding in the wagon. Sooner or later they would stop, and when that happened he couldn't be in this wagon any longer. Easy enough to slip out, he supposed, but where would he go?

West. That was all he needed to know. He had to get to the west and he had to go quickly.

The river ran to the east. There were boats that could travel the other way, of course, and they seemed fast enough. He could hire one, he supposed. Might be better and faster than a horse. Certainly safer, though he couldn't swim, either. Not much call for it in Goltha, unless you were a fisherman.

He peered out the back of the wagon, sticking his head past the covers. It was still light out and would be for a few hours. He could try waiting it out and hope no one needed supplies. There were advantages, of course. Risks, yes. The soldiers wouldn't appreciate him being with their foodstuffs, even if he didn't pilfer any. It was the thought, of course.

He might have stolen something; even if he left everything exactly as it was, there would always be a few who'd claim he took from them. That was always the case. Do nothing and get accused, so you may as well take what you need. He thought about that as he was gathering enough food for a few days. There were scars on his back from where he'd been caught a few times and given the lash.

When he'd gathered enough to keep his belly full, he checked again and then slipped out of the wagon. His timing couldn't have been much better. He could see an area where the ground dipped toward the waters and the docks.

Fast fingers had earned him enough coin to get a boat if he was careful. Whistler took a bite of hard cheese that was slightly too bitter for his preference and chewed it anyways, because food wasn't always as plentiful as he liked. That was the problem with stealing things. You never knew what you were going to get for your efforts.

There was a line of people waiting at the docks, looking for boats to take them west. The only good news was that there were several boats lined up to take on passengers. Most of them looked like they'd sink if they were on water for too long, but it was take a boat or risk stealing a horse, and the boat wouldn't be considered a hanging offense if he was caught.

Really, it was hardly a choice at all.

Kallir Lundt

Three days and nights they rode through the ice storms, searching for the Pra-Moresh, but whilst they heard them that was as close as they came to finding any of the great beasts. If the truth had to be known, Kallir was fine with that notion. The creatures were terrifying. His hand moved unconsciously to the line where flesh and metal met at the edge of his face, and his fingers touched the thick scars where the claws of the Pra-Moresh had peeled his features away like the rind of an overripe fruit.

Tarag Paedori, the King in Iron, sat astride his mount and sighed. He wanted more.

A wailing cry of sorrow and what sounded like children arguing came from the direction of Ordna. Without a single word spoken, the group sat more alert in their saddles and Tarag and Desta both reached for the long, barbed spears most commonly used when hunting the beasts.

Kallir contemplated his weapons for a moment and instead chose to grab a throwing axe. It was his intention to stay farther away than a spear from any of the beasts that came along. His last effort with a spear had not gone as hoped.

The best plans often fall apart like sand sculptures in a hard rain. The first of the Pra-Moresh might well have been in the direction of Ordna, but the responding mix of laughter and outrage came from much closer, almost immediately to Kallir's left.

He spun hard toward the sound and saw the shadowy form rise out of the endless sandstorm, towering above him and his mount alike. Frakka let out a rumbling growl of his own and turned to face the new threat. Kallir looked, aimed and threw his axe. The weapon rolled exactly as it should and bounced off the thick fur of what the Sa'ba Taalor called a cackler because of the laughter that went along with their roar.

The Pra-Moresh giggle-wept and charged toward them on all fours, moving with unsettling speed.

Kallir felt his blood singing and grabbed for his spear. He would have never reached it in time, but Frakka was fast enough. The mount rose up and balanced on his hind legs as his forepaws lashed out, swiping. The Pra-Moresh was armed with truly savage claws and protected by a layer of rough fur that could stop anything short of an arrow with relative ease. The claws of the cackler tried to cut Frakka and the mount returned the favor. Frakka had an advantage. He was wearing the armor that Kallir had made for him. It saved the mount's life. Metal and leather took the blow that likely would have disemboweled the mount otherwise.

Frakka's claws tore through the thick hide and drew blood. The Pra-Moresh scream-moaned and retreated a few paces.

Kallir didn't wait. He drove Frakka forward and drove the tip of his barbed spear into the great animal's chest. Meat pushed aside, but bone did not. The spear anchored itself in flesh and went no further, but at least he had a good grip on the spear and could use it to keep the roaring nightmare away from him.

Frakka backed up and then lunged forward. The shift in weight would have been disastrous on a horse, but Frakka could offer warning of his action through their mental link, and Kallir had a chance to compensate for the changes.

Desta came in low and drove her spear into the cackler's thick left thigh. The thing let out a screech and sobbed as it rose from its previous stance and charged forward on its hind legs.

Desta held on to her spear and used it to keep the thing from clawing her. The shaft of the spear bent but did not break, and she retreated as the cackler charged.

Tarag's spear took the Pra-Moresh in the throat, driving

in on one side and pushing through on the other with a fountain of bright red blood.

More cries from cacklers came from three different directions.

There was no time for panic.

Kallir and Frakka moved forward and Kallir twisted his spear and pushed hard, felt the barbed tip slide past bone and between two of the monster's ribs. The creature sobbed and wailed and tried to retreat, but the barb did its job and kept Kallir attached. The strength of the thing was enough to lift Kallir from his saddle, and he held onto the spear for a moment before letting it go and falling back.

Despite the raging sandstorm, the damned thing seemed to sense that he was at a disadvantage, and it came for him again, claws spread wide apart and head turning at an angle while it tried to decide where to bite down.

The whole beast pulled hard to the side as Tarag and his mount came closer and yanked at the spear through its neck. At the same time, Desta hauled on her spear and went in the other direction, pushing the legs of the beast off balance.

Kallir moved, grabbed his spear while the creature was fighting to maintain balance, and shoved for all he was worth in the opposite direction of Desta. The cackler went down hard on the ice.

His spear slid deeper into the thing's chest and the tip cut into the heart of the cackler. The thing shuddered and wept like an infant, the sounds disconcerting as they came from so large a creature.

There was no time to celebrate. There were more of the damned things around them, and they were hungry. They were always hungry. That was part of what made them so dangerous.

Frakka bounded closer and waited. Kallir jumped into the saddle and then urged Desta closer. She took the hint and moved up behind him as Frakka spun toward the closest of the cacklers.

Desta said something, but between the winds and the myriad sounds from the massive beasts, the words were lost.

She held her spear in her bloodied hands and prepared for the onslaught as best she could.

Kallir grabbed for a javelin, his spear lost to the fight that had already taken place. Barbs were good for keeping a weapon locked in. That was also the disadvantage. Once in, the spear wasn't easy to remove.

Tarag Paedori rode past as they were still seeking the right target. The spear in his hand was properly braced, and impaled the Pra-Moresh that was charging them. The point drove through the neck and collarbone of the creature and he held onto the shaft until half the weapon's length was buried in the torso of the beast.

The King in Iron let go of the weapon and rode past as the cackler realized it was dying. For a change, the beast made no sounds. It merely fell forward and expired.

Just that quickly the hunting was done. The rest of the hunting party had killed two more of the cacklers, leaving enough to make for a proper feast.

Kallir's spear worked well enough to hold the body. The ropes tied to the spear were strong enough to hold the weight and soon the hunting party was headed home through the ice and wind and dust of the Blasted Lands.

They were not lingering in the hopes of finding prey and so they moved quickly, hauling their prizes behind the mounts that carried both their usual riders and the others who had walked while actively hunting. Desta rode behind

Kallir and settled the long spear across her lap as they moved along.

"This is your first hunt?" She had to yell to be heard.

He nodded. "My first hunt for cacklers. I hunted for tamer prey in Fellein. Deer and wild boar." He chuckled. "I used to think boar was as dangerous as an animal could get."

"What changed your mind?"

"Having a cackler ruin my face."

"Ah. I had wondered."

"You could have asked."

"I knew you would say when you were ready."

"Among my people, the Fellein, everyone would ask."

"Among my people, that's like begging a person to brag about their victory."

"What victory. I had my face torn away."

"You lived through it. That is a victory."

He smiled. "That philosophy is very different from what I grew up with."

"The gods rewarded you. They gave you a new face. They do not always offer that form of reward." Which he knew was true. Bullara was a warrior he'd met several times, and the woman had only one eye and what was left of her mouth was a gaping hole on one side of her face. He could count her broken teeth through the long-healed wound. She'd been mauled in the battle with Fellein, had taken a blow from a farmer's war club. The damage she sported would have repulsed any man in Fellein, but here? Among the Sa'ba Taalor? She was considered extremely attractive. It was common enough to see the Sa'ba Taalor sporting scars that showed their history of combat, and he knew several who were missing fingers, or even full limbs. They did not let those injuries slow them down often. If they did, they didn't live long.

Five years and he still hadn't adjusted to that way of thinking. He lived in a land that may as well have been forever away from his homeland.

One moment they were walking through the storm and the next the air was calm and much warmer. He'd been distracted as they approached the edge of the Blasted Lands.

Frakka spoke, *You worry too much about appearances.*

"I have an iron face. I have reason."

"Reason for what?" Desta's voice surprised him.

"I was speaking with Frakka, who says I worry too much about appearances."

"You do. You are very handsome."

"I have an iron face."

"Yes. Like I said, very handsome. A gift from Truska-Pren. You must be very honored."

"I am." And he was, but he'd never thought that his face would be considered a sign of prestige. For as long as he could remember, he'd assumed the sight was repulsive to women and men alike. Even when he considered Bullara, and how she was received, it never crossed his mind that his appearance would be anything but unsettling at the best of times.

And here was Desta confirming the beliefs of the Sa'ba Taalor. Which made him wonder if she found him a worthwhile companion because of his face, or in spite of it.

Best not to consider that sort of madness for long.

The air was calm, but there were noises aplenty. Several of the hunters with him let out cries as they stared to the south. He followed their gaze and found the reasons for the noise.

There was a party of over a score of men, rugged types by the look of them, hard men who were likely sellswords.

What made them different was that they had several Sa'ba Taalor with them. Four, possibly five, each of them riding a horse instead of a mount.

From what he'd heard, that was a bit of a rarity in itself.

Tarag Paedori called out to the strangers in the language of the Sa'ba Taalor. "What is this then? Why are you so far from home?"

The strangers looked at their gathered force, nine warriors, with six mounts and a few fresh kills. A hunting party to be sure, but one that was less unusual than the gathered mixture facing them.

One of the Fellein called out in the common tongue, "Speak your foul language in the forges, you bastard, but speak the language of Fellein in my presence."

Tarag responded by baring his teeth in what was very obviously a challenge. When he spoke, however, it was in Fellein. "Watch what you call me. I have never taken insults well."

The Sa'ba Taalor standing with the other group did not interfere, and he'd have been very surprised if they had. First, the gray skins were not known for stepping into a challenge issued to another. Fights were often personal. Second, they were very likely Godless, and that meant they were effectively outlaws being spotted by enough of their own people to constitute a serious threat to their continued freedom.

Lastly, unless they were truly foolish, they would recognize Tarag Paedori as the King in Iron. They were outlaws, the Godless, facing the personal emissary of one of their forsaken gods.

Tarag looked at the gathered Sa'ba Taalor facing him and spoke clearly in his own tongue again, switching from one to the other language with practiced ease. There was a reason that Kallir and the King were friends, and one facet of that was helping the man learn to speak with the Fellein.

"You are the Godless. Return with us and all is well. Turn away from me and you turn away from the gods. You will not find them forgiving on this day."

The five of them did not look at each other. Two rode forward and moved past Tarag as they did so.

The other three stayed where they were.

"This is your decision?" He waited without moving, looking at each of the three.

One more rode forward and nodded once, sharply, as he passed the king. The other two stood their ground.

Kallir watched on, knowing that the end would be bloody.

Tarag stayed where he was. When he spoke, all of the Sa'ba Taalor listened carefully.

The Fellein looked at each other and shook their heads. They did not understand, and so Kallir translated for them. "I do not punish you today. The gods punish you."

The two Sa'ba Taalor who rejected the gods screamed as they burned. One of them fell from his horse and the other stood up in his stirrups and howled his pain out into the air as if it might free him from his damnation.

Eyes bulged, and teeth were bared. Hair smoldered and skin blistered. The heat started somewhere deep inside of them. Kallir saw it start, watched the light that seemed to grow from their bones, watched as that light grew and the flames burst through their skin, roasting meat, boiling blood and incinerating hair in a sudden explosion. He did not let himself look away. The gods had blessed him with a new face; it was only right, only proper to watch as they cursed others.

All around them the Fellein retreated, horrified by the punishment the gods cast upon the Godless. Several of the horses bolted and took their riders with them, fighting to remain in saddles, struggling not to be thrown.

No one spoke. No one looked away. The gods made their judgement known and they watched the suffering as was their sacred duty. One does not turn from the gods as easily as from mortal judgements.

It took several minutes for the Godless to die. Long after they should have been dead, they continued to writhe and crawl across the ground as fat was rendered from flesh and bones crisped into little more than blackened char. When they were finally deceased, Tarag turned on his mount and headed back for the mountain where Truska-Pren resided.

It was not long before they were home. Once on the mountain, the Godless were led to the throne room of Tarag Paedori. Because he knew it was expected of him, Kallir walked the path to the throne and waited as the king made his next judgements.

Tarag Paedori did not speak. It was the god who spoke through him. Kallir heard the words in his head even as Tarag uttered them to the Godless. "You were given life by me. You were granted a place to live, food to eat and the blessings of the Daxar Taalor, and you turned away from us when we were silenced. You are forgiven and you are welcome, but now you must be humbled."

The three stood their ground and did not look away from their king. Tarag Paedori, the King in Iron, walked before the first of the men and covered the two Great Scars on his face with his hands. It was not easy to see, but each of his hands held a strip of iron that could almost have been a shadow in the great man's palms. The first of the Godless screamed with his mouth and held still as Tarag's hands smoldered. When he released his grip, the scars were sealed shut, the flesh around them blistered, cauterized by lines of glowing iron. There is only so much a man can tolerate. The pain was simply too much and the poor bastard fell to his knees and shivered as the metal cooled.

The second man stood his ground, though he shivered at the thought of what was to come. There were four Great Scars on his face. They were sealed in the same way, and before it was done, he was unconscious on the stone floor of the throne room.

The third of the Godless to return was fortunate. He had only one Great Scar on his face. He remained conscious and stood his ground even after the hot metal seared shut the marking placed upon him by a god.

"The gods have forgiven you. For one year you will bear the marks I have placed upon you. For one year the gods will not speak to you, unless it is through the mouths of the kings. This is your punishment."

Tarag said no more. He left his throne room to return outside, where the hunting party was already busy.

All around him the Sa'ba Taalor got busy with their kills, and Kallir followed suit. With Desta's help he hauled the carcass of the cackler onto chains and lifted the body, preparing it for cleaning. Before he could consider where to start, the woman was already at work with her long skinning knife, cutting a massive slit in the belly of the thing and letting the guts spill out.

There were plenty of hunters he knew personally who would be offended by the help, but he was not. He was grateful, for one, and also accepted that Desta, Frakka and Tarag had all been a part of the hunt. He had never understood why anyone took offense at an offer of assistance, especially when he was simply grateful for it.

Not far away Tarag Paedori, the king, hauled his kill onto one of the long posts, and prepared to start cleaning and skinning the body. He gave several orders to others nearby, and soon a dozen people were building fires.

There would be a feast, soon enough. Before then there would be time to bathe, and to relax. The best cooks would season and prepare the great carcasses. Frakka was already feasting on cackler entrails and several other mounts joined him. The heart was set aside to go with the carcass. It would be prepared differently, he knew that, but he couldn't have said what the preparations would be, only that the end result would taste wonderful.

The Sa'ba Taalor would be eating and drinking, and he would join them and be grateful for the feast and the companionship.

It was not the world he'd been raised in.

It was a better world.

Trigan Garth

The sounds that crept up from the cave were exactly the sort that made Trigan curious. He considered entering the cave and seeking out the source of the noises, but did not. They were not his concern, unless the sounds became bothersome enough to distract the soldiers he was training.

If he could call it training. Some listened and others complained. The loudest protests came from the worst of the soldiers. That was the part that made no sense to him. There were hundreds of mercenaries. No, thousands. They were passable as soldiers, he supposed, but few of them seemed capable of thinking for themselves, and those who did the most thinking were those who had the smallest thoughts. That was the problem with the Fellein: they were foolish in their hearts as well as their minds.

One of them was calling to him even as he considered the cave where Jeron often hid and the noises that came from it.

"Are you listening to me?" The man stepped closer, staring hard at him.

Trigan sighed and stared at the man. He was cooking over a small fire. The air was cold and dry; the fire was a comfort and he was hungry. What he was not was ready for, was another argument. Trigan looked at the Fellein. "No. What do you want from me?"

"There are too many people here. Supplies are running low."

"I don't care."

The man looked at him as if he'd grown another arm out of his forehead. "But you're in charge."

Trigan smiled. "Yes. That is why I don't care. I am here to teach you to fight, not to make sure you have a tent."

The man's brows drew together over his potato-like nose. It was a very large nose, and had been broken several times. "I have a tent."

"Then why are you complaining?" Several people who'd been listening to the fool talking all laughed at that.

"What are we supposed to eat?" His eyes roamed down to stare at the roasting meat Trigan was cooking. "Where is fresh water?"

"Eat what you can hunt. The water is outside and down that way, to the river."

He could see the man considering whether or not to say

anything else. That made him a fool. He should stop before Trigan took offense and responded with a challenge.

"Who am I supposed to talk to about these things? You are useless."

And that was exactly enough for Trigan. He reached out and punched that potato of a nose, spreading it across the man's ugly face.

That should have been the end of it. From what he'd seen of most of the Fellein, that *would* have been the end. They did not like confrontation and often retreated at the thought. Several people called out and rose as if offended by his attack against another. They did not move against him, wisely, but they watched on and spoke out.

The man with the now ruined nose shook his head and coughed, and then came forward, intent on hurting Trigan. Rather than stop him, Trigan simply stepped out of the way and let him blunder past, squawking indignantly. Several of the Godless laughed at the fool's efforts. The fool grew angrier and pulled a dagger from his belt.

Trigan waited as the man circled. "Do not do this. I will kill you."

Undeterred by the warning, the man came forward and crouched slightly at the knees as he started to circle.

Trigan waited patiently.

The man charged forward, handling the dagger better than Trigan expected. He finally took a chance and stabbed forward with the blade and Trigan again made certain not to be where he struck. A man with a knife was a dangerous man, but only if he connected.

The second time his new friend tried to stab him, Trigan pulled his own, considerably larger blade, and shook his head. "Defend yourself."

Potato Nose tried. He backed away and started to apologize, but it was too late for that. Trigan used his larger blade to knock aside the dagger and then stabbed the point of his blade into the fool's chest. It was easy enough. The Fellein were not, as a rule, very skilled with their weapons.

Potato Nose grunted as he died.

Trigan withdrew his blade and wiped the blood from the weapon and held it firmly.

"Hear me!" He made certain his voice was loud enough to be heard, even over the grumbles from a few of the pale-skins. "I do not care if you are tired, or if you are hungry. I care if you can fight." He looked at the people around him, made certain that they were looking back, and then nodded.

"We are preparing for war!" Trigan lifted his blade above his head. "I will not cook your meals or gather your water. No one is here to help you wash yourself. We are here to fight and to win! If you are not strong enough to do these things, you should leave before you end up like this fool."

That said, he sheathed his blade and reached down for the spit where his roast was cooking.

"What a lovely speech." Jeron's voice was different these days. He'd sounded like a stranger and looked like one as well. Even hidden away in his robes, the changes were evident. He was taller than he had been, and his shoulders were narrower. He had changed so much that his clothes no longer fit him properly.

"Where have you been?" Trigan tried to see the sorcerer's face, but it was lost in the shadows of his hood.

"Taking care of matters that needed my direct attention." Something moved inside the cowl, but Trigan couldn't quite make out what that something was. It did not look like a chin.

"These soldiers of yours. These mercenaries, they are restless. They want a fight. They want more food and water. They complain constantly."

"So I see." The sorcerer's leg moved his robes enough to let him prod at the man Trigan had made dead. "Perhaps not killing all of the mercenaries might work to our advantage."

"How? They have proven to be weak. If they are alive, they will die when we fight the Fellein."

"Then they die when we fight the Fellein! That's one more enemy the Fellein have to kill, or the Sa'ba Taalor for that matter."

"They will not survive my people."

"That's not the point. We need soldiers."

"We need warriors. Not fools who can't hold a weapon."

"They've been trained, Trigan."

"No." He shook his head. "They have been given a weapon and told which end to hold and some of them barely manage that."

Jeron stood still as something shifted under his robes, moving slowly across his left side and then up his back. Trigan watched the progression with curiosity. He had seen many strange and wondrous things in his life, but the wizard's transformation remained a mystery.

"What is happening to your body? You are changing."

"The Overlords are remaking me. I don't know much beyond that." The man spoke, but his words were not completely truthful. "They need me to be more than I have been."

The Overlords, again. He had not met the rulers of Jeron. They were hidden away. Perhaps deep in the cave where the wizard spent so much of his time. "Where are these Overlords? Where do they hide?"

"They have slept for hundreds of years, Trigan." Jeron's voice grew softer, and Trigan had to strain to hear him. "They spent a lot of time and energy fighting Fellein before, and they were defeated." The sorcerer shrugged uneven shoulders. "They did not die, but they were wounded."

"And so now they would try to defeat Fellein again?"

"They do not care about Fellein, Trigan. They care about all of the land from one ocean to the other. They would control everything."

"They would control the Seven Forges?" Trigan frowned at that notion. There were *gods* at those great mountains. He knew from experience how great those divine beings were. They would not simply retreat from a possible battle.

Jeron laughed. When his hand came out from his robes it reached out and patted Trigan's shoulder. The hand had the wrong number of fingers to it, and they were long and spidery. "No, Trigan. They would control everything. Fellein, the Seven Forges… everything."

Trigan considered those words carefully.

"Trigan. You should come meet them."

"Meet them?"

"The Overlords. Come with me. See them. Meet them. Understand what it is that they want." Jeron's fingers squeezed at his shoulder with surprising strength. "Come."

Trigan wondered for a moment why the man had decided to show him the very secret he had been keeping so closely. Still, he needed to understand these Overlords. They were a mystery and he did not want to follow them without knowing who and what they were that they thought they could challenge the Daxar Taalor.

Trigan took his food with him. He would eat as they walked.

The pathway into the cave was easy to discern but changed. The cave was simply a cave. The ceiling above was a dozen feet tall, and the walls were smooth from what seemed centuries of existence, though the cave had not been in this spot for very long.

"I have been gathering the power that the Overlords need to awaken. That time is finally here, I think."

"You do not know?"

Jeron laughed. "I could consult the Sooth, read the entrails of a hundred dead men, beg the answers from the gods themselves, and still I would not know with any certainty." He sighed and looked back toward Trigan. "Portents and omens. Nothing is ever certain until it is done."

Trigan nodded and walked on, his curiosity growing as they began descending a long spiral path deeper into the earth.

"The Overlords believe that they are destined to rule this world," Jeron spoke casually. "They are not alone. There have been plenty of rulers and would be rulers who believe it was their destiny to rule. Only a few hundred years ago the emperor swore that the very gods chose his family to rule over Fellein. As if any mortal could dictate what the gods believe."

Trigan, who had spoken with all seven of the gods of the forges, knew better than to think he could read the minds of gods. He could, at best, guess their intentions, and even then only after they spoke to him.

They walked further down the spiral, led by the flaming torches resting in several sconces along the wall. Like the very cave itself, the sconces seemed born of ancient times. There were deep scorches above each torch-holding device, smoke stains discolored the stone. Still, none of this had been here in the past, if Trigan had to guess. The cave had not been here. The ground had been unbroken when he arrived.. That was how he knew how powerful Jeron was. The man had created this or brought it from another place. He had done something that only gods should be capable of.

"How old is this cave, Jeron?"

The wizard looked his way. "I have no way of knowing. The Overlords have slept here for nearly a thousand years."

"They created all of this?"

Jeron nodded. "I expect so, at least. They have been here, in this place, since they were defeated."

Trigan considered that as they continued descending.

Finally, after long enough for Trigan to finish his meal, they reached the chambers where the Overlords rested. The entrance was blocked by two heavy doors. Jeron waved a hand and the doors swung open revealing a vast chamber carved from white stone. The walls were thirty feet or more in height and faded into the distance, lost to the lights around the center of the chamber. Vast fires burned here, fueled by the gods alone knew what. There was no wood, there were no supplies, but still the fires roared and flickered and kept the darkness and the cold at bay. The center of the cave was nearly as hot as an oven, though Trigan found the heat easily tolerable.

Trigan had been in the presence of gods. He was not especially impressed, but acknowledged that the chambers were of a grand scale.

In the very center of the vast chamber was a patch of darkness. In that black pool something rested. Perhaps several somethings, but they were hidden in the ebon shadows that surrounded the area.

They walked slowly, and Trigan had plenty of time to see

that the darkness they approached was more than a lack of light. The darkness nearly seemed to absorb the illumination from the fires. It was not shadows. It was more than that.

He stared at the closest forms, puzzled by them.

"The Overlords have slept. They awaken now, Trigan. After so many years, they are finally ready to emerge." Jeron's voice held a note that was familiar to the Godless. It was the sound of a fanatic. He had been among them for his entire life before coming here. To the Sa'ba Taalor, the gods were incapable of making mistakes. Their words were law. This was all very familiar to him.

He looked toward the darkness. It had shape, form and dimension. Unlike the shadows, there was life here, not merely an imitation.

It was not life as he understood it, but it was life.

The darkness held secrets. Those secrets moved, he could sense that. The darkness seemed shapeless, but if he looked long enough he could make sense of that formlessness, see the hidden forms within it. Here, a hand reached out, there a body twisted in a parody of birth. Solid shadows stretched away from the center of the darkness and pushed to escape their prison.

"Do you feel them, Trigan Garth?"

He nodded. "Yes."

"Are they not magnificent?"

Were they? He had seen gods, spoken with gods, been touched by them and changed by them. His hand ran along the Great Scar on his right cheek, feeling the mark left behind when Ydramil first touched him and rewarded his faith.

Still, he nodded again.

The darkness moved and breathed. The hairs along his

neck stood on end. Not because he was afraid but because shadows were not supposed to move that way.

Trigan stared at the darkness where the Overlords were supposedly waking and frowned.

"The Overlords have spoken to me about you, Trigan. You and your people. They are impressed by you." Jeron's voice was soft, lulling.

Trigan was not lulled. In his experience, when a Fellein spoke in those tones it was an attempt to put a man at ease. Usually when they tried to put a person at ease, it was because they were planning something against that person's better interests.

"I am paid. I serve."

"How have you lived without your gods in your life, Trigan? Has your world been better or worse?"

"Different."

Jeron stepped closer, and Trigan made himself relax. Tense muscles did not move as quickly.

"Perhaps you need different gods for different times, my friend."

Trigan turned his head enough see Jeron from the corner of his eye.

That was when the shadows attacked.

CHAPTER TWELVE

Whistler

Old Canhoon was not what he'd expected. Everyone had heard the tales of how the capital city had lifted from the ground and drifted through the skies on the way to Lake Gerhaim. He had even seen the vast city floating in the skies, had watched it crash down into the waters of the lake and been as surprised as everyone else when the island of stone stayed where it was instead of sinking into the waters.

What he had not truly considered was how large Canhoon was. Old Canhoon had lifted from the ground and left behind so much of the city that had grown around it over hundreds of years. The Sa'ba Taalor had attacked what was left and burned a great deal of it, but they had not taken everything, and apparently what was left had decided to grow back, like a garden growing in a field of weeds.

Whistler walked around the city, amazed by what he saw. Here and there he could see the remains of burnt out buildings, but mostly he saw new structures, rebuilt houses and more. The ruins he'd expected were not to be found. Instead a city thrived and grew larger around a small lake that had, near as he could figure, once been the resting place of Old Canhoon.

This new town had a different name. These days it was called Tyrne, after the city the gray skins had ruined with one of their mountains. He knew nothing of that. He'd heard of the original Tyrne, but that was all. It was as far from his world as any place could be, and he was farther away from his world than he'd ever thought of going. Goltha was days away from him, and he'd never imagined that happening, but the voices were still saying he had to head west, and so he did.

So far he'd seen amazing places, like this new Tyrne, but the need to move on still pulled at him.

Not far beyond new Tyrne, he could see where the Jeurgis River and the Freeholdt River met each other and crossed paths. The waters were different shades of blue and the merging spots muddied into each other. He'd hoped he could take the boat he'd hired as far west as the voices said he needed to go, but that was no longer possible. The rivers did not travel into the Wellish Steppes, whatever they were, and that was all that lay west of him until a person ran across the valley of Trecharch. Say this if nothing else: he'd learned a great deal about the land where he lived, just by talking to strangers heading in the same direction as he was.

The people heading to the west were the sort he'd spent a lifetime avoiding. Strong men who carried swords and looked like they'd kill a fellow as soon as talk to him. They were rough types, the sort the City-Guard grew wary around, and there were a lot of them heading the same way.

If there was one thing Whistler was good at, it was not being seen. A talent he'd long ago acquired. The trick wasn't to hide so much as it was not to get noticed. Not getting noticed was a skill that had kept him alive many times and he took advantage of it now. No more smiling, no more standing out like a cocky young fighter. Better to simply exist for the present time, and so he changed the way he stood, the way he looked around and the way he smiled. There was less of an air of menace to him now, and that was for the best, because the men and women around him were exactly the sort that would cut a man's throat for looking too menacing. They were also the type that would do the same to anyone who looked weak. It was a challenging situation, but one he could work with.

He walked with the mercenaries, for that was what they were, and he moved to the west. Some rode horses, most were on foot. Those with horses had, for the most part, already moved on.

This lot moved quickly, because rumor had it there were empire soldiers heading the same direction. Had any asked, Whistler could have confirmed it, but no one asked, and he certainly didn't volunteer the sort of information that would catch a man's attention.

There were plenty of rumors, but near as he could figure, everyone around him was looking to make coin as mercenaries. There was someone hiring swords and knives. He had plenty of knives, but never once in his life had he used a sword. Hardly needed one, now did he? Knives were just fine as far as he was concerned, and he'd stick with what he knew. Near as he could figure, a sword was just a bigger knife, and in his experience, it was the edge on the blade that made the difference.

Didn't mean he had any plans of taking a dagger against a sword, mind you. Just common sense there.

Not that it mattered. Not that he cared. The plans of the many had nothing to do with his personal goals. It was the voices, really, that made the difference. They never stopped talking, not as long as he ignored them. They kept on and on, endlessly, singing, whispering, humming, whatever it took to get his attention, until he gave a little and went along with them. Then, when they had him obeying, they'd let him have a bit of peace.

That was what he wanted most. Peace. He could remember what it was like not to hear the voices, and he wanted that again. Wanted it bad enough he'd do almost anything to get it.

For now, that meant walking west. Not much choice to it if he wanted his calm back.

One of the men walking near him kept looking in his direction. It wasn't an aggressive look, but it was nearly constant and starting to annoy Whistler. His experience in life said that a man looking that hard wanted something, and most likely he wouldn't like that something, regardless of the intent. He'd known a few men wanted to take from him. His money, his possessions or his body. So far, he'd managed to avoid the last one, but the first time he killed a man it was because the fellow was feeling a mite lonely and wanted his company. Didn't matter that Whistler had no interests along those lines. Seemed a foolish thing to kill over, but on the other hand, he wasn't the sort to force himself on anyone.

The dagger was in his hand as easy as running his fingers through his hair, and he felt better for the blade. They were old friends, weren't they? They'd been some places together and done a few things.

When he looked again the fellow with the staring eyes was gone from his sight. That didn't make him more comfortable. He resisted the urge to look in all directions, and instead started slowing his pace, looking around as carefully as he could. Best not to let it be known he was aware of the change. Best not to alert the stranger who just might have taken an interest in him.

One thing you could count on was a sense of commerce. Find a hundred people in one area and three more will show up in short order to see if they can't provide comforts for a profit. It was as true as the sun rising in the east.

Several wagons and carts had been set up for that very purpose, and Whistler stopped at a stand selling roasted meat long enough to buy a skewer of lamb and to survey the situation. He found the man who'd been giving him looks easily enough. He was standing off to the side with three others, looking right at Whistler. It wasn't a good sign for the way his day might go. Sostice, a lad he used to work for, always said one man was a challenge. Three or more were a problem. One you could face off against and have good odds. Two might be more challenging but if you knew the land, you'd likely get away safely. Three meant they could block any route for escaping, and more than that? You were on your own, you were as good as dead.

He didn't know if he completely agreed with that philosophy, but it was a good starting point to work from.

"You're in trouble." The voice came from his left and he looked that way. The man standing there was young, dark, and had one lazy eye.

"Am I now?"

"Befter is looking at you. He thinks he knows you from his time in Stonehaven."

"I don't know Befter and I've never been to Stonehaven."

Uneven teeth flashed white against dark skin. "Befter isn't very smart, but he makes up for it by being stubborn."

"Doesn't mean I know him any better."

"I do. He'll be coming for you. Thinks you owe him money."

Whistler chewed at the lamb on his stick and offered to share. The man talking to him took him up on the offer. "Thing is, Befter shouldn't want to confront me."

"It's not that he wants to. He thinks he has to in order to prove himself. Befter is like a goat, really. Once he sets his eyes on locking horns it's a done thing. He won't stop until the fight is over with. I've seen him lose a few fights, but I've seen him win more. Mostly because he has others willing to fight with him."

"Befter the one with the angry eyes?" Whistler pointed with his chin as he wiped grease away from his mouth. The man with him took a largish piece of lamb and offered the stick back, but Whistler motioned he should keep it.

"Aye, that's him."

Befter saw him looking and started in his direction.

"Be ready to run." It was all the warning Whistler gave his new friend.

Befter came two paces closer and Whistler threw his dagger. It arced through the air lazily, and Befter stared at it, watching, surprised, until the dagger buried itself in his left eye.

There was nothing lazy about Befter's response. He let out a howling shriek and covered his bloodied eye with both hands.

"By the gods! What did you do?" Lazy Eye stared on horrified.

"I stopped him, didn't I."

Befter fell to the ground, still screaming, and writhed in the dirt.

"He was going to beat you, but I don't think he'd maim you."

Whistler had two throwing knives ready by the time the three with Befter were looking his way. They didn't come to Befter's defense, but instead vanished into the crowd. All the better, in his eyes. They didn't vanish away, trying to find an advantage. They ran away not wanting to get caught up in the violence. Anyone couldn't tell the difference was a fool.

"I don't want to get beaten." He looked at his new friend. "I don't like getting hit."

"Well, no one does." Lazy Eye stared at him for a moment and then looked away.

"Yes, but if I have a choice between taking a man's eye or having his fist in my face, I'll take his eye every time." He shrugged and looked around again. Several people had seen him throw the knife, had seen it land, but not a one of them came forward now. There was no sign of City-Guard or soldier and that suited him just fine.

"So I can see, friend."

Befter was alive. He'd likely recover well enough, but he'd have one less eye. Might be he'd even learn a lesson from it.

Whistler didn't much care what the fool did as long as he stayed away.

He walked over to Befter and pulled the blade from his face. The man screamed and sobbed and curled in on himself, because the pain had to be a massive thing, having an eye cut open like that.

Not that it mattered. Not really.

And then he walked on, because those damn voices wouldn't leave him be, not even for a minute.

Whatever was going to happen in the west, he had three days left to get there. The voices made that very clear.

CHAPTER THIRTEEN

Jeron

The Overlords were pleased.

Jeron had called Trigan Garth to his side and, after him, he called for others of the Godless and walked them down to where the Overlords stretched and woke.

None of them had a chance to escape before it was too late. None of them understood that sorcery didn't have to be flashy to be effective. Most seemed to expect clouds of smoke and gouts of flame, especially after the war. There were very few who hadn't seen Gerheim frozen by magic. There were even fewer who hadn't at least heard of Desh Krohan calling lightning from the skies and destroying an army summoned by the Sa'ba Taalor and their gods. Certainly, there were plenty who claimed to have witnessed the spectacle themselves, and that was on both sides of the war, near as he could figure.

Each of the Godless followed him because he willed it, and his sorcery was strong enough to ensure it. Perhaps if they had still been connected to their gods they'd have been warned, but that wasn't the case. They were called the Godless for a reason.

The Overlords waited patiently and then took their

prizes, and though Jeron worried about losing his greatest warriors, he also knew that they served at the whims of the Overlords, whether they were aware of it or not.

Like him, they were at the will of their new masters.

Like him, they were taken in and though he had no idea what was happening to Trigan or the others, he understood that they were being changed by the Overlords. They had been caterpillars and now they became something more. He had studied metamorphosis. He understood that tadpoles became frogs, caterpillars became butterflies and that the Godless were now becoming something else, just as he himself was changing. What they would be by the time the transformations were complete was a different story.

Darus Kestle had not yet finished his transformation, but it was close. He had been a trusted aide and Jeron had sacrificed him to the Overlords without hesitation. They said they wanted him and so he was offered up. At first he thought the man dead, but after a time he started understanding that the black, shadowy substance surrounding Kestle was his cocoon. He was changing, becoming something different and, if he was lucky, he was becoming something better like Jeron himself.

The Godless called Vendtril fought hard as the darkness swallowed him. He fought as hard as any person Jeron had ever seen in his life. When the darkness came for him, the Godless drew his sword and an axe and tried to cut it down, to whittle the darkness away. He had no luck. Each slice hacked into the shadow-stuff was as effective as a blade against a fire. The darkness fell away but was not extinguished, and the wind of the blade seemed only to feed fuel into the shadows. He tried and in the end was consumed.

But that wasn't really the case, was it? Fire took in fuel and feasted. The blackness wrapped itself around Vendtril but failed to diminish him. He was still there, still struggling, still failing, and Jeron could feel the transformation beginning to take place, even if he couldn't fully comprehend just what that change was.

Not far from where Vendtril struggled and strained, the shadows had coalesced into a hard shell, a barrier wrapped tightly around Trigan Garth. There was no longer any sign that the Sa'ba Taalor continued to strain and fight, but Jeron could feel him, still, could sense the fury with which the man continued his fight.

The struggle had to cause him pain. That was all there was to it. Jeron had not fought the same way, but his transformation had not been painless.

Roledru stood back a distance, not coming any closer to the shadow stuff that writhed over the Godless, the mercenaries and the Overlords alike.

"You are not trusting, Roledru."

"I'm trusting enough." The man's voice was subdued. "I just don't want to be changed."

"How can you be certain?"

"I've only just grown my hair long enough to pull it back and tie it. That's a large enough change for me."

"I have been given so much by the Overlords," Jeron spoke softly, his voice trailing off. It was hard for him to comprehend how much he had changed already. He still didn't know when the transformation would stop, but he was in no hurry to see the miraculous changes come to an end, either. Unlike Roledru, he had complete faith in what was happening.

He had faith in his new gods. He wondered idly if the

Godless would feel the same when they emerged from their chrysalises. He expected they would. The Overlords seemed to take everything into consideration.

"Why does it feel like the world is holding its breath, Jeron?"

"Not the world. Just the world we see," Jeron shrugged. "I expect the rest of the world is merely scratching their heads and trying to understand what's happening out here."

"What do you mean?"

"I mean we've had over a thousand mercenaries come here and not return. According to the Sooth we have caught the attention of others."

"The what? The Sooth?"

"Spirits, my good man. Spirits that can often tell the future."

"Oh, right. The liars."

Jeron laughed. "They can lie. They often do, but that doesn't mean they always lie. The trick is to know what they consider important, I think. They tell the truth about the things they think matter. The trick is to convince them about what matters."

"And how does one convince a spirit about what matters if they're so far different from us?"

"That's the trick. I've spent lifetimes learning the answer."

"Not sharing it then?"

"I am not. If you'd like to become my apprentice, I might be able to teach you, but it would take lifetimes for you as well."

"Hmmph. No. That's alright. I'll just keep working for you if it's all the same."

"It's your decision to make, Roledru."

The man nodded, and stayed well away from the pool of shadows that had taken in over fifty bodies already.

"So what happens now, Jeron?" He gestured to where Trigan and others lay in their slow suffering.

"We wait. Not much longer." Jeron walked over to where Trigan struggled and placed his many-fingered hand over the cocooned flesh. "Most of the pieces are already where they need to be. We wait for one more person."

"And what's so special about this one?"

"I've no idea. The Overlords want him. That's enough for me."

Roledru sighed and nodded. He was nothing if not content with his lot, it seemed.

That was a good thing to see. So many wanted more, hungered for new challenges and victories. Roledru was that rare person who was satisfied with what life offered him. Most would be better off if they followed his example. Of course, if they did, life would be harder for Jeron.

Nachia Krous

Being the Empress might have many advantages, but holding court was not one of them. The affair she was hosting was a perfect example of what she hated most. Oh, to be sure, there was a lot of fun to be had, but it wasn't being had by her, and that was annoying.

The purpose of the soirée, as far as she could figure, was to help her find a suitable paramour. So far it was a complete failure. Most of the men she was seeing were as far from her idea of a good companion as anything she'd seen in the years since she'd ascended to the throne. Most of them were full of themselves, or simply hungry for her attention. There seemed little space in between the two extremes.

Desh Krohan was sequestered in one corner of the room where the celebrants gathered. He was speaking quietly, and she couldn't hear the words, but she had no doubt they were words that would annoy her to no end if she could. If forced to guess, she suspected he was talking about the need for an heir to the throne.

Sometimes she hated the man. Mostly she loved him like an uncle, but now and then the thought of beating him held a certain appeal.

Brolley, her brother, was talking with Queen Lanaie, who doted on his every word. Lanaie was popular among the courtesans. She was a lovely young woman with a quick wit who was also the ruler of Roathes.

Roathes was not what it had once been. The people there were wedged between two of the Seven Forges, Wheklam to the west and Durhallem to the north, but the land was also fertile, and just warm enough to allow some of the more exotic crops to grow easily.

Lanaie was also very likely going to marry Brolley if nothing changed. They'd spent the last few years together, nearly inseparable, and Brolley adored her. While Lanaie would never be her favorite person, she was good for Nachia's brother.

Brolley was looking her way and offered one of his bright smiles and saluted her with a glass of wine, whilst a vacuously handsome young man was doing his best to be witty just for her and failing by a stretch. She nodded and smiled at the appropriate time. Surely her actions were enough to please Desh. It was all she could hope for, really.

Desh approached, his eyes casting about the room as he walked. She smiled in his direction and pretended to pay more attention to Prince Hammond. The man was a relative, however distantly, and she'd known him most of her life. He'd been a spoiled brat as a child – though that was hardly fair, as she had been one herself – and he remained a brat well into adulthood. Hammond was precisely everything she hated most in a man. Pretentious, handsome enough to distract, and well on his way to sitting on a throne. Back before she'd become Empress he'd have been exactly the sort of company she would have enjoyed. Now? He was a problem waiting to happen. He was the sort that wanted to be the center of attention far too much and she, being the Empress, would never be able to give him the sort of devotion he craved.

The fact that he was considered a hero didn't help in the least. Despite his personality, he had fought in the war and actually won a few minor victories against the Sa'ba Taalor. Of course, minor victories were still victories, and against the gray skins they counted for twice as much.

He was one of the best of the lot Desh offered on this, his third attempt to find her a suitor. The previous nights had been a waste of time.

Hammond smiled in her direction, his eyes expecting a response. Desh moved closer and nodded, saving her from a potentially awkward moment. "Majesty, may I have a moment of your time?"

"Yes, of course." She smiled an apology, and Hammond and the rest of her suitors moved quickly and quietly away. That was one thing about her long-standing reputation that worked to her advantage. Her earlier years were peppered with tantrums and scandals. They had been so much a part of her world that even years after her ascension, people still expected her to react the same way.

"I'm sorry to disrupt what I hope has been a fruitful

meeting, Majesty, but we have news from Elda." Elda was one of the countries heavily affected by the relocation of the Seven Forges. The volcano had blown the edge of the country into shreds, but the seat of power was untouched, and their loyalty remained strong.

"What news?"

"There are black ships amassing near Ordna. Certainly nothing to indicate any unexpected attacks, but worth noting in these troubling times."

"Are the times suddenly so troubling?"

He rolled his eyes at her, but did so discretely. "You know what I mean."

"Have we heard anything from Merros?"

"Only that the regiment has reached the edge of the steppes and will continue on their path. They should arrive within two days if all goes according to plan."

She nodded. "Ask Merros what he thinks of the situation here. I want him returning immediately if he sees the ships as a threat."

"He won't like it."

"I certainly see no reason for that to change things." Anyone listening in would have been scandalized. They'd have assumed her words were a condemnation of the general's skills. In truth she was just keeping with her usual humor. Not that she much worried about the opinions of others. Once again, there were a few advantages to being the Empress, and one of them was that she still had more power than most of the people around her. The only good news was that no one was listening in closely enough to hear them. Neither she nor Desh Krohan were foolish enough to let their voices carry very far.

From halfway across the ballroom she could see Ahdra

holding court. The priestess to Vendahl had become something of a celebrity of late, gaining support among the more powerful members of society in Canhoon, much to Nachia's disgust. She made a mental note to do something about that sooner rather than later. The notion that the churches were continuing to gain power was not comfortable to her, but she also wasn't quite certain what method would work best for stopping them.

Ahdra laughed and smiled, waving one hand to fan herself as she used the other to touch Dholmen Karza on the arm. Karza, the ambassador from Brellar, was laughing in return, his eyes shining almost feverishly at the contact. Ahdra had that effect on a great deal of the men and a few of the women who surrounded her.

"I don't like her." She tried not to sound petulant but was not sure if she succeeded.

The First Advisor nodded. "Nor should you. As we've discussed, she is pure trouble, her and her whole lot."

The Sisters entered the room, and half of the conversations around them faded away to whispers. The Sisters were, collectively, among the most stunning women in the court. Many people spoke of them, and just as many feared them. They were sorcerers and very powerful. They were also very nearly the personifications of men's desires. One blonde, one brunette and one redhead, a great many people assumed their appearance was enhanced by sorcerous means. It was a fair assumption and completely accurate. That did not dilute their appearance in the least. When they entered a room, everyone looked. When they spoke, everyone listened. Men lusted after them. Women lusted after them. Even when they were dressed in casual clothing or hooded, people noticed them. Seeing them under these circumstances, dressed in finery, they were nearly impossible to resist.

Desh Krohan paid them not the least attention. It was his way to avoid looking at anyone around him with interest. Nachia heard his claims of extreme age and ignored them for the most part, but she was impressed by his ability to not stare at the women who were his closest companions. When she saw him avoid casting the same looks that most every man in the area threw their way, she was more inclined to believe he was too old to notice how desirable they truly were. That, or he was so used to seeing them that it simply didn't matter anymore.

"Desh, your Sisters are here."

"Really, Nachia, I'm too busy trying to find you a suitable suitor to spend my time protecting you."

"I assure you, all of your would-be suitors are staring at your Sisters."

"That works to your benefit. You have a chance to consider any of the men in the room without being seen to be staring."

"I don't particularly care if I find a suitor, but must they look so damnably attractive all the time?"

"Their particular looks also work to keep me safe from attack."

"That might be funnier if I knew you were joking."

"Why on earth would I joke about that? I'm really quite fond of moving through my days without being attacked."

There was a disturbance on the far side of the chamber. As she watched the doors to the hall were opened, and a retinue of ten Sa'ba Taalor came through the threshold, moving with the casual grace of big cats. There were men and women alike in the group and none of them wore weapons, or any form of uniform. They never did. They preferred their flashy garments to the regimented looks of the military. That was one of the things she liked the most about them, though it often confused her. Uniforms at least let her know who was the highest in rank. Though they were without any regalia, they were dressed in finery, the sort she expected from the Fellein in the room. Where they had found the clothes she would not guess, but someone had been paid well to dress the gray skins in the latest fashions of the court.

"Well, that's… unexpected."

The Sisters moved closer to her, never once revealing any possible tension at the arrival of ten potential assassins.

Desh slid smoothy to her side and watched the procession, slipping his hood over his head in the process.

Nachia found herself wishing she'd brought her throne into the chambers. If it truly offered protection, she'd have taken it.

She couldn't tell if she'd ever seen any of them before. When she'd met the Sa'ba Taalor the first time they'd still been wearing their veils, the better to hide the Great Scars on their faces.

No one actually screamed, but more than one man reached for a sword, or cursed the lack of one. Very few sported weapons in the presence of the Empress these days.

The retinue continued toward the Empress. Four men and six women. The Fellein parted before them, though a few did so reluctantly.

Hammond moved closer to her side. Unlike many of the others, he was wearing a sword at his hip. The advantages of being royalty, she supposed. He waited with his hand on the hilt of his weapon.

The first four to approach her were the men, who stepped

to the sides and bowed at the waist, their hands held out before them palms toward the skies. The women stepped forward and did the same, all except the last of the lot, who stopped in front of her and nodded.

"I am pleased to see you, Empress Nachia Krous of Fellein. I am Swech Tothis Durwrae, Chosen of Paedle and King in Mercury."

This one she remembered, by name if not by face. There was no proof that Swech had killed her cousin, the previous emperor, but there was a strong belief that she did. Still, that couldn't be seen to matter, not when faced with one of the seven kings from the Seven Forges.

"Why are you here, King Swech Tothis Durwrae?"

The woman held her hands before her to show that there were no weapons.

"My gods have asked me to come before you at this time and offer peace between our people."

Nachia remembered her conversation with Andover Lashk. She arched one eyebrow. "What has changed that the gods of the Seven Forges now want peace?"

"We will face a common enemy in the near future. The gods foresee this, and would have you consider a joining of our forces and yours against the common enemy."

"What enemy is this?"

King Swech stared into her eyes. The woman was covered in scars. She had three of the marks they called Great Scars on her face. Her gray hair was pulled back in a ponytail and held in place by a silver clasp that looked like nothing Nachia had ever seen used to hold back hair. Her eyes gave off a silvery light, the same that marked the Sa'ba Taalor that she had met over the years, including Andover Lashk. She was dressed in finery, yes, but the fashions were more for a man than a woman. All of them dressed appropriately for men, the better, she assumed, to allow them to fight easily if it came to that. There was nothing of the fashions for women that made fighting easier. Though she was hardly a skilled warrior, she doubted that the long skirts she wore would make combat more comfortable. Certainly, the preposterous hats that half the court sported would only get in the way. Even her crown, a small enough affair, was unlikely to be worn onto a battlefield.

Swech did not wear a crown. Her arms were covered only because the weather was cold. Her exposed flesh – more than most women would deem proper – was marked by scars old and new, and her hands were callused.

"We call them the Nual-Moresh. The Deathless. I believe your people called them the Overlords."

All around the room the courtesans looked at each other in the hopes of getting answers. There appeared to be no one who could offer those answers up.

Desh Krohan remained silent, an intimidating, shadowy form who offered no words of wisdom or consolation.

The Sisters remained nearby but did not speak.

Hammond scowled, but seemed uncertain as to what he should do.

That just left her to make the decisions.

The disadvantage of being in charge, she supposed.

Swech

She had not expected the gods to call on her to speak to the Empress of the Fellein. Still, if she only responded to what was expected of her it would be a very different world.

The Empress Nachia Krous was thin. She was fair skinned with reddish brown hair and she wore clothing that hid much of her shape. She smelled of flowers and was powdered. She held herself just so, and if there was a single scar anywhere on her body it was hidden away, under many layers of clothing.

Despite all of that, Swech promised herself she would not underestimate the woman. The Empress' eyes were critical. Despite how she looked, it was obvious that she was studying each of them and looking for flaws. Swech did not doubt that she saw the flaws she was looking for and remembered them all. She was wise enough to choose Merros as her commander of armies, and despite the odds against them, Merros had led his armies to more victories than expected in the war.

She pushed those thoughts aside. Merros was not present. She did not have the luxury of looking for him. For now, she had to concentrate on the Empress and the sorcerer.

Nachia Krous spoke. "There were beliefs that yours was the blade responsible for killing the previous emperor. Is that true?"

Swech only briefly considered lying. "Yes. My gods commanded that he die by my hand and so I killed him."

"He was my cousin. I loved him dearly."

"Your loss pains me, but I would not have changed anything. When my gods command me, I listen and obey. If they told me to kill you at this moment, I would do everything within my power to kill you."

"And have they?" The woman leaned in closer. "Are you supposed to kill me?"

"You are alive." It was all the answer she had for the woman.

Nachia Krous nodded and turned her back on the

procession. The sorcerer loomed, a wave of destruction held back, a raging storm only moments way. Swech contemplated him very carefully.

"Follow me." The Empress walked away and Swech followed. Swech's retinue started following but she stopped them with a gesture. They would be hostage to whatever desires the Empress had.

Desh Krohan wanted to follow, but Nachia forbade him with a glance. If the king of the Sa'ba Taalor walked alone, so would the Empress of Fellein. Nachia would not show weakness before her potential enemy.

The chamber they entered was as large as the ballroom, but almost empty of people. Several great tables were decorated with finery, set for a feast. Twenty or more servants were making certain that every table was fully stocked with eating utensils that were barely comprehensible to Swech, and those servants stopped as one when they entered the room. With a single look, the Empress conveyed her need for privacy, and the four armored men who'd come to attention the moment the door was opened moved to different positions in the room, far enough away that they could not hear when the Empress spoke.

The other servants walked quietly and efficiently to a set of doors on the far side of the room and left.

"Why would your gods seek to work with me, after previously murdering my predecessor?"

"I do not question the gods."

"Are your gods always this fickle?"

"I do not understand this word. What is 'fickle'?"

"It means do they always change their minds?"

"No. They never do anything without a reason, but they are gods. Their reasons would likely mean little to us."

"Why?"

"For the same reason that our decisions make no sense to earthworms." Swech shrugged. "The reasons are there, but beyond our abilities to understand."

"I've been accused of being very wise."

"I have been accused of being a capable killer, but that does not change my abilities to comprehend the gods." Swech moved her hand in a waving motion, imitating the sea. "I *am* a very capable killer. I have killed many, many people, but I still do not understand the reasoning of the gods. The Daxar Taalor told me to kill Pathra Krous, after I had befriended him and given him gifts. I did not want to kill your cousin. I liked him. He was a kind, gentle and funny man. Still, one does not question gods if one is wise. The gods have given me everything that I am, and to do less than obey is to do less than my best."

Nachia Krous stared at her.

"I will always do my best for my gods. Always. If they told me to kill every last one of my people, I would not stop until my task was finished, or my people killed me."

"Your faith in your gods is admirable." The Empress crossed her arms. They were thin arms, and Swech wondered if the woman would manage to hold a sword without dropping it. "I do not have that sort of faith in my gods. If they told me to fight you right now, I would question why."

"Your gods have been absent. Mine are always with me. I had this very conversation once with Merros Dulver."

"Was that before or after you murdered my cousin?"

"Before. We have not talked as much after."

"Well, that's not quite true."

"As I have said, I do as my gods command me." For a time she had worn another face, another body, and she and

Merros Dulver had spent a great deal of that time together.

"Then how am I to trust you?"

"You must do as you see fit, of course. I could lie to you and give you promises that I might later break, but that is not my intention. I can only offer you what I am. I am faithful to my gods above all other things in this world, Majesty."

The Empress sighed. "Very well. What assurances can your gods give me?"

That was an interesting question. Swech had no answers.

The same was not true of the Daxar Taalor. Before Swech could respond, the Great Scars on her face spoke in unison, in the language of the Fellein. "Those you call the Overlords are a great threat not only to you and your people but to our people as well. For as long as the Overlords are undefeated, you will have nothing to fear from the Sa'ba Taalor, our children. This is our vow. We offer you a token. Swech Tothis Durwrae is yours to do with as you will. You may kill her. You may torture her. You may do as you please. She is yours."

There was only one possible answer to the situation, of course. Swech plucked a long dagger from beneath her tunic and offered the hilt to Nachia Krous. At the same time, she raised her head and bared her throat in supplication. The gods offered her life to the woman whose cousin she had murdered.

Swech kept her eyes on the eyes of the Empress and waited.

Nachia Krous took the offered blade.

Swech remained where she was, her eyes unmoving, her body unflinching.

Nachia Krous placed the tip of the dagger against Swech's neck. The point pushed against the flesh, and every beat of her heart pushed the very tip against her artery.

The Empress stared at her with hatred in her eyes.

"He was the kindest man I have ever known. No matter what I did to act a fool, he forgave me my sins."

Swech remained where she was. There was a part of her that had already assessed the situation. Disarming the Empress would have been very easy. Killing her would have taken only the smallest effort, and crippling her would have been easier still, but she meant what she had said. She was the servant of her gods and if they demanded her life, it was theirs for the asking.

"You took him from me."

"I did as my gods demanded." Swech took a fraction of a step forward, until she felt the skin on her neck stick and then bleed ever so slightly. A drop of warmth ran down to her collarbone. "I hurt for you, but if my gods asked again, I would kill him again. I would kill you. I would kill your wizard. I would even kill your general." She pushed again and let another drop free from her body. "And I care for Merros Dulver. He is the father of my child."

The blade eased away from her neck. "You have a child by Merros Dulver."

"Yes."

"Does he know this?"

"No."

"You are mine. Is that correct?"

"Yes."

Those eyes, those dark, dark eyes, stared at her and the Empress slowly nodded. "Then you will stay with me. I want you to choose two of your people to leave here. They are to go back to your kingdom. They are to bring your child to me. Do you understand?"

"Yes." Was that fear in her belly? She thought of her

boy, her only child, and understood the meaning of fear.

"You will remain here. You are my *guest*."

"Yes."

"Make it so." The Empress lowered the dagger and walked back to the doors leading to the gathering.

Swech followed quietly.

Desh Krohan

"I do not like this. Not in the least." Desh spoke but wasn't quite sure who he was talking to. The Sisters, most likely, though they hardly seemed to be listening. "The last time we left a Sa'ba Taalor alone with our ruler..."

Pella spoke softly. "We were not as prepared as now."

"I still don't like it."

Nachia came back into the room, King Swech following behind her.

"Well, so I was wrong." Desh shot a glance at Tataya, who was nearly constantly telling him that he worried too much.

"How unsettling." Tataya smiled brightly in his direction, but the smile never reached her eyes. She was far too busy assessing the situation for herself. That was why he loved her. She was just as much a worrier as he was, even if she would never admit to it.

The whole of the room breathed easier, it seemed. The Sa'ba Taalor were the only ones who seemed unworried by the notion of Empress and king walking into another room and being left to their own devices. Then again, their king was a capable assassin and Nachia, despite her years of training, would never be Swech's match.

Nachia Krous had been trained by some of the best

swordsmen in the land and had been given numerous lessons by Andover Lashk as well. She could very likely handle herself in many cases, but against one of the gray skins she had as much of a chance as a kitten against a Pra-Moresh. It was simply a different level of training. She could spend every waking hour for a year being trained and never come close to the levels of combat that the Sa'ba Taalor took for granted. They were trained from birth, it seemed. According to what he understood, certainly from the time they could walk they were being taught how to defend themselves and how to fight. He'd actually seen one of their children, no older than ten and not particularly tall or well developed, cut a seasoned Fellein soldier down in a matter of three strokes of an undersized sword. Savage didn't begin to describe them.

Andover Lashk, whose absence worried him more by the day, had been trained by the gods of the Sa'ba Taalor until he was among the best of them. According to what he'd told Desh, he fought in literally thousands of battles, was killed again and again and resurrected repeatedly until he could hold his own against any opponent. As he'd damned near killed Desh when they fought, it was easy to believe.

Nachia came closer. "You've got that look on your face."

"What look?"

"Like you just chewed and swallowed a rotten Pabba fruit, seeds and all."

"Where did you go?"

"Sometimes rulers need to have private discussions."

"Some rulers speak with their weapons."

"I opted to behave myself."

He opened his mouth to make a comment and she waved her hand. In that hand was a dagger that most decidedly was not part of her formal attire.

"For the present time, Swech is my guest here. She is to be afforded every consideration."

He looked at the king, who in turn looked at him and nodded her head in lieu of a curtsy. Swech then turned to her people and spoke calmly and quietly. Two of her people nodded and then left the room as quickly as they had entered it.

Sometimes he wanted to strangle the Empress. This was no exception.

"Really, Nachia."

"Her gods gave her to me as a sign of trust. I'm certainly not going to give her back."

"I... We... We don't have slavery in the empire."

"Who am I to argue with gods?" She stared at him with a blank expression, and while he was amused, he was also very annoyed. "They say that we have mutual enemies in the Overlords. For the present time they want us to work together."

"Then I suppose we'll work together, Majesty, if that is your decision."

"It is. For the present time we'll all work together against a common threat. I'd like you to communicate to General Dulver that King Swech is my guest. I'd also like to hear his latest reports on his current whereabouts and anything that they might have discovered. I would also very much like you to inform him that the Overlords are, indeed, awakening."

Ahdra, the wretch who was currently in favor with the god of prosperity, looked their way with keen interest. Despite his dislike of using sorcery, despite the personal cost, Desh cast a simple glamour over her. The words she heard were not the words they spoke. She'd remember nothing but a conversation about the local fashions.

"Majesty, might I suggest we take this discussion elsewhere?"

Swech answered. "What is there to discuss?"

"What to do with you, for one thing."

"I am here at the request of the Empress. I am hers to do with as she will."

Nachia said, "I could kill her if that would be to your liking, Desh."

"No, no." He shook his head. "I think we can do without the scandal, currently."

"What scandal? She's mine to do with as I please."

"Might I suggest something less permanent? Perhaps finding her a room to call her own while she's here?"

"If that's your preference."

Ahdra wandered slowly away, once again chatting with several dignitaries. Prince Hammond watched the conversation as if he were watching a gathering of ruffians preparing for a knife fight. That made him slightly more observant than Desh had actually expected of the man. So far, he seemed the most likely to keep Nachia's attention for more than five minutes.

That was important. She needed to find a proper husband, and she needed to produce an heir. There was more at stake than she realized and he knew all too well that she would never take his word for that. As was often the case she seemed to take things too lightly, as if both she and he were indestructible and would be around forever.

He knew better. The Sooth had warned him.

He looked toward the Empress and found her once again in discussion with Swech. The Sisters surrounded the two women, worked as buffers against the other people in their vicinity.

That was good. Nachia needed as much protection as she could get, and not just from the Sa'ba Taalor.

The gray skins were also working as buffers, their bodies strategically placed around their king, though they hardly seemed aware of how they had positioned themselves. Like as not it was automatic with them. They were in a foreign land, and not that long ago their people had been at war with literally everyone around them. Small wonder they moved to protect their ruler.

Desh considered the latest changes and knew that before the night was done, he'd be consulting the Sooth again. Oh, to be free of the possibilities. But that would not happen. There were no guarantees of what the future held, it was true, but glimpses and promises of what might be were better than facing the unknown without any preparation at all.

"Are you listening to me?" Nachia's voice cut through his musings.

"No, Majesty. I fear my attention drifted. Apologies."

"I said I've spent enough time here. I need to leave. I have things to consider."

He wanted to disagree. She had a social game to play, a need to be here, where people could see her and be reassured, where she could be courted and adored by the very people he'd carefully selected to be around her at this time.

"Of course, Majesty." He bowed formally. "Shall I entertain your guests for now?"

Nachia offered a very small smile and nodded imperceptibly. "If you could make apologies for me, Desh. Swech and I have a few issues to discuss."

Goriah asked a question with her eyes and Desh nodded

as imperceptibly as Nachia had. A moment later the Sister was gone as if she had never been there, and he felt better knowing that she would be following Empress and King alike.

CHAPTER FOURTEEN

Andover Lashk

The blade cut across his midriff and Andover hissed, retreating.

The deck swayed beneath him and the winds roared, even as waves tried to wash his feet out from under him. Donaie Swarl stepped in closer and pushed her advantage. Andover's left hand blocked her blade and he felt metal scrape across his palm and fingers, and was grateful for the nearly indestructible gift he had been given of iron hands.

Donaie Swarl, not to be deterred, dropped low and swept his legs. He almost managed to save himself but the ship tilted beneath him and he crashed to the deck again.

"Better! Get up!" She called the words and stepped back, giving him a chance to regain his feet. In a true combat situation, he'd likely have been dead a second after he fell. The King in Lead was dangerous, and struck as fast as a venomous snake. She kindly did not kill him.

Andover groaned inside but remained calm and quiet as he rolled his body and climbed to his feet. As soon as he was standing, she came forward again, feigning with her sword and dagger alike. He moved, not certain how she would attack, only that she would, indeed, be willing to kill him when she did.

It was a brutal fight, to be sure, but he had been trained to deal with nothing less.

The weather was nightmarish, and the great black ship under them rocked with each wave that crashed along the hull. Donaie had sought the storm in an effort to teach him what it meant to fight on the deck in a turbulent sea, and she had done very well at finding what she searched for. He had a deep desire to vomit, but that didn't matter. What mattered was staying alive when a madwoman was trying to kill him.

She offered no quarter. None was expected.

The blade that hit his arm turned just enough to avoid cutting muscles and sinew. The flat of the blade slapped hard and the edge sliced through his skin easily. He stepped in closer and drove his elbow into her ribs with enough force to stagger the king, and all around them sailors cheered and jeered as they watched the combat.

Donaie Swarl fell back as he pushed into her, and her knee tried to crush his privates. He managed to block the blow, but barely, and in the process she struck with her dagger, shaving skin from his ear.

He grunted and then tossed his sword at her face. While she was knocking the weapon aside he struck a hard blow to her sternum, pulling back from what would have been a killing strike at the last possible second. The impact was enough to send her staggering backward and he moved in closer, striking again before she could recover herself.

He'd have celebrated the blow if he could have, but somehow, he found himself on his back, on the wet deck of the ship, just as a wave washed over and smashed into him hard enough to roll his entire body sideways.

Donaie held up her hands. "Enough."

Andover coughed half a wave of ocean water from his mouths and shook his head. He was winded, sore, wounded and exhausted and he loved every second of it. The Sa'ba Taalor around them sounded their approval, and as Andover rose again, Donaie Swarl came closer and thumped him on his chest with one callused fist.

"That was invigorating!" She smiled, and he smiled back. Had he fought that hard in Fellein, they'd have called him a monster. Here, among the People of The Forges, it was just another practice session.

Another wave rolled over the side of the ship and slopped across the deck, washing detritus away and staggering Andover. No one else seemed the least affected by the water. They were used to the worst the seas had to offer. Andover was still a novice. There were children on the ship who did a better job of standing against the waves.

Donaie put a companionable arm on his shoulder and slowly slid it down towards his elbow, her fingers trailing over his bicep. Andover sighed, and stood carefully as the ship swayed under him. He feared he would never get used to the motion. Still, he would do his best to adapt.

"Where are we going, Donaie?"

"Where the seas take us. Where Wheklam commands. We gather the fleet to the east, on the far side of the land. Near Elda."

Andover nodded. He had been to the mountain before, but not since it had relocated to Fellein. It would be a long trip, as he understood it, though he had never been that far from his place of birth.

The vast black ship rolled with another massive wave and then abruptly settled. The change was so strong that everyone on the ship was thrown off balance by the sudden transition from rocking back and forth to motionless. The waves that had been throwing the ship so easily were gone as if they had never existed.

Andover looked to the seas and found the waters nearly as smooth as a still pond. He frowned at the concept. Though he had never been much of one for traveling to the ocean, he had seen rivers, lakes and the vast waters, and never truly seen them calm.

"What is this?"

Donaie Swarl, who had lived at least as much of her life on the waters as she had on the land, shook her head. "I would call it impossible if I were not experiencing it." She stared at the waters and moved to the edge of the ship, looking down at the calm sea. "Wheklam did not cause this."

"There are other gods."

She nodded. "Yes, there are." She agreed, but he suspected she did so only because she felt obligated. The Sa'ba Taalor seldom acknowledged the other gods of the world; or if they did, it was grudgingly.

A dozen commands came from the King in Lead and the crew of her ship began hoisting sails and preparing. The waves were unsettlingly calm, but the winds had not faded away. In short order the ship was sailing into a heavy fog, pushed along by a favorable breeze.

Andover was capable of following the orders given and did his part, though he had never truly been trained on a ship. When they were under way he started below decks. It was not long before Donaie found him and ushered him into her cabin. He was inexperienced in many things, it was true, but he was not a fool.

While Andover and Donaie were otherwise occupied, the

source of the sudden calm on the seas slipped past the great black ship, lost in the heavy fog.

Jeron

He held the short staff in his hands and contemplated it. The wood was dark. The details on the serpents carved into the walking stick varied from shape to shape, but in all cases were superior craftsmanship. The oil from countless hours of handling had worked its way into the wood over time, and even without benefit of a sanding and oiling session, the wood was smooth and polished.

It was almost enough to make Jeron regret killing the Inquisitor when he was caught out on the streets of Goltha.

There were many rumors about the Inquisitors that he found interesting, but one of the greatest was that the seat of their power came in the form of their walking sticks. Not quite true, of course, but there was an element of truth in the words.

He was a necromancer, he could feel the power in the stick, could feel the portions of souls used as the source of that power. Desh Krohan had long since showed him how to take his own power and store a fraction of it at a time in carved stones. He expected what the Inquisitors did was similar. A little portion of the energies available, locked away for later use.

The difference was simply that this was like benevolent necromancy. Not a single life force stolen, but tiny fragments of a hundred or more lives, caught in wood and held until needed.

Sorcerers used stone because it could hold the power. The Inquisitors used wood, which he'd have thought would be ruined by the power. How strange that they had managed what the wizards could not.

Jeron's hands moved over the wood, seeking to understand what made the staff a useful tool for the Inquisitors and not the sorcerers. He had only minimal success, and that bothered him.

Roledru watched him skeptically, but was wise enough not to comment. The man's discretion was admirable.

They were currently sitting in Jeron's tent, which was off limits to everyone else. Well over a thousand mercenaries were with them now, and more trickling in every day. It was inevitable that at some time in the near future, Desh Krohan and his fellow sorcerers would learn Jeron was alive. When that happened, his descent into necromancy and his connection with the Overlords would become common knowledge.

He was not pleased by the notion. He'd rather enjoyed being believed dead. It made his experiments into the forbidden sorcery much easier. There was little he feared in the world; Desh Krohan was one of the exceptions, and if he were being truthful, there were a few other sorcerers he had concerns about, like the Sisters and Corin.

He had one advantage. He had the Overlords, and if he could work out the secrets of the damned stick in his hands, he'd have a second advantage, power to charge his abilities. Magic always came with a price, and if he could find a different method of paying that price, he would indeed be a source to contend with.

"You have that look on your face. You are considering the wizards."' Roledru was sharpening his long knife.

"Yes, of course I am. They'll soon be considering me."

"Can you not continue to hide from them?"

"There is already a strong chance that they will not recognize me, Roledru. I have changed a great deal."

"This is true." The man nodded and pulled his hair back, tying it in place with a strip of leather. "You do not look at all the same."

"I do not look human." He marveled at that. His body had changed so very much, become something he had never expected. When he was away from his tent, the robes covered him completely. There was no way he could allow himself to be seen without them and not expect a reaction from the very people he paid to follow him. His form had never been seen before, or if it had, not in a very long time.

Roledru did not seem bothered, but he was the exception. He had watched the changes taking place.

"You have not looked human for some time, Jeron."

"Yes, but I am less human now, I think."

Roledru looked at him critically, and then nodded. Then he went back to sharpening his knives.

Jeron contemplated the staff again and moved his thumbs over the wood.

Roledru grinned ruefully and shook his head. "It's wood. Not a mystery for the ages."

"How would you know what I'm considering?"

"Because you mumble when you think, and I am fluent in mumbling."

"I mumble, do I? What was I mumbling about?"

"The difference between a sorcerer and an Inquisitor. The difference between stone and wood."

"I shall have to be more careful what I say in the future."

"As you will, I suppose. But it's still just wood."

"Wood is not supposed to hold sorcery."

"It doesn't hold sorcery, Jeron. It holds life. Wood holds

life when it grows from the ground, yes? Why should it be different now?"

"You are remarkably observant, Roledru."

"No. I am simply not as foolish as you think I am."

Jeron laughed and moved his head in something between a shake and a nod.

"Why are you so worried about the wood?"

"Because it holds something I want."

"You want the life force held within it."

"Yes, of course."

"So just take it, like you did from the people."

"That might destroy the staff."

Roledru nodded. "And did you want to save it for later? Use it if you grow feeble and need a staff?"

"Well, no."

"You killed every person you took life from, Jeron. Why are you worried about a stick?"

"And that's precisely why I keep you around, Roledru. You always get to the heart of the matter." It only took a few words to pull the life from the staff, the same incantation used to open a passage from the body to the spirit. The same markings in the wood worked as surely as they did on flesh, and soon the collected power within the walking stick was entering Jeron's body, pouring into him as easily as wine pours into a goblet.

So much power! Jeron shivered as the energies flowed from the walking stick, as the wood grew pale, decayed and destroyed by the power that was drawn from it. He knew from experience that the exact same power ripped from a person left that person screaming, whether they were dead or alive.

Was there a way to measure the power? He was not

certain, but he suspected it was no less than the life force of a dozen men he drew into himself. It was more than one human form could hold, but not more than his new shape could contain. Not more than one of the Overlords could capture within themselves.

Roledru studied him as the power flowed into his body, filling him, satisfying him in ways he didn't know could happen.

The man did not speak, he merely watched.

When Jeron was done draining the walking stick, the wood he had so admired was ruined. What had been a thing of beauty was no more. Instead, he held little more than flinders, which he let fall from his fingers and collapse on the ground.

"You see?" Roledru shrugged. "Just wood."

Jeron nodded. "You were right, my friend."

Roledru nodded and resheathed his knife after wiping the blade clean. "You keep all of this for yourself? Or do you share with the ones below?"

It was a powerful temptation.

Still, "I suppose a wise man would share it."

"If one is to have gods, one must make sacrifices, yes?"

Jeron sighed and rose from his seat. "Indeed, and these days I have gods."

Roledru said nothing, but he nodded his head and watched as Jeron moved from the tent, pausing long enough to grab his robes and drape them over his shoulders and head.

The trek down the long, curving slope that led to the Overlords was uneventful, save for the thoughts that filled his head. Calculations and considerations took most of his time, and thoughts of what came next took the rest. There were situations to consider. The army he'd amassed was of fair size, but hardly more than a defensive force if he were to be honest. The biggest advantage he had for now was anonymity, and by all of his calculations, that would be gone soon. Merros Dulver and a force of a hundred of his best were on their way, and they'd soon see that an army was amassing.

An army. He laughed at the notion. The Overlords were powerful, he knew that, but his army was small, far smaller than he wanted to think about. Less than two thousand soldiers, all told, and most were mercenaries of dubious skill.

Something had to be done. A change had to be made, or surely the Overlords and their servants would be finished in short order.

What he needed was more than he had, and likely more than he could accomplish on his own. There was simply no denying that any longer. To be sure, his soldiers could take on General Dulver and his lot, could handle them easily enough. There were well over ten to one odds in his favor, but even if he killed every last one of them, there would be tens of thousands more waiting to be called forward. If nothing else, the war with the Sa'ba Taalor had increased the size of Fellein's Imperial Army.

He was still considering that fact when he entered the great chamber of the Overlords.

He felt them as soon as he entered the chamber. He had sensed them before, of course, the Overlords and their growing power, but this? This was a different thing altogether.

What he felt now was the difference between the breeze before a storm and the full undaunted rage of a hurricane.

Jeron stopped and spread his arms far and wide, basking in the presence of the Overlords.

"You have awakened, my masters!" His smile was broad enough to actually hurt his face. "You are awake!"

"We are awake," the voice confirmed. "And we hunger."

For the moment that was enough.

Jeron was grateful for Roledru's counsel. The Overlords were hungry and he had the sustenance they demanded.

Desh Krohan

The books were spread out across his offices, with manuscripts, scrolls and a seemingly endless array of notes in his own tight scrawl, ranging from new messages to notes he'd made hundreds of years ago and kept for whatever possible reason. Sometimes, often really, he was his own worst enemy.

There was information there, if he could find it. He didn't have all of the knowledge of the world, the gods knew, but he had some, and buried in the books and tomes there was information about the Overlords. There simply had to be, hadn't there? He had always been meticulous to a fault. It was one of his better failings in life. He needed to find all that he could and, while the Sisters were very useful, some things he had to do himself. Still, his eyes ached from reading and his head pounded with a dull, painful cadence.

One passage held his attention:

The Overlords are not human. They are not, I suspect, of this world. Be they gods, demons or something altogether different, the closest I can find as a comparison is an insect. They are not in human form. They have never been human. They are as far removed from man as man is from a fish. There are bones in their bodies, but they resemble nothing I've seen before. The powers they can summon are not known to me. They have called the dead to a parody of life. They have peeled the powers from my predecessors as easily as a sail captures the wind, and left the sorcerers before me dead or worse in every encounter. I'm only alive because I ran when the opportunity presented itself to me.

Abrantsis is dead. Olento is dead. Great Phinney is dead, killed with ease by the Overlords. We have summoned armies to fight them and watched armies fall before them. The gods are silent in the face of the Overlords, though they have been silent for some time, near as I can figure. The Revelent are defeated, destroyed where they stood, their faith as useless to them as their armor. The bones of the Revelent are scattered, broken and made as dust before the servants of the Overlords. Hundreds of the finest warriors of Felayne, crushed and killed as if they were toddlers before Knights Imperial.

I fear even the greatest sorceries of our age are useless before their magics. These Overlords use powers we have never encountered before, and they do so without the great draining effects of our own magics. I fear the worst. I dread the worst. We may well have found a power that is simply too great to counter.

He read the passage again and shook his head.

All had seemed lost, for certain, and somehow they had prevailed against the Overlords once, but he could not understand exactly how. What had been different? What had changed when Fellein was at the edge and ready to fall?

He had no idea.

The smallest of sounds, just exactly enough to catch his attention, and Desh turned toward the doors to his chamber.

Swech stood at the entrance to his private offices, standing before the closed doors.

"How did you get in here?"

"I opened the doors and walked in."

"The doors were closed."

"Yes. That's why I opened them."

"Yes, but how did you open them?"

"Carefully. You are a wizard. I do not know what you are capable of."

Desh raised one eyebrow. "Well, for one thing, when I close a door it tends to stay closed."

"Yes. Well done. The door was closed when I approached it, and I had to turn the latch."

"I don't think you're understanding. I had the door closed and sealed against entry."

"No. There was no seal."

Desh closed his eyes and slowly counted to ten. It was a trick that was supposed to help with frustrating thoughts. It wasn't working.

"How may I assist you?"

"Paedle has asked me to answer you."

"I beg your pardon?"

"You have questions about the ones you call the Overlords. I have been asked to answer your questions."

For a moment he considered asking how she knew he had questions, and then he paid attention to what she had said. A god had sent her to answer his questions.

"I'm puzzling out how we defeated them before."

Swech looked him in the eyes. "You did not. The Daxar Taalor called upon the Sa'ba Taalor to fight the forces of the Overlords. The Daxar Taalor fought the Overlords on their own and beat them into a deep sleep."

The stories of the faithful often reflected tales of gods fighting on their behalf. He'd have considered the claims ludicrous had he been able to recall any methods he used that had helped drive the Overlords and their followers back. Despite his hours of research and the help of the Sisters, there was nothing he'd found that explained how the Overlords had been stopped.

"Why didn't they kill the Overlords?"

"They are gods, but at that time they were weakened from fighting the gods of your Fellein."

"So, they were too weak to finish what they started?"

"No. The Daxar Taalor were still engaged in combat with the gods of Fellein when the Overlords came into the war. They were not strong enough to kill the gods of Fellein and the Overlords at the same time. So they satisfied themselves with beating both groups and allowing them to retreat."

"Are you saying that your gods defeated the Overlords and the gods of Fellein?"

"Yes. That is correct."

"Well, that seems rather bold."

Swech smiled. "Gods are bold by their nature."

"I suppose there's some truth to that notion."

"I follow gods of war. If there are subtle gods, they are not among those I follow, not when it comes to politics."

"There are too many gods, Swech. I couldn't hope to keep them all separate."

"I only follow seven of them. I do not concern myself with the rest."

"Probably a wise decision on your part." He sighed and moved ahead. "How did your gods defeat the Overlords?"

"I could not describe the battle as it happened. I only know that it did. The Daxar Taalor won. The Overlords did not. Your gods did not."

"They're not my gods. I choose not to have any."

"That will not go well for you."

"It's done me well so far."

Swech shook her head. "You take these situations for granted."

"I haven't got time for gods. I have other concerns."

"Ask what questions you would of Paedle."

"Can we stop the Overlords from waking?"

"No. They are awake now. They are regaining their power."

"Can we defeat the Overlords?"

"They can be defeated. They were before."

"How did the Sa'ba Taalor defeat the servants of the Overlords before?"

"With swords and steel."

"How did the Daxar Taalor defeat the Overlords?"

"With unexpected brute force."

"Will they fight the Overlords again?"

"It is very likely, I cannot say for certain because the Daxar Taalor have not decided as yet."

"What will make them decide?"

"The faith of their followers. They are uncertain what is happening with the Godless."

"Who are the Godless?"

"They are the Sa'ba Taalor who have not yet returned to the gods. They remain an uncertain aspect."

"And how does that change things for the Daxar Taalor?"

"How does faith affect the gods?" Swech shrugged her shoulders and moved closer. "How does your lack of faith affect your gods, Desh Krohan?"

"I've never given it any thought."

"The gods have never considered the Sa'ba Taalor without faith. It is impossible to say how the faithless will change the way that gods consider their world."

"I fear we have moved away from the question at hand."

Swech tilted her head to the left and then shook it, "We have not. Gods react to faith as people react to the air we breathe, the water we drink and the food we eat." Her hands spread out before her and her fingers waggled. "What we need and what we have are not the same things, not for people or gods."

"So the gods are waiting on the decisions of the Godless?"

"It is not for me to say what the gods wait on."

"You are frustratingly vague."

"The gods would, perhaps, say the same of you, sorcerer."

"What can your gods say that will help the current situation?"

"We are too late to stop the Overlords from rising. We are not too late to defeat them, but it will take great efforts on the parts of the Sa'ba Taalor, the Fellein, and the gods themselves."

"And what happens with your Godless?"

"They will face the judgement of the gods."

"That hardly tells me anything."

Swech smiled again and stepped closer. Desh resisted the urge to panic. If she wanted him dead, he suspected she could have entered his room without him knowing, a thought that offered no comfort at all.

"Are gods not notoriously vague? Like your Sooth?"

"The Sooth are as honest as they know how to be. They do not see the world as we see it."

"And you think the gods do?"

He had no answer to that.

"We are as children to the gods," Swech said. "We are as infants. They explain what they can, but we are not ready for their explanations, I think. We are too young, and do not live long enough gain their wisdom."

"I've lived over a thousand years, Swech."

"Then, perhaps, you should speak to the gods yourself."

"I've yet to figure out how to speak with gods. I am always given an intermediary."

"You see? If you had my faith, the gods would speak to you directly, as they do to me."

"And how does one simply find this faith?"

"It is not simple and it is not found. It is sought throughout a lifetime, sorcerer. You have sought the answers to the universe in your books. I have sought the same information from my gods."

"And have they taught you sorcery?"

"No. But I have not asked to understand sorcery. I have asked to understand combat and war."

"Well, there are gods of war and combat. I have yet to find a god of sorcery."

"Perhaps you have simply not asked the right questions."

"And can your gods understand sorcery?"

"Can you use sorcery to win a war?"

"Of course."

Swech moved closer still. "Then at least one of my gods understands sorcery."

"Which one?"

"If I were to choose only one god who would understand sorcery, I would choose Ydramil, the god of reflection and contemplation." She tilted her head. "Yes, Ydramil."

"And is Ydramil a god I could speak to?"

"If he deems you worthy, yes."

Desh Krohan crossed his arms. "And how would I know if he deems me worthy?"

"You could ask him."

"And how would I do that?"

"How do you ask anyone for anything?" With that she turned on her heel and walked toward the doors of his chamber. "He chooses to be the god of reflection. His chosen metal is silver. Find a silver surface, and reflect."

A moment later she was gone from his chambers, and Desh Krohan was left to consider her words and to reflect on their conversation.

Kallir Lundt

The gods spoke to Kallir Lundt. He woke in his bed, very abruptly, and faced the window in his chambers.

IT IS TIME, KALLIR LUNDT. FIND YOUR KING AND SERVE HIM AS YOU WOULD SERVE ME. The voice was that of Truska-Pren and not to be denied. Kallir rose from his bed and dressed quickly in the darkness of the predawn light. Within ten minutes he was heading for the king's throne room. There were others heading for the same destination, and in all cases they looked as alert as he felt. When gods speak, it is best to listen.

Tarag Paedori stood before the iron throne, the walls behind him glowing a dull red as the heat of the great forge burned and pulsed, and waited with surprising patience. In short order that room was filled to capacity, and still more people came to listen.

"The enemies of old have come back to us." Tarag's voice carried easily and the followers of Truska-Pren listened in silence. "The Nual-Moresh waken and they are ready for war!"

The words were spoken as a call for celebration. The Sa'ba Taalor longed for war, longed to celebrate the violence and bloodshed that would honor their gods. Throughout the vast chambers, the people around Kallir cheered and roared their approval.

"Gather your armor! Prepare yourselves for battle!" Tarag raised his arms high above his head, holding the great sword he'd forged himself. The metal gleamed and reflected the red light of the iron forge.

"There will be no mercy! There will be no forgiveness! The deathless would see us fall and would strike down our gods! Let them know us! Let them fear us! We will ride with the first light of the dawn!"

Kallir's blood sang! His heart thudded harshly in his chest, ready for the combat that would bring joy to the gods themselves.

There had been a time when the thought of combat sent shivers through him, but that time was long past. The gods wanted blood to flow and if it was his blood or that of his enemies, Kallir would gladly give them their offerings.

A single look at Desta and she nodded her head. She would ride with him into combat.

The sun was rising by the time the forces of the King in Iron started moving, riding into the great wall of storm that surrounded Truska-Pren's mountain. Kallir was near the front of the line, riding to the left of his king.

Tarag Paedori's face was hidden behind a mask of iron. Kallir's face was not hidden but shone with the same dark colors.

Morten Dunraven

Tuskandru looked down his mountain with a strange expression, and Morten found himself wondering if he had offended the man in some way. It wasn't a comfortable thought. If he was being perfectly honest, the notion terrified him.

"Your horses, are they ready for battle?"

"They're well-trained, your majesty, but your people are not so prepared."

The man nodded, and his face broke into a strange smile. "The gods call for war this day!"

"Against Fellein?" He had a sudden image of the massive brute reaching out and pulling his head clear from his body. There was nothing comforting about that notion, not in the least.

"No. We are not at war with Fellein, not now. We must ride against the Deathless."

"Who are the Deathless?"

"Our enemies!" Tuskandru slapped him on the shoulder and sent him stumbling for a moment. Then the man looked his way and asked again, "Can your horses ride into war?"

"Yes, of course. They're trained for combat, but they need seasoned riders."

"You have four trainers. They will teach us as we ride!"

"I don't think this will go the way you want it to, your highness."

"I want my people to ride your horses. If they fall from the animals they are not learning well."

"It's not that easy. There are signals they must learn. Ways to ride."

"Teach them as we go!" He called out to another of his people and the man lifted a bone horn and blew a sharp note that carried up and down the mountainside. The people around them cheered, and Morten looked up and down that very mountain as he saw the Sa'ba Taalor begin moving.

The great beasts that some of the gray skins rode moved, called by the horn or some other means. The animals found particular people and joined with them. The riders climbed aboard the vast saddles on the large beasts, and in short order they were lining up.

Morten looked at the horses and shook his head. There was simply no way that this could work.

And yet, even as he thought that, the Sa'ba Taalor gathered, hundreds of them, closing in on the corrals that they'd built to hold the horses. Tuskandru's second came closer, placing her horned helmet on her head.

"You will ride with us into combat. It is a great honor."

"I'm not ready for war." He shook his head.

"You will ride with us. You do not have to fight, but you need to lead the riders on their new horses." Her tone made it clear that she was speaking to someone who was not very bright. He'd have considered taking offense but was afraid that all of the damned gray skins might take offense as well. There was no simple way out of the situation.

"I don't think they can keep up with you, Stathsha. They've never ridden a horse before, not a one of them. They'll fall off and break their necks."

"Do this thing, and whatever you ask, Tusk will grant it to you. You will have the gratitude of a king."

He thought for all of two seconds. "I'll do what I can. I make no promises."

"That is enough for now." She turned her mount. "Show them how to climb on the horses and then follow me."

What else could he hope to do? He nodded and called out to his trainers and the others who'd ridden with him, speaking in the common tongue. "We do our best to show them how to climb on a horse and then how to ride one."

"And if they kill themselves?" It was Erig who asked.

"Then they die."

"Fair enough."

There were no deaths, but more than a few fell from the horses on their first attempt.

CHAPTER FIFTEEN

Jeron

The Godless came free from the shadows.

The servants came free from the shadows.

None of them came forward unchanged.

Trigan Garth was darker than before, as if the shadows had stained his skin. His eyes were no longer silver, but burned with just as intense a light. A smoking darkness drifted from his skin as if the shadows burned him and dragged themselves after him.

"You are alive, Trigan Garth."

"Yes." The man's voice was a hiss. He sensed the anger that seethed just beneath the calm exterior of the Godless. "I live, but I am no longer what I was. You have forced a change on me, Jeron of Fellein, and I am not well."

"It was the will of the Overlords."

"It was deception." Those odd, yellow eyes glared their hatred toward him and Jeron nodded.

"It was a necessity. The Overlords are not to be denied."

"I served you, Jeron, not your Overlords."

Jeron looked away, not concerned about being attacked. No one could resist the Overlords, and certainly not a barbarian fighter. Trigan would serve.

"The world is more complex than you think, Trigan Garth." He walked from the chambers and the reborn followed him, remade in the image of their masters. "You will come to appreciate the changes made to you as I have come to appreciate my transformation. Now is the time of our ascent. The one we've waited on has arrived."

To prove his point, he called on the power of his new gods, and showed the world what they could do.

Whistler

The voices very nearly deafened him as he climbed the hill. There was no longer a consideration of his place among the people he traveled with, only of the voices.

For a while, Whistler thought he was being called to be a mercenary, but no, the strangers traveling with him didn't seem to be called in the same direction. They moved up the hill and to a single tent that waited there. He felt no calling to head in that direction, and when he tried the voices screamed.

Instead he climbed beyond them to the very top of the hill and he stood on a stone etched with ancient markings that rested at the apex.

When he settled himself on that spot, the voices calmed down.

"I'm here," he said, expecting no response.

The voices stopped.

It was the closest he'd been to true peace in a very long time.

He should have known it would never last.

Merros Dulver

He wanted to like the Inquisitor, but it wasn't easy. For one thing, the man performed dark sorceries – necromancy, no less. For another, he was always smiling, and his smile could best be described as enigmatic.

Darsken Murdro nodded. "You have mentioned this, yes."

The Inquisitor adjusted his hat and looked at the looming hill before them. It was a largish hill and it had not been there when last either of the men had traveled the area. That was the very situation they were discussing. The hill shouldn't have been there.

"This is where you fed the Overlords to keep them asleep?"

"It is, yes." He sighed, "There was no hill."

"Hills do not grow on their own."

"Not in my experience, no, they don't." Darsken shook his head and then shrugged. "I am not a sorcerer. I don't know the limits of their powers."

"I rather wish Desh Krohan or one of his Sisters was here."

"You brought a sorcerer with you."

"Yes, but I prefer to deal with someone I know."

"You've had several days to get to know her better."

Merros looked over his shoulder and stared at the adept. "That's a woman?"

"Yes."

"Are you absolutely certain?"

"I am."

"This is awkward. I've called her 'sir' no less than five times."

Darsken Murdro laughed and put a hand over his mouth to try to stifle the sounds. "This is only awkward for you. I am merely amused."

He liked the man much more at that moment.

When the ground started shaking, he was unprepared for it. Merros was a soldier; he was prepared for swords, for combat, even for the occasional army, but not for earthquakes. His horse felt the same way and started dancing impatiently the very moment the ground began shaking under them.

The hill they were staring at shook, and Merros scowled, worried that it might do something even more unexpected. He hadn't been prepared for it to be there in the first place, despite the news he'd received from the Sisters.

Also, there were mercenaries in the area. He'd heard several reports of them, though for the life of him he couldn't imagine where they were hiding. There was a single tent on the side of the hill. Surely they weren't hiding in there.

The horse under him bolted, and Merros had no choice but to either hold on for dear life or fall on his posterior. He managed to hold on. Ahead of him, the Inquisitor fell from his horse and rolled quickly to his left as the animal he'd been riding ran away from the hillside. Several of the cavalry with him fell from their horses too. Others had already dismounted and were saved from the Inquisitor's fate.

Moments later, the horse beneath him was running as fast as he'd ever seen an animal move, and Merros was grateful to the beast.

The ground split behind him and lifted higher into the air, pushing, straining toward the skies above. Slabs of stone broke through the rough soil, grinding toward each other, shattering into the hill and pushing, thrusting upward as the ground split and roared and made way for more stones.

Merros rode for all he was worth, keeping his seat despite the vibrations shaking the world around him. The damnable horse ran, and he rode, and prayed to gods he barely believed in.

And behind him the world continued to rage, the earth rose and crushed and rose again, splitting, falling away and then crashing together in defiance of all common sense. The world roared and changed and there was nothing he could do to stop it, and so he rode and wished, despite himself, that Desh Krohan was there to force reality to make sense again.

The horse danced and panicked, and Merros was forced to dismount.

From the ground the great mountain rose, forced itself into the world, was birthed by the flat lands of the steppes. How long it took he could not have said, how long he and the horse charged away he could not have expressed.

A mountain rose, and when it was done he could no longer see the steppes for the sheer size of the newly risen edifice.

Merros Dulver stared long and hard at the great form, and wept in confusion, for no mountain should ever rise from the ground so suddenly, and the last time he'd seen a mountain rise it had signaled the rising of a war god.

"What is this then?" He screamed the words, was barely aware that he spoke.

In response the mountain roared, and from its crest a great cloud of black smoke erupted amidst a towering pillar of flame.

Merros Dulver was a general and a soldier. He did not understand in that moment that the world had changed, but he would come to understand it all too soon.

He'd soon understand that the Overlords had awakened and that they were very, very angry.

EPILOGUES

Whistler

The very ground beneath him boiled.

Whistler stepped back as the earth around him shook, collapsed and burned.

He kept his balance and retreated from the hole that split and swallowed the rock he stood on. He retreated and avoided what seemed a certain fall to death.

He had lived long enough to know when danger was trying to pull him in, and he'd lived long enough to understand that where he was couldn't get much deadlier. The air roared, and the ground continued to split, to open, a wound in the earth that bled noxious gasses and steam.

The world itself pushed upward in an angry fit. Whistler fell backward and stared in horror as the ground before him continued to open and the world behind him thrust toward the sky.

There would be no escape. He was young and he was strong, but next to the mountain rising from the ground he was also so very tiny. Might as well be an ant trying to escape a well-placed boot. Might as well be a tiny spider as its web was swept away by a broom.

The ground split beside him and bled steaming vapors.

That jet of heat lashed out at Whistler's face and burned him, seared his skin and peeled muscles aside with all the gentle kindness of a ravenous Pra-Moresh.

Whistler screamed as his face was destroyed. The air roared loud enough to muffle his screams, to silence his wails of agony, and Whistler fell back, his body captured by fingers of stone that caught him as easily as he might snap a leaf from a tree.

Oh, how he cried out, how he burned as the mountain held him, cradled him, even as it was born into the world, raised higher and higher into the air.

Whistler burned. His senses were overwhelmed by the superheated gasses that pushed into his face, boiled into his lungs, and should have, by all rights, killed him.

But, oh, the voices were singing now, a lullaby, a litany of joy and sorrow, of chances missed, and opportunities not yet explored.

He supposed he was ready to die. The pain was overwhelming, and even his eyes burned in his ruined face.

Dead. He should be dead or dying. He probably would have been if not for those voices that called to him, drew him back from the gathering darkness around him and sang away the endless agonies he knew he should be feeling.

The pain flowed away from him. He felt his flesh restored, though it hardly seemed to feel the same as before.

"Would you live this day?"

"Yes." What a foolish question. Who doesn't want to live?

"Would you serve us if we give you back your life?"

"Yes. Of course." What's one master over another, really, and surely everyone serves someone.

"Think carefully." The voices spoke his true name, the name he was born with, the one he never spoke, because

he'd heard once that names have power. Some people, it seemed, would learn those names in any event. *"If you vow to serve us, it will be forever."*

"I serve you and I live. If I don't serve you, I die, is that correct?"

"Yes." He sensed anticipation from the voices, as if this moment was one they'd waited for, for a very long time. That made no sense to him. He was not that old, and the feeling he got was that they'd waited centuries, perhaps longer.

"I'd rather not die. I'll serve you."

"There will be a cost."

"There's always a cost. There's a cost if I serve you, too. Life alone isn't enough." Everyone always wanted to negotiate.

Around him the mountain exploded. Fiery molten stone vomited forth from the throat of the mountain and black ash belched into the skies and rolled down the side of the mountain like an avalanche of snow. The lava flowed past him, the smoke moved away from him like cobwebs caught on tree branches.

"What else would you have from us?"

He considered that very carefully while flames and smoke moved around him in his sheltering stone grip.

And then he answered.

And the voices agreed.

And so he was changed forever.

Tuskandru

Tuskandru's armies stopped when they saw the mountain rising from the ground. The world shook and the air burned and the horses reared and threw many of the riders. Most got back to their feet. A few lay broken on the rugged ground.

From almost exactly the opposite direction, Tarag Paedori's armies also slowed and stopped, watching as the mountain rose, pushed forth by the gods alone knew what. They were not afraid, the people of the forges, for they understood the way mountains grew when pushed. They knew the ways of the earth and easily comprehended the raw tectonic power needed to birth a fresh mountain in the world.

They were not afraid, but they could respect the new power that rose in the Wellish Steppes that day.

Two kings and their armies watched as dark stone pushed forth, ripping at the ground, stabbing at the skies and weeping molten earth. Birth is seldom an easy thing.

Seven times in recent years the world had given birth to new mountains, and on each of those occasions the Sa'ba Taalor had celebrated the events as a joyous occasion.

This time was different. This was no cause for celebration. This was a bastard born, an unwanted child forced upon the land.

Still there was cause for happiness. This child brought with it the possibility of war, and for the people of the forges, that was always a wondrous event.

The vessel was small and it only carried four figures with it, each as different from the next as stones washed upon a shoreline.

The first was a woman with blonde hair and blue eyes. In her time, she had caught the eye of more than one young man, though that had never been her intention. She was far more interested in learning the secrets that the world and the stars had to offer, and to that end she had even studied sorcery once upon a time.

The next was a lean young man, sure of foot and quick to smile, though seldom heard to speak. He was swarthy, with dark hair and dark stubble that grew back almost as quickly as he shaved it. His hair was kept short, and though he was younger even than the woman, his hair was shot through with grey.

The great predatory beast that was third of the four was the mount of the last traveler. Dark fur and bright eyes, massive claws and teeth as long as daggers, the beast was more than it seemed and remained calm as the waves moved around the boat. Its great mane whipped in the wind and its tail lashed slowly side to side.

The last was a man with grey skin, dark hair, and seven mouths, each a slash across the healed wound that had once been a larger mouth, now sealed shut. His left arm was not gray but instead was silver, a smooth metallic hide that looked flawless, save for several scars.

In his time, Drask Silver Hand had been many things and followed many leaders. He was loyal to gods and kings alike, at least when the mood struck him.

He looked upon the continent of Fellein and the distant volcanic island where Wheklam rose from the sea, and to his north lay Durhallem, the Forge of the Wounder, who was as unforgiving as any steel blade had ever been.

For five years they had traveled, seeking answers in distant places, from different people and sources. In some ways it hardly seemed a week they'd been gone. In other ways it seemed a lifetime.

ABOUT THE AUTHOR

JAMES A MOORE is the award-winning, bestselling author of over forty novels, thrillers, dark fantasy and horror alike, including the critically acclaimed *Fireworks, Under the Overtree, Blood Red,* the Serenity Falls trilogy and the Seven Forges series.

Fancy some more James A Moore?
Take a look at another series, The Tides of War, starting with The Last Sacrifice

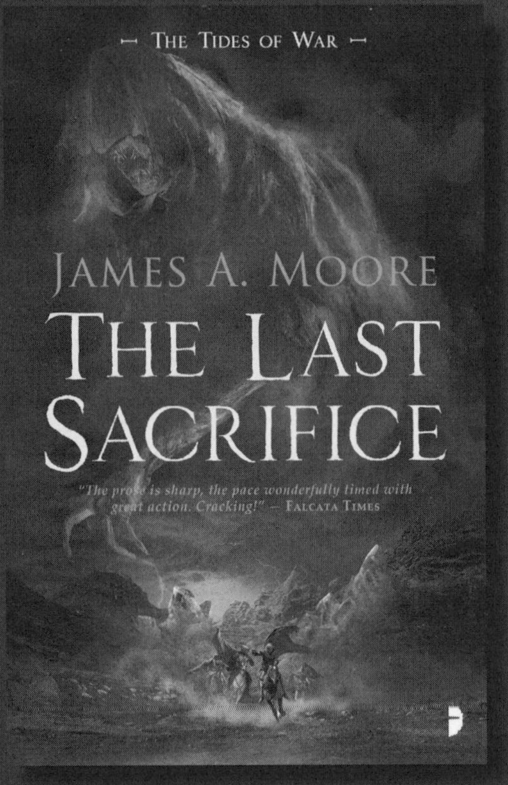

Read the first chapter here!

CHAPTER ONE
Four Coins

Home.

Was there ever a finer word?

Brogan McTyre and his cohorts had spent the last eight weeks riding along the Hollum trails and the plains of Arthorne, serving as guards and guides alike to the merchant trains. It was hard work, and it was unfulfilling, but it put enough coin in their purses to keep them through the worst of the winters.

Now, after two months' travel, they were heading back to where they all wanted to be – except for Harper, who seemed perfectly content wherever he settled. Back to their homes.

The leaves had started their slow burn, and to counteract the oranges and yellows that imitated a hearth's fire, the air had grown cold, and frost covered the ground every morning.

That meant the air was chilled enough that every breath offered a gust of steam and every intake sapped just a touch of the internal heat.

Still, they were heading home.

The Broken Swords were behind them. According to the legends Brogan's father had told him when he was a lad, the collection of mountains hid the remains of old giants, and the gigantic spears of crystal that thrust from the earth and stone of the area were supposed to be fragments of the giants' swords.

He didn't believe the tales, but he remembered them fondly and had shared them with his own children more than once.

A smile crept across his face as Brogan thought of his little ones. Braghe was his pride, of course, a hearty lad who at only five years was already an adventurer and constantly getting into battles with whatever monsters his imagination could summon. His daughters, the twins, were as lovely as their mother and happily too young for him to worry yet about the sort of lads who thought as he had before he married. Leidhe and Sherla were eight, and their hair was spun from the same fire as his. They had his locks and their mother's looks. A combination that would doubtless cause him plenty of grief, as they became young women. Also like their mother, they were fighters. When they weren't trying to be prim and proper they were out fighting imaginary beasties with Braghe.

Much to their mother's chagrin, they were seldom prim and proper.

His smile grew broader as he thought of their mother. Nora was reason enough to come home and the thought of being with her again took a great deal of chill from the morning.

"You're thinking of your woman again, aren't you?" Harper's voice cut through his thoughts and he looked toward his lifelong friend. Harper was the only man he knew who looked as comfortable on a saddle as he did on the ground. There was something of a cat about the man. He seemed perfectly relaxed all the time, until you looked at his eyes. They were constantly moving, roaming even when his body seemed incapable of doing more than stretching lazily.

"Why do you say that?" The thing with having Harper as a friend was you never knew when he was going to tease ruthlessly or try to provoke a fight. He looked perpetually calm – but that meant nothing.

"Because you've got that dreamy smile on your face again. You only ever get that smile when you've just been laid or when you're thinking about Nora."

"How would you know how I look when I've just had sex?"

"Because I've seen you *after* you get home to Nora as well as when you're thinking about getting home to her."

Brogan shook his head and smiled. If nothing else he could always trust Harper to observe the world around him very well.

"What are your plans for the winter, Harper?"

"I'll be finding a place to stay and a woman to keep me warm, I suppose."

That was always Harper's plan for the future. It was as reliable an answer as could be found in the Five Kingdoms.

Up ahead of them Mosely was rounding the final curve in the road leading to Kinnett. Not far from him stood Volkner, who owned the homestead nearest Brogan's.

The look on Volkner's face when he saw Brogan was enough to cause panic to set in.

Brogan urged his horse forward and kept his eyes locked on his neighbor, a dread sinking into his stomach that was deep and abiding.

Mosely looked back over his shoulder as Brogan rode forward.

Volkner's dark eyes were wide and filled with sorrow. "Brogan, lad, I'm so very sorry. We've been trying to reach you. I sent Tamra to find which path you were on. He must have chosen badly."

"What is it, Volkner?" His voice shook.

There are rules all people follow. Most of those rules are made by kings.

Volkner's hands were empty.

"There are coins, Brogan. At your door. Four of them."

"Coins?" Brogan frowned and shook his head. "What are you talking about?"

Volkner spoke again, carefully, with great emphasis, his eyes blinking wetly as he made sure Brogan was listening. *"Coins,* Brogan. There are *coins* at your doorstep. Four of them."

"No." Brogan could barely speak.

Harper came up from behind, his voice calm and cold. "Are you sure, Volkner?"

The older man looked to Harper and a faint contempt painted his broad features. "Oh, I've seen them before, Harper. Not as many as you, perhaps, but I've seen them."

Brogan's ears rang with a high, sweet note that tried to seal all other sounds away. "Have you looked in the house?"

"It's forbidden, Brogan. You know that." There was regret in the words.

"How long ago?" Harper again, asking the questions that Brogan would have asked if his heart wasn't trying to break.

Volkner shook his head and spread his arms in a gesture of his sadness and frustration. "Five days since, that I know of. I visited two days before that and all was well."

"Five days?"

The winter grew in Brogan's chest. Without another word, he drove his horse forward, brushing past all of them. The gelding charged hard and the familiar landscape nearly blurred but it was not fast enough.

His dismount was more of a leap than a proper climb from the saddle. Brogan only took five strides toward the door before he saw them.

He had heard of the coins before. Had seen one as a child, but only the one and he had never touched the thing.

That they were valuable was impossible to deny. Brogan

could see the weight of them where they lay on the ground in front of his home. They were large and heavy and worth far more than he'd made in the last few weeks of travel. He stepped over them and opened the door, calling out to Nora and each of his children as he entered.

It was a good place. He'd built it himself with the assistance of Harper and others. The people around him had helped as he had aided them when the time came. The town was good that way. He left Kinnett and knew that all was well with his wife and children, and that people as good and solid as Volkner were always there.

But the coins were different, weren't they?

No one answered his calls.

No one was home. He'd known they wouldn't be. There were four coins, one for each of his children and one for his wife.

When they came, when they took from a family, they always left one coin behind for each person they stole away.

One coin for each and every sacrifice.

"No."

He backed away from the door and shook his head, that feeling of dread growing more profound.

"No. No. No. Nonononononononono…"

The coins.

He looked to the ground again and saw them properly. Four coins. Just as Volkner had said.

Without thinking about the possibilities, he bent and touched them. They were weighty, to be sure. The largest gold coins he had ever seen or touched. The metal was as cold as the air, colder, perhaps, as he held them in his hands. They were marked with unfamiliar images and symbols.

As he held them, Harper dismounted and came toward him.

"Brogan…" Had he ever heard so much sorrow in his friend's voice before? No, surely not. Harper was not a man who held onto his grief. He was gifted that way. When his mother died as a child he'd cried for fifteen minutes then never again that Brogan knew of. When his father grew ill and withered five years later there were no tears at all.

"Harper." He could barely recognize his own voice. "You know the Grakhul. You've dealt with them."

"Aye." Harper did not turn away from him, did not flinch, but held his gaze. "What you would do, it's forbidden. You know this."

"Four of them, Harper? My entire family?"

"Brogan, it's the law in all Five Kingdoms. 'When the Grakhul offer coin it must be taken.'"

"My entire family, Harper." Brogan's voice was stronger now. Louder.

"Brogan."

"My entire family! How many do they take at a time?"

"Four. You know this, too."

The world did not grow gray, as he feared it might. It grew red.

"How long do they take to offer up their sacrifices?"

"How would I know that, Brogan?"

Part of Brogan knew Harper was trying to make him see reason. But where it mattered, Brogan did not care.

"Is there a chance that my Nora is still alive?"

Harper licked his lips. He looked as nervous as he ever had.

"There is a chance, yes, but it is slim." Harper held up his hand as Brogan started for his horse. "You don't know where they are, Brogan."

"No. I do not." He looked away from the gelding and toward his friend. "But you do."

"I cannot. You know this too."

"My entire family. All of them. Has that ever happened before?"

"No one knows how they make their choices." Harper shook his head as Brogan started walking again.

"Take me to them. Maybe I can make them change their minds."

He could see Harper wanting to argue again. He knew his friend well. They had fought side by side on a score of occasions and traveled together long enough that even if they had not grown together in the same town they'd have claimed fellowship.

"I have to try, Harper." His hands clenched into fists around the four cold, metal coins. They were of such a size that his fists could not completely close. "I have to."

Harper stood completely still for one more moment, then he sighed. "So let's go see if we can get your family back."

"I owe you."

"I've owed you for a lifetime." Harper shook his head and spat. He was not happy. There was nothing to be happy about.

Volkner was coming his way, his ambling stride leaving him swaying one way then the other. Brogan knew exactly how much the man ached inside for failing to stop Nora and the children from being taken.

"I am so sorry, Brogan."

"You could not have stopped them." It was all he could manage as a defense for his friend. It was the truth. No one could stop the Grakhul. They were called by many names, not the least of which was the Undying. Every story of anyone trying to prevent a family member from being taken ended poorly for the would-be saviors.

Brogan climbed back into the saddle and turned toward

the Broken Swords. The sun gleamed off the distant shards in a display of colors that was the envy of rainbows, and Brogan did not care in the least.

Somewhere beyond those mountains his family was being dragged to their deaths.

He would save them or he would die trying.

Niall Leraby walked through the woods and let himself commune with the world around him. Not far away he could hear the Weeping River living up to its name, the waters sighing and crying as they pattered over the crystalline rocks and worried their way past the thick roots from the garrah trees that leaned over the river as if to protect their young.

A dozen paces away a doe looked at him and froze, waiting to see what he would do. He nodded in her direction and ignored her otherwise. He loved a good cut of venison, but he wasn't here to hunt for meat. He was looking for the proper herbs to satisfy Mosara's needs. The master gardener was not a hard man to work for, but he expected nothing less than perfection in what was brought to him. Less than that, he often said, would lead to a person dying.

There were some gardeners who tended to the trees on an estate or two, and then there were gardeners like Mosara, who handled the landscape at the palace. Some day, if he were bright enough and learned his lessons well, Niall would take his place there. For now he learned and in the process he wandered the woods outside of the city and plucked this root or that leaf or even an occasional berry, because Mosara told him he had to.

"All and well," he said to himself. "There are worse ways to spend an afternoon." That was the truth of it, too. He was happy with his lot in life. There were few who could say that in his estimation.

The deer was almost behind him now, and he had let her drift from his attention when she suddenly bolted, charging past him and leaping a distance that was startling to witness. She did not wait around, but continued her rapid escape from the area.

He turned to see what might have startled her, and saw the cloaked figure a dozen feet away.

Niall was not a fool. Upon occasion he was accused of being too trusting, but he seldom let himself get caught unawares.

His fingers tightened on the walking staff in his right hand and he made himself appear calm.

"Well met."

The cowl was filled only with darkness and whomever it was that looked back from under it made no response.

"Was there something you needed help with? Are you lost?" It happened from time to time, even away from the city. People could get lost. In the woods if they ate the wrong things they could easily get addled and forget where they were going.

Instead of speaking the figure tossed a glittering trinket into the air and Niall watched as the shining metal arced toward him. No. Not a trinket.

A coin.

The metal hit the ground in front of Niall and landed on its edge. The loam under his feet was soft, and the heavy coin cut the surface of the stuff and stood at a nearly impossible angle, like a dagger driven into flesh.

"What are you doing?" Niall asked, but he already knew the answer.

He took a step back and shifted his balance. The staff rose

up from the ground and he held it in a two-handed grip.

"I do not follow your gods." He did his best to sound stern. "Find another."

The cloaked figure shuddered and came toward him, moving quickly. "No." The word was not spoken, it was hissed.

Niall brought his staff around in a brutal arc and aimed the thicker end of the hard wood at the blackness of the cowl's depths. Somehow he missed. His aim was good, but the stranger moved too quickly and dodged his attack.

Niall shook his head. He wanted this done and sooner rather than later.

While he was contemplating what he wanted something hit him hard in the back of his head. The wooden staff fell from his hands and he grunted then fell forward.

When he hit the ground, the cold coin of the Grakhul scraped along his jaw and narrowly avoided drawing blood.

There were more of them. Not one shape, but half a dozen or more, and they moved around him, cutting off any chance of escape.

He would have risen if he could have. The cloaked figure leaned over him and spoke again. "The gods do not need your faith. They need your life."

They fell on him then, their hands feverishly hot, their breath rancid and diseased. He did not know how many of them attacked; he could not tell for certain, but he saw their faces and knew a fear deeper than he ever had before.

After that the darkness swallowed Niall whole.

They rode hard, and as they went they gathered more riders to join them.

They did not manage an army, but there were enough folk

who either owed Brogan for past deeds, had suffered from the same loss in the past, or would work for coin, that they gathered twenty in all. More would have been too cumbersome.

Harper led the way.

Harper, who could be so secretive and who had spent time among the Grakhul, protecting deliveries to their nameless keep in the forsaken northeast. The laws of the Five Kingdoms forbade travel to the area. It was the land reserved for the Grakhul, and unless those very people offered safe passage, the foolish that trespassed did not live long to speak of their journeys.

"We have to follow the proper passages across the land. Stray too far and death will follow."

Harper's words dragged Brogan from his thoughts.

"How do you know these paths?"

The man's smile was thin and unreadable. "I was trained to be here. I'm betraying a trust."

"Do you think I don't know what I've asked of you?" Brogan's voice was soft as the finest leather. "Do you think I ask it lightly?"

"If I doubted you, I would not be here." Harper did not flinch from his gaze. "She is your wife, and they are your children, but I've loved them too. They're as much my family as you are, Brogan."

"Why do they take them, Harper?"

"Why does the wind blow? The gods make demands and those who follow them obey those demands."

Really there was no more to say and so they rode on as quickly as they safely could.

The land they finally reached was bleak, a dismal collection of black rock and broken shale that fell toward a dim, gray shoreline of more shale and dark sands. The ocean beyond it was equally uninviting and violent besides. The waves at high tide slammed themselves furiously against the shoreline and dashed into the blades of rock with murderous force. The vibrations from the impacts could be felt through the leather of his boot heels.

According to Harper more than one fool had attempted to attack by that route but none had succeeded. Few had ever approached the nameless keep of the Grakhul and come back. Those that did were never the same. Strong men were broken by what they saw and their flesh sometimes withered where they had strayed too far from the proper path.

Harper pointed out the Gateway to them. The place that the Grakhul claimed led to the home of the gods.

At a distance the monolithic Gateway rose from the night time waters, a massive bridge of dark stone that sometimes was merely an arch and other times revealed the land beneath it. They had heard of the Gateway before, but only one of them had ever seen it. Few saw the Gateway and fewer still saw the keep. These were forbidden things, as ordered by the royal families of the Five Kingdoms. Those rare few given permission to visit were allowed only because the Grakhul deemed them worthy. Harper was one of the fortunate souls trained to find his way through what seemed like an unremarkable terrain.

None of them looked at the Gateway for long. There was something about that odd stone bridge over the waters that hurt the eyes and made the mind ache.

After a scan of the area Brogan McTyre pushed aside the idea of attacking from the shore below. There were other ways that might prove slightly less dangerous.

"Well, now we know why no one ever attacks this place." Laram scowled as he spoke.

The keep was built into the side of the dark stone cliff.

Somewhere in the distant past madmen had decided to risk life and limb and carve the damnable place into existence. The very structure gave off a feeling of extreme age, even if one didn't take the time to notice where the winds had smoothed a few of the edges.

Brogan looked toward Laram and nodded. He felt exactly the same way. The difference was that he was the one leading the assault and couldn't actually voice that opinion.

He shook his head and spat into the cold sea air. If he thought too much about the dangerous air of the place, if he let himself worry, he'd lose his anger. He needed that right now to keep him warm and to keep him brave.

Unconsciously he let his fingers roam into the pouch secured on the inside of his broad leather belt, where the four coins rested. He did not need to see them. He'd memorized every detail of their surfaces. They'd been pressed between his belt and the fabric of his kilt for days, but when his fingers touched the heavy gold coins they still felt cold. He understood cold as he never had before.

"Enough. The sun's up in a few hours." He squinted into the wind and looked toward the east. "Though around here it might be hard to tell. Let's find a way in. We've bloody work to do."

A few voices muttered agreement but most were silent. They were here because they owed Brogan a debt or because they had experienced similar pains. Brogan couldn't hope to offer enough to offend the gods. Where others had allowed the old ways to continue, Brogan intended to get his family back or make sure it never happened again.

Harper spoke up, dark hair flipping lazily around his lean face, dark eyes staring intently at Brogan. "You are sure you want to do this? It breaks all of the laws."

Brogan knew the man was trying to be the voice of reason, but anger and reason have never been close associates. "I did not ask you here to stop me, Harper, and you know that."

His thin mouth broke into a crooked grin that made the man look younger by years. "I never said I would stop you, Brogan. Only that I would aid you in any way I can. Sometimes that means saying the things you do not want to hear."

Brogan put a heavy hand on his friend's shoulder and nodded. "I thank you for that, but I mean to have my family today. Will you join me?"

Harper licked his lips. "I have never been one to turn away from blood. No reason to start now." The leaner man looked toward the shore and the odd, rough stone that marked the top of the Grakhul keep. "There is a pathway. It's right at the edge and it is steep. If you are afraid of heights, you might wish to turn back." Almost as an afterthought he added, "The horses will have to stay behind. They'd never manage to keep their footing."

"How do the Grakhul manage it?"

Harper looked at him for a long moment and barely even seemed to breathe. The man was seldom bothered by much. "They aren't human, Brogan. Make no mistake of it. They are not like us, no matter how much they might look the part."

Brogan spat again. "No turning back. Let's go."

Harper, the only one of them who knew the ways to enter the keep without dying for the effort, led the way with that same half-smile on his face.

Harper sighed. "No turning back, indeed, Brogan. No turning back now. Not ever again."

Brogan had heard the warnings before. They had all been raised on admonitions about what it meant to defy the Grakhul. Those had always been enough in the past.

Everything changed when it happened to your loved ones. He understood that now. There would be no forgiveness for whatever happened. For that reason alone he owed a debt of blood to each of the men with him.

They were mostly mercenaries. They'd fought at one time or another for each of the kingdoms. The thing about being sought for crimes was first people had to know you had committed them. None of them were foolish enough to admit to the crimes. Well, except possibly Harper, but he could only hope the man kept his tongue.

"Harper?"

"Yes?"

Brogan looked to his friend and took a deep breath. "I don't know what I'll do if we're too late."

"I'd say we should pray, but that might not go the right way. I mean who would we pray to?"

He could always trust Harper to find the most challenging part of a quandary. Who indeed?

The others would not talk. Like him they were here for personal reasons. Blood sometimes calls for blood.

Harper was right. Madmen had surely designed the slope down into the keep. The stone was slicked with algae and nearly too smooth to allow a man to walk. Instead they clutched at the wall of the winding, twisting path, and half-walked, half-slid toward the plateau below.

Brogan, a man bent on either salvation or revenge, could feel his heart hammering in his chest. After ten minutes of doing their best to keep their footing, Harper and the men he was leading made it to the flat land of the keep itself.

The ground here was just as damp, and the green slime that had been under their feet coated the walls of the ancient structure as well, lending it an unsettling level of camouflage.

The winds along the cliff face were rough and those men who had long hair and had not already tied it back began the task almost immediately. The sole exception was Harper, who remained as calm as ever.

For one moment Brogan pondered whether the man would betray him, then crushed the thought. They had grown up in the same town and been friends as long as he could recall.

Harper looked his way and drew his chosen weapons. In his right hand he carried a long blade with a hook at the end. In his other hand he gripped a thin sword that was perfectly designed for a man of his leaner stature.

Harper broke the silence. He spoke softly, but did not whisper. The wind would have stolen his words away too easily. The men moved closer to hear him. "We move around the first wall here, and we'll see their sacrificial pits. There are four of them. They are large, but they have no decorations to let you know they are there. Be very careful. You have already felt the surface of the ground here. Those pits, they are where the bodies go." He didn't have to say which bodies. They all knew.

The Grakhul had always come and they demanded their sacrifices.

The Grakhul did not ask. They took. They left only the coins. The weight of them pulled at Brogan's belt.

Harper looked his way and Brogan realized the man was still speaking. "Beyond the pits is the great hall. It's where the prisoners are kept and where all of the Grakhul feast." He looked at the ground ahead. Dark and green and damp against a gray sky that showed no sign of a sun. There were clouds out there, a gathering black bank that rose up the gods alone knew how far. The waves raged and threw themselves at the land.

Brogan knew how they felt.

"Lead the way, Harper. Let this be finished." His words were low, but heard by all.

Harper nodded, and that smirk marred his features as he turned and moved forward, sliding across the ground with a grace that Brogan envied.

Brogan strode across the level deck, with stone on three sides and a severe drop to the sea below on his left, and pushed his boots into the thick slime, balancing himself with each step he took. After only a few paces the slippery surface lost its coating of green and became a surer, safer footing.

Harper moved around the last corner and he followed. Five steps and Brogan saw the first of the pits. They were vast, indeed, and dark: cavernous holes large enough to easily swallow a fully loaded wagon and as perfectly round as anything he had ever seen. The walls were completely smooth and as far as he could tell no lichen or moss touched the stone. He had no idea how far they went down, but the cliffs ran for a few hundred feet before they met the ocean and he could feel a breeze rising from the pit. The breeze smelled of the sea and darker things.

Some moments take forever. There was so much to see, so much to absorb, and Brogan's mind was a sponge at that moment, thirsty for information.

No more than three heartbeats to take it all in, but only one was needed before Brogan was screaming.

There were four pits. The edges of three of them were coated in a residual wash of crimson that painted the dark stone.

At the pit closest to them a single man dropped a small, bloodied body into the well and looked up at the sound that came from Brogan's mouth. The shape that fell into the pit was tiny, no larger than a young boy. Brogan recognized Braghe's face before the figure dropped.

The second pit had already been abandoned, and the man who'd been standing there was walking toward the farthest of the four deep holes.

At the third, a man was looking down into the depths of the well – and turned toward the group as Brogan screamed.

At the fourth of the sacrificial pits seven men still stood. They held a woman by her wrists, by her ankles, to stop her from escaping. She tried, too. She thrashed and struggled and wailed at them.

Tears stained Nora's face. Through the markings they had painted on her flesh, he could see the tears as they cut at the colors that tried to hide her beauty from him. A hundred strides and more away and he knew Nora's face, her shape, as well as he knew his own hands. She was his world, his breath, his light.

"No!"

Brogan charged forward, barely looking at anything beyond Nora.

She looked his way, her mouth an open wound showing her pain. Despite it all, his warrior's brain calculated. There were four pits. Only one was still untouched. The sum was painfully simple. His children were dead. But there was still a chance, wasn't there? There was the possibility that he could reach Nora in time.

He ran for Nora, and Harper ran beside him and raised his chosen weapons. As a unit the rest charged forward, spreading out in an effort to block any attempts their enemies might make at escape.

The single man standing at the first pit looked their way. He was dressed in a dark tunic and boots. His head was shaved clean and his skin was pale. He stared without any comprehension, an expression so completely shocked by the appearance of strangers that it bordered on comical. His eyes flew wide, his mouth dropped open and his hands raised up to clutch at his chest. And while he goggled in their direction, Harper ran a blade from his clavicle up to his nose, splitting everything between in one stroke.

The dead man fell as Harper pulled the sword free, never missing a step in his stride.

Brogan ran past the corpse and continued on. There would be time to look at bodies when the living had been sorted.

The wind roared and threatened to push him aside. The wind did not matter. There was Nora and nothing else.

As he went, Brogan pulled his axe from its sheath.

Four of the men around Nora came their way, most of them dressed much like the corpse left behind by Harper. Not a one of them was armed and as a whole they looked confused by the idea of anyone attacking them in this place of ritual and sacrifice.

Brogan sneered and raced toward them, his axe hefted up in his thick arms, his eyes locked on the closest of the pale bastards that had taken his family from him. He charged, a roar building in his chest. Four men stood between him and Nora. They would not stand for long.

The axe cut deeply into pale flesh and brought forth a river of crimson. He did not stop as the first of the bodies fell. The second man died where he stood. The next in line flinched back, tried to escape, but never had a chance. The blade cleaved through his chest and only stopped when it reached his backbone. A hard kick wrenched the body away from his weapon and Brogan roared again, the fury consuming him.

And up ahead Nora let out the smallest of sounds as a blade from the man beside her pierced her heart.

There was no thought left in him. Brogan smashed into

the next fool between him and his wife and barged him into the pit. Another came too close and suffered the same fate as he reached for Nora.

The man who'd killed her – for even then, much as he wanted to believe otherwise, Brogan knew the truth of the matter – looked his way and tried to speak out a warning. His words were in a language Brogan did not know, but whatever he'd been saying in any tongue would have been wasted breath.

Brogan brought the axe up above his head and cut the man in two.

Whatever the plans, whatever possible ideas the Grakhul had in mind, they were forgotten when Brogan came forward. They fled from him, backing away and chattering in their foolish tongue as he dropped the axe from his grip and barely felt the sway of it on his wrist. Brogan moved to take Nora in his arms.

His wife looked at him. Her dark eyes rolled in their sockets and she looked his way, and whatever she might have wanted to say, whatever she might have been feeling, it faded from her, unuttered, as her ruined heart stopped beating.

There were only a dozen or so men. They never stood a chance against his gathering. If he had been alone Brogan would have died and never even noticed. He was lost staring at the remains of his beloved for a time. Who could say how long? Surely not Brogan himself.

He rose slowly, Nora in his arms, his axe swaying against his wrist, held in place by the heavy leather strap. It tapped against him several times but if it cut he did not notice.

Harper looked his way with haunted eyes and shook his head in sorrow.

"I am so very sorry, Brogan."

Brogan had no words.

Around him his men stood guard and looked on. Not far away the ocean roared and the wind howled and Brogan understood all too well their fury.

For a moment he considered the possibility of taking Nora's body home with him and giving her a proper burial.

Instead, he kissed her sweet face one last time and let her fall into the deep pit. A mother, he knew, would want to be with her children. "Let this be your last sacrifice."

Harper put a hand on his shoulder with great care. "Brogan, there are more of them. There is a *city's* worth of people here."

As he spoke, their enemies made themselves known. They came running from the great hall Harper had spoken of, most of them dressed much like the corpses around them. None were armed. None had even contemplated being attacked in this place.

The axe found its way back to his hands. It felt weightless as Brogan contemplated his enemies.

The closest of them bellowed in his gibberish language and Harper held out a hand, stopping Brogan for a moment.

He called to the strangers and they quickly exchanged words. Harper turned to his friend. "Truly I am sorry, Brogan. All of your family…"

"I know this." Four pits and now all four were painted with blood.

"They say the gods demand fresh sacrifices or they will tear this world apart."

Brogan's voice was hoarse with tension. "Let them."

The time for considerations and discussions was done. Brogan charged toward the speaker and cut into his stomach with one hard swing. Before him, the gathered men of the Grakhul stared, horrified, and did little or nothing to defend themselves.

Around him, behind him, he heard more battle cries. They owed him debts and so they came. They had lost to the Grakhul and so they shared their rage. They all had their reasons for breaking the laws and not one of them felt any regret.

The battle was brutal and fast; a reaping of bloodied wheat that fell to the stone floors without much protest and few attempts at defense.

When it was done, all of them were winded – murder is exhausting work – and Brogan looked at the corpses and frowned. It made no sense. These were not, could not be, the Grakhul he had heard so much about.

Laram said it for him. "These are the brutes who demand sacrifices?"

Harper shook his head. "No. They must be out and seeking their next sacrifices." He frowned. "The women, the children, they are hiding somewhere below. What do you want to do about that, Brogan?"

Brogan looked at the corpses. For as long as anyone knew, the Grakhul had come and taken and left their coins. For as long as he could remember it had not mattered. Now, however, his family, his entire family…

"We gather the children and the women. They come with us."

Harper looked at him with one raised eyebrow and that damnable smirk. "What will you do with them?"

"Give them to those who lost their families." He shrugged, not completely certain what he planned. "They can decide for themselves what should happen to scum who took their loved ones."

"And the bodies? What if the families see the bodies?"

His face in that moment, he knew, was not the face of a loving man. "Let them know my loss. Our loss. Let them grieve for their loved ones before they are given to the people who will judge them."

Laram spoke again. Laram, who was always a more decent man than Brogan. "We could push them into the pits."

Brogan shook his head. "No. There will be no more bodies in those damned pits. They've had their blood."

That was all there was to say about the matter.

The women and the children of the Grakhul did not go gently. They were not the least bit intimidated by the gathering of men and if they grieved for their loved ones they showed it by taking up weapons and fighting against the invaders.

The first attack came from a boy of perhaps ten who charged out of a darkened doorway with a knife in his hand and came at Brogan. One step out of the way took care of the knife. One fist to the side of the boy's head left him reeling on the ground.

The second attack came from the boy's mother, who charged at Brogan, swinging a small axe. Laram tripped the woman in midstride and sent her sprawling. She let out a cry and dropped her weapon. Rather than stopping, she came back up a second time with a dagger drawn from her belt.

Harper stopped her with a word. She froze and looked at the men around her, her eyes wide. By the time she was done assessing the situation Harper had placed the blade of his weapon to her throat.

Harper's words were a mystery but his tone clearly offered a warning. There were several exchanges between the woman and the soldier and when it was done he put away his sword.

"They'll come with us."

"What did you say to her?"

"They could come with us or they could die." Harper eyed the woman for a moment. "I also told her we'd make sure the children suffered before they died." The woman sighed, put her hand around her mouth to amplify her words, then bellowed out in the gibberish language of her people. Within minutes, a very large group was forming. Twenty men, all told. If the families got serious, Brogan's group would never have a chance, despite the fact that half the women had little ones gathering around their knees. There were twenty able-bodied and well-armed men. There were hundreds of women and children.

Brogan shook his head and spat. "If we're taking them, we need to be able to control them."

Harper shook his head. "No reason. They'll follow us."

"Why would they?"

The very woman who'd tried to attack him answered. Her voice was thick with the strange accent of her usual tongue, but he understood her well enough. "Because you have damned this place and the people here. Our only hope, no matter how small, is to be away from here."

She would say no more. Instead she soothed her child, the boy he'd punched in the head, and then she and the rest of her people followed after Brogan and Laram and the rest.

Harper and four others did not immediately leave. They caught up instead. Brogan noticed but said nothing.

Another exchange with one of the women and he and the others left again, coming back with a few wagons that had seen better days and horses to draw them.

One of the women led the horses and found a different route that wound upwards, to the top of the plateau. The exit point was nearly impossible to see and Brogan wasn't surprised that Harper had not known of it.

Within an hour they were on their way from the keep and moving in a very large serpentine across the nearly barren land. A few of the women had gathered possessions, but most did not bother.

As they left the sky roared with a hundred strokes of thunder and fingers of light ripped through the darkening clouds, cutting their way across the skies and bullwhipping strokes across the horizon. Brogan turned to look at the great Gateway. He watched as tongue after tongue of lightning stroked the thing but did it no harm.

"How often does that happen?" Laram was making conversation, nothing more. The woman with her son was walking nearby and looked at them but did not answer. Her smile was not pleasant.

The sea behind them raged on, hammering at the shoreline. The winds blew harder, as if inviting them to leave the area even faster than planned.

Brogan should have felt victorious. He had avenged his family and stopped the bastard Grakhul from ever doing to another what they had done to him. Instead he felt hollowed out and left to wither and die.

ANGRY ROBOT

We are Angry Robot

angryrobotbooks.com

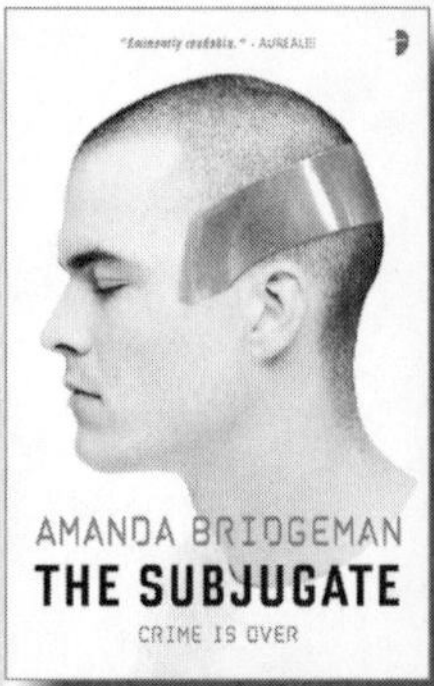